PHASE THREE ALERT

Other Books by John Ball

Last Plane Out
The Van: A Tale of Terror
A Killing in the Market
The Kiwi Target
Rescue Mission
Phase Three Alert
The Fourteenth Point
Mark One: The Dummy
The Winds of Mitamura
The Murder Children

Virgil Tibbs Mysteries

Five Pieces of Jade
The Eyes of Buddha
Then Came Violence
Singapore

Chief Jack Tallon Crime Novels

Police Chief
Trouble for Tallon
Chief Tallon and the S.O.R.

PHASE THREE ALERT

JOHN BALL

SPEAKING VOLUMES, LLC
NAPLES, FLORIDA
2014

PHASE THREE ALERT

ISBN 978-1-62815-077-3

For Chaplain (Major) Alvin C. Durham,
United States Air Force-Civil Air Patrol, with admiration and respect

AUTHOR'S NOTE

THIS BOOK WAS MADE possible by the generous and essential cooperation of the United States Air Force. My particular appreciation is tendered to the West Coast Office of Information (SAFOI) and to the other Air Force agencies that lent their help.

I would like to offer my very special thanks, and deepest appreciation, to the many friends I was fortunate enough to make at Thule Air Base. The American military personnel and the Danish civilians who were stationed there were unstinting in their guidance, their patient digging-out of research material, and their unfailing hospitality. There, 840 miles from the North Pole and at one of the most isolated and fearsome sites anywhere on earth, they took time from their essential duties to give of their best. The High Arctic is a harsh and unforgiving environment almost impossible to imagine without experiencing it. Despite the constant rigors to which they were subjected, they did not allow even the violence of Phase Three conditions in the middle of the Arctic night to deter them.

I have now shed my parka, my mukluks, my arctic boots, my thermal long johns, my felt innersoles, my arctic gloves with their mittens and liners, the several pairs of socks I wore each day, and the Phase Warning Card that I carried at all times. But I have not shed Thule, surely one of the most exotic places in the world. There I found a camaraderie and an awareness of a vital mission that have become a part of me.

It is a great privilege to share them with you.

For the benefit of those readers who may not be familiar with the technical aspects of flying, the nature of the High Arctic, or the operations of the United States Air Force, there is a glossary, beginning on page 293, which defines many of the specialized terms used in the text.

John Ball
Thule, Greenland, February 1975
Encino, California, May 1976

PROLOGUE

Presque Isle, Maine, March 1943

DAYLIGHT WAS A LITTLE more than two hours old. The hard nip in the air was only slightly relieved by a frosty sun that glittered off the exposed ice and hard-packed snow. The air itself still had the cutting edge it had developed during the night; it hacked away relentlessly at the exposed flesh of the men who were out of doors and working. The sky lacked the crisp clearness that normally follows the passage of a cold front, but both ceiling and visibility were satisfactory. By the standards of the ten-month-old United States Army Air Corps Air Transport Command, it was a good day for flying.

The airfield was crowded with planes, most of which had been cold-soaked for at least twelve hours and were therefore difficult to start. The engine oil was cold and congealed, cylinders had contracted, and pistons were reluctant to move.

The job of the crews and mechanics working with them was complicated by an eighteen-knot wind that cut across the field, dropping the chill factor down to where numb fingers could not hold wrenches securely and cowl fasteners resisted all reasonable efforts to get them open or shut.

There was some illusion of warmth in the sharp sounds that cut across the wide open areas: sounds of engines being run with manifold pressures of eighteen inches and up. The discs cut by the propellers took on hard outlines and the air they hurled backwards generated dozens of snow eddies that danced like wintery spirits behind the tail surfaces of the planes. Three B-17's had all four engines going and the combined cacophony of their power plants hurled defiance at the numbness of the cold air. Their sustained roar was augmented when a fighter turned onto the end of the working runway and opened up, the whine of its propeller adding powerful overtones to the basic thunder of its power plant. It moved down the field, gaining speed, until near the end of the runway its pilot pulled back and the aircraft lifted off into the sky. It was heavily loaded and did not climb rapidly.

As he walked toward the operations building, Major General Walter Lippincott was acutely aware of the activity of the base. He surveyed what was going on with a professional's eye and despite the cold and the sharp wind, he breathed deeply of the smell of the Air Corps facility. It was a mixture of exhaust fumes, fuel, lubricants, and the unique aroma of aircraft themselves, something duplicated by no other man-made objects. He paused to watch as a lumbering B-17 began to turn slowly onto the end of the runway. His trained ears told him that the engines were running well; unconsciously he had heard them during the run-up when the separate magnetos had been checked. He knew without being told that she was headed for Goose Bay, a ferry hop of 569 miles that was the first leg of the North Atlantic Route that eventually ended at Prestwick, in the British Isles.

4

As the big bomber began its roll, General Lippincott lowered his eyebrows and wondered how competent her pilot was. The general had earned his own wings the hard way in the old biplanes that depended for their aerial lives on the tough wires that held them together; it scared him profoundly to see some of the inexperienced young flyers who were setting out to cross the Atlantic guided by navigators who had never been over an ocean before in their lives. The early estimates had called for a ten percent loss of the planes and crews due to raw personnel, sometimes acute weather phenomena, the usual hazards of military flying, and the unrelenting wartime conditions.

As the B-17 gained speed, for just a moment her port main landing gear lifted up. The pilot corrected quickly, rolling his aileron into the wind and holding his aircraft straight down the runway at the same time. General Lippincott clenched his teeth; with a crosswind like that the pilot should have had his aileron into the wind before he even started to roll—thank God he had corrected in time. If he lived long enough, he would learn. The general continued watching until the twenty tons–plus that the B-17 represented at last parted from the ground and the wheels began to retract. Two and a half to three hours should see her safely on the ground at Goose Bay, the shortest, and in many respects the easiest, leg of the transatlantic route behind her. It was a marvel that the ten percent loss rate had not materialized, considering the greenness of the crews. The new flyers lacked experience but not guts; they did their best and it was usually good enough. Before long they would be in the skies over occupied Europe and the German fatherland. There they would have to tangle with the swarming fighters of the *Luftwaffe* that would pour death at them from every angle while the bursting flak would take over the moment the fighters withdrew. Then many of the brave young bodies would be torn apart and the fine new aircraft would be crumbled and blasted by the vicious ground fire. Compared to that, the North Atlantic ferry was a Fourth of July holiday.

That's what they were flying into; they knew it, but still they went. They would go and they would keep on trying, and that was their enormous strength.

Lippincott stamped his feet to dislodge the excess snow as he paused just outside of Operations. A four-man crew coming out saw him; the young men stopped in their tracks and saluted — all but the navigator, who, contrary to regulations, was carrying his octant in his right hand. Since his left was already burdened with his heavy flight kit and his high-altitude 214 tables for celestial navigation, he was automatically excused.

"Good morning," the general said.

"Good morning, sir." The crew commander did not look a day over twenty-five, but he was precise and businesslike. As he pushed open the door to go inside, Lippincott blinked his eyes once as a token subservience and said a quick silent prayer, asking that the crew he had just met be allowed to survive. Having done the best that he could for them, he walked rapidly down the corridor and into the operations commander's office.

The colonel jumped to his feet, but General Lippincott waved him down again. "What have you got for me?" he asked.

The colonel picked a waiting folder off his desk and handed it to his superior. "This should fill the bill, sir."

Lippincott dropped into a chair and crossed his legs. "Give it to me verbally," he directed. "Have you any coffee around this place?"

The colonel raised his voice. "Hank!"

A side door popped open. "Yes, sir."

"Two coffees, please. The general likes his black, a little sugar."

"Right away, sir."

6

Lippincott knew that the coffee would be terrible, but it would be welcome, just as poor visibility was better than no visibility at all.

The colonel spoke clearly, with the air of a man who is sure of his subject. "The crew commander is a Captain Miller. He's a professional and was in the Air Corps well before Pearl Harbor. He was in the top tenth of his class at flying school; his personal record is also very good. Married, an infant son. Close to an ideal career officer with over twelve hundred flying hours without accident. He has a reputation for being cool in the face of emergency: he's had a couple and handled them well."

"Of his own making?"

"The reports said not."

"Good. Get him in here."

"He's standing by; I told him to wait for possible special orders."

The sergeant who had taken the coffee order came in, two steaming mugs in his hands. He served the general, set the second mug in front of the colonel and then asked, "Anything else, sir?"

"Yes, I have a Captain Miller standing by in the crew section. I want to see him immediately."

"Yes, sir." The sergeant left quickly and closed the door behind him.

"How about the rest of the crew?" General Lippincott asked.

"Copilot and radio operator a little better than average. The navigator isn't a pro, but Miller has a good opinion of him."

"When a pilot thinks well of his navigator, that's a good sign. How's that boy in the fighter crash?"

The colonel shook his head. "The prognosis isn't good. If he does make it, he may be crippled."

"His fault?"

"Partly — partly ours, I supposed, for not having given him

7

more seasoning. He pulled up too sharply on takeoff and stalled out."

The general also shook his head. "A man with ten flying hours should know better than that. I hope he makes it, but he probably was showing off — to himself." He stopped talking in order to drink his coffee. The hot brew was overstrong and its acid bite hit his stomach with a reminder that he had had no breakfast. He had not had time to eat — there had been too much to do.

A knock sounded on the door. The colonel barked, "Come in," and waited.

The young captain who responded was precisely the sort of person Lippincott wanted to see. He was perhaps twenty-seven and had about him the air of a professional who has found his career and is proud of it. He stood a shade under six feet and as he saluted, Lippincott noted that he mercifully lacked the brand-new brightness that characterized so many of the freshly commissioned officers who passed through Presque Isle in a steady flow.

"You sent for me, sir," he said.

"Yes, Captain. General Lippincott would like to speak to you."

In the presence of the general the young captain stiffened a little more. Lippincott was used to it and with little egotism on his own part, he approved of it.

"I understand that you are scheduled out at fourteen hundred hours over the North Atlantic."

"That's correct, sir."

"Off the record, how competent is your crew?"

"The best, sir. My copilot is relatively new, but he's capable. Our radio man was a ham operator before the war."

"How about your navigator?"

"Exceptional, sir. Lieutenant Mafusky taught high school math before he joined up. He went into navigation by his own

8

choice—he isn't a pilot washout. At his experience level, I doubt if there's a better man in the Air Corps."

"Have any of you any over-ocean experience?"

"No, sir, but we'll all have some shortly."

Lippincott was satisfied. "Captain, I understand that you are a career man."

"Yes, sir."

"Captain, what is the condition of your aircraft? Any squawks?"

"None, sir. She's a more or less brand-new B-17, but she's well rigged and the power plants are fine."

"Have you named her yet?"

"Yes, sir. *The Passionate Penguin.*"

Lippincott smiled to himself; the names became more fanciful every day. He suspected that there would be a fairly graphic illustration painted on the plane's nose, but that didn't concern him at the moment.

"Captain Miller, there is a piece of highly classified cargo that has to be delivered to Prestwick as soon as possible. I mean it when I tell you that if it fails to reach England promptly, our entire war effort might be affected. But more than that, under no circumstances, regardless of any risks or sacrifices that may be involved, must it be allowed to fall into enemy hands. That would be disastrous."

"I understand, sir."

"I'm planning to have this piece of highly sensitive cargo put on your aircraft for delivery in England. On your arrival, it will be picked up personally by General Falkenberg; you are to give it to no one else."

"Right, sir." The tightness was back, which was good.

The general handed over a photograph. "This is General Falkenberg. Also, don't hesitate to ask him for his ID."

"Thank you, sir. I would have done that anyway."

"Good." The crate contains an explosive device that will

9

operate if an unauthorized person attempts to open it. However, it is not hazardous unless the crate is dropped or otherwise badly mishandled."

"Could you give me the weight, sir?"

"Eighty-six pounds."

The captain was relieved. "Then it won't figure on our weight and balance."

"It shouldn't. There will also be two or three other crates, as decoys. Stow them somewhere up front. I'll arrange security for your aircraft at Goose and the other stops. You're going via Bluie West Eight?"

"Correct, sir."

"That's all, Captain, except for the fact that you will tell your crew as little as possible about the cargo. It was something you were asked to take and you have no idea what it is. Which is true. Your guess is that it is an urgently needed part that ran out of stock overseas—a part for an experimental aircraft somewhere in England."

"From now on, sir," Captain Miller said carefully, "that is precisely what it is."

"Excellent, Captain. The crates will be color-coded; the sensitive one is yellow."

"We'll take it there, sir."

Lippincott stood up and shook hands. "Have a nice flight, Captain."

The youthful aircraft commander saluted, turned on his heel, and left.

The departure of the B-17 at 1400 hours was without visible incident. With four small crates stowed aboard she ran down the runway, her ailerons properly into the wind, and lifted off precisely when she should. She had a good solid feel about her and as she climbed upward to her cruising altitude, her crew sensed her strength and stability. Although she was a new aircraft, Miller felt a real affection for her as she answered his commands and bored her way through the sky with her great wings reaching out over a hundred feet and her four engines sounding a unison chorus of almost perfectly synchronized power.

As Miller flew her on, he saw her not as a war bird, but as the prototype of some future great airliner that would be able to carry 50 or more passengers at speeds approaching three hundred miles per hour. With perhaps 40 passengers and a greater fuel load, transcontinental nonstop flights were a definite possibility. Give her the same wing and engines, but a different fuselage, and she could handle twelve rows of seats—48 passengers as contrasted to the 21 carried by the ubiquitous DC-3, the pride and joy of Douglas Aircraft.

He was still thinking about that as he guided her down the approach path to Goose Bay, flared just short of the runway, hung her wheels an inch or two above the surface, and let her settle on. When she had found the ground, he slowed her up and let the tail wheel settle on with hardly a bump. The first leg was behind him and he had enjoyed every minute of it.

As soon as everything had been secured to his satisfaction, and the classified cargo had been properly cared for, he headed for the crew ladder and climbed down into the sub-Arctic cold of Labrador. The impacted snow crunched hard under his feet as he walked out from under the nose of his aircraft, remembering as he did so that he was scheduled for an 0800 departure. Getting everything started up, warmed, and ready to go in the morning would be a difficult task after what promised to be a long and frigid night. That thought was fully occupying his mind as he led his small crew across the hardstand toward the operations building.

By 0730 everything was in shape; Mafusky's flight plan showed five hours and forty minutes for the slightly more than 1,000 miles they had to go. It would be the longest leg and in some respects the most hazardous. Bluie West 8 was at Söndre

Strömfjord, well up on the west coast of Greenland, and had only one runway. It had to be approached by flying at low altitude up a fjord and the go-around, in case of a missed landing, was reportedly one of the worst in the world. Also, departing traffic would be coming down the same narrow fjord in the opposite direction, which was a mental hazard if nothing else.

Those were some of the difficulties he had heard about. He also knew that German submarines had been sending out false navigational signals. They had caused a number of planes to fly off course and some of them had crash-landed on the dreaded ice cap as a consequence. He considered these things carefully, but he was not afraid of them. He simply was cautious, as befitted a pilot, no matter how experienced, who was about to take his aircraft and his crew into a difficult situation he had never faced before. By knowing what lay ahead of him, he would be able to deal with whatever problems arose. He had great confidence in his B-17 and that was by far the most important factor in his planning.

The weather briefing had been generally good. The forecaster had seemed confident as he had laid out the expected winds at the altitude and anticipated conditions at Bluie 8. Nevertheless, Miller had ordered full tanks on the sound theory that you can never have too much gas when you are flying into a possibly uncertain situation. The *Penguin* was an E-model, which meant that she had more than four times the range necessary to reach her next destination, if you discounted the need for holding reserves. In a pinch, she would be able to go straight on through to Reykjavik, Iceland, another 847 miles across Greenland and the hostile North Atlantic. He didn't fancy that, particularly since it would mean an unfamiliar night landing after ten or eleven hours in the cockpit, but he was prepared to do it if he had to.

At 0755 he called the tower and asked for taxi instructions. Although he tried not to let it show, he took a genuine pride in the fact that his crew was on time to the minute; it was doing things right that won wars. His satisfaction grew as the *Penguin* rolled slowly over the hardened snow toward the end of the business runway. At that moment he loved every rivet in her. She was a living thing to him, and she was going to bomb the hell out of Hitler's Germany.

At the end of the taxiway he turned into position and ran up all four engines, making sure that everything checked out properly. That completed, he called the tower and reported the *Penguin* ready for takeoff.

Despite her eight tons of fuel load, she did not take too long to get off. The cold air suited her wings and its increased density helped her. As she bored steadily upward, her wheels tucked up for the next several hours, she was more than ready to accept the challenge of the High Arctic. Mafusky passed up a heading that Pat Ryan, the copilot, clipped in place where they could both see it clearly. Miller glanced at his twenty-four-year-old second-in-command and read out that he too was taking pride in their bird and what she was doing.

Fifty minutes out of Bluie West 8, the base reported deteriorating weather conditions and advised all aircraft in the vicinity to stand by for further data. Miller checked that the whole crew had heard the transmission, then he spoke into the intercom. "Don't any of you forget that German subs have been active up here sending out false weather and navigational information. This could be our first contact with the enemy."

He glanced around and received back a series of approving nods; no one was visibly nervous. He turned his attention back to the sky ahead and watched for any signs of changing weather.

Ten minutes later the radio operator sent in Mafusky's position report and ETA. Bluie West 8 came back with a further advisory that the weather was worsening and to expect possible holding.

"Keep a careful watch out," Miller ordered. "I want to know as soon as you see anything."

As he flew on, he glanced at the instruments only occasionally, keeping his major attention on the sector of sky visible through the windshield.

Three minutes later he caught a change in the visibility. It was dead ahead and a trifle ominous. At almost the same moment the radio crackled and Bluie 8 advised all aircraft in the vicinity to be on the ground within fifteen minutes. Miller knew without asking that the *Penguin* could never make that deadline; he picked up the intercom and told his navigator to repeat their arrival time to the base and to ask for instructions. He looked again at the sky directly ahead and studied the visible evidence of possible trouble. For the first time he accepted the weather transmission as genuine.

His opinion was reenforced by the radio operator, who advised that the signals were coming from the right direction.

Greenland was in sight by then, an apparent vast mountain of unbroken snow and ice. He knew he was seeing the edge of the ice cap, the incredible phenomenon that covered almost all of Greenland. An enormous monolith of incalculable weight, it soared to 10,000 feet and went on for hundreds of miles. Despite the weather problem facing him, Miller took time to look and to think about what he was seeing. Tomorrow they would fly across it, if the weather had cleared up enough to permit a takeoff, and he would see it closeup in detail. It was one of the most astonishing sights in the world and he wanted to enjoy it while he could.

His thoughts were interrupted by another radio call: Bluie 8 reported that the field was closing and would remain closed for an indefinite period due to an Arctic storm. Miller called back for instructions.

Bluie advised him to proceed, but to make all possible speed. In response he began an immediate letdown, inching the throttles forward instead of easing them normally back.

The *Penguin* dropped her nose and the airspeed began to build up rapidly.

Ten minutes later, while the aircraft was passing through altitude 4,000 feet, the air suddenly became rough. Trusting the structural integrity of the big Boeing, Miller kept his throttles where they were for another minute and a half, but by the end of that time the *Penguin* was bucking so badly he was forced to ease off. As he did so, he checked behind him and saw that the radio operator was reaching for the urp bucket, which was a bad sign. Miller glanced at Ryan to see if he was all right; his copilot was holding himself in, but the turbulence was beginning to get to him and he might not last another two minutes.

Bluie called and advised that extreme conditions were building up in the fjord. Approach control wanted to know how much fuel he had remaining. Miller read the gauge as best he could and reported back that he had enough for another five hours. That was an understatement, but he was playing it safe—it still gave Bluie the option of ordering him on to Iceland if it was deemed necessary.

Approach control advised him to begin a climb immediately on a northeast heading and to report weather conditions being encountered at five minute intervals.

Ryan gathered himself together and after a nod from his captain he advanced the throttles as much as was feasible under the turbulent conditions. Miller pulled the nose up and set a rapid climb; the bucking of the aircraft was getting his crew sick and while he still felt all right, he knew that he had his own limitations as well. One element of airsickness was fear; that emotion he blocked completely.

The *Penguin* climbed up through 7,000 feet without any improvement in the conditions she was encountering. Two minutes later she should have crossed the coast of Greenland, but there was no way to tell; visibility was drastically reduced and flying by hand required Miller's complete attention. As a means of keeping Ryan in responsive condition, he passed the actual flying over to him. The youthful copilot took over his task and overcontrolled somewhat as he fought to minimize the constant heavy turbulence.

It was bad and Miller knew it. He had been briefed about Arctic ice storms and had been told how they could come virtually without warning. He had no doubt that he was flying in one and what was more, it was steadily getting worse.

At 9,000 feet he came on the controls along with Ryan to help do what he could. He reported to Bluie, but he could not hear any response.

At 10,000 feet he breathed a quick sigh of partial relief; they would soon be above the ice cap and he had been worrying about that. If it had suddenly loomed up before him, with the poor visibility he had, it would have been impossible to turn in time. It would have been finis for the *Penguin* and all aboard her.

At 11,000 feet he had major difficulty in controlling his aircraft. He was flying her now with Ryan pretending to follow through on the controls. Bluie called with a message, but he could not hear anything more than a background voice shattered into distorted fragments. To spare his suffering ears, he cut off the radio. He glanced back and saw that both the radio operator and the navigator were so airsick they could not function. He did not blame them; they had to ride blindly while he, at least, could make the pretense of doing something to ease the strain.

As the *Penguin* climbed, it seemed to him that the turbulence was growing even worse; in response he leveled off and pulled the throttles back to minimum cruising speed. That, at least, would relieve some of the strains on the airframe. A moment later a fearful updraft seized the *Penguin* and flung her almost onto her side, as though she had been a toy; Miller got control, but as he held hard aileron to return her to an even keel, the number four engine began to lose power. He did not

16

detect it at once, but as soon as he was able to scan the engine instruments once more, he knew the fresh problem he was facing. Ryan should have been taking care of it, but his copilot had turned visibly white and his face was covered with a fine sweat.

Miller applied full carburetor heat and enriched the mixture. That should have produced a fairly fast response, but as the continuing gusts pounded against the aircraft's structure, the power output steadily dropped. He reached for the throttles and tried to coax more life out of the power plant, but while he was still making adjustments, a sharp, quick shuddering told him that it was too late. The engine was quitting and there was nothing he could do to save it. He pushed the feathering button to streamline the propeller and cut the ignition. Then grasping the throttles once more, he pulled back on engines one and two and fed a little more fuel to number three to help maintain the trim.

He glanced again at Ryan; his stomach knotted when he saw the trace of blood that tinged his lower lip and the hard stare in his eyes.

Miller made a decision; they could not remain in these conditions on three engines, he had to find something better. He dropped the port wing and turned until he estimated that he was headed more or less true north. If he could break out of the worst of the turbulence, then the *Penguin* would be able to hold at reduced speed until the killer storm had cleared Bluie West 8. There were no emergency strips available anywhere and he knew that northern Greenland was almost utter desolation. Thank God he had started out with full tanks!

Ryan reached out a hand and managed to use the intercom. "It's getting worse," he said. It was a plea for help, combined with a hope that Miller could perform some sort of miracle. As if in answer, the heaviest gust that she had as yet encountered seized the *Penguin* and flung her nose up into a position that could lead to a complete stall within a few seconds. Miller

17

rammed the yoke forward with all his strength and with locked elbows held it hard against the firewall. The *Penguin* rose as though she were on the crest of a mighty wave, climbed, and then plunged downward as the gust let go. Miller pulled back and steadied her, then read the engine instruments once more during the second or two of respite granted him. They told him that number three had fallen off more than twenty-five percent.

Almost frantically he fought to clear the vital engine and get it running properly once more, but in a matter of a few more seconds he knew that it was a no go. That left him only one possible decision; he rammed the yoke forward once more and yelled, "I'm setting her down!"

If the rest of his crew heard him, he got no reaction. Only Ryan was still in communication and he looked as though he would have sold his soul for three minutes of smooth air.

The depressed elevators fought to raise the tail at the same moment that another savage blast hit the underside of the wings. For a horrible few seconds it seemed that the *Penguin* was doomed to be flung into a whipstall or possibly a spin; then, fighting for her own life, she escaped from the murderous gust, sharply tilted on her side, but with her nose safely down once more.

With the carburetor heat on full, Miller pulled the throttles back to an estimated eighteen inches — he was no longer attempting to read the gauges. Then he pushed the nose hard down and prayed to God that the atmospheric pressure setting he had on his altimeter was somewhere near the truth. If it wasn't, it could mean their lives.

He brought the *Penguin* down quickly, as fast as he dared, until the altimeter read 10,500 feet. He was pushing his luck desperately to go that far, but he had not deemed that he had any choice. He slowed her descent and she responded as he had prayed that she would; now he knew that she was a living thing like himself and that they had formed an inseparable bond between themselves; they would live or die together.

The turbulence was still merciless, but possibly it was slightly diminished. Holding onto the yoke with fingers that were locked like steel, he flew at the utmost limit of his skill. He took one second to look at Ryan; his copilot was staring dead ahead with his mouth partway open.

As the number three engine quit, Miller made an instantaneous decision. "Gear down!" he ordered.

Ryan jerked his head around in disbelief. He saw Miller and knew that he meant it, but his mind had already set its course. "*No!*" he protested. Their only hope was to belly in; that had been pounded into him at flying school.

"*Gear down, God damn it!*"

Across the edge of fear, Ryan reached out and started the wheels down. Miller rolled the trim tab, then checked the indicator until he saw that the gear was down and locked. After that he shut out the rest of the world and flew like a man in a trance. With the aid of his remaining two engines, he guided his aircraft down through the violent air until he felt a sudden smoothening and knew that it had to be ground effect. At once he pulled the yoke back and tried to hold in a level position, the descent arrested, but not stopped. In a quick flash he seemed to see something through the windshield: a slightly different texture within the all-encompassing whiteness. He came back harder on the yoke, trying to set up a partially nose-high attitude.

The turbulence abruptly let go. For a second or two he was airborne in a whirling snowstorm that filled the entire universe around him with its mad dancing, then he felt the gear hit.

He pulled hard back and held, risking a horrible bounce and knowing it. For a deadly three seconds the aircraft tried to climb back into the sky as she believed she had been ordered to do, but with very little power and a deadly drag on her wheels, she was helpless. At ninety-two miles an hour she absorbed the shock of the touchdown, softened as it was by a mass of loose snow, and ran blindly ahead.

In the cockpit Miller continued to pull back with all of his strength, fighting to hold her tail down. Despite him, the heavy drag on the gear tried to throw her onto her nose. The instant he sensed it he countered by pushing forward partway on the throttles. The fresh blast blew the tail down hard until, despite the added power, the speed lessened. Then Miller eased off on the live throttles and almost sedately *The Passionate Penguin* ground looped, struggled during a few more desperate seconds of life, and then came to rest at 9,100 feet altitude, somewhere on the Greenland Ice Cap.

BOOK ONE

PROJECT

CHAPTER ONE

AFTER MANY WEEKS of hibernation, the Arctic sun had at last reappeared; as it hung low and brilliant in an almost cobalt sky it gave out abundant light if very little warmth. The long period of almost total darkness was over, a welcome respite for those who, for one reason or another, had spent the barren winter months north of the Arctic Circle. The welcome sunlight threw back the curtains of the long-lived night and gave fresh promise of an eventual springtime, at least in name.

In the crisp cold of early morning Technical Sergeant William T. Stovers walked across the sharply crunching snow, his parka hood safely protecting his neck and ears and his thermal boots insulating his feet from the twenty-four-degrees-below-zero (Fahrenheit) temperature. As he breathed in the biting air he noted that it had warmed up somewhat during the past twenty-four hours. The blessing was academic because he would be leaving Sondrestrom shortly and he did not know when he would be back.

Sergeant Stovers knew that he was in a somewhat dour mood and that fact in itself he found upsetting. Deeply within himself he had a determined pride in his professional skills and he had schooled himself to keep free of any involvements that might interfere with his efficiency. As he continued on at a steady pace, he concentrated on the thought that he had work to do and banished all other considerations from his mind.

In a matter of another two minutes he reached his airplane, which was out on the ramp awaiting him, and climbed up into the main cargo hold. It was one of the few C-130 Hercules turboprop airlifters in the Air Force that was equipped with auxiliary ski gear. Because it was normally used to support the DEW Line sites far out in stark isolation on the ice cap, it required a loadmaster of more than ordinary abilities. In that capacity Sergeant Stovers knew precisely how to allow for the added weight and drag of the cumbersome ski gear. In addition, he had an expert's knowledge of snow and ice cap operations that few men shared. The aircraft itself was in superb condition, he had no concerns there. Two things, however, were bothering him: the first, that his aircraft commander happened to be Lieutenant Scott Ferguson and, the second, that as far as he could see in any direction, it was a bright and beautiful day.

Normally he was highly in favor of lovely days. He had enjoyed many of them in Europe. In the tropics he had made the most of them in a variety of different ways. In the Orient he had used them to pass out candy to eager youngsters or to go walking with the pretty and polite girls who still found a frequent place in his thoughts. In the Arctic they inspired him to draw in deep lungfuls of the crystal-clear air, except when he happened to be in Greenland and in Lieutenant Ferguson's crew. Then, experience had taught him, they could be a portent of possible trouble.

Sergeant Stovers liked Greenland, not because he was inspired by low temperatures and the total absence of anything at all that could be called a tree, but because of the towering, incredible ice cap that was a professional challenge unmatched in the world. To him it was greater than the Grand Canyon, both as a spectacle and as evidence of nature's ability to do things on a scale that mere humans could never dream of duplicating. Not even the Great Wall of China could challenge it.

The ice cap, which covered all but the edges of the immense island, kept the nature of the inland terrain forever shrouded in a perpetual mystery. The vast frozen monolith rose from the bare ground near the shoreline to a maximum thickness of 10,600 feet — more than two vertical miles of solid ice that exerted a pressure almost beyond calculation. It had been variously estimated that if the Greenland Ice Cap were to melt, all of the oceans and seas of the world would rise from 23 to 30 feet.

Because of the fantastic pressure, the ice at the lower edges was continuously forced to break off and become the icebergs that harassed vessels using the North Atlantic sea lanes. Some of it, he knew, formed the basis for a new industry — it was cut into small cubes and shipped under refrigeration as far as Tokyo to cool drinks with the pristine purity of the ice age. In the central region the vast sea of ice, the only true Arctic desert, remained largely static—an immensity of size, bulk, and weight which, even when seen from the panoramic heights of a pressurized aircraft, was beyond the capabilities of the human intellect to comprehend.

The C-130A, which at the moment was Sergeant Stovers's main responsibility, could land on the ice cap. The 6,200-pound ski gear, in addition to the wheels, made it possible for the powerful turboprop to fly to the isolated DEW Line sites, which perched like spacecraft on some far-removed planet, and to set down on the marked-off landing areas known to be free of crevasses and other hazards common to wilderness ski flying. There the airlifter could deliver tons of supplies for the men who manned the cubical structures with the bulging radomes on top. They perched above the ice on massive steel legs which constantly sank, inch by inch, into the frozen sea underneath. To keep the stations in position, they were lifted every few days; when the tops of the steel supports were reached, fresh sections were bolted on and the process continued.

Taking off on skis from the ice was not a simple matter. The impromptu runways were not smooth, but hilly. The skis themselves added very substantial weight and drag. The altitude was usually 9,000 feet, plus. The friction was much greater than that of wheels rolling down a clean paved runway. The four mighty engines kept their turbines scream-ing and their propellers torturing the air during those takeoffs, and every one was a thrill. Adjusting and securing the load each time so that the plane would make it successfully took knowledge and talent. That was Sergeant Stovers's job.

To him the ice cap was a permanent adversary; to Lieuten-ant Ferguson it was a plaything.

Ferguson was a good pilot—no one had officially doubted that. Personally Stovers liked him; he only resented the fact that he sometimes seemed to forget the seriousness of the business in which he was engaged. One really bad mistake and the ice cap could assimilate plane and crew somewhere out on a wilderness of such vastness, with total lack of any possible food or fuel, so as to make it a terrible enemy.

Lieutenant Ferguson, having discovered the ice cap and having read as much as he could find about it, was apparently determined to explore it every time he got the opportunity. Whenever the weather permitted and he was present to do so, he would find a suitable excuse to go off flying over the never-visited areas just to look at a part of the vast frozen emptiness that possibly no one else had ever before seen. He had never been known to go out on the same heading twice.

On this particular morning the flying weather was close to Arctic perfect and the C-130 was ready to go. It was programmed to take out three of the locally attached personnel to get in their required flying hours before returning to base. That meant at least a half-day trip and, since Ferguson would be in command, it meant that as much time as possible would be spent over seldom-if-ever-visited areas atop the great hostile desert. That was why Sergeant Stovers bemoaned the fact that the day was so brilliantly clear and suitable for long-range observation. It would have been far more sensible to have stayed on the Thule airway and perhaps practice an instrument approach or two on the way back.

There was no load to be carried other than the required arctic survival kits and equipment, the mandatory sleeping bags, and the other emergency supplies that a careful crew chief, and the equally cautious loadmaster, always made sure were on board.

After a final check of all equipment and gear, and a verifying inspection of the weight and balance figures, Sergeant Stovers glanced at his watch. Takeoff was scheduled in twenty-two minutes, so the rest of the crew should be coming on board shortly. He looked out of the entrance doorway and almost collided with Lieutenant Jenkins, the navigator, who had chosen that moment to come in from the other side.

"Where to?" Stovers asked, just to be sure.

The lieutenant came on board and sat down heavily in his arctic gear on a stack of parachute pack survival kits. Because he was, at twenty-eight, not only already balding, but also notably overweight and unable to do much about it until he left the Arctic, he was short of breath. He gathered himself together and began a mock lecture. "Our route this morning has been scientifically chosen. Careful study of existing documents has revealed the fact that there is a considerable area of the ice cap, located approximately halfway from here to Thule, which is virtually unexplored. At least it has not been visited under conditions of good visibility within the memory of man. We are going there."

The lieutenant looked around and noted with approval that both coffee jugs and the flight lunches were on board and secured.

Sergeant Stovers did not comment, there was no need. Instead he climbed down the four steps to the ground in order to feel the solid, safe, firmament of Greenland once more under his feet. He was wearing three pairs of massively thick wool socks, over them mukluks, and then arctic thermal boots with added double-felt innersoles. Even on the ramp area there was a good bit of snow, under that a substantial layer of ice, and beneath that, concrete. Nonetheless Bill Stovers felt that the soil itself was as good as pushing its way between his toes, and the thought gave him an improved outlook. After more than 6,000 hours of professional flying he knew the high reliability of properly maintained and flown aircraft that stayed out of lethally bad weather. In another five or six hours he would be back at the same spot and free to go his own way. At Sondrestrom for all practical purposes there was nowhere to go, but at the moment that thought did not disturb him.

Down the ramp a vehicle was approaching; that would be the Fearless Leader and the rest of the crew. He stood by the door and watched them unload. Ferguson, he noted at once, was in a particularly pleasant and optimistic mood, which made matters slightly worse. Stovers recalled his happier days with the considerably more cautious and conservative Major Sams, who had had twenty years in the cockpit behind him and who had insisted that everyone on board wear parachutes during all takeoffs and landings.

28

Ferguson was tall and lean, the very picture of the popular man about campus who had won his letter in basketball. His long arms were made for waving carefree greetings and his somewhat skinny rear for fitting into the bucket seats of sports cars. His hair was thick and bunched on the top of his head so that he appeared at least eight years younger than his true age. He did not look the part of an aircraft commander and he often refused to act it according to the long-accepted script.

Fortunately, he made up for his lack of appearance and decorum by a youthful skill at the controls that at times approached the phenomenal. He made dead-on-the-button instrument approaches and he had once set his C-130 down during a snowstorm whiteout with both ILS and RAL unavailable. They still talked about that one, how he had apparently smelled the ground and the comforting safety of the runway with no radio aids at all to guide him on final approach. When he had been asked about it by his superiors, he had simply answered, "I knew where it was."

In ten years, Stovers thought, he would be one hell of a pilot. Maybe even sooner if he settled down.

As Ferguson ducked his head to climb on board, Stovers said a proper, "Good morning, sir." It pleased him that he put into the words exactly the intonation he had wanted: official correctness, but with subdued undertones of professional restraint.

In fifteen minutes they were airborne. In the cold air the props took hold with abrupt suddenness and the heavy airlifter fairly jumped off the ground. Once they were clear of the fjord and the surrounding hills, Jenkins passed up a climbing heading toward the northeast, one that would take them over the long upper reaches of the timeless frozen desert that deserved recognition as one of the true wonders of the world.

When they had been out slightly under an hour, Ferguson evicted his regular copilot and put one of the Sondrestrom men in his place. "When you fly one of these things," he explained, "don't let the fact that there are skis hanging on underneath bother you too much. They only cost about four miles an hour of cruising speed. Actually, if anything, the aircraft is overpowered and you don't have to worry about hot, thin air up here. Let me show you."

After that he began a series of maneuvers close to the ice cap that caused Sergeant Stovers to withdraw well back into the all-but-windowless fuselage so that he would not have to witness what was going on. He felt the pull of the G's in the steep turns and knew that Ferguson was flying the big empty transport like a fighter. Fortunately the sergeant had a strong stomach, otherwise the abrupt changes of attitude and almost continous turns would have had him reaching for one of the urp buckets in a hurry. As it was, one of the Sondrestrom crewmen who was along for the flying time did not look too happy.

Stovers shut his eyes and thought of the navigator, who was supposed to be keeping track of the position of the aircraft over an area totally without any possible points of ground reference. At the moment, he reflected, he did not care where they were.

Another steep turn revealed itself in the pull on his stomach; the Sondrestrom man reached for the wax-lined bag. Stovers watched him as the thought touched a corner of his own brain that he, too, was beginning to feel certain symptoms of distress.

At that moment Staff Sergeant Andy Holcomb, the flight engineer, craned his neck down from the flight deck in some position he found possible and called back, "Hey, Bill."

Stovers unbuckled and got up to answer the summons; as he started walking forward the pull of another steep turn hit him and he hoped that the overlong demonstration of flight tactics would soon be finished.

He reached the short ladder and climbed up onto the flight

bridge to answer whatever schoolboy question Ferguson wanted to put to him for the benefit of the local men. As soon as he was able to straighten up and take hold of the back of the engineer's chair he sensed at once that his initial guess had been wrong. There were five other men in the good-sized cockpit and all of them were concentrating their attention out of the windows. The C-130 had excellent visibility, even down at the sides.

"Look," Holcomb said, and pointed ahead. Stovers looked and in a matter of seconds picked up a dark object half-buried on the ice cap. As they came up on it and it swept underneath, Sergeant Stovers was already prepared with the answers. Since he was the senior man in the crew, both in terms of age and experience, he expected that his opinion would be asked.

It was. "What do you make of it, Bill?" Ferguson inquired.

"It's a World War II B-17, sir. It's one of a flight of nine, I believe it was, that took off on a ferry flight to England and ran into impossible weather as they neared Greenland. As I recall, sir, some turned back, one ship made it to the destination airport, one or two got in along the coast line, and this one made a forced landing on the ice cap. Colonel Bernt Balchen subsequently rescued the entire crew—no casualties. It was lost for something like twenty-two years, then a few years ago it was rediscovered."

"Are you describing the *My Gal Sal?*" Ferguson asked.

"Yes, sir, that was the name of the aircraft."

"Tell him, nav," Ferguson directed through the intercom.

"That isn't it," Jenkins answered. "I know where the *My Gal Sal* is—it's on the ice cap south of Sondrestrom. We're way north of there now."

The loadmaster was not given to being impulsive; he waited until the C-130 had been racked around again, then, with thoughts of discomfort forgotten, he took another close look. Definitely it was a B-17 with its nose vaguely pointed toward the west, apparently the direction in which it had gone in. It appeared to be in reasonably good condition, which suggested that the crew had probably at least survived the landing.

"Have you seen the *My Gal Sal?*" Ferguson inquired. Although the question appeared to be open, Stovers knew that it was meant for him.

"Officially, no, sir, actually, yes. We swung by it a time or two when Major Sams was out supplying the DEW Line. Naturally we all wanted to have a look at it."

"I'm with you," Ferguson responded. "Then you remember that *Sal* had her fuselage broken just back of the wing, right?"

"Yes, sir." Stovers looked again at the object on the ice cap which was coming up once more and saw that it was definitely not the same wreck. The wing was not tipped forward at the same drunken angle and it appeared to be a little deeper in the wind drift lines that patterned the loose snow on the surface.

"My apologies, sir, I was mistaken. That isn't the *Sal;* I don't know what it is. When we get back we can check with the Air Rescue people and see if they have it charted. If not, then its a new find and we can report it as such."

As soon as he had spoken he realized that he had given justification to all of the many exploratory trips that Ferguson had made over rarely visited sectors of the ice cap, but the man had possibly made a discovery and he was entitled to the satisfaction that went with it.

Ferguson studied the surface of the ice cap less than 500 feet below his aircraft with fierce concentration. He seemed to be memorizing and analyzing every detail. When he spoke again into the intercom, it was for everyone's benefit.

"I remember what happened when the *My Gal Sal* was found; they located the pilot in California and brought him all of the way back up here to revisit his aircraft. Colonel Balchen came too. Then, at the last minute, somebody issued an order that they couldn't land out there. The idea was that the pilot — he was a doctor named Stinson, I believe — was to go back on board and see if he couldn't find something of his own to recover after all those years. *Life* magazine had photographers on board the aircraft and there was one correspondent. Well, they flew around in circles, took some pictures from the air, and then came home."

"Sounds like a fizzle," Jenkins said.

"No, not quite that bad, but nothing to what it might have been. Colonel Balchen, who knew more about those things than anyone, said at the time that a landing would have been easy."

Sergeant Stovers, who was definitely not slow witted, was already engaged in making a series of mental calculations. He had them completed to his satisfaction before another low-level pass close to the downed bomber had been completed. After that last flyby, Ferguson eased back on the yoke and pulled the C-130 up to a comfortable 1,000 feet above the seemingly endless ice plateau.

"I think we should take a vote on this," he said. "It looks very good to me, but I can't deny an element of risk. All those in favor . . ."

Corbin, the youthful copilot, nodded his approval; being a copilot, he knew he had better.

Jenkins, the navigator, lifted a thumb in the air.

"Andy?" Ferguson asked.

Aware that he would have to make any repairs required if something went wrong, the flight engineer hesitated. "As far as I can see it looks all right," he hedged.

"Bill?"

Sergeant Stovers knew that if he, as loadmaster, issued a veto, it would be respected. He had only to say that in his opinion the fuel load made it unwise and that would be that. Ferguson had not asked for his vote as a man as much as for his professional opinion. The fuel load was well within tolerances

33

and the big freighter was all but empty. With a slightly light-headed feeling, he drew breath into his lungs. "OK by me," he declared.

Ferguson did not even look at him, which would probably have been a mistake. Instead he concentrated totally on the wind lines that marked the top of the ice cap. Then he issued a crisp command.

"Skis down."

CHAPTER TWO

WHEN THE SAFETY of his aircraft and the welfare of his crew were involved, Ferguson did not underestimate the ice cap. He was acutely aware that if anything happened to disable the C-130, the consequences could range from serious to disastrous. Therefore, once having decided to land, he proceeded with such obvious caution that Sergeant Stovers was amazed.

After deciding on the area which looked most promising as a runway, he inspected it minutely during a flyover in each direction at minimum safe speed and altitude. When he had done that, he pulled up to give himself a little more maneuvering room, swung around 180 degrees, and then set up a long, slow approach at a very shallow rate of descent. He timed it almost perfectly so that he arrived at the beginning of his selected landing area just as he was at flaring altitude. He eased back on the yoke and then rested his right hand on the pitch controls as he waited for the two rear skis to touch. When they did so, the harsh, loud scraping sounded through the whole aircraft. He did not drop the nose ski on; instead he added a fraction more power.

Nose lifted, the big turboprop moved across the ice cap just under takeoff speed with its rear skis tracing a firm pattern on the snow cover. Concentrating intently, and ready to add power the moment there was any evidence of a possible snow bridge that might give way, or any other unseen hazard, Ferguson felt out the surface without committing himself to a landing. When he had covered a good 8,000 feet, he eased back on the yoke to increase the angle of attack, added additional power, and lifted quickly back into the security of the air.

When he had sufficient altitude, he turned back at reduced speed and inspected the tracks he had just made for any evidence of a possible dangerous area. Satisfied at last, he climbed again to turning altitude, swung around once more, and established his final approach. He flared with extreme care, but as the rear skis made contact the airframe shook gently and the noise was abrasive throughout the fuselage. This time Ferguson eased the nose ski down and the heavy airlifter was fairly on the ice. It was as good and smooth a ski landing as he had ever made. As soon as the speed began to drop and it was evident that everything had been successful, a certain constrained excitement began to be felt by every man on board.

Ferguson let the Hercules slide across the snow cover at partial power until the old B-17 was only a short distance ahead. Then he chopped the power back and his airlifter slid to rest less than seventy yards from the end of the wing of the old bomber.

Sergeant Stovers opened the crew door and swung it down to form the four steps that led to the surface of the snow. As he

36

did so, he had an odd, undefinable sensation. He had made many ice cap landings at DEW Line sites, but always in marked-off and established areas. Now he was hundreds of miles from any place he had ever been on the ice cap before and the ghost of the abandoned B-17 hulk added a sense of unreality.

Although he was far from a romantic, the thought did come to him that if he had had a space suit on, it might have been something like stepping onto the surface of a different planet. Against his own well-seated conservative judgment, he was for a few stimulating moments glad that Ferguson had decided to set down.

In the hold, the rest of the crew and the three riders from Sondrestrom were busy getting into their parkas and other arctic equipment. When everyone was ready, Stovers included, by common unexpressed consent they all waited for Ferguson to be the first to step out onto the virgin snow. Sensing this, the youthful aircraft commander ducked his head, thrust his shoulders through the doorway, and climbed down. Despite the invitation of the silent, frozen bomber, he first made a careful inspection of his ski gear and assured himself that the C-130 was standing firmly on the ice and was in no possible danger of sinking in. Satisfied, he went back to the crew door where the others were still waiting.

Together the nine men who made up the party walked abreast the short distance to the old bomber. As they drew closer it seemed to grow a little in size—a patient piece of relatively complex machinery which, in utter solitude, had stood there for more than three decades. Once it had been able to fly, now it was a hopeless derelict totally without any power whatever to help itself.

Perhaps out of respect for the flying machine it had once been, the little party walked completely around it to inspect its condition. Jenkins, the navigator, had his Rolleiflex that had been modified for Arctic use. With it he took a number of pictures, squatting down for better camera angles and then backing away to get in some of the sweep of the ice cap which now formed almost all of the visible world.

"Shall we go on board?" Holcomb asked.

Ferguson paused by the nose before he answered. "I've got to respect the man who flew her," he said aloud, but largely to himself. "He put the gear down before he landed. The easy and safe way would have been to slide her in on her belly, but he wanted to give her a chance."

Corbin, a redheaded Californian who had once had thoughts of trying to organize an Arctic skin diving club, felt the miasma that filled the sharply cold air close to the old warplane and asked a reasonable question. "Do you think he had ideas about taking her off again? Otherwise, I don't see why he put the wheels down. It was a lot riskier way to land."

"I think he couldn't bring himself to do the thing that he knew would permanently wreck his fine new bird," Ferguson responded. "He must have been almost certain before he set her down that she would never fly again, but there's always that one outside chance. Suppose he iced up in bad weather and couldn't climb above it. Probably he knew almost nothing about the ice cap, but he could well have believed that with improved weather, if it came soon enough, he would be able to clear up the trouble and get her airborne again. It must have been a pretty desperate hope, but he took a calculated chance without too much added risk." He stopped and looked again at the ghost ship half-buried in the compacted snow. "I'd have done the same thing," he added.

Sergeant Stovers was interested in the fact that the design which had been painted on the nose was still partially visible despite the cruel weathering it had endured. It was far from intact, but it could be made out. Some of the letters of the name were totally gone, others were readable. By making four or five patient trips to first one side and then the other of the nose, he was at last able to decipher what the words had been.

As is characteristic of many senior NCO's, he did not volunteer the information, but waited to be asked.

Ferguson finished his inspection of the nose area and walked around the wing toward the rear of the old fuselage. He felt very strongly the magnetism of the derelict aircraft, at last receiving visitors after such a long and hopeless wait. Over the years the snow had gradually built up into a semi-solid mass against the fuselage until it was almost level with the top of the main structure.

One of the riders from Sondrestrom, a captain named Finch, came up to stand beside him. "Want to go on board?" he asked.

"I think so," Ferguson answered.

"I'll get an axe from the C-130," Finch said. "We can chop a hole through the top. It's the easiest way."

"We'll do nothing of the kind," Ferguson came back. "This may be an old wreck, but it's still an airplane and entitled to some respect. If we go on board, it'll be properly through the crew door."

For some reason that proclamation warmed Sergeant Stovers. He gladly went back to the C-130 and broke out the two shovels he kept on board against the time that a ski might plow in somewhere and have to be dug out. It was up to him to think of things like that.

When he came back with the tools, he handed one of them to Andy Holcomb. Then he allowed himself the honor of chopping out the first shovelful of snow and throwing it aside. For five minutes he and Holcomb labored to make headway through the hard-frozen snow that had gathered against the gear and had piled up underneath the bomb bay. When the captain tapped him on the shoulder and offered to take over, Stovers handed him the shovel and let him work out his penance.

It took some time to chip away enough of the stubborn stuff, but the wind was light and there were plenty of fresh

39

hands to keep the work going. Ferguson did his share as did everyone else until, after a good thirty minutes, enough snow had been removed to give access to the underneath crew door.

As everyone had expected, it was frozen rigidly shut.

"Maybe it's locked," Corbin suggested.

Ferguson shook his head, "The pilot wouldn't do that, he'd leave it open. There aren't any sneak thieves around here."

The Californian pressed his lips together, wishing that he had had the sense to see that before he had made a fool of himself. His embarrassment was relieved when Andy Holcomb returned from another trip back to the C-130; this time he was carrying a thin red signal flare in his left mitten and an empty canvas bucket in his right.

"Bill," he said to Stovers, "fill this with loose snow and stand by. I'm going to try and free up the door without setting fire to the whole wreck. If anything starts to sizzle, get the snow onto it fast."

When everything was ready he pulled the cap off the flare and struck it expertly despite the cumbersome arctic mittens he had on his hands. When the hot chemical flame appeared, he brought it slowly close to the door handle and latching mechanism. He spent more than five minutes of cautious careful work, testing continuously, trying to get even the slightest sign of movement from the unyielding handle. Then, quite abruptly, it gave way and turned. Holcomb looked over his shoulder with a grin on his face. "It still works," he announced. "It should. Nothing corrodes on the ice cap. It's virtually impossible."

Carefully wiping away the melted ice as fast as he got it to yield, he worked his way around the door jamb. By the time he finished the latch was again immovable, but the application of a little more heat released it once again. Like a magician presenting his climactic illusion, he jerked, yanked, used the flare at several points of resistance and then with one last concerted effort pulled the protesting door open. His success achieved, he threw the still-burning flare well out onto the ice cap where it could do no harm.

At Ferguson's motioned invitation, Holcomb climbed in first. As he elbowed his way up through the opening, it seemed to him that he was invading a stark relic of a bygone age. Everything was in rigid, frozen immobility. A thick layer of snow covered everything that was flat enough to offer it a bed. Something about the scene seemed familiar, then he remembered. He had seen a movie not too long before in which part of the earth was shown after it had been presumably seared by a nuclear blast. It had been the same way—a kind of frozen animation, as though men had been here and then had suddenly gone a long time ago.

There was no odor whatever inside the old wreck, not a trace of the familiar aircraft smells of fuel, oils, metal, heavy fabrics, electrical insulation, hydraulic fluid, spilled coffee, and the coming and going of many human bodies. The absolute absence of any kind of scent gave the whole fantastic scene a strong aura of unreality. For the first time he realized how utterly and hopelessly dead the old bomber was. He was inside a cadaver.

Ferguson had come up and was looking inside the cockpit. It was mute and empty, still waiting for the skilled hands of the pilots who would never come. Despite three decades of merciless exposure, a few of the fittings still looked new, proof that the gallant old bird had been born only to meet an almost immediate and undeserved death. Ferguson felt the controls and found them as rigid as stone.

He wondered, if some great crane were to lift the wreck to a warm climate and let it thaw out there, how many of the multiple levers, switches, and handles could be made to move. It was idle speculation, because the Arctic was unrelenting in its grip, particularly at this high latitude. It might be another twenty years before any other human beings would visit this tragically deceased four-engined bomber.

He turned away to find Holcomb watching behind him. "Would you like to fly it, sir?" the sergeant asked through his thick white breath.

"If I could, I would," Ferguson answered. "She deserved better than an end like this. I hate to go away and leave her out here."

Holcomb thought about that for a moment. "Sir," he inquired, "do you think we could take back something, some part of her, as a souvenir?"

"I was thinking the same thing, but I'd hate to hack her up to do it."

"Certainly not," Holcomb agreed. "No butchery. I won't have it on my conscience."

"Then anything you can get loose and out the door, I think we can have. But don't take too much time, we're expected back."

"Yes, sir."

While Holcomb returned to the C-130 once more to get what few tools he might need, the others in the party took their turns visiting the old bomber hulk. There was a mixed reaction; two of the Sondrestrom pilots were already bored and clearly wanted to get back home. Holcomb, on the other hand, and Jenkins, seemed willing to remain all day if it were possible.

Remembering his responsibilities, Ferguson set a twenty-minute time limit for the collection of souvenirs from the wreck. At the end of the allotted time, plus a five-minute dispensation to complete a job on hand, Jenkins had proudly recovered the ship's octant; and Holcomb, with Stovers's patient if not particularly sympathetic help, had a real prize—a communication set he had succeeded in removing from its brackets by heating them with a candle flame. The candle itself came out of a personal survival pack which Stovers had devised to contain everything that the regular equipment did not include.

The adventure over, Holcomb fired up the APU on the C-130 and the desolate ice cap echoed with the shrill scream of the turbine generator.

"I wonder if she can hear it?" he asked, only half in jest, of Jenkins, who was making a measurement on his chart.

"I'd like to think so," the navigator answered as he plotted his best estimate of their exact position.

After the engines were started and the checklists completed, there was no real point in taxiing back to where they had first touched down; the ice cap appeared equally firm and solid ahead of them and there was still a good 4,000 feet of ski tracks to show where the surface had been tested.

Without a load on board, and in the cold, heavy air, the Hercules required only a short run, even at the high altitude and on skis. With the combined howl of four great turbines, the C-130 moved forward, gathered speed, and returned to her element.

"Did you get the tail number?" Ferguson asked his navigator over the intercom.

"Yes, sir," Jenkins answered. "And I have her exact position plotted as closely as I could determine it. I'm within a five-mile circle, I'm sure of that."

"Don't forget that that octant you have is technically government property, although I expect they'll let you keep it. The same goes for your radio, Holcomb—it won't be of any use now, but let's keep everything proper and above board."

"Absolutely," Jenkins agreed.

"Scotty, do you know Sergeant Murphy up at Thule?" the copilot asked.

"I'm not sure, what about him?"

"He hates the Arctic like the devil, but he's an electronics genius. I'm going to ask him to get this thing working again, just to prove that it can be done. My money says that he can."

"Five bucks," Jenkins cut in.

"You're on. Any time limit?"

Jenkins pressed his intercom button once more. "No, but he has to get the original set working and get a recognizable signal on it. He can use a reasonable number of new parts, if he can find them, but he can't build the whole thing over."

"Fair enough."

Sergeant Holcomb made a contribution. "The instrument shop might be able to get that octant in shape again. It's a Bendix Mixmaster and they won't be able to get any parts for it anymore, but those guys are pretty sharp."

Ferguson touched the intercom switch on the back of the yoke. "No bets on that; it may not be too hard. The thing has been in a weatherproof case and the fuselage gave it some added protection."

During the quiet that followed for the next several minutes Sergeant Bill Stovers fought an invisible battle with himself. He had been incubating an idea ever since the takeoff, but his better judgment told him to forget it. He walked back and forth a few paces each way in the big empty cargo hold, pretending to inspect various pieces of equipment that he already knew to be in perfect order, while he thought the matter out. At last he overcame what he knew was his better judgment and returned to the flight deck.

He plugged in a headset, adjusted it, and then used the intercom. "Sir," he asked, "do you think it's possible that we might go back to that B-17 again sometime? If we took the proper equipment along, we might be able to salvage a propeller or something like that for the NCO Club."

"I can't see why not," Ferguson answered.

CHAPTER THREE

THE DISCOVERY of the B-17 made the return to Sondrestrom a minor event. Although he kept it from showing, or thought that he did, Lieutenant Ferguson had the fiery hope that it was, indeed, a new find. He had his own private reasons for that and they had nothing to do with a desire to put his name on file as the discoverer.

Together with Jenkins, his navigator, he went to Operations, and through the communications available there reported to the Aerospace Rescue and Recovery Service the location of the downed bomber and the tail number by which it could be identified — if any records were still available after thirty years. One of the functions of the ARRS was to keep careful track of every known aircraft wreck anywhere in the free world.

The Operations NCOIC was interested. "How well were you able to see it?" he asked. "How close did you get?"

"We landed," Jenkins answered. "The area was ideal for it and we wanted to determine if there were any bodies on board that should be returned to the States for proper burial."

"What did you find?"

"Nothing except the old bird itself. We were able to check inside and there was no evidence of the crew."

The sergeant behind the counter nodded. "That may save some headaches later on. Thanks a lot, Lieutenant."

"No sweat."

The NCOIC checked the board behind him. "You know that you're scheduled out to Thule at ten hundred hours tomorrow."

"Yes," Ferguson answered, "but we still don't know why."

"They'll tell you, sir—eventually."

"I'm sure they will. Call us a taxi, will you?"

The sergeant nodded and picked up a phone.

Lieutenant Ferguson's mind was churning as he lined up the runway, five minutes early, and ran through the last few pre-takeoff checks. Behind him he had a six-pallet load that had been checked and secured by Sergeant Stovers. Up near the front of the cargo hold the crew's personal gear had been stowed and strapped down. The four turbine engines were howling their song of power; the rugged airframe was closed up and ready.

As soon as the tower gave the word, Corbin eased the power forward and the engines surged. The wheels began to roll down the snow-covered runway at exactly 0957. As he always did, Ferguson enjoyed, the gathering speed of the Hercules; with a little more than 4,000 feet of runway behind him he rotated and the big airlifter came smoothly off the ground. When the wheels and flaps were up, and he had sufficient altitude, he turned her north toward Thule—the furthest

46

outpost of the United States Air Force and perhaps the most extraordinary military base in the world.

Sondrestrom was well north of the Arctic Circle, but Thule was hundreds of miles beyond that. Its desperate isolation and extreme latitude had justly earned for it the ancient name *Ultima Thule* — the end of the earth.

Below the wings of the aluminum bird there was nothing but snow, a vast eternity of it, and occasional rocks that broke through like the lost souls in Dante's frozen sea. In the left-hand seat, Ferguson looked out at the fantastic panorama and almost shuddered because of the thoughts that were tumbling through his mind. Each time that he flew this route he remembered again his great ambition to be an astronaut and the defeat that had been forced upon him simply because he was too tall. There had been no measurement of his abilities or of his determination, only the bare fact that he was too far over the height limit and therefore, by accident of birth, cut off from the great adventure into space. Instead of an exotic spacecraft traveling to the far reaches of the solar system, instead of the red deserts of Mars or the shrouding cloud cover of Venus, or even the totally hostile — yet attained — moon, he had to settle for a chunky freighter, a flying truck condemned by its special equipment to remain forever in the limited areas of the Arctic. Free bird that it was, it could not even roam its own planet as it had been built to do.

He had been sentenced to earth because of three inches nature had added to his frame. The C-130 had been sentenced to the Arctic because Lockheed had fastened a set of cumbersome skis to its underbelly — more than three tons of added weight it must always carry, three awkward objects perpetually out in the slipstream to add punishing drag and cut down the streamlining of the clean wing and the otherwise trim fuselage.

He took hold of the control yoke and touched the red button that disconnected the autopilot. Flying then by hand he

47

breathed his understanding to the aircraft that was his partner in flight. So far and no further they could go together. The destiny of man always seemed to rest with a privileged few who somehow managed to be standing in just the right place at the right time, with the right degrees, the right attitudes, the right aptitudes, the right ages, the right reactions, the right rank — and the right dimensions.

Ferguson wanted to wrench the transport around in a barrel roll, to work off his emotions by soaring high, topping out, and then plunging downward, by pulling up onto his back in a half loop and rolling out in a stomach-wrenching Cuban 8. But you can't do that in a loaded C-130; a fine bird she is, but built to fly straight and level. Her job is to plod on down the highway of the sky and deliver so many tons of freight at the other end — mission accomplished.

Probably the pilot of the old B-17 had had some of the same feelings, because he had been a flyer too. He had had no aspirations toward becoming an astronaut, they had been all but undreamed of in those days, but he had known the wonderful freedom of the skies and had experienced the subtle patterns of ever-changing clouds that only the airman can witness. Perhaps he had been green and inexperienced, and therefore had wrecked the beautiful new bird they had given him to fly because he hadn't known where in hell he was going. But he *had* put the wheels down, proof that he had hoped to fly it out again, one way or another. That was the mark of a man willing to take an added risk to try and save his airplane, and Ferguson mentally reached across the span of years that had passed since then and saluted him for it.

Corbin tapped him on the shoulder and broke his reverie. With a gesture of his hand his copilot indicated that it was time to descend. For a second Ferguson was disoriented; he had been flying mechanically with his mind preoccupied. Swiftly he pulled himself back to reality. He checked the heading, read the DME, and saw that he was fast approaching Thule;

48

the C-130 was already within 900 miles of the North Pole. As Corbin reported in, Ferguson set up a standard rate descent. His daydreams were gone now — he was fully occupied in bringing in his aircraft despite the fact that the traffic that close to the top of the world was negligible; he was given number one to land while he was still above 10,000 feet.

The business of the checklist began as the Hercules continued to unwind its altimeters, coming steadily closer to the frozen world that lay below. Presently the distinctive round shape of the Arctic mesa known as Mount Dundas lay directly ahead and Thule was within visual range.

He banked the C-130 the allowable amount, put it on the glide path, brought it down the track, and greased it on without giving a thought to allowing Corbin to test his skill. Ferguson was not in a mood to relinquish anything.

When he checked in at Operations, there was a message for him. He was to call General Pritchard in the Pentagon immediately upon his arrival.

The sickening thought hit him that he was to be chewed out from on high for having landed without authority on the ice cap. In a way, despite the careful precautions he had taken, it could be argued that he had unnecessarily risked his aircraft and his crew. Normally his orders came from Scott Air Force Base in Illinois, the headquarters of the Military Airlift Command. If the Pentagon wanted him, then something out of the ordinary was definitely afoot.

Good-bye command.

Fortunately there was a phone he could use without the embarrassment of having others tuned in and listening. He informed the base operator of the order he had received and then patiently waited for the moment when the axe would descend.

The pattern of communications was woven and the general's aide came on the line. "One minute please, the general would like to speak personally with Lieutenant Ferguson."

The one thing Ferguson most feared at that moment was the thought that Sergeant Stovers would be able to hitch up his pants and silently say, "I told you so," for the rest of his life.

The general came on the line. "Lieutenant Ferguson, I understand you are the crew commander of the C-130 that discovered the wreck of a B-17 on the ice cap yesterday."

"Affirmative, sir."

"Am I correct that you actually landed next to the hulk and explored it to some extent?"

Here it came. "Yes, sir, after checking the area first, of course. If there had been any bodies . . ."

"I understand. How much risk is involved in landing out there, Lieutenant?"

How decent of him to put it that way!

"Apart from the possible dangers inherent in all unconventional operations, sir, I would say almost none at all. Landing out there is like landing on the dry lake bed at Edwards. Not quite that good, but very nearly, sir."

Now let him chew him out, the stinger had been pulled.

"All right, Lieutenant, there is something I would like to have you do. I've already cleared it with Scott, so that's taken care of. You know approximately where the wreck is, don't you?"

"Yes, sir."

"Good. Weather permitting, I'd like to have you go back there tomorrow. If the tail number we received here is correct, there may be something on that B-17 I'd like to have you recover if possible."

"Would you describe it, sir."

"Yes, of course. It's a wooden box, or crate, unmarked. I don't have the exact dimensions, but it should weigh about a hundred pounds, plus or minus. There may be two or three other crates stowed somewhere on board; if by any chance you find them, it would be prudent to recover them all. I realize that they may no longer be there—it's been a long time."

"It's still possible, sir. It's an extremely isolated area with no surface traffic at all to my knowledge."

"I don't presume that you saw anything like that when you explored the wreck."

"No, sir, but everything was covered with a thick blanket of snow and we weren't there very long. If those crates are still on board the aircraft, we'll get them for you, sir."

"Fine, so ordered. When you do, bring them back to Thule and then report immediately to Colonel Kleckner, the base commander. He will direct you where they are to be stowed. They are not to be delivered to anyone else."

"Understood, sir."

"Now if for any reason the weather isn't good, or if you need your regulation crew rest, it doesn't have to be tomorrow. I would say, however, that now that the plane has been rediscovered, there is some urgency in getting this errand done as soon as possible."

"You can depend on us, sir."

"One more thing: I realize that the word is out on your having found that old bomber and it can't be recalled. That's all right, but concerning your errand, keep it as quiet as you reasonably can."

"How about the crew, sir?"

"They will have to know, of course. Once that piece of freight is safely in your possession, the major risk will be over. By the way, handle it with some care. It was originally equipped with a protective device that would destroy the contents if an unauthorized person attempted to open it. I'm sure that it's no longer operational after thirty years, but try not to put a crowbar to it if it happens to be frozen down hard. Chop a piece out of the airframe if you have to."

"I understand, sir. We'll treat it as hazardous cargo, sir, and take all of the usual precautions."

"That won't be necessary, Lieutenant. The protective device, even if by some chance it thawed out and functioned, would not endanger your aircraft. It was expressly packaged for air shipment."

"Sir, may I ask a question?"

"Go ahead."

"We'd be very grateful if you could tell us anything about the fate of the crew that flew the B-17. We'd like very much to know if they made out all right."

"The crew made out fine. They got pretty cold, and hungry, but they were able to send out some radio signals. Have you heard of Colonel Bernt Balchen?"

"Of course, sir. The great Arctic expert."

"Right. Colonel Balchen rescued them off the ice cap, just as he did the crew of the *My Gal Sal*. I assume you know about that."

"Yes, sir."

"They were out there several days before Colonel Balchen got to them. They were pretty far gone, but they all made it. Shortly after they were picked up, a major storm closed the area and laid down a fresh blanket of snow. After that, no one was able to find the plane. There was a shortage of equipment and too many other things to do at the same time."

"Thank you very much, sir. I understand now why they weren't able to bring that piece of cargo out with them."

"Don't underestimate that crew, Lieutenant; they tried their best, but they got the wrong crate. It wasn't their fault. This isn't for publication, but the crates were color-coded. The pilot was conscious and he asked that the right one be brought."

"Then what fouled it up, sir?"

"A color-blind Eskimo. Such things happen, you know."

"Sir, were you by any chance there?"

"Negative, Lieutenant, but since this is a semi-secured line, I will tell you that at one time we were quietly looking for that bird. For some reason, we didn't find it; fortunately you did."

52

"Thank you, sir. Weather permitting, we'll be out early in the morning."

"Thank you, Lieutenant. Good-bye."

Chief Master Sergeant Perry S. Feinberg relaxed expansively in the warm interior of the Thule NCO Club and took his ease in the grand manner. He was a big man, six feet tall and of impressive bulk which was not all muscle, despite the fact that he liked to think it was. His mind was alert, his professional competence legendary, and his discretion absolute. Although the tour at Thule is only one year, at that moment Sergeant Feinberg could not comprehend how the base would manage to operate once he had departed. In full justice to his remarkable abilities, it needs to be added that during occasional fleeting moments the base commander shared the same thought. Sergeant Feinberg invariably got results.

There are certain men who have such unbounded confidence that no challenge appears too great, no proposition too tough to be handled. Sergeant Feinberg was such a person. He had his full measure of ego and took justifiable pride in what he was able to do. He was also in full possession of the well-known fact that the United States Air Force is directed and run by those mighty and potent men who are addressed professionally as "Sergeant." Generals he considered excellent for making plans, awarding decorations, and appearing as required before various committees of the Congress. When it came to supervising the maintenance of complicated aircraft, for example, and seeing that even thumb-fingered mechanics did things right the first time, practically all generals in his opinion would be out of their depth. Chief Master Sergeant Perry Feinberg would not.

Despite Sergeant Feinberg's outgoing personality, Bill Stovers found him much to his liking. As in the case of the

Mikado of Japan, when he said a thing would be done it was as good as done; virtually it *was* done, and it was safe to say so.

With a gesture that Gregory Peck would have recognized as beyond his powers, Sergeant Feinberg summoned the waiter, who was a moonlighting enlisted man, and ordered another round of drinks. When it came, Stovers picked up the tab because it was his turn.

"Tell me more; give me the details," Sergeant Feinberg demanded.

"After we scraped across the deck once to see if there were any potholes in the way, we set down and had a look at it. You could still read the tail number clearly."

"Did you get inside?" A gleam of unusual interest was visible on Feinberg's face.

"Yes, we did. One of the deadheads wanted to chop a hole in the upper deck, but Ferguson wouldn't allow it. He said it was still an airplane and entitled to respect."

"That's more sense than I gave him credit for," Sergeant Feinberg said generously.

"Andy Holcomb thawed out the crew door with a small flare and we got inside. We looked around a bit, but there wasn't too much to see. We recovered the navigator's octant and a communications set. There's a bet on about that."

"Let me guess." Sergeant Feinberg sampled from the newly provided glass and found it satisfactory. "Of course the bet is whether it can be made to work after all these years."

"Specifically, the bet is whether Sergeant Murphy can get it going and bring in a recognizable signal on it. He can use a reasonable number of necessary parts, but he can't rebuild it from the ground up."

Sergeant Feinberg lit a cigar like a Spanish grandee. "It's a losing bet, because Murphy won't do it. My money says he could if he wanted to, but forget it. He's only got a few weeks to go and then he's out. He keeps track — hour by hour."

"I never saw the countdown chart above his desk."

"The only man without one. He objects to it because it depicts a nude female. Sergeant Murphy has principles; he belongs to a very conservative church."

"But he still keeps track, you said, 'hour by hour.' Is he stir crazy? The Thule Twitches?"

"How well do you know Mike Murphy?" Feinberg asked.

"Not too well."

Perry Feinberg blew a smoke ring that floated like the nebula in Lyra until the sergeant sent a thin jet of smoke after it and it dissipated. "Mike Murphy, apart from his family, has only two major interests in his life and the commanding one is gardening."

"Gardening," Stovers repeated.

"Gardening. He made a perfectly serious proposal to build a heated greenhouse, equip it with artificial lights, and raise some of our own fresh vegetables up here. He felt sure he could do it. Since the soil is virgin, he thought it would be fascinating to plant it for the first time. Most soil has produced thousands of crops — weeds if nothing else. The soil up here hasn't produced anything since the ice age, possibly not since the earth was formed."

"That is a thought," Stovers agreed. "With no rotted older plants to put nitrogen into the soil, would it bear?"

"Ask Mike Murphy, maybe he has the answer to that one. Anyway, Mike can't wait to get out of here; when he retires, he's all set to go into the nursery business."

"I still don't see, though," Stovers persisted, "why his plans to go into business would interfere with his fixing a radio set. That's his job, isn't it?"

"Not that World War II set; that would have to be a labor of love. Look at it this way: when a man is crouched down, with his fingers on the line ready to start a hundred-yard dash, that's a helluva time to try and sell him any life insurance."

Sergeant Holcomb appeared and joined the party without waiting to be invited. Mercifully, the jukebox was quiet, and across the room there was little activity at the bar. "I thought you'd like to have the word," he said to Stovers. "Tomorrow we fly."

"We just got here!"

"Well don't count on too much crew rest, because we're going back to the wreck we found yesterday."

"Back to the wreck?" Stovers was genuinely nonplussed. "How did the boy wonder ever get permission to do that? Or did he set it up on his own?"

The waiter appeared and Holcomb ordered beer. "All I know," he said, "is that Sergeant Withers in Ops had a message for him when he came in to call General Pritchard in the puzzle palace immediately upon arrival."

Perry Feinberg leaned back in his chair with a considerable satisfaction showing on his broad face. "It's time I let you guys in on something," he began expansively. "For a while it was classified, but it couldn't be anymore. Do either of you guys know Ed Scott? Well, he was at Sondrestrom during the war when it was Bluie West Eight. He was a corporal at that time and was in the communications end. One day the word came in that a high-priority B-17 flight was coming through. They caught an unexpected Phase Two and the bird had to overfly. The crew crash-landed somewhere north of Bluie on the ice cap. Fortunately some radio gear was still operational and they were able to put out a signal. They were saved after about four days. Colonel Balchen pulled them off."

"The same B-17?" Holcomb wanted to know.

"I'm not sure, but it could be. When Ed finally told me about that incident, he remembered the name of the aircraft; it was called *The Passionate Penguin*."

Bill Stovers took his time; when he did speak, it was without emphasis. "It's the same airplane," he announced. "I read the name on her nose when we were out there. That was it, *The Passionate Penguin*."

"Then . . ." Sergeant Feinberg paused clearly for dramatic

56

effect, "you'd probably like to hear the rest of the story."

"If it isn't still classified," Bill Stovers cautioned.

"A restricted flight over an established route covering friendly territory couldn't still be under wraps after thirty years," Feinberg replied, flicking an ash from his cigar.

"All right," Stovers conceded.

"According to Ed Scott, who didn't tell me until *he* was satisfied that it was no longer secret, the *Penguin* was carrying a package of important war dispatches, or so it was rumored, and when the crew was rescued, they left it on the airplane."

"They couldn't have been that careless," Holcomb said.

"They weren't careless; they came out lugging something they thought was their secret cargo. But they had the wrong container."

Bill Stovers said nothing until he had lit a pipe and had it going to his satisfaction. "Probably they were given a fake container while the real one was marked 'mechanical parts'; it was a familiar dodge and a very stupid one. Where's Ed Scott now?"

"Japan," Feinberg answered. "I'm going to write to him when I get back to my quarters. There's a C-130 coming through tomorrow that's going over the top to Alaska. At Elmendorf they can hand the letter to the flight engineer of the next C-141 headed for Japan. Scotty should have it in three or four days. If he answers promptly — and he will unless he's on TDY — in a little more than a week I should know a lot more about the B-17."

"It could just be," Holcomb said slowly, "that with the hurry-up call from the Pentagon right after we found the old wreck, we might be going out to recover that secret shipment — even after so many years."

"You are now the last man at this table to have thought of that," Feinberg informed him. "Not that it's secret anymore, but they might like to have it back, just the same."

The glasses were empty and Holcomb bought a round.

"So when you go out there tomorrow," Sergeant Feinberg continued, "I think I'll come along. Just in case the boy wonder doesn't have orders to pick up that container, I'll latch onto it, if I can find it, and bring it back. The colonel just possibly might be interested."

"I would say so," Stovers agreed.

"In addition to which," Feinberg added, "I plan to take along a few of my boys and some light maintenance stands. You suggested, Bill, that a prop from the old bird would look nice all shined up on the wall there." He indicated the proper spot. "Any objections?"

Holcomb shook his head. "Not as long as you can handle the boy wonder."

Sergeant Feinberg casually flicked the ashes from the tip of his cigar again and made a neat mound in the ashtray. "A mere bagatelle," he said.

CHAPTER FOUR

LIEUTENANT SCOTT FERGUSON had no intention of carrying any extra personnel on his return to the carcass of *The Passionate Penguin*. Because his active imagination would not be stilled, he had allowed himself the luxury of considering his special assignment to be a particularly sensitive classified mission of the type that seldom falls to the lot of first lieutenants. The idea of carrying any additional sightseers did not at all fit with his conception of the thing he had been asked to do. Sergeant Feinberg sensed his attitude at once and proceeded according to plan.

"May I speak with you privately for a moment, sir?" he inquired at the appropriate moment.

Ferguson handed in his flight plan to the Ops man on duty and then glanced at his watch. "Certainly, but if it's about coming along with us this morning, I'm afraid that I can't approve it."

Sergeant Feinberg led him away from the counter and toward a private corner of the Operations area. "Sir, there is a consideration involved about which you may not know."

"What is it?" Ferguson asked, trying not to appear impatient, but at the same time suggesting that he was a busy man.

Sergeant Feinberg became confidential. "A few years ago I attended the NCO Academy at Orlando with Sergeant Edmund Scott, who is now a close friend of mine. Sergeant Scott was on duty in Greenland at the time that the B-17 was lost on the ice cap."

"Could we skip the ancient history?"

"Not very well, sir, if you're to be fully informed."

"Then go ahead."

Sergeant Feinberg managed to suggest with an invisible gesture that Lieutenant Ferguson had just made a very wise and prudent decision. "The point is, Sergeant Scott mentioned to me on one occasion that the flight of that aircraft was quite heavily under wraps; it was reputed to be carrying something of a significant nature as an item of special cargo. Of course, since it had been more than twenty years ago at the time, the classification had been removed."

Ferguson looked at him for a long moment.

"I am now confiding in you, sir, the fact that to the best of Sergeant Scott's knowledge, the sensitive item on that aircraft was never recovered. I believe I can recognize it. What I plan to do, with your approval of course, is to pick it up quietly and secure it on board the C-130. One more thing, sir: so as not to be obvious about it, I've dropped the suggestion that it might be interesting to recover one of the propellers from that old crate — I beg your pardon, sir — I mean aircraft and display it properly refurbished in a place of honor in the NCO Club. Some of my men would like to do that."

"A smoke screen," Ferguson said.

Feinberg beamed his appreciation of Lieutenant Ferguson's astuteness. "Exactly, sir. It will also explain, if anyone happens to be interested, why we went back to the B-17 in the first place."

Ferguson thought and considered three possible responses before he spoke.

"All right, you and your boys can come along in order to create a suitable diversion. Pass the word to Sergeant Stovers to load some maintenance stands—you will have to have them to get a prop off. And possibly an A-frame to get it down without dropping it."

"Yes, sir."

Just as Feinberg was turning away, apparently to follow his instructions, Ferguson had another thought. "That is, if it won't take too long," he added.

It was the moment for truth and Feinberg recognized it. "I believe that they're already on board, sir," he said. He was careful to keep his face wooden as he spoke.

The takeoff at 0840 hours was uneventful. The C-130 rolled down the runway hardly more than 3,000 feet, rotated, and surged up into the cold sky. After leveling off at 15,000 feet Ferguson passed control to his copilot and went down into the main cargo hold to see precisely what he was carrying. There were several light maintenance stands, a large heater unit, kits of tools, four sets of skis, and, including Sergeant Feinberg, a total of six additional crew members.

Ferguson signaled to the chief master sergeant and spoke to him above the howling of the turbines just outside. "Did you need this many people? All this gear?"

Feinberg managed to show respect and radiant confidence at the same time. "I tried to think of things that would be useful, sir. For example, the heater unit will thaw out the door quickly for us and then make the inside of the B-17 a lot more comfortable. It occurred to me that some of the things we might like to recover will be frozen down pretty solidly. The heater should handle that problem without attracting undue attention."

Ferguson admitted to himself that he hadn't thought of that solution.

"Two of the troops are ski experts," Feinberg went on. "While we're at the aircraft, they will survey the landing strip and check it for safe operations."

"Is that what those markers are for?" Ferguson asked, nodding his head in the direction of some additional supplies he had just noticed.

"Yes, sir. It's expendable equipment, and knowing how these things sometimes work out, it seemed like a good idea to secure the landing area."

Ferguson decided to be candid. "In other words, to support my judgment when I landed there in the first place."

Feinberg gave him a significant look. "Well, sir, there's no harm in protecting youiself, as it were, when you have the chance. Not that I'm suggesting that you need it, sir. . . ."

Ferguson returned to the bridge and the left-hand seat. He did not even pause to speak with his loadmaster, who had carefully remained at a deliberate distance to let Feinberg do the talking.

Less than an hour later, the Hercules was three minutes short of Lieutenant Jenkins ETA when the redheaded copilot came on the intercom. "There she is," he said, and pointed ahead at a two-o'clock angle. Ferguson chalked one up for his navigator, who had fixed the position of the wreck so accurately on their first visit and had relocated it so efficiently. The possible embarrassment of having to report to General Pritchard that they couldn't find the B-17 again would have been overwhelming.

Once more he checked the area carefully before putting the skis down. His former tracks were clearly visible and there were no signs of any landing hazards he could detect. Satisfied, he ordered the pre-landing checklist, extended the skis, set up an approach, and when everything was ready, slid the big airlifter onto the ice cap almost as gently as though it had been a dead-flat paved runway.

"You were right," Perry Feinberg said in the cabin to Bill Stovers, "Junior can fly."

"Damn right he can," Stovers responded.

This time, remembering the relatively heavy equipment that would have to be moved by hand, Ferguson taxied up until the left wing of the C-130 almost reached over the hull of the old bird whose long desolation was being broken for the second time within forty-eight hours. As Sergeant Holcomb shut down the engines and silence returned to the lonely ice cap, Ferguson felt again the sensation that he was on the surface of some other planet and about to explore the ruin of what had been an early spaceship—one of the first to land here. He kept his private romantic imaginings to himself and maintained a matter-of-fact, commander's exterior for the benefit of the others who were present.

By the time that he had donned his arctic gear and climbed down the four steps into the hold, the rear ramp had already been dropped and two men on skis were just exiting out onto the snow. They were roped together in the manner of mountaineers and had a small sled on which the runway markers had been loaded. That phase of the operation was well underway and Ferguson dismissed it from his attention.

The heater unit was next; it too had been sled mounted in order to make it reasonably movable on the surface of the ice cap. Sergeant Stovers was busy supervising its unloading and no additional help was needed. Ferguson chose the open crew door and stepped out himself into the sterile cold of the fantastic plateau. Comfortable in his arctic clothing, he looked with renewed wonder at the old hulk that had been standing in such total desolation for so long. He could not help wondering if, in some strange manner that humans could not grasp, she understood that she was once more receiving

63

visitors; that her all but endless vigil, waiting for her pilots to return, was, for the moment, over.

Since it would take a while to get the heater operating and the door thawed out once more, he walked around to the front of the old bird and drank in the contrast between her and the C-130 turboprop that was poised almost wingtip to wingtip. What a change in twenty-odd years of aircraft design!

Now that he knew what her name had been, he studied the nose of the old bomber and made out the letters for himself. The tail number was still quite clear, but the paint that had been used to christen her had not been of equal quality. There she sat, dead without knowing it, still putting up a pretext that she was an aircraft with her nose lifted toward the sky.

Ferguson's imagination frequently took off on its own without filing a flight plan as to its intentions. As he looked at the outdated wreck, he wished that some good fairy would grant him three wishes. He stood quietly in the snow, ignoring the splendid C-130 that was his to fly, and thought about the abandoned aircraft that had never lived to fulfill her destiny. She was a hulk, but she still looked like an airplane, and that was enough to win his sympathy.

Sergeant Feinberg approached, a huge bear of a man in his heavy arctic clothing. "We've got the heater going and we'll be inside shortly," he advised. "I told the boys that you'd given the order she was not to be chopped up and that whatever was taken off was to be removed properly. Is that right?"

"That's right!" Ferguson replied, and he practically barked the words.

Almost as though they had been working on that type of aircraft all of their lives, three of Perry Feinberg's boys were busy removing the number four propeller. The powerful portable heating unit threw a steady stream of warm air inside the fuselage as Lieutenant Jenkins and Sergeant Holcomb

64

scraped the encrusted snow off the places where it had lodged and pitched it down into the bomb bay. Ferguson lent a hand on the job, but as each bit of the interior was cleared, he paid close attention to what was being uncovered. With his arctic gloves on his hands he prodded the banked-up snow along the bottom sides of the fuselage. When he uncovered the corner of something that was clearly a wooden crate, a savage thrill of discovery took hold of him. With two or three minutes additional work he had it clear and as far as he could tell, it was the sensitive cargo he had been sent to recover.

As anticipated, it was frozen down as firmly as though it had been riveted in place.

He continued with his exploration and within a matter of minutes he had unsnowed two additional crates not too different from his initial find. He was satisfied then that one of them would be the critical item, safe and sound after three decades of unguarded isolation.

The heater would have all of the crates thawed out within a reasonable time, he postulated. Inwardly he was secretly glad that it would probably not be too soon; in a somewhat strange mood that he himself could not recognize, he was in no hurry to leave. He had the thought that he would never be returning here again and at his age he disliked to close any door behind him finally and forever.

He paid another visit to the cockpit, planning to content himself by simply looking at the frozen controls. For a moment he put his right hand on the four throttles and imagined that he was indeed pushing them forward. Then he remembered; he couldn't do that — they were working on one of the props.

Ferguson wanted some part of her to keep for his own, as a symbol of a new-found friendship between man and machine. He had not even been born when she had last flown, but they met now as adults.

The cushion on the pilot's seat probably would be thawed

out in a little while. The fleeting heat would warm up the old bird a bit before the perpetual cold would return. It was one amenity she had been granted as a kind of posthumous salute. He promised silently that he would use the cushion whenever he could and in that small way help the aircraft to regain her self-respect.

He looked out and saw that the number four prop was already off; loaded on the heater sled, it was being taken on board the C-130. After all, it was a reasonable thing that they had done, even though he didn't like to see the B-17 dismembered like that. He sat down inside the still-warming fuselage and contented himself with doing nothing.

At 1212 hours Bill Stovers brought him a box lunch and a cup of hot coffee. It had been a helluva long time, Ferguson thought, since anyone had sat and drunk hot coffee inside that old bird.

He looked out and noted that part of the crew was back in the Herc, presumably eating and using the head, but the rest were still at work. A substantial A-frame had been rigged over the number four nacelle; it took him a while to awake to the fact that they were also removing the number four engine.

Taking off an engine was hard work, particularly under the existing circumstances—it was cold out there. He watched and marveled at the fact that the men at work seemed to be genuinely enjoying themselves. With a small blast heater, which was another piece of cargo he had not noticed on board, they were thawing out the bolts and connections. No one was using a hacksaw; everything was being disconnected properly.

Dammit, maybe he wasn't the only sentimental slob in the whole stiff-necked Air Force! He got up and tested one of the crates for movement; it showed some signs of loosening. He finished his lunch and gathered up the small amount of trash. Feeling a little guilty that he had absented himself for so long, he redonned his parka and climbed down the crew hole into the sharply cold air outside. He had to move a piece of canvas

66

that had been used to block the space between the heater hose and the door frame to do it. As he dropped into the snow, he noted that the door itself had been removed.

Two men were carrying what appeared to be the left elevator into the back of the C-130. The passion for souvenirs appeared to have no limit.

Sergeant Stovers, quite suddenly looking like a man who had emerged from his shell, came briskly toward him. "Sir," he said, "we'd appreciate it very much if you'd give us a hand. We're trying to get the number four engine off and it's going to take every available man to do it."

Ferguson went willingly and ignoring the matter of rank joined Jenkins and Corbin in helping on the ropes that had been expertly slung around the power plant. He estimated quickly: the engine delivered 1,200 horsepower and therefore it would weigh something like 2,400 pounds. A careful look at the block and tackle hung from the A-frame satisfied him that the ratio was right, three men would be able to do it.

Sergeants Holcomb and Stovers climbed into position and took off the last set of nuts as Perry Feinberg kept a critical eye on the job and served as ground anchor man. With enough men to do the job it was comparatively easy; at the right moment the A-frame took the strain and then it was a relatively simple matter to lower the cumbersome piston engine down onto the sled that had been placed to receive it. The sled itself was piled with blankets to reduce damage to a minimum.

After all hands had pushed and hauled the engine to the rear of the Hercules and had muscled it up the ramp, Ferguson had the feeling that things had gone about far enough. He returned to the ancient B-17, whose crew door would never be frozen shut again, and tried once more to move the most accessible of the wooden crates. It yielded to his reasonable persuasion and he slid it over to the crew door opening without undue difficulty. Waiting for him there was Sergeant Feinberg and one of his men; the senior NCO relieved him of it without a word.

When the last of the wooden boxes had been retrieved, he checked the now comfortably warm cabin of the bomber and satisfied himself that there were no more crates on board. Then, with reluctant steps, he returned to his own living aircraft and suggested that it was about time to return to Thule.

As he had anticipated, Sergeant Feinberg asked for a brief dispensation to allow a small piece of work that was under way to be finished. The small piece of work proved to be the number one propeller which was hauled on board to join the number four that had already been secured by Sergeant Stovers.

Just in time, Ferguson remembered the seat cushion he had decided to appropriate for himself. Trying not to look conspicuous, he returned to the B-17, went back up inside, and shortly reappeared with his modest prize. The skiers who had checked the landing area had long since completed their job. The last of the maintenance equipment was being stowed under Sergeant Stovers's direction. Within the next minute the hydraulic actuators lifted up the rear ramp and moved the upper section down to form the rear seal. Everything was on board and everyone seemed quite happy.

As soon as Andy Holcomb had the outrageously noisy APU going, the C-130 pulsed with life. The airscrews began to rotate and then whirled into discs as the turbines took hold. When the checklists had been completed, Ferguson moved her out into the center of the newly marked runway area and then headed into a takeoff run down the long snow path. Even with all her power, the mighty bird was a little slow to come off because of the altitude and the friction of her skis. She broke loose at last and climbed up into the sky while the whine of her power plants echoed over the endless empty vastness of the ice cap.

Inside the C-130 the parts of the old aircraft began to give out thin trickles of water as the ice within them melted slightly in the heat of the cargo hold. The men themselves were tired and lay sprawled on the horizontal canvas benches along the sides of the fuselage. Even Sergeant Feinberg set aside his dignity and let his bulk overflow the narrow pallet while he slept.

As airmen do everywhere, they awoke in time to buckle down for the landing. Once again Ferguson slid the Hercules expertly onto the white-painted Thule runway. At the tower's instruction he parked a little past Operations, a somewhat superfluous gesture since there were no other aircraft anywhere on the ramp.

Half an hour later Ferguson was still aboard his command. In spite of the cold, he had elected to remain to attend to the necessary paper work and to make sure that the wooden crates he had brought in would not be removed without his knowledge. When he had finished his work, he climbed down onto the cargo floor as a six-pack truck drew up outside. Moments later Sergeant Feinberg entered the aircraft, closely followed by Sergeant Stovers, the loadmaster.

"Colonel Kleckner is aware that we're back, sir," Feinberg reported. "We're instructed to put the crates in this truck; Sergeant Ragan, the head of base security, will take over from there."

"Thank you very much."

"Also, sir, the commander is in his office and I believe that he's expecting you. A taxi will be here momentarily."

"Good." Ferguson paused, wondering if he should ask the question that was on his mind. "Sergeant," he began finally, "now that you have them, what are you going to do with all of the parts from the B-17?"

At that moment Sergeant Stovers found it necessary to check something on the outside of the aircraft; he left without a word.

Perry Feinberg paused himself before replying, which was a rare thing. "I think you have already guessed, sir," he said when he was ready. "Forgive me, but I saw you when you were standing in front of the nose of that abandoned old bomber, and I believe I know what you were thinking."

Feinberg paused and carefully read out the reaction to his words. When he was satisfied, he went on. "We're going to clean them up and put them in good order. We have quite a bit of time on our hands up here, sir, and sometimes without too much to do. It may take a while, but I think, and the others agree, that we can bring that old bird in, piece by piece, and put her back together again."

CHAPTER FIVE

COLONEL JAMES KLECKNER put down the telephone by means of which he had been talking with the Pentagon and gave his attention to the NCO who had appeared in the doorway of his office. "Lieutenant Ferguson is here, sir," the man reported.

"Ask him to come in."

Since he had not yet met Ferguson, the colonel got to his feet to receive his newest junior officer. The colonel was a tall, well-built man who wore a suitably impressive array of ribbons on his uniform, and atop them, the wings of a command pilot. His features showed that he was used to carrying responsibility, but like most good commanders he was, under normal circumstances, an affable man with a quick smile and a relaxed manner.

Ferguson came in, offered his salute, and then took the hand that was extended to him. "Sit down, Lieutenant," the colonel invited.

"Thank you, sir." Ferguson took his place with a proper amount of dignity.

The colonel sat down behind his desk. "Welcome to the top of the world," he said. "I understand that you've been to Thule before."

"I've passed through several times, sir, but we've never been on the ground here more than an hour or so."

"Have you and your crew had the Thule briefing?"

"No, sir."

"Then I'll attend to that. There's no place on earth like this, Lieutenant. For example, even during the very coldest days in the middle of winter, we have a heavy requirement for air conditioning."

"For what reason, sir? The hospital, perhaps?"

"No; as a matter of fact, it's outdoors."

The colonel paused as two cups of coffee were brought in. "You see, Lieutenant, this whole base is built on the permafrost. There is a comparatively thin layer of soil that thaws somewhat during the summer, but below that the ground is permanently frozen like a solid block of steel that may go down a half mile or more. It makes an excellent foundation and it will bear enormous weight as long as it remains frozen. But when you put a building on it and then heat the building, the next time you look the building may be five or ten feet lower. So the buildings here are all well above the ground and we use air-conditioning units to prevent the permafrost from melting underneath them."

"It's fantastic, sir."

"Indeed it is. That's why the runway is painted white, incidentally — to reflect away the sunlight in summer. As it is, there are some rough spots, as you may have noticed."

Ferguson decided that it was time to ask his question. "Sir, would you care to tell me why we've been ordered to report here? Frankly, we're all very much in the dark about that."

The colonel relaxed back in his chair. "I'm glad that it hasn't leaked out. While it isn't classified, I'd like to see as low a profile as possible maintained concerning the assignment you've been given. Is that quite clear?"

"Absolutely, sir. I'll pass the word to the rest of the crew."

"Good. The news gets around pretty fast up here, so the whole base will know what's going on, but the less you emphasize it, the less attention it will be given. How much do you know about Camp Century?"

Ferguson recalled something he had once heard. "Is that the city under the ice?"

The colonel nodded. "Correct. Several years ago, with the permission of the Danish authorities, the United States Army went far out on the ice cap and built a considerable installation, literally under the ice. Instead of tunneling, the Army engineers cut a series of very deep trenches and then installed prefabricated buildings in them, complete with plumbing, electricity, heat, and everything else that was needed. Then the top was closed over."

"How did they power it, sir?"

"With a nuclear reactor. Camp Century at the time seemed like something out of science fiction; actually it was used as a research station until the programmed studies were completed. Then it was abandoned and certain of the equipment was removed. But the basic installation is still there— approximately a hundred and fifty miles from Thule."

"I take it that there is a landing area, sir."

"Definitely," the colonel answered. "The location for the camp was well chosen and there certainly was enough space on the ice cap available. All around the camp the area is very smooth. As you have probably guessed by now, the Army is very shortly going back to Camp Century to make some

73

further studies on the ice movement, if any, and certain other things. Army personnel will be out there for at least several weeks — it may be longer. Your job will be to support them."

"It sounds very interesting, sir."

"It certainly should be. By the way, I understand that you were successful in your mission this morning."

"We believe so, sir. Lieutenant Jenkins, my navigator, relocated the B-17 on the first pass. We went on board and recovered three medium-sized crates that were still there. Base security has them now."

The colonel nodded his approval. "You won't discuss anything about that, of course. If anyone asks, you went back to the B-17 to salvage a propeller for the NCO Club. You got it, I suppose."

Ferguson thought very quickly before he answered that. "We did, sir, and one or two other things."

The colonel flashed an agreeable smile. "Yes, I would suspect so. By the way — one of the Danish workers here is quite a good artist. His name is Viggo Skov; he's over at the mess hall. Perhaps he could do a painting of a B-17, on the ground or in the air, and it could be permanently displayed with the propeller as an artifact beside it."

Ferguson found himself on the only patch of thin ice in northern Greenland. "I shall certainly keep that in mind, sir," he promised. Before he committed himself any further, he stood up. "Thank you, sir," he said.

The colonel smiled once more. "I think you'll have an interesting time while you're with us here."

"There's no doubt of that, sir," Ferguson replied. "No doubt at all."

Chief Master Sergeant Perry Feinberg stood with his parka unbuttoned surveying the vast interior of hangar number eight on the Thule flight line. Large enough to contain a B-52

74

easily, the big structure was all but empty. Along the west wall an assortment of maintenance stands were stored against the time that they might be needed. The floor of the hangar was solid concrete, but not far from where the stands were parked there was a wide, gradual depression that covered a considerable area. Although it was approximately eighteen inches deep at its center, the concrete itself was not broken.

A staff sergeant was explaining the layout. "There's plenty of vacant hangar space; right now eight, nine, and ten are all virtually empty. They're kept on the ready in case SAC wants to use them on short notice."

Sergeant Feinberg already knew all that, but he had his reasons for letting himself be informed once more. Meanwhile he was taking everything in with an expert's eye. "Just in case SAC did come in unexpectedly," he said, "would they park a B-52 or anything like that on the low spot?" He lifted his arm and pointed.

"No, the '52's weigh too much to stand on anything but the strongest areas. And it wouldn't be needed."

"But that doesn't mean that that spot is necessarily weak."

"No, not at all — it means that the permafrost somehow melted and gave way a little. The only thing wrong with it, actually, is that it isn't precisely level."

"Do tell," Sergeant Feinberg commented. "I have some stuff I want to park inside for a while; all right if I use that area?"

"No problem, go ahead. I'll clear it with Major Eastcott if you'd like."

Feinberg lifted his shoulders slowly and then eased them down. "I don't see any reason to bother him about it right now," he declared. "Now, do you happen to know off hand if Supply has any propeller stands available?"

"Propeller stands!"

"I have a use in mind for them."

"Possibly in cold storage, Perry; Supply will know. There's a lot of gear down there, but it's been locked up for some time and there'll be two feet of snow on everything."

"Who's the right man to talk to, in your opinion?"

The sergeant thought for a moment. "For efficiency, Baker, but if you want a favor done, see Atwater."

A satisfied smile appeared on Sergeant Feinberg's broad face. "Precisely the way I see it myself. Meanwhile, this little discussion is just between ourselves — right?"

The other man waved a hand. "Of course. Off the record, what's up?"

Perry Feinberg had been ready for that question for some time. "You may have heard that they are planning to start a Thule flying club."

"Yes, I did catch some wind of that. And you want to park an airplane there." The sergeant nodded.

"We may have one coming in," Feinberg told him.

Sergeant Stovers carried his burden under one arm as he opened the heavy outer door of the building and then the inner one that provided a double seal. Safely inside, he hung up his parka, stashed his arctic hand coverings, and then without difficulty found the desk where Sergeant Mike Murphy was at work. Murphy's desk was piled with a considerable work load of paper; on top of the largest pile, and weighing it down, there was a four-month-old copy of *Better Homes and Gardens*.

Stovers set down his load and dropped into a chair without ceremony. "How are you doing, Mike?" he offered.

Sergeant Murphy gave him his attention. "Hello, Bill. What in hell have you got there?"

"A communications set. It belongs to Andy Holcomb; he'd be here himself, but he's down helping to get some things off the C-130."

"That's your job, isn't it?" Murphy asked.

76

"Normally yes, but in this instance, Andy is the right man.
What do you think of the set?"

Murphy barely glanced at it. "World War II," he said
flatly. "A relic."

Bill Stovers was patient—a virtue that had been noted
many times by others. "I'd like to plug it in and try it," he
stated calmly, "but I don't want to blow the damn thing up. So
I came to see your first."

"Where, for the Lord's sake, did you find it?"

Stovers stuck to the strict truth. "We were down in
Sondrestrom," he answered.

"I hope you didn't pay anything for it."

"No, but we would like to get it working. Can you give us a
hand?"

"No," Murphy answered.

Bill Stovers did not appear ruffled. "Somehow I got the
notion that anything electronic was more or less up your
alley."

Murphy mellowed. "Look, Bill, nothing personal. First, to
put it bluntly, the set isn't worth fixing. Secondly, I've got a
lot of work to do and not much time to get it done. I'm leaving,
you know."

"How much longer, Mike?"

"Just over six weeks. And I'm using every minute of my
spare time. Do you remember Ted Funakoshi?"

"Yes, I met him in Frankfurt."

"That's the man. His family is big in the nursery field out in
California. He's retiring soon and so am I. We're going to go
into business together on the Coast. That sort of thing takes a
lot of careful planning; I won't be half-finished before it will be
time to leave here. So understand, Bill, I don't have either the
time or the inclination to put several hours of work into
checking out that antique set you have there."

"All right," Stovers said. He picked up the set and left;

minutes later a base taxi deposited him in front of the personnel door to Hangar 8. He went inside with the communications set and discovered that some workbenches had already been set up in the back. Two men were inspecting the elevator that had been taken off the B-17. He put down the radio, studied the two propellers that were temporarily laid out on the floor, and then walked up to Perry Feinberg.

"Do you remember the discussion we had at the club about Mike Murphy and his ability to fix electronic gear?" he asked.

"Very well indeed," Feinberg answered.

"At that time you said that there were two things that interested him. One of them was gardening."

"Right."

"What's the other one?" Stovers asked.

A base taxi pulled up in front of Supply and Andy Holcomb got out. He opened the first door, stamped the excess snow off his feet, and then went inside. He didn't know Atwater, but he found him sitting in civilian clothes at a desk that was comfortably covered with forms and requisitions. Because he was cheerful and outgoing, Andy had no trouble establishing contact with the man he had come to see. "I'm going to be stationed up here for a while," he explained, "and I thought I'd drop in and see what your setup is like. I may be needing some things."

"You name it, we've got it," Atwater answered. "There's a story that when Thule was first built back in 1951, somebody shipped up fifty lawn mowers to keep the grass cut. We don't have any lawn mowers—if the story's true they were sent back—but is there anything else on your mind?"

"I was thinking about some propeller stands."

"We've got 'em; we used to have C-54's in here. But I don't know if you can use them; you're on the C-130 aren't you?"

"Right."

"Our stands may not be big enough, those are pretty large

props you've got. We can try; if they don't fit, we can have one made up."

"Let me try the one's you already have," Holcomb suggested.

"Fine. They'll have to be dug out of cold storage and, believe me, that means cold. But we know just where they are. How soon?"

"Are you busy?"

Atwater got to his feet. "There's something here you haven't told me yet," he said, "but let's go and look at the stands if you'd like. I've got a truck outside."

Atwater got his parka, donned his heavy gloves, and then led the way. His vehicle was nosed up to the building in a row of others. He went to the front, unplugged the electric heater, which was standard equipment in every car and truck at Thule, and then climbed inside. Andy joined him and they were off.

The flight ramp was well cleared of snow and there was little trouble getting to the large building where the seldom-used equipment was stored. Once inside, Atwater threw a switch and overhead lights revealed a remarkable scene. It too could have been a small corner of the earth after an atomic holocaust had wiped out all remaining forms of life. It was dead and inert; a heavy blanket of snow that had somehow found its way inside lay over everything with a virgin purity that seemed to forbid trespassing.

It was at least twenty below zero inside; because of that fact, Atwater's breath was clouded in front of his face when he spoke. "I think I know right where to find them; I was looking at the diagram just the other day. A lot of stuff that's here will probably never be used again, but we keep it—the rent is cheap."

He led the way across the floor, his feet sinking to below the ankles at every step. He had a broom he had picked up close to the door, one that had obviously been left there for the purpose he intended. When he reached the spot he wanted, he

79

set to work with the broom and in a few seconds he had uncovered the top of a stand that made Holcomb's heart sing with joy. "That's it," Holcomb declared.

"We've got some engine stands here too," Atwater said. "A little bit of everything."

"Engine stands!" Holcomb could not keep the excitement out of his voice.

Atwater turned toward him. "Yes, engine stands. For piston engines. You can't use them."

Holcomb made a decision. "Just possibly I can," he confided.

Atwater remained calm. "Suppose you tell me about it," he invited.

"Make one guess," Andy said.

The supply man thought a moment. "Everyone knows that you guys found another B-17 out on the ice cap."

Holcomb nodded. "You've got it."

"Good God!" Atwater thought some more. "I don't think it's possible."

"Why not — there's no corrosion out there. And the bird's intact; she's sitting up on her gear just as though she was on the ramp right here."

A long pause filled the strange, frigid warehouse. "Does the colonel know about this?"

"He probably will, in time."

"You'll need hundreds of parts; that stands to reason."

"You said you had everything."

One more time Atwater thought. "Yes, as a matter of fact we do — even tubes for 1943 radios. But . . ."

Holcomb put his thumb on the scales. "Since you know, how about it — are you with us or not?"

Atwater gave another swish with the broom and more snow toppled off the long-unused propeller stand. "Count me in," he said.

After the evening meal in the mess hall, a line equally made

80

up of Danes and Americans formed in front of the base theater. A few men went to the immaculately maintained base library, which contained the newest books, as well as many on esoteric subjects. The two Danish librarians on duty were ready to transact business.

A small but steady flow went into the base gymnasium, a converted hangar that offered surprisingly good facilities. The karate class was due to meet and the NCO who taught it was warming up, loosening the tendons of his body.

Under the same roof the base bowling alley had a most unusual attraction—a woman. Captain Carolyn Yang from the base hospital was taking part in a foursome. She commanded all of the attention she could possibly desire. In addition to the nurses, there were also two female officers at the BMEWS installation at J Site, the massive radar installation that was the reason for Thule's existence. They were never at a loss for invitations to go out, going out being somewhat limited 690 miles north of the Arctic Circle.

On the flight line, where no activity was scheduled, darkness had fallen. It served somewhat to cover the movements of several men who manned two trucks and drove toward the cold-storage area. Within half an hour the trucks were on their way back, this time being reasonably careful to keep out of sight. No one appeared to notice them, not even when they turned onto the ramp and then disappeared into the vaulting interior of Hangar 8.

Major David Valen, United States Air Force, was a tall man of slender build who was happiest when he could communicate with his fellow human beings in a quiet, nonspectacular way. No one at Thule could recall when he had raised his voice. He was also an excellent listener; he listened as Sergeant Stovers sat, fully relaxed, in his presence.

"So that's it, sir," Stovers concluded. "Now, may we count on you for a little help?"

"Of course. I'm not a mechanic, but any way that I can lend a hand I will. I'm in the resurrection business. What do you want me to do?"

"Well, Chaplain, we've hit a small snag. To restore the old aircraft just as she was, we have to fix the radios."

"Of course."

"Sergeant Mike Murphy is the man to do the job, but he's a short-timer and he doesn't want to get involved."

"Then he should be persuaded. Suppose I talk to him about it."

"Excellent, sir, but we also had another idea."

"Speak."

"Mike has two main interests apart from his family: gardening and a certain Hollywood actress."

"I've heard him refer to Monica Lee," the major said.

Stovers nodded quickly. "You've got it, sir. As you know, she makes a specialty of playing the wholesome girl next door — a sort of professional virgin if you'll pardon me. That's why he likes her so much. With all the stuff that's been coming out lately, she's the only one who meets his standards of what a young woman should be. Mike has some very strong convictions."

The major thought on that. "Yes, I know — he's a fundamentalist all right, not that there's anything wrong in that. But I do know that he doesn't have any pinups on the wall, and that's a decided novelty around here."

"Now we're on the same frequency, sir. To come to the point, Sergeant Feinberg mentioned to me that you know someone in Hollywood."

Stovers paused at that point. He had never met the Protestant chaplain before, but the word was out that he was a solid citizen.

"What do you think will turn the trick?" Valen asked.

"In Perry Feinberg's opinion, an autographed picture from her would be dynamite. If you could possibly get one for us, we will tell him that it's his—as soon as the radios are working properly."

"Ah, so." The major reflected. "I don't know if my friend in Hollywood knows Miss Lee or not, but he could probably arrange to see her without too much trouble."

Stovers warmed to the good news. "Sir, since time is very short in Mike's case, would you phone your Hollywood friend? We'll pay the charges."

The major shook his head. "In a good cause I'll pay them myself. However, one question: when are you next going out to that abandoned B-17?"

"Tomorrow morning, sir. Quite early. A proficiency flight, you understand."

"Perfectly. Now, am I invited to come along?"

"I was just about to ask you, sir."

"How fortunate. In that case, perhaps I'd better book the call right away." He reached for his telephone, but Stovers raised a hand.

"That's already been done, sir. Sergeant Feinberg took care of it. He knows the base operator quite well, so you'll be called on the first open spot." He remembered his game plan. "If she could just sign it 'To Sergeant Mike Murphy' or something like that, then the problem is solved."

"My contact is a pilot; may I tell him about the airplane?"

"Yes, sir, but please ask him to keep his mouth shut; we don't want any publicity at this point."

"Understood." As if to punctuate that comment, the phone rang.

Sergeant Stovers discreetly took his departure. He was so quietly elated, he was all but unaware of the thirty-one-below-zero temperature he encountered as soon as he stepped outside. As he walked across the crisp snow, he noted that there was very little wind. For Thule, it seemed quite warm.

The shallow sun had long since painted a High Arctic

83

twilight on a segment of the sky and then had silently and inexorably disappeared. A very deep cobalt blue formed the infinite sky overhead; not even a wisp of cloud interfered with the brilliant display of thousands of stars of varying intensity that proclaimed the night.

Venus hung brightly almost exactly due south, a beacon planet that shone from its own probable lifelessness down onto the sterile immensity of the timeless desert of ice. Throughout the ages the great ice cap had been building, inch by relentless inch, as the loose snow was solidified and then pressed down by successive layers until it at last surrendered its own identity and became part of the homogeneous mass that would endure until the end of earthly time, or until the coming of some overwhelming disaster that would boil the seas and unlock the ice cap's trillions of tons of petrified water.

In the southern quadrant, where the vast sea of ice met the almost black sky to form the horizon, a three-quarters moon steadily rose — a cold light cast on an eternally frozen world. As the night slowly passed the moon climbed higher into the sky until it gave a faint illumination to the endless whiteness. Not within a radius of more than two hundred miles was there any living creature to witness the phenomenon; the wan beauty and stark reality of the spectacle were as wasted as the "gems of purest ray serene that the dark unfathomed caves of ocean bear."

Standing outlined in the cold moonlight, the remaining bulk of *The Passionate Penguin* was motionless and still. It had once been a machine capable of flight, a creation of the twentieth century, but as it stood effortlessly opposing the moderate wind that blew unfelt over the total desolation, the resistance it offered to the elements was totally passive. It was, or had been, only a machine, one of many thousands that had been built under the glowing hot stresses of war to fly and fight until it was shot down or the enemy capitulated. It felt nothing and it knew nothing.

84

The Passionate Penguin did not know and could not know, because it was incapable of feeling the pain of living things, that its partially amputated framework only gave the illusion of wholeness. Underneath, in the vital area where its basic structure was centered, the main right landing-gear fitting only barely still supported the weight above it. The impact of the final landing had been such a merciful release to the men who had been on board, they had been unaware of how severe it had been. The gear had not collapsed, by a blessed mechanical miracle, but the vital structural component had been broken.

During three decades of ice accumulation, and more than ten thousand days of drifting snow, the cracked section had gradually sealed over in a frigid embalmment. *The Passionate Penguin* was eternally grounded and the fatal rupture of her structure did not, of itself, make any material difference.

CHAPTER SIX

BY 0800 HOURS the sun was up; it was still low on the horizon, but after the two-hour morning twilight it was providing abundant daylight even in northern Greenland. The long weeks of the unbroken Arctic night were over and the astonishing maze of Thule's above-the-ground plumbing was fully revealed for all to see.

On the flight line, despite the fairly early hour, a good bit of activity was under way. Several trucks had already brought supplies to Hangar 8, where a large accumulation of gear was being built up. A diesel-powered generator was delivered, all sled mounted and ready to go. Almost two hundred separate tools had been laid out in a systematic pattern on the floor; they ranged from light wrenches and screwdrivers to two heavy sledges that had been produced from somewhere. There were also maintenance stands, A-frames equipped with block-and-tackle hoists, two large heating units and several smaller ones, various power tools, and even a small self-propelled crane that would fit inside a C-130 with four inches to spare.

The organization was remarkable. The advance planning had been brief, but thorough. As the best-qualified member of the team, Sergeant Holcomb was in charge of engineering. He had a list on a clipboard; as each piece of equipment was delivered and put into position, he carefully checked it off. He had to face only one disappointment — a meticulous search of the base library and all available records that might in any way supply the necessary data had failed to turn up any information at all concerning the structure of the B-17 bomber. All he had to work with were superficial facts: the wingspan was 103 feet, 9½ inches; the length was 74 feet, 4 inches; the height 19 feet, 1 inch; and the total gross weight, fully loaded, was 54,926 pounds. After making some careful calculations he had come up with an empty weight of 34,000 pounds, but that could not be considered more than an informed guess.

Another small truck arrived with some specialized tools that had been borrowed from the BMEWS installation. Andy checked them in and then noticed an item on his list that had not been crossed off. "Penetrating oil," he called out. "Anybody got it?"

"Coming," someone answered.

He turned to find Lieutenant Ferguson at his elbow. "Andy, if you take all of this stuff, there won't be any room left to bring anything back."

"It's not all coming back, not on this trip. We're going to leave some of the stands out there this time. They won't be needed here; we have plenty more."

"How many ACM's are coming with us?"

Holcomb referred to his list. "We have twelve additional crew members and one deadhead — Major Valen, the chaplain."

"Deadhead my ass," Ferguson retorted. "If he comes, he works."

"Don't worry, sir, he will. He already has."

"Why the sledges?"

"To drive out driftpins. We're not certain, but they may be needed to get the wings off."

Perry Feinberg, immense in his parka, appeared. "The last of the gear is here," he advised. "Bill Stovers wants to start loading ASAP."

"Begin now," Holcomb authorized. He turned to Ferguson. "Sir, it would help like hell if we could have the Herc backed up to the main door so that we could go right up the rear ramp. We've got a lot of stuff to secure."

"As of now," Ferguson answered, and headed for the door. The whole spirit of the thing had his emotional batteries fully charged. Within ten minutes he had the powerful airlifter backed into position ready to receive her cargo. As the hangar door was opened enough to permit all of the equipment to be moved out, there were at least twenty men on hand to help with the work. Only the fact that it was Saturday made that many willing hands available.

The loading was half-completed when a staff car drew up. For a sick moment Ferguson thought it was the colonel, then he remembered that the base commander had a red light atop his own vehicle. The base Information Officer climbed out carrying a large bag of camera gear. He slung the strap across his shoulder and then came over to Ferguson.

"Morning," he said. "I'm Tilton, the IO. We met at the mess hall."

"Yes, of course," Ferguson acknowledged.

"You know the motto of the information branch — Last to

88

Know, First to Go. I only got wind of this last night. Good God, Scott, this is the biggest story we've had since the B-52 crash; you should have told me."

"We've been trying to keep it quiet," Ferguson admitted. "Nothing personal, Frank."

"Forget it; you can't. Anyway, you've got to have some pictures. I checked with the photo lab and found that no one had been assigned. So here I am."

"No one is assigned to anything," Ferguson explained, "not officially. This is a spare-time activity — call it a recreation project."

"All right, but how about adding an ACM? You can't leave me out of this one."

Ferguson saw an opening. "Will you help cover for us if it becomes necessary?"

"Absolutely."

"Then tell Perry Feinberg that you're on the list; he's handling personnel."

The maintenance stands were being moved rapidly into the Hercules. The crane operator fired up his vehicle, preparatory to driving it on board. Because of the close fit, it would be the last thing to be loaded.

The crane went on six minutes later. Sergeant Stovers supervised its careful progress up the rear ramp and then had it come forward, almost literally inch by inch, until it was in position. Chains were waiting to secure it solidly, an operation that took an additional five minutes. Then, at last, everything was loaded and ready to go. Perry Feinberg checked the selected personnel on board and waved his thanks to others, all of whom held a first priority on the next trip. Stovers operated the controls that raised and sealed the rear ramp.

The APU was already splitting the morning air with its blasting shrillness. On the bridge Ferguson was going through the checklist with the aid of Corbin, his copilot. Lieutenant Jenkins spread out a chart and spun his computer to determine a climb-out heading.

"Weight and balance?" Ferguson queried when that item came up on the checklist.

"Satisfactory. Way under max gross; less than twelve thousand pounds."

"All cargo and ACM's secured?"

"Secured and briefing given."

Four minutes later the first of the four powerful turbine engines began to rotate; as it gained speed the next one came to life. Presently the third started to whirl and the APU was shut down. The fourth propeller began to turn and then as the fire was lit it accelerated and became a visual disc. Corbin pressed the switch on his yoke and called the tower. In response he was given clearance to taxi and take position at the end of the runway. Ferguson released the brakes and the C-130 began to move forward across the ramp.

Corbin made the takeoff. He did a smooth job of it and climbed out steadily until he had enough altitude, then he set up a standard left turn toward the ice cap.

Captain Tilton loaded his cameras and prepared them for action. They were especially equipped with arctic batteries and were taped over wherever possible to avoid any contact between bare metal and the hands of the operator. Major Valen stood between Ferguson's left seat and the side of the fuselage, looking ahead at the spectacle of the ice cap. Ferguson was flying then, with the autopilot disconnected. As his fingers gripped the yoke, he seemed to feel through them the life of the aircraft he commanded.

Corbin spoke over the intercom. "Do you think the colonel knows about this?"

Ferguson had thought about the same subject. "If he doesn't he will shortly—that's for sure. But he may not know *officially*."

"In other words, we don't mention it to him unless he asks."

"Right! If he orders me not to fly out here any more . . ."
He left the sentence unfinished.

The remarkable visibility from the cockpit of the Hercules offered a panorama of the ice cap that no camera ever devised could capture. As far as the eye could see, over an arc of more than 180 degrees, the vast whiteness extended unbroken—a desert devoid of any form of life for more than 1,500 miles of stark grandeur. Ferguson had seen it many times, but like a schoolboy experiencing his first wonderful discovery of Sherlock Holmes, it held at that moment an almost hypnotic fascination. And it was going to be made to give up something that it had unlawfully seized and had held for more than a generation.

Or perhaps the ice cap was not to blame. Viewed another way, it had provided a haven—a resting place almost two miles up in the sky where a distressed aircraft had found sanctuary of a kind and her crew the opportunity for survival. Without the ice cap, it could have had a different ending. Perhaps, far underneath, there was jagged, hostile terrain that would destroy any aircraft that tried to find a place where it could get onto the ground. At some other part of the globe, in a jungle somewhere, the gallant old B-17 would have been destroyed by a hundred natural enemies within a few weeks or months. Only on the ice cap had she had a chance.

He flew on, a strange tingling running the length of his spine. He was insensitive to the passage of time.

"Dead ahead."

Ferguson came to abruptly; he had been wool gathering more than he had realized. He scanned through the windshield and saw the B-17, little more than a tiny dot, a mile or two directly in front of him. "Pre-landing checklist," he ordered.

He was alert as he planned his final approach. By rights it was Corbin's turn, but he did not want to risk even the slightest mishap, good as he knew Corbin was. Tilton leaned over his shoulder to snap a picture. To accommodate the information officer he circled the wreck once, then put the skis down and set up his approach once more. With the power reduced he crept closer to the surface of the covering snow until the runway markers swept back underneath; then he eased the throttles back still farther and lifted the nose into a landing attitude. The Hercules slid onto the ice cap with hardly a quiver of the airframe.

With delicate skill Ferguson guided his aircraft to a position within a few feet of the right wingtip of the abandoned hulk and then stopped when the rear ramp was at a minimum distance from the nose of the World War II bomber. Well satisfied, he shut down and secured the flight controls and systems.

The rear ramp opened up and within two minutes the crane backed out. It's huge tires sank a little into the hardened snow, but it was quite able to maneuver. As the first of the maintenance stands was being unloaded, Andy Holcomb began a detailed inspection of the B-17's structure.

It was cold on the ice cap; a fair wind was blowing and the chill factor had to be somewhere around thirty below. That did not deter Holcomb, principally he was concerned with the work that had to be done.

In front of the nose of the bomber a large canvas was spread, on it a wide assortment of tools was laid out. Stands were placed around the number three engine and two men fired up a small heating unit to thaw out the propeller hub fastenings. Similar attention was being given to the other remaining propeller. Three more men equipped with another of the portable heating units spread a second canvas near to the tail and set up stands to reach the high rudder and vertical stabilizer. After five minutes of careful inspection, one of them called to Holcomb.

"Andy," he reported. "Good news — it comes off. I was afraid that the fin was an integral part of the fuselage."

"Need any help?" Holcomb asked.

"One more man would be welcome." In response, Major Valen climbed up from where he had been standing on the snow. "I'm not a mechanic," he said, "but I'll lend a hand."

Perry Feinberg started one of the big heating units and fed the large-diameter hose up into the fuselage. The ice cap came comfortably alive with noise.

Captain Tilton circulated, taking photographs as rapidly as he could get himself into position. He snapped one of Ferguson as the young aircraft commander stood near to the hull of the B-17 and then paused for a moment. "I want to record all this," he declared. "It's the first project of its kind I ever heard of. Whenever you need an extra hand, I'm available."

"We'll let you know," Ferguson promised.

Stands were being placed around the number one engine and the remaining heater unit was spotted on top. All four engines would have to come off, but that should be no problem since one of them was already safely stored back in Hangar 8 and now there was the crane to help.

When the last of the gear had been removed from the C-130, Sergeant Stovers rigged a substantial canvas curtain to close off the front twenty feet of the hold. That done, he set out some of the food he had obtained from the mess hall and connected a good-sized coffee maker. He also laid out a kit of first-aid supplies in case of accident. Five minutes after he had finished, the crane moved into position to take the propeller from the number three engine as soon as it was freed.

Inside the fuselage of the B-17 Andy Holcomb was making a careful inspection; Ferguson was with him. "Hot damn!" the sergeant said. "Look, skipper, the fuselage breaks here, right behind the trailing edge of the wing. That should make it possible to bring her in in two approximately equal sections. What I'm saying is: neither section can be much more than forty feet long, which means that they will fit inside the C-130."

"That's great," Ferguson replied. "Terrific — *if* the wings come off at the root. That's the big question."

"I know," Holcomb answered. "There are fillets that will have to come off; we may have to drill out the rivets, but there are worse jobs."

"Oh, sure." Ferguson was checking the control cables that ran down the inside of the fuselage. "Andy, these appear to be in duplicate, but there are turnbuckles — they can be opened right up."

"Boeing sure in hell knew what they were doing when they designed this baby. Simple and easy maintenance. That's what you need for a war bird like her."

"Let's get all of this snow out of here," Ferguson suggested. "Then we ought to be able to take up the flooring without too much trouble."

"Do you feel strong, sir?"

"OK, I'll do it."

Holcomb dropped through the crew door opening down onto the snow and moments later passed up a broom. There was hardly room inside the cramped quarters of the B-17 to use it. "Let's have a shovel," Ferguson said.

As soon as he had the tool he wanted, Scott Ferguson set to work. The interior was growing warmer from the heater and he took off his parka. He worked willingly, pushing the snow up to the crew door and then shoving it down out of the aircraft. Because it *was* an aircraft and at the moment, it was his aircraft.

It was a tight fit in the center of the fuselage, between the wings. From in back he pitched the snow up onto the narrow walkway; when he had a sufficient pile, he climbed over it and cleared it off from the other side. When he had finished to his satisfaction, it was quite warm inside the old hull and he was mildly sweating. He knew the danger of that in the Arctic and stopped to let his metabolism return to normal.

Outside he heard the crane laboring; he looked through the part of the windshield that had partially defrosted and saw that the number one engine had just been detached and that the crane was backing away from the nacelle with it in a sling. Then the crane turned and headed toward the C-130.

A visual check told him that both of the remaining propellers had been removed. He was missing too much; he had to see what was going on. Forgetting the fact that his pores were still open, he dropped down onto the mound of snow he had made and walked out from under the belly of the aircraft.

He could hardly believe it all. The rudder was gone and the vertical stabilizer with it; the dorsal was still in place and he correctly assumed that it was an integral part of the rear fuselage. The empennage had almost been stripped clean, only one horizontal stabilizer was still in position and two men were working on that.

Andy Holcomb came up to him, smiling despite the penetrating cold wind. "Can you stand some good news?" he asked.

"Let's have it."

"Two things. First, the wings do come off right at the root next to the fuselage. We can't do that yet, of course, but it doesn't look too tough. We've already got penetrating oil on the driftpins. Also there are only about twenty connections, all told, between the main hull and the wing—that's including mechanical and electrical. Secondly, the outer wing panels come off—about twenty feet from the tips. It's simple; once we get the connections thawed out, we can take off the wingtips. That cuts each wing down from about forty-five feet to only twenty-five for the root sections. It makes everything a helluva lot easier."

"Hurrah," Ferguson said. He could hardly believe how well things were going.

"Now, sir, I've got to tell you that we also have an almost insurmountable problem." Ferguson felt a sudden sinking feeling, but he did not dare to show it. "What is it?" he asked.

The flight engineer was suddenly quite grim. "Sir, you'd better brace yourself for this one. We are keeping on with the work, and we aren't going to stop, but we're afraid that we're licked. It's the wing root sections. You see, sir, we measured them. At the point where they attach to the fuselage, the chord is almost exactly nineteen feet."

Ferguson tried to absorb that. "I didn't realize they were anything like that wide," he said.

"That's how it is, and we can't help it."

Ferguson fought against what he already knew. "Andy, we're going to have to split them some way."

Holcomb shook his head. "No way, skipper. To split them you would have to take the whole wing literally apart, spars and all. Take off all the skin and if we did that, there's no chance we could ever get them back together again without jigs and the whole lot. And the rear opening of the C-130 is just about nine feet square, as you know. It's out of the question to try and carry those wing sections on the outside; it would be dangerous as all hell."

"In other words?"

"In other words, we've got two vitally essential wing root sections out here on the ice cap, a helluva long way from Thule, and absolutely no way at all to bring them in. We've had it."

CHAPTER SEVEN

LIEUTENANT SCOTT FERGUSON sat alone, his forearms resting on the table, his head tilted forward as he communed with his own thoughts. It was very quiet in the dining room of the NCO Club; the blare of the jukebox across the hall in the bar seemed not to penetrate. The Officers' Club was open and available, but Ferguson was awaiting the arrival of Sergeant Feinberg, who had promised to join him. Meanwhile an almost untasted drink rested before him; he was in no mood for any temporal pleasures.

Everything had gone so splendidly until the wing root chords had been measured. Somehow everyone working on the recovery of *The Passionate Penguin* had known; the job had gone on, but it had become a mechanical exercise — something that had been started and therefore everyone went through the motions of continuing until such time as it was formally called off.

The ice cap had won.

Or the *Penguin* had lost: the ice cap hadn't made her wings too big to load even into the wide-mouthed C-130.

Another young officer entered the room and looked about him. Ferguson inspected him, but as far as he knew, they had never met. Ferguson definitely did not want any company, but he was also acutely aware of how close-knit the Thule community was—there was no other air base like it. The extreme Arctic isolation brought everyone together and he could not afford, as one of the newest officers aboard, to appear less than cordial. Therefore when he met the man's eye, he gestured an invitation.

The other lieutenant came over, drew out a chair, and sat down.

"My name is Collins," he said. "Tom Collins."

"Yes, sir," a waiter said, directly behind him.

Collins raised a hand. "That's my name, not an order. Bring me a martini." He looked again at Ferguson. "What are you drinking?" he asked.

"I'm fine, thank you. Scott Ferguson." He held out his hand.

"Are you on the C-130 that came in?"

"It's my airplane."

"Welcome aboard. You don't look too happy."

"I'm not."

"Brace yourself; Thule isn't that bad. One year and it's all over. And in summer, the scenery is pretty spectacular."

Ferguson didn't want to pursue that topic any further. "What's your job?" he asked.

Collins sat up straighter and assumed an attitude. "I am one of the chosen few," he replied. "The gods of fortune have smiled upon me. I am a helicopter pilot."

"Sit down anyway," Ferguson said. Collins was already sitting, but that was an unimportant technical detail.

"Someday," Collins continued, "you may have to ditch in the drink. When that happens, do not despair. We'll be along to fish you out."

"There isn't any water up here," Ferguson noted. "It's all ice. Unlimited masses of ice."

"So much the better — that way you don't have to get wet."

The waiter reappeared with the martini and set it down. Close behind him Andy Holcomb was approaching. Ferguson waved him to a chair. "Lieutenant Collins, Sergeant Holcomb. My flight engineer."

"My pleasure," Collins said, and shook hands.

Holcomb had some notes he spread out on the table. "Sir, do you feel like talking?" he asked.

"Go ahead. Tom here will keep his mouth shut I'm sure."

"About the B-17? Everybody knows, but whatever goes on at this table is under the rose, OK?" Collins signaled the waiter and pointed to Holcomb. Andy ordered a beer.

"I've come to discuss some possibilities," Holcomb began. "First, I reviewed the idea of disassembling the wing root sections, but finally and absolutely that's out. I can quote a dozen engineering reasons, one of them being we don't have any jigs to put them back together in. Forget it."

"All right," Ferguson agreed.

"So we've got to move them in as is — or as will be when we get them off the rest of the airframe. The nacelles don't come off; possibly we could drill the rivets out, but it would be a hideous job to try and disassemble the engine frames and then get them back together again. Nyet."

Ferguson tried his drink at last; he needed it. "I won't argue; they've got to come in as is. If we get them in at all."

"I know, sir, I feel just the way you do. But there's got to be a way. Alternative one — dog teams. Det. Four, the helicopter outfit, flies regularly to an Eskimo village north of here, seventy or eighty miles up the coast. It's called Kanak, I believe. They have dog teams. And dog teams, I find out, have been regularly moved by helicopter. So we get the whirlybird boys to bring in a couple of dog teams and drivers. We take them out on the ice cap. Then they go to work."

"Andy, I don't want to be the devil's advocate," Ferguson said, "but that's an awfully long shot. It's a helluva ways out there, you know that. Secondly, I don't know how much a dog team can handle, but remember that those damn root sections are nineteen feet wide and twenty-five feet long, more or less. Plus the nacelles. I don't think they can do it; they won't have sleds anything like that size."

"How much do they weigh?" Collins asked.

Holcomb had been working on that. "I've made an estimate," he replied. "I can't get the exact data; maybe Boeing has it, but it would take two weeks at the least to try and find out from them. Basically there are three elements: the skin, the spars, and the fuel cells. The skin won't amount to much. There are two spars and they are rugged as hell, so they will weigh up. Then there are the fuel cells and they can't be removed without taking the whole wing apart. I figure four hundred pounds for them. So all told, I make it about twelve hundred and fifty pounds. That's an informed guess, no more."

"I don't know how much distance a dog team can make in a day, but thirty miles should represent a limit," Ferguson said. "That means a minimum of ten days at maximum output. And we'd have to drop supplies all along the way. Plus the fact that there are two of those root sections. Forget the dog teams, Andy, they'd never be able to do it."

"All right, we come to that noble organization, the United States Army. The Army built Camp Century; tons upon tons of stuff were hauled out onto the ice cap. They built a whole city, remember, and our wing roots can't be the same load as,

100

say, a nuclear reactor. They must have the sleds that can do it, and the snow cats to pull them." By the time he had finished there was a decided look of hope and expectation on his face.

"The Army could do it," Collins agreed, "but none of that gear is here. Getting them to bring it back again for an unofficial project would be hell. Even if it *was* here, asking them to go out that far would be tough. They might, but none of that equipment is anywhere closer than Sondrestrom at the best."

Perry Feinberg appeared and was introduced to Collins. He sat down and, in a drastic departure from his usual form, displayed a hint of discouragement. "The troops are dis-spirited," he reported. "The stuff is all unloaded and in the hangar, but it was a chore."

"How do we stand?"

"We've got both outer wing panels, all four props, three engines, and the complete tail assembly. And some miscellaneous bits and pieces. But those damn wing roots . . ."

"We've discarded the idea of dog teams," Holcomb told him. "And the Army has taken away the stuff it used to build Camp Century."

Perry Feinberg began to recover. "I covered the same ground and got the same answers. However, we do have Trackmasters here for use in phases. If we built a sled that would hold them, we might be able to airlift the sled out there and also a Trackmaster. Of course the colonel would have to approve that and he is a bear about keeping all rescue equipment on the ready at all times. The Trackmasters are rescue vehicles."

Ferguson was looking hard at the table top, hearing nothing. The others noted his condition and waited. Finally, he looked at Collins. "What kind of choppers do you fly?" he asked.

"Jollies. Jolly Green Giants. HH-3's."

"What kind of an operating range do you have?"

"Maximum, about a hundred and seventy miles."

That figure was a blow, but Ferguson persisted. "How many do you have?"

"Two. That was the full complement of aircraft here at Thule until you arrived with that fixed-wing monster."

Ferguson ignored the jibe; greater matters were on his mind. "How much weight can a helicopter lift?" he asked.

"The sky crane can hoist ten tons with no sweat."

"How much can a Jolly lift?"

"That depends on the fuel load and what equipment is on board. Normally we carry six thousand pounds of fuel. And because we are rescue vehicles, we have to have eight hundred pounds of rescue gear on board at all times."

"But with full tanks and all the rescue gear, you still have a reserve capacity?"

"Oh, sure, we carry a full load of passengers, their baggage, and the crew."

"With a half–fuel load, then, you could pick up a piece of hardware that weighed twelve to fifteen hundred pounds."

"With a sling, no sweat. I know what you're thinking, but we don't have anything like the range to go and get those wing roots for you."

Perry Feinberg had a thought. "Just suppose," he said, "that we were out on the ice cap and stranded where the B-17 is. For some reason, we couldn't fly. What then?"

Collins shrugged his shoulders. "Then we'd come and get you, that's all."

"How?" Holcomb asked.

"Several ways. When an active rescue is on, and lives are at stake, we do a lot of things that aren't in the book. We have a midair refueling capability, but that calls for a tanker, of course."

"What kind of a tanker?"

"A C-130."

"*Ah!*"

"But it has to be specially equipped and yours won't do."

Ferguson was thinking intensely. "Maybe it will," he declared. "Not for midair refueling, but we sure as hell can spot fuel bladders or drums for you along the route."

"And put beepers on them so you can find them," Holcomb added.

"You'd have to talk to the major," Collins said.

"I am acquainted with the major," Feinberg said. "A splendid gentleman and of course a superb pilot, but something of a stickler for the rules."

"That he is."

"One last question," Ferguson interjected. "Tom, suppose somehow we could get this set up — do you see any *technical* reason why it wouldn't be possible?"

Collins thought. "No, none that we couldn't overcome. You know the reputation of the Jollies. It would be a helluva operation, but we could probably hack it."

Andy was not satisfied. "And if we did manage to get approval, would the guys at Det. Four go for it? Would they give us a hand?"

"Oh hell yes," Collins answered.

To Sergeant William Stovers, a problem was not something to worry about — it was something to be solved. It was in that context that while the others were talking in the NCO Club, he pushed open the series of doors that gave access to the hangar where Det. 4 was housed, stamped the snow off his feet, and hung up his parka. Then he went inside. With a sure instinct he avoided the section where the commander and the other officers would be found and instead located the area where the working NCO's were busy.

He was made welcome. A mug of hot coffee was placed in his hand and a chair was put at his disposal.

"I've got to admit," he said, "that I know very little about helicopters. Since I'm going to be up here awhile, it seemed like a good idea to come down and find out a few things."

"That's a helluva good idea," the chief of maintenance responded. "Have you had any rotary-wing experience at all?"

"A couple of superficial rides," Stovers answered, "but all I did was sit on my butt in the cabin."

"Let's go look at the airplanes," the chief suggested.

Stovers was so well attuned to what he was doing, he did not even flinch when he heard the word "airplanes." He followed his guide into the main hangar area, where two of the big helicopters were sitting in perfect alignment side by side. There was plenty of space between them, Stovers noted, and the housekeeping inside the hangar was immaculate.

"We always maintain an alert posture," the Det. 4 man explained. "Of course, we never know when a call may come in, but when one does — we're ready. If we have any reason to expect one, we have one of the airplanes fully cocked so that all the crew has to do is to jump on board and hit the starters."

"How do you cock them?" Stovers asked.

"We go through all the preliminary checklists — and they're quite complicated — and take everything up to the 'start engines' stage. After that no one touches the ship or changes anything. If any work becomes necessary, we go through the whole thing again."

"They must be very complex machines."

"That's right, Bill, they are. They have all kinds of special systems and flying them isn't that easy."

Stovers began to lead into his subject. He looked carefully inside the cabin and counted the available seats. He measured the remaining cargo space with an experienced eye. Then he studied the size of the airframe and tried to relate the physical dimensions to the machine's ability to lift. "I see that you can carry ten or twelve pax," he commented.

"Yes, easily. Plus all their gear and baggage. We do that all the time when we go out to the Eskimo villages."

"You carry a lot of semi-permanent gear."

"Yes, that's all rescue equipment. It has to be on board at all times. If we get a call when we're going someplace, we can divert right then and there and we'll have everything with us. About eight hundred pounds worth."

"Isn't it true," Stovers asked, "that you can also carry things externally?"

"Absolutely, that's one of the advantages of a helicopter. They use them, for instance, in erecting high tension towers. When they want to build a cross-country electrical trunk line, they assemble the tops of the towers on the ground, which is a lot easier. Then a helicopter picks them up, one after another, and puts them in place. A skyhook in other words."

"These aircraft could do that?"

"Yes, the H-3 could, depending on the size of the towers of course."

"Is there anything in particular that you carry?"

"Yes, Firebees for one thing. They're pilotless drones that we recover and carry externally."

"How big are they?"

"Almost twenty-three feet long, a little less than thirteen feet in span."

"How much do they weigh?" he asked.

"Empty, about fourteen hundred and fifty pounds, but they can gross up to thirty-two hundred."

A half an hour later Bill Stovers left the Det. 4 hangar and took a cab to Hangar 8. It was a short distance, but he had already been at Thule long enough to know that wandering around in severe sub-zero temperatures was definitely not recommended. That was one reason why the free taxi service had been set up.

The driver did not mind at all. He dropped Bill at the doorway and then asked casually, "What's going on in there?"

"Some repair work," Stovers answered.

Once inside he turned on the overhead lights and then spent ten minutes surveying all of the parts and components that had already been brought in. The wing panels had been laid out in their approximate positions on the floor. The four propellers were in a neat row. One engine had been mounted on a stand and two of the cylinders have been taken off.

When he had inspected everything to his satisfaction, he walked over to the workbenches that had been set up. On one of them he found the first real piece of aircraft structure that had been brought in — the left stabilizer. He examined it minutely, as though it had some special secret that it could reveal to him. When he was at last satisfied, he checked carefully to see what sort of tools were at hand.

From a hidden corner of Supply someone had unearthed aircraft cleaning compound. Placed next to it there was an electric buffer with several spare discs.

Sergeant Stovers took off his parka and folded his sleeves back above his elbows. Then he set to work. He tried a small test area first, carefully rubbing the cleaner by hand until the accumulated patina of soil had been loosened and partly wiped away. Then he switched on the electric buffer and guided it carefully over the metal. The results were satisfying. As soon as the test section had been thoroughly cleaned, he looked for polish, found some, and applied it to the same small area. When it had dried sufficiently he used the buffer once more. This time the aluminum brightened until it shone like new — each individual rivet head a tiny bright eye studding the surface of the Alclad.

That was all that he had to see. He worked on for more than three hours, carefully and systematically, until he was finished. Then he replaced the tools and threw the waste into a barrel. He knew why no one else had come to put in some spare time and he was glad for his own reasons that he had not been interrupted. When he had finished putting everything in order, he checked over his handiwork.

The left stabilizer shone more brilliantly than it probably

had when it had been indeed brand-new. The transformation was phenomenal; no one looking at it would call it anything other than a fine aircraft part; even by the not too brilliant hangar lighting far over head it showed highlights on its almost dazzling surface.

Bill Stovers was satisfied. When the others saw it, they would get the message. He got back into his parka, called a cab, and then waited outside in order to let the icy air cool the fire in his brain.

It was almost an hour later when another vehicle pulled up before the door of Hangar 8. The tall man who got out was alone. After shutting the door of his staff car, he looked around to be sure that he was not observed. When he saw no one, he went inside and found the switch; once more the overhead lights came to life.

He did not bother to take off his parka, but he did walk around and look at the various parts that were laid out on the slightly concave floor. As he surveyed them and appraised their condition, he pressed his lips silently together and without realizing it, shook his head.

He was about to leave when he looked toward the work-benches and saw the bright reflections from the stabilizer. He walked over, at a slightly faster pace, and stared down at the polished aluminum. He ran a hand over the surface and examined it by touch as well as by sight. Then he lifted one end and sighted down the edge to be sure that it was straight and true. He checked the fittings and found them all to be in apparent good order.

Despite himself, he began to revise his thinking. He drew breath and spoke aloud, to himself. "Maybe they can do it," he said. "Just possibly they can."

Almost at once he discovered that his mood had improved. He definitely felt better as he snapped off the lights and emerged once again into the frigid Arctic night. As he walked toward his car, a small brown shadow shifted position on the snow. He stopped and watched the movements of the tiny Arctic fox.

"Hello, Archie," he said, fully aloud this time. He felt in the pocket of his parka, but he had nothing to throw to the little animal.

It came a few steps toward him, hoping for food, but the man it was trying to approach backed away. He liked animals, but he knew that the Archies were almost all rabid, despite the fact that they showed none of the symptoms. Many of the husky sled dogs also carried the deadly disease, and had to be treated accordingly.

When Archie was convinced that his new-found friend had nothing to give to him, the little creature ran off into the night, its very thick fur making it possible for it to survive under the severe conditions that were all that it knew.

Regretting that he had had nothing to offer to the hopeful little animal, the colonel got back into his vehicle and drove away.

CHAPTER EIGHT

THE VISITOR who enters the Non-Commissioned Officers' Club at Thule will find the bar to his right, immediately after the checkroom, where he can leave his parka. To his left there is a dining room which offers an unexpected degree of elegance in the almost desperate isolation in the High Arctic. Straight ahead there is a large room, with a bandstand at the west end, which can serve many purposes. It was toward this room that Chief Master Sergeant Perry Feinberg made his impressive way.

When he entered the room he found, as he had expected, that some ten of his colleagues were gathered, seeking consolation. At once his broad face illuminated in a beaming smile; he suggested Franklin D. Roosevelt listening to the election returns whenever he happened to be running for President.

Without waiting for an invitation, Sergeant Feinberg seated himself. "Gentlemen," he announced. "Our troubles are over. I have reached a decision."

Sergeant Steele, from Operations, looked at him from under heavy lids. "Would you care to favor us with your conclusions?" he asked.

"Certainly." Sergeant Feinberg was expansive. "After carefully reviewing all aspects of the matter, I have decided that the boys in Det. Four are going to bring in the wing root sections for us. Sergeant Prevost, who owns one of the Jollies, has advised me that they can do it. I regard his opinion as final."

Bill Stovers said nothing, content to wait and see what was coming next.

Atwater, from Supply, filled in as straight man. "Now that it has been decided that the splendid gentlemen from Det. Four, which includes the junior officers, are going to accomplish this miracle a couple of hundred miles beyond their normal operating range, has anyone been so thoughtful as to notify them of this fact?"

Sergeant Feinberg lit a cigar in the grand manner. "All in due time," he answered. "A few minor details remain to be resolved."

"The colonel for one," Holcomb suggested.

"Quite possibly, yes," Feinberg concurred. "But I regard the colonel as a most enlightened man of great capability. It's the dunderheads who usually bollix up the works. They lack imagination."

"If he needs to get someone in line," Steele said, "the colonel can be highly imaginative."

"Now," Sergeant Feinberg expounded, "what we need to do is to impress on the commander of Det. Four the somewhat urgent need for a realistic, long-range training exercise."

By a fortunate—and carefully arranged—coincidence, two of the younger helicopter pilots from Det. 4 developed a sudden interest in the C-130 airlifter and in its forthcoming mission on the ice cap. They were, therefore, on the flight line quite early the following morning, in arctic flight suits, prepared for an orientation ride in the big Hercules. Ferguson welcomed them and after a brief preliminary agreement, he took them into Hangar 8. Four men were working on the engine that had already been stripped of two of its cylinders. "It's been there thirty years," Ferguson said, "but it's been in a deep freeze—no corrosion, no rust. It can be overhauled."

"That's incredible," one of the helicopter pilots declared.

"If you can freeze a steak, why not an airplane?" Ferguson asked. "And the airplane is a helluva lot more durable. Think of it this way: a lot of planes are tied down outside the year around in all weather and they still last for twenty years or more."

"That's true," the other pilot agreed. "I used to own part of one."

Ferguson made the most of the carefully shined-up left stabilizer. He exhibited it and let his two guests look it over in detail. When they had done so, he knew that he had them sold. "Another thing," he added by way of further explanation. "Just because aircraft are few and far between up here right now doesn't mean that we're short of good mechanics. Some of the best in the business are here, many of them in other types of jobs. This isn't being undertaken by a bunch of amateurs."

"Obviously not," the first pilot agreed. "Let's get going, we're ready."

"Sergeant Stovers is the loadmaster," Ferguson told him. "He'll let us know when the gear is loaded. The bird is cocked, so it won't take us long to fire up."

Less than fifteen minutes later the Hercules lifted off the

Thule runway with a total of twenty persons on board and a considerable amount of equipment. A small tractor tug with a snowplow attached sat close to the rear ramp opening. Its nineteen-year-old operator had a wide grin on his face: he knew that he was good and he was anticipating the chance to prove it.

Even Sergeant Feinberg had to admit that the cockpit drill was beyond reproach; it was a premium quality crew all the way. He still thought so after what remained of *The Passionate Penguin* showed up, within one minute of Lieutenant Jenkins's estimated time of arrival. Ferguson put the skis down and executed another of his near-perfect ice cap landings. There was a moderate crosswind, but that did not trouble him at all. When the big Herc slid to a stop, it was again almost wingtip to wingtip with the derelict B-17, an arrangement that was spoiled only by the fact that the World War II bomber had no wingtips left — they were back in Hangar 8 at Thule.

The work for the day had been carefully laid out in advance. Enthusiasm had returned; it was assumed that somehow the helicopter detachment would solve the problem of the oversize wing root sections.

A large A-frame that had been left at the site was rigged over the outer end of the right wing root and a sling was fitted under the wing section. When that had been done, the line from the block and tackle was attached to the small tractor that was fired up and ready for action. As the tractor backed away, its driver cautiously obeying the hand signals of Andy Holcomb, the sling tightened and for the first time in more than a generation, the right main wheel lifted off the ground.

A canvas was spread underneath it to make the job easier and four men began to disassemble the landing gear. In the sub-zero temperature and moderate wind high on the ice cap, it was a difficult job, but a large portable heater helped greatly by unfreezing the fittings and by offering a warmed area in which to work.

While that was going on, the remaining engine was being removed with the aid of a smaller, but powerful, heater-defroster. The remaining large heater was once more at work pouring warmed air into the fuselage.

Meanwhile the fairings at the wing root were being taken off to expose the heavy driftpins that held the wings on. They would have to be sledged out and it would be, at the best, a difficult task.

But nobody minded. Least of all Sergeant Holcomb, who was foreman for the whole job. Inside the fuselage, Lieutenant Jenkins was busy carefully removing the bolts that held the front and rear sections of the fuselage together. He was not alone: the two helicopter pilots joined him in his labors while Bill Stovers carefully undid the turnbuckles that held the complete double set of control cables in position.

In one hour and twenty-two minutes that job was completed; *The Passionate Penguin*'s fuselage had been separated into two sections just behind what remained of her wings.

For the next forty-five minutes the tractor operator was in his glory. With his snowplow blade he built a ramp at the rear of the C-130 up to the interior floor level. When the ramp on the aircraft was raised to the level position, he pushed some snow onto it to make sliding easier. Then he drove his powerful little vehicle across the snow toward the tail of the old bomber.

It took ten minutes to rig the ropes properly. When Sergeant Holcomb was at last fully satisfied, the tractor was ready to pull. At that moment someone remembered; he yelled, *"Stop! You forgot the tail wheel!"*

It took forty-five minutes to correct that oversight. The wheel could not be raised into its well, so it was taken off after enough snow had been shoveled away to make the work possible.

The rest was almost anticlimactic — the tractor pulled, the fuselage shuddered slightly, and then the rear section slid slowly backwards, an empty tapered cylinder that had been stripped of all of its tail surfaces — only the dorsal remained in position.

With expert skill the tractor driver turned the section around, then pulled it across the loose snow to the end of the ramp he had made with his blade. Then he unhitched and drove around to the open end so that he could push the half-fuselage section into the C-130, tail end first.

Sergeant Stovers saw to every detail of that. He had a freight pallet waiting on the 463L tracks that were fitted into the floor of the Hercules. At very slow speed, and with extreme care, the fuselage half was pushed on board, a wooden plank cushioning the contact between the tractor and the fuselage itself. It took an hour to do it and to fasten the section down, but when the job had been completed, despite his temperament Bill Stovers wanted to cheer. They had been bringing back bits and pieces; now they were bringing back an airplane.

The right landing gear went in on a sled; the remaining engine came down off the nacelle that had held it so long and was carefully rested on another sled that was waiting to receive it. The nose section of the old bomber remained exactly where it had been except for the tilt of its wing; the snow packed underneath its center section was enough to hold it in place.

There was a break for lunch aboard the C-130, then the other main landing gear was recovered. "I wonder about the tires," Atwater said to Andy Holcomb. "Those we haven't got in Supply, of course, and I don't know where to get any more."

"Somebody must stock them," Andy replied. "I've been reading up — did you know that there are several B-17's flying in California right now? They use them to drop retardants onto forest fires. That means lots of landings and takeoffs, which means they have to have a source for tires."

"It sounds logical," Atwater agreed. "I'll start nosing around."

The toughest part of the work was separating the wing root sections from the main fuselage forward section, which was all that remained. The heavy tapered pins were rammed home so securely that repeated attacks with a powerful sledge did not seem to budge them a bit. Heat was applied, and more penetrating oil, but the stubborn pins would not let go. Everything else was ready; the service lines into the wing had been uncoupled and only the driftpins stood in the way of progress.

Still they refused to yield. "No wonder the B-17 was so tough," Ferguson said to Perry Feinberg. "Even the right way, it's almost impossible to get it apart."

The massive chief master sergeant smiled. "It is obviously now time," he declared, "for me to get into the act. We should have brought Angelo from the weather service; he's a weight lifter and a muscle man. But since he is not here, I shall have to attend to it personally."

In his heavy arctic boots and other equipment, Feinberg climbed up into position, took off his two outer pairs of gloves, and fitted a smaller leather pair into position. Then he hefted the sledge, calculated his stance, adjusted his position minutely, drew a deep breath, and swung the sledge in a mighty arc through the air. The whole remaining aircraft shuddered from the impact, but the pin did not visibly move. On the sixth swing it did; it shot out of its socket and was very nearly lost in the snow.

After the first victory the rest seemed easier; it had been proven that it could be done. Two hours and twenty minutes later, which was a longer time than Ferguson had intended to spend on the ice cap by a considerable margin, the last pin on the left side let go. The wings were off. The tractor pulled them a little to one side. As the sun threw the last of its light into the sky, all that remained of *The Passionate Penguin* on the ice cap was half a fuselage section and the two huge wing root sections. The back of the massive job had been broken.

Thirty-five minutes out of Thule, at 16,000 feet, Ferguson received notification of a Phase Alert. Although he had not spent much time at Thule, he had been thoroughly briefed on the intense Arctic storms that occurred there during eight months of the year. They were highly dangerous, so much so that going out under Phase Two or Phase Three conditions, except in pairs and on specifically authorized missions, was a court-martial offense. He radioed back at once, giving his position and ETA, and asking for further advice, if any.

Thule reported that Phase Alert was in effect, but that he could continue his approach at best possible speed. Phase One, the first drastic level of the expected storm, was estimated to be an hour away. Ferguson began an immediate letdown at close to red-line speed; at the same time he asked Jenkins to work out immediate headings for Sondrestrom, in case he would have to divert there, and for Alert, the Canadian military facility at the extreme northern tip of Ellesmere Island, some 420 miles from the geographic North Pole—a place he was eager to see. This northernmost permanently occupied point on the globe had a landing strip that could handle a C-130; he knew that because the Canadians passed through Thule with their C-130's on their way up to the ultra-isolated station. Normally Alert was closed to all visitors, but a United States Air Force transport forced to fly there, and with only military personnel on board, would probably be accepted. Meanwhile, as Jenkins worked out the headings, he continued his approach to Thule and communicated with the ground people there every few minutes.

When he was fifteen minutes out, he was advised that Phase One was definitely coming, but it was likely he would be able to get in all right before it hit. He was cautioned to watch out for strong and possibly rapidly shifting winds.

Ferguson put out of his mind the thought that he was

carrying a considerable portion of the *Penguin*'s fuselage in the cargo hold; he passed back the word that an emergency landing might be in the cards and ordered all personnel to fasten seat belts. Sergeant Stovers made another thorough check—as he had twice before—of the lines securing the cargo and equipment on board. When he was satisfied, he seated himself once more and pulled his seat belt as tight as he was able. He knew what a phase was.

As the C-130 came down from over the ice cap, Ferguson did not waste moments by setting up a conservative formal approach; instead he asked for clearance, got it, and then racked his aircraft around in a steep turn that pointed his right wing almost directly at the ground. Gear and flaps down, he swung over the end of the runway, chopped the power, and put the Hercules on, halfway down the strip. He had 10,000 feet to work with and half of that was more than adequate under emergency conditions. He encountered a sharp gust just as he touched down, but reacted quickly and successfully. He was clear of the runway in seconds, and headed for the shelter of Hangar 8. The ground people raised the door so that it was fully open just as he arrived on the ramp outside. Ferguson fed in a little power and taxied directly inside. By the time that the props had stopped turning, the door was closed and sealed.

The extreme High Arctic base of the United States Air Force was located in northern Greenland by permission of the Danish government. Since Greenland is a county of Denmark proper, very close cooperation between Denmark and the United States is both a pleasant fact and an absolute necessity. Thule Air Base is owned and used by the United States, but the physical operation of the facility is a Danish responsibility. All of the Danes who work there are required to be able to speak English. It is a voluntary, civilian service suitable only for men who enjoy the very high Arctic and who can adjust without difficulty to that demanding environment. Some of the Danish civilian personnel have been on the job for many years. A few actually find comfort in the solitude that Thule provides, and they empathize with its wild and stark scenery during the daylight months.

After two years at Thule, Danish citizens are excused from paying the very substantial income tax imposed by their country. For as long as they choose to remain, they continue to enjoy tax-free status — it is one of the major inducements to serve in the Arctic.

The architecture of the base is not another. Most of the buildings are low, cubical, prefabricated structures designed for maximum utility and zero aesthetics. The only concession to decor is the Thule Christmas tree. Enjoying its eminent status as the only tree in Greenland, it rises some twenty feet in front of the headquarters building. It is lit as a symbol of the holiday festivities in November when the long Arctic night settles in and it continues to spread holiday spirit until late in February when the sun begins to be visible once more. In the unbroken blackness of high noon in January the Christmas tree shines out its message and offers good cheer. It is undoubtedly the longest-lasting Christmas tree on earth. Constructed of pipe that has been carefully welded and then painted, the tree can withstand winds of more than 150 miles per hour — and it has.

Building 708 at Thule is known as "the high rise" because it towers a dizzying three stories against the background of the not-too-distant ice cap. It is an officers' billet that houses the base commander, VIP guests, the executive staff, the pilots of Det. 4, the Catholic and Protestant chaplains, and a superb collection of fetching and heartwarming pinups. There is also a small indoor garden that draws its nourishment from fluorescent lights hung overhead.

There is a closed and restricted room, which becomes an immediate command post in the event of Phase Two weather.

During Phase Alert and Phase One it is not activated, but if Phase Two conditions are declared, the command post goes into action. One of its major functions is to account for every person on the base, Danish or American. Since phase weather can be swiftly fatal without the fullest protection, the head count is vital. Widely known at Thule is a powerful Dane, a bearded giant of a man who, some years before *The Passionate Penguin* was rediscovered, was caught out of doors in a Phase Three and survived. Only indomitable will, tremendous physical toughness, and fantastic luck had made it possible.

During Phase Alert, all preparations for severe weather are made, time permitting. All loose equipment or materials outside must be secured.

During Phase One, indoor activities may continue, but outdoor pedestrian travel is by the buddy system only. Trips to the great BMEWS installation that is commonly referred to as J Site may be made only if authorized.

If Phase Two is declared, all personnel must remain in whatever building they are in. Those outdoors must seek immediate shelter in the nearest possible place. Vehicle traffic is limited to authorized emergency equipment *only*. The buddy system is mandatory.

Phase Three requires every person on base to report his whereabouts. Outdoor travel of any kind is forbidden — with the sole exception of authorized rescue efforts. For this purpose the Trackmasters, which resemble tanks as much as anything else, are called into use. Designed to operate under the most violent of Arctic conditions, they can maneuver on and off roads with their very wide, multilevel tracks. They are low to the ground and can go almost anywhere to seek and, if possible, rescue personnel caught stranded in conventional vehicles or out in the open.

Phases can last a few minutes or several days. They can come with very little warning and great violence. Along the road between Thule proper and J Site, there is a series of phase shacks built to give emergency shelter and to withstand whatever the Arctic can throw at them. Phase shack number seven was equipped with an anemometer until the instrument finally blew off the roof—but not before recording a wind velocity of 207 miles per hour, the second highest wind speed ever measured on earth. How much higher the wind got after that no one knows.

Lieutenant Ferguson and his crew members, regular and added, were still in the hanger securing the C-130 when Phase One was declared. As the loudspeaker repeated the news, Andy Holcomb rushed to the phone and requested three cabs for the trip from Hanger 8 to the mess hall. None of the men had eaten, and if Phase Two were to come, the mess hall was as good a place to be trapped as any.

The dispatcher could not promise immediate service. At that point Chief Master Sergeant Feinberg made his presence known over the line and suggested urgency. The cabs, in the form of six-pack pickups, arrived within five minutes.

The wind was vicious as the men climbed inside the sturdy vehicles. The weather was already unflyable; sharp gusts picked up clouds of loose snow and flung them wildly against the sides of the hangars, against the trucks, and against the parka-clad men as they scrambled to get inside the cabs. When the taxis started out, they had to go slowly because of the drastically reduced visibility.

The air was sharp and biting when the men got out and covered the fifty feet from the roadway to the first of the triple doors that led inside. Within the brightly lit hall that served all comers, a massive meal was waiting. As Ferguson spooned up the first of his hot soup, he offered a half-prayer that Phase Two, if it was coming, would hold off until after they had eaten and made their way to quarters. He remembered the weather outside and the cruelties that it inflicted on the Archies and the huskies that remained in the open all of their lives. It would be even worse far up on the ice cap, almost two miles above where he sat, where what remained of *The Passionate Penguin* was totally exposed.

He finished his soup and tied into a huge portion of meat loaf. The Danes made it their own way, but no one complained that it wasn't good. There was even some Thule ice cream and reconstituted milk that was a vast improvement over the mixtures that had been served during World War II.

Because they had been working together all day on a joint project where rank had had little meaning, the men sat in groups of four around the tables ignoring the slightly more comfortable section that had been set up for ranking civilians and officers.

"I tell you, Det. Four can do it," Andy Holcomb declared with some heat. "Bill was down there and checked their lifting capability. The damn things can set down almost anywhere on the ice cap to refuel. On the way out, they can set up their own caches. And another thing—when they start bringing the sections back, if they're mounted properly in the slings, they can carry their own weight. They'll fly."

"I don't think they want them to," Ferguson answered. "It would raise hell with their weight and balance. Suppose one of the wing sections lifted itself right out of the sling, or up against the bottom of the chopper. My guess is that they'll fly them endwise."

A phase announcement came over the PA system. It was still Phase One, but a worsening of the storm was expected. "Let's get the hell out of here," Ferguson said. "I want a night's sleep."

Taxis were summoned. The men climbed into their parkas one more time, stuffed their hands into their liners and mittens, and then into their arctic gloves. Sergeant Stovers pulled a wool knit cap over his head. When the taxis came, the men were ready. Ferguson was the last to leave; just before he pushed open the first of the doors, the PA system began: "Attention all personnel, this is a phase announcement . . ."

To keep his conscience clear, he ran outside before he could hear what was going to be said. As it was, the taxi ride was a nightmare. Visibility was hardly more than five feet; the truck crept slowly, finding its way by the reflective phase markers that lined both sides of every Thule roadway. Somehow the driver found Building 708 and pulled up directly in front of the center door. Ferguson got safely inside and closed the massive outer door. After he had fixed the heavy bar that held it shut, he paused for a minute and gave thanks — not in a formal prayer, but remembering that if he had delayed even a little longer on the ice cap, he could have ended up anywhere. Perhaps even forced down as the *Penguin* had been, thirty years before.

But it had been worth it, nonetheless. One more trip would bring in the rest of the fuselage; that left only the wing root sections that Det. 4 would somehow have to be persuaded to airlift. Then, by God, the ice cap would have been stripped of its prey and the job of restoration could begin.

The brass couldn't stop that; there would be no reasonable way. One more trip, two chopper missions — those were the only hurdles. And after that . . .

Tired as he was, he climbed the steps to his quarters two at a time in full arctic gear. As he passed the open door of the command post, he saw that twelve or fifteen men were on duty at their stations, verifying and adding up the head count.

His mind was full of the airplane and it kept him awake long after he had hoped to be asleep.

CHAPTER NINE

THERE WAS LITTLE work done at Thule the following day. The Phase Two storm kept up its unabated fury so that the base personnel could only be grateful that at least it wasn't getting any worse. No one was able to go anywhere, not even to the mess hall. The emergency phase rations were broken out, overdue letters were written, and books that had been waiting weeks to be read were picked up at last.

On the third floor of Building 708 three of the junior officers of Det. 4 were hard at work on a problem. As they labored, their efforts were inspired by an almost solid wall of pinups. None of the captivating young ladies depicted would have lasted outside for half a minute in what she was wearing — which, in practically all cases, was nothing whatever. The pinups were one of the few amenities that helped to make life at Thule a bit more endurable.

First Lieutenant Ron Cunningham was laying out the project. "If we leave an hour before dawn, then we should be able to make our fuel drop on the ice cap in late twilight. That's no problem."

Lieutenant Mike Turner, who combined a string-bean physique with a mathematical mind, punched an electronic calculator in his hand. "If we pick just the right spot," he announced, "we should be able to do it with one refueling. That is, if those damn wing sections don't weigh a lot more than we think."

Tom Collins was deeply absorbed in the chart of upper Greenland that he had spread out before him. "If they do, then we might need two drinks to get back. Roughly, we'll be able to lift more than eight hundred additional pounds that way."

Turner, who both knew the performance regulations and believed in them, shook his head. "That would make matters a lot worse," he said.

"I know," Cunningham agreed, "but what we can do once we can do twice if we have to."

Mike Turner still had his reservations. "It isn't what we *can* do—it's what we can get away with."

"Absolutely," Collins agreed. "However, the necessary delicate negotiations are in the hands of Sergeant Feinberg. I trust you known him?"

"I do," Turner answered.

"We'll have to pass it off as a training exercise," Collins said. "The problem is there are *two* of those damn things."

"So we train two different crews," Cunningham answered. "It will increase pilot proficiency and qualify us to do difficult lifts off the ice cap—just in case the Army gets into trouble out there."

Tom Collins was thoughtful. "If only Major Kimsey will buy it, then we've got it made."

A captain from Administration had wandered over in time to pick up some of the discussion. "Frankly," he said when he had an opportunity, "I think the whole thing's nuts."

Rank meant little while in barracks during a phase. Therefore Collins did not hesitate to contradict him. "The hell it is. Look — they've brought the whole damn bird back here except for the nose section and the two wing roots. The nose section comes in on the next trip — we do the rest."

The captain was not satisfied. "And what will they have when they're finished? Basically junk. They might make the thing into a display, but there's no one to come and look at it."

"Eskimos," Mike said mildly.

"All right — how would you like to fly a chopper that's been out in the Arctic weather for thirty years? Sikorsky couldn't fix it. A B-17 is a four-engine beast that's got to have all kinds of systems and circuits . . ." He shrugged his shoulders. "Nuts," he repeated.

Cunningham went back to his planning. "The C-130 gang will have the sections in position for us to lift. Once the slings have been rigged, the rest should be relatively easy. Well, not easy, but would anybody care to put up any bets?"

Mike Turner was thinking again. "One of us ought to go out there in the C-130, at the risk of life and limb, to see that the sling setup is done properly. The fixed-wing types won't know anything about that."

"Good idea," Cunningham agreed. "One of our flight mechanics would be the boy."

"About Major Kimsey —" Collins began.

Cunningham nodded to cut him off. "That, of course, is the problem. But I'll think of something."

The colonel had the door of his quarters part way open so

that Major Valen had no trouble announcing his presence. "Come in, Dave," the colonel invited. "How about some hot cocoa?"

The chaplain dropped into a chair. "A godsend," he said. After that he kept quiet until the colonel put a steaming mug into his hands.

"Anything on your mind?" Colonel Kleckner asked.

That was a tough one because something certainly was, but the major didn't want to discuss it too directly. And he would not lie. "Some general ideas," he prefaced. "I've noticed some things recently."

"Such as?" The colonel seated himself, in amiable mood, with his own cocoa.

"There's quite a difference in the way that various people react to the life up here," the major began. "Some of them adjust very well. Others have a hard time of it."

"I know," the colonel agreed. "But on the whole, I think you'll have to agree that this is a remarkably fraternal community. More than any other place I can name."

"True, sir, and that helps a lot, but basically this is still tough duty."

"Is it getting to you?" Colonel Kleckner asked.

The chaplain shook his head. "Only in that I'm concerned for some of the men. Which, after all, is my job."

The colonel was well ahead of him. "Have you any suggestions, Dave?" he asked.

That was the moment and Valen took the ball. "I can reach some of them from the pulpit, but not everyone comes and there is a practical limit to what words alone can do."

"Of course." The colonel continued to listen.

"Summer isn't too far off; when the weather warms up a little, some additional recreational activity will help a lot. Climbs up Mount Dundas, baseball when it's possible, some photography — there is certainly some spectacular scenery to shoot up here."

126

"You feel that more recreation is the answer?" the colonel suggested.

"Part of it, certainly. Almost anything that the men can get involved in—something that will take their minds off the isolation and the constant presence of the High Arctic. And the separation. Someday, I'd like to see a program for family visits up here—in summer, of course."

"We don't have very much summer. And no warm weather."

"Right—but if perhaps the extra achievers might be rewarded by a visit with their wives or girl friends . . ."

"But not both at the same time," the colonel noted.

Major Valen smiled. "I doubt if any of our guys would make that mistake."

Colonel Kleckner took his time drinking his cocoa. Then he looked up. "I'll keep what you've said in mind," he promised.

By 1700 hours the storm had subsided enough to be downgraded to Phase One. That made trips to the mess hall possible and life at Thule brightened immediately as a consequence. The Danish supervisor of the *messen* saw to it that an especially good meal was prepared; the scheduled beef stew was canceled and steaks were set up instead. All hands showed up for the meal and the big hall was well filled. The movie for the evening was announced. The staff librarians prepared for an extra run of business.

Shortly after 1800, Weather advised that the storm could very well intensify and that a Phase Three was possible. Following that grim pronouncement, the dessert bar did a land-office business. Thule ice cream was consumed by the gallon and the iced-tea containers were drained dry.

Immediately after eating, Colonel Kleckner stopped at the library and asked if there were any books available on the air aspects of World War II. The catalog listed several, but for some unstated reason, all of them had been recently checked out.

After selecting some titles off the shelves, the colonel returned to Building 708. There he shed his parka, got out of his arctic footgear, and washed the used cocoa mugs. After that he went upstairs and casually wandered down to the Det. 4 end of the building.

The poker game was already going strong. Lieutenant Mike Turner sat, shirtless, with the relic of what had once been a hat pulled partly over his eyes. He surveyed his cards and found them about as encouraging as a communication from the Internal Revenue Service.

Tom Collins kept changing the order of the cards in his hand, as if by doing so he could either increase their value or encourage them to blush forth in the same suit.

Ron Cunningham opened with a determined effort to appear casual. Major Richard Mulder, one of the two Det. 4 field grade officers, checked.

The colonel surveyed the board with an expert's eye and then declined an invitation to sit in. Instead he continued down the hall and then paused by the door of Major Forest Kimsey's room.

The Det. 4 commander got to his feet. "Evening, sir, come in," he invited. "Have a beer?"

"By all means."

A cold can was extracted from a refrigerator and popped open. The colonel sat down to enjoy its contents. "Tell me," he began, "if you were to get a medevac call right now, how would you handle it?"

"First, I'd check with Weather and get all the poop that I could. Then, if it was still Phase One, I'd have all hands report to the hangar on the double. I'd cock one of the birds and get ready for takeoff."

"Would you go?" the colonel asked.

"Two things would decide that: the exact level of the

weather activity and the urgency of the mission. If lives were at stake, and if it was humanly possible to get airborne under the existing conditions—yes, we would go."

"Off the record, Major, how well is your outfit tuned up right now?"

"We're in pretty good shape," Kimsey answered. "I lost two of my best pilots when they rotated back stateside last month. Their replacements are younger men—not quite as sharp. But they're good boys and they'll shape up."

The colonel drank some of his beer. "With you to teach them, I'm certain that they will," he said. "When the weather lets up, it might be a good idea to put on a good stiff training exercise. A hypothetical rescue off the ice cap, or something like that. I'd like to see you make it as realistic as you can; I never believed in handing a man a broomstick and asking him to pretend that it's a rifle."

"Really go out and do something," the major confirmed.

The colonel checked the fetching dimensions of the young lady posted on the bathroom door and approved. "Sharpen them up as much as you can. Someday, perhaps under severe conditions, they may have a damn important mission to fly."

"And the Arctic is merciless," the major added. "I'll lay something on that will be realistic and make them sweat a little."

"Good." The colonel nodded his approval and then finished his beer.

While the storm outside continued its ferocity, another of a different kind was raging inside the mind and body of Lieutenant Scott Ferguson. He could not get *The Passionate Penguin* out of his head and even thinking that the vital wing root sections might be impossible to bring in was enough to make him break out in an emotional sweat.

There was one more trip for him to make—he still had to get the forward fuselage section. It was automatically the

129

head, the heart, and the torso of the great bomber and careful measurement had proven that it would fit inside the C-130. He was determined that it would fit even if he had to chop a hole in the powerful airlifter to make it possible. Once that major component had been salvaged, virtually the whole aircraft would be safe and secure in Hangar 8, awaiting only the ministrations of skilled and dedicated mechanics. With the help of God, it was possible that they might be able to give her back her life and her glory.

The wing sections — the damn wing sections . . .

He paced up and down his room, keeping an ear tuned to the PA system. The inactivity was killing him; he was so anxious to get down to Hangar 8, he could hardly contain himself. He wanted to do something with his hands. Deep within himself he had the solid conviction that the World War II wreck was *his* airplane; perhaps it wasn't by accident that he had found it, alone and abandoned on the ice cap but otherwise apparently in perfect condition.

Once, when he had been a boy, he had gone wandering in the woods near his home. He had been perfectly safe; the woods were familiar territory and he had been in them many times before. Then he had found a trap that someone had left, and there was a tiny animal in it. One of its legs had been cruelly caught in steel jaws and had been lacerated when the little creature had struggled to get away. When he had found it, it had been in obvious agony.

He had had no idea whose trap it was, but he had hated him nonetheless. With some difficulty, because the trapped animal was crazed with pain, he had managed to get his hands into position and pry the trap open.

The little animal he had freed had let out one final cry of heartbreaking hurt and then had limped off, too frightened to spare itself by going more slowly.

He remembered that he had gone home with a strange new

feeling in possession of him — he had felt an almost unearthly happiness. He had believed firmly at the time that the Lord had guided his footsteps so that he would rescue the trapped animal, and it had frightened him a little. He had wondered what he was destined to do with his life, because that had seemed like a preview — a tiny foretelling of his future. The incident remained fresh and sharp in his mind; he knew that he would remember it to his dying day. It had implanted in him the strong desire to save things — to spare the hurt of living creatures and to forestall the destruction of worthy objects that deserved a better fate.

The same strong, unreal sensation filled him now. For the first time, he saw the whole picture clearly. It had started out only as a visit to an abandoned wreck. After that it had become a souvenir hunt. Somewhere in the process it had been transformed into a recovery project in the form of a challenge or, perhaps, a game to be played.

Not anymore; the game was over. Somehow, some way, those wing sections would be brought in. Then, if he had to do it alone, by God, that airplane was going to be put back together again. And in the process it would be overhauled until every bit of its structure was restored to its original condition and airworthiness. When all of that had been done, he was going to take it out and fly it. He had never said that to himself before, but he had thought it all along. He was going to roll that airplane out of its hangar in perfect condition, fire it up, taxi it out to the end of the runway, and take off.

There had been some talk about making it an exhibit. It would be assembled just to look at — the world's largest static model airplane.

Not the *Penguin* — not her. He refused to accept the possibility that for some unforeseen reason what he planned couldn't be done.

There was a knock on his door.

He opened it to find Tom Collins and Mike Turner from Det. 4, both of whom had been out on the ice cap with him on his last trip.

"Shut the door," Mike said.

"We've got some dope," Collins declared, and sat down. Turner planted himself on the edge of the bed. He was suitably dressed for scaling fish and his hat, as usual, was down to his eyebrows. It had started out as a semi-disaster and had descended from there. His mind, however, was functioning.

"Listen," he began, "at periodic intervals we're supposed to put on a significant training exercise — something that will really challenge our capabilities. Another one is coming up and Major Kimsey has detailed the two of us to develop a suitable problem."

Tom Collins continued. "So after deep and profound deliberation, we have decided to propose going after some large pieces of debris that are cluttering up the ice cap and bringing them in. Such a task will give our exercise a little actuality."

"We talked to the Danish commander and he liked the idea," Mike declared. "He said that it would improve the ecology of Greenland. Get that — the ecology of Greenland. We've got more ecology up here than anyone knows what the hell to do with. Anyhow, he approves. Now, from the limited viewpoint of a fixed-wing pilot, can you think of anything suitable that might take a bit of doing?" The grin he produced shamed the Cheshire cat.

Ferguson was almost unable to speak. "How soon?" he asked.

Tom Collins answered. "After the weather lifts. This forced inactivity has given us some time to do a little planning and work out some weight and balance figures. We're estimating the wing sections at fifteen hundred pounds each. If they weigh a helluva lot more than that, then no dice."

"Normally," Mike continued, "whenever one of our airplanes goes out, the other remains here on standby in case anyone gets stewed and falls through the ice. But since all he would do in that event would be to hit still more ice, we think it would be reasonable to take both birds out on the exercise with the understanding that if we're called, we jettison whatever we have immediately and hightail it back in a hurry. We get about one rescue call a month. Just before we go, we plan to check with the Danish doctor at Kanak to make sure that he doesn't have any business coming up for us as far as he knows."

"Just what is the range of a Jolly?" Scott asked.

"Over seven hundred miles with a partial load, but you'll still have to haul some fuel out there for us. We'll plant some more ourselves along the way and fix it so that we can find it again."

"Would you like me to fly cover — just in case?" Ferguson asked.

"No, thanks," Collins answered. "We'll manage. If anything does go wrong, we've got good radios and we can yell 'help' as fast as anyone."

The whole prospect was too good to be true; it had Ferguson a little dizzy. "I think," he ventured, "that I'll go down the hall and see Major Kimsey. He might appreciate a few words of thanks."

"If you'll allow me," Turner retorted, "my advice to you is that now is a damn good time to keep your mouth shut." He lifted his chin to improve the angle of his vision from under the edge of his supposed hat. "Just be sure to remember Det. Four when you say your prayers," he added.

As soon as the storm passed and the weather returned to Arctic normal, a flurry of fresh activity began almost immediately at Thule Air Base. The first arrival on the field was a heavily laden C-141 carrying many tons of supplies earmarked for the use of Camp Century. Three-quarters of an hour behind it another of the heavy jet airlifters flared onto the runway with a full load of pallets bearing additional Army gear.

The great bird was hardly safely blocked on the ramp when there was a whistling overhead and the Eastern Air Lines contract rotator came down out of the sky. The Boeing 727 greased on and pulled up in front of an empty hangar where the reception committee was waiting.

First off was an Army full colonel who headed a party of some twenty other officers. Colonel Kleckner was there to welcome them all. So also were Commander Kure of the Danish Navy — the ranking representative of his government — and a considerable number of other Thule regulars. Captain Tilton, the Information Officer, was on hand with a photographer. This was news for the *Thule Times*, the newspaper that scooped the world on northern Greenland events each time that it appeared — which was every other week.

The rotator also brought some fifty men who were arriving to begin their one-year tours at the Arctic outpost.

In the morning, when the rotator would return to McGuire Air Force Base, it would carry a load of happy men who had at last completed their tours and could look forward to reassignment in warmer and far less hostile climates. In most cases they would be able to have their families with them, a blessing they were fully prepared to enjoy to the utmost.

The airline captain, whose accumulated experience totaled more than 32,000 flight hours, knew most of the Thule senior staff very well. He quickly spotted Major Valen and drew the chaplain aside at the first opportunity. "I have something for you," he said. "It was handed to me by Jim Mock, a close friend of mine who flies for TWA. He brought it in from the Coast. He asked me to see that you got it personally." He handed over a mailing tube that was carefully sealed at both ends.

"Do you happen to know where Captain Mock picked this up?" Valen asked, just to be sure.

"Not for certain, but he came out of Los Angeles the day he brought it to me."

The major expressed his thanks while visions of perfectly functioning radios danced through his head. He was certain he knew what the tube contained. He was slightly jostled, and looked up to see Sergeant Feinberg there. "I beg your pardon, Major," the sergeant said. "I wasn't looking at what I was doing. Is that what I think it is?"

"I believe so," the chaplain answered. He looked at the tube more carefully and then nodded quite calmly. "It has the right return address."

"Sir, I am buying."

"Perhaps Lieutenant Ferguson . . ."

Feinberg beamed. "Shall we say at the club in forty-five minutes. The powwow should be over by then."

Major Valen glanced at his watch. "I shall announce that you are buying," he said.

Feinberg raised a hand. "Please pass that word with some restraint, sir," he implored. "Otherwise the turnout will be more than the club can hold. We don't want to be responsible for the first Arctic riot."

"No, indeed. Only the regular team members."

"Done," Feinberg agreed.

The small party that gathered around a table in the otherwise deserted big dining room at the NCO Club was in a more than festive mood. The horrible problem of the massive wing root sections was about to be solved, no one doubted that, and the means of getting the complicated radios fixed was at last at hand. Andy Holcomb touched on that point while the rest of the group awaited Major Valen's arrival. "The communications were a lot more involved than you might think," he explained. "I got some dope on it out of the library.

The B-17 had an intercom, of course, and in some cases it was redundant to protect against battle damage. Then there was a communications system to maintain contact with the rest of the formation — the '17's seldom flew alone. And, of course, there was all of the usual ground communications on top of that, both voice and CW. So there was quite a lot of electronics for that day. Sergeant Murphy should have a nice time with it all."

Two minutes after that the chaplain came in with the mailing tube in his hand. As the men gathered around, he opened it with loving care. He knew that its contents were valuable and he was not about to let any slip of his pocket knife deface what it contained. He opened both ends and then carefully removed what was rolled up inside.

It was not a glossy print; it was something on heavy coated paper much larger than he had expected. Silently he weighted down one edge with salt and pepper shakers, then he opened it out.

Even to the little group of men who were more than acclimated to Thule and its decor, it was a startling picture. Beyond any doubt it was Monica Lee; the lovely face that was known to millions smiled with utterly winning charm. She was looking directly at the camera — at the person who was in turn looking at her.

There was quite a bit to see. Both the photographer and his exquisite model had disdained even the thin gauze covering that some of the Thule pinups had seemed to find necessary. For the first time Monica Lee revealed to her vast army of fans an unexpectedly spectacular pair of breasts. Without artificial aid they thrust out, firm and erect, from her body. Their dimensions were impressive and their molding sublime. If that were not enough, they were tipped at the end by upraised nipples that would have fired Praxiteles with the fervent desire to exceed himself.

But they were no more than the rest of her nude figure — it

was totally revealed down to her knees. There were many many other nudes at Thule, but this one possessed a symmetry that was unbeatable. The chaplain looked at it and quoted Samuel Finley Breese Morse. "What hath God wrought," he said.

"Oh man!" Ferguson answered.

"Hardly that," Holcomb commented.

"That is absolutely the most woman that I have ever seen in my life." Sergeant Feinberg spoke in hushed tones. "And that is not a statement to be lightly dismissed."

"It *is* autographed," Bill Stovers noted.

Indeed it was. It had been signed with a brush pen and in elegant style:

> To Sergeant Mike Murphy
> My loyal, valued fan.
> From all of me.
> Monica Lee

An awed hush fell over the assembled men. The chaplain was the first to recover; he explored the inside of the tube and found a note addressed to himself. It was from his friend in Hollywood conveying the news that this was a unique item indeed. In a desire to break her too-constraining image as Miss Purity, Monica Lee had accepted an urgent invitation to become the pinup of the month in an internationally popular men's magazine. The photographic results, in the form of an advance color proof, were enclosed.

Unfortunately, Miss Lee's agent had had a fit upon finding out about the startling picture and had frantically phoned a large covey of lawyers in a desperate effort to kill the deal. The pinup would not appear—hence the extraordinary value of the enclosed proof, the only one that Miss Lee had consented to autograph. She had done so after much persuasion and a plea for special consideration for Our Boys in Uniform.

That was all and that was enough.

Quiet fell once more after the reading of the letter. All eyes remained fixed on the spectacular picture, but no one dared to speak.

Finally Sergeant Stovers did. "What I'd like to know now," he said, "is who in the hell we're going to be able to get to fix the damn radios."

Corbin agreed. "It's fate, gentlemen: a picture like that, autographed — and addressed to the only man in the Air Force too square to appreciate it."

After that, no one said anything. No one could.

CHAPTER TEN

WHEN SCOTT FERGUSON got out of his warm bed shortly before five in the morning, he was infused with the feeling that this was to be the most momentous day of his life. As he went through the mechanical motions of shaving and showering, oblivious to the pitch darkness outside, he was acutely aware that before nightfall the ultimate fate of *The Passionate Penguin* would be decided. She had been pulled to pieces on the ice cap until very little was left out there, but what was by far the most difficult part of the whole recovery operation lay directly ahead.

As he dressed he knew that the men from Det. 4 would be getting up too. Because they were a rescue outfit, they were used to hitting the deck at all hours of the day and night — with or without advance warning. He had a silent, unexpressed blessing for them, because if all went well during the next several hours, they were going to pull off a rescue that was probably unduplicated in flying history.

When he was almost ready he called a taxi and then went down to the center entrance, where he found both Jenkins and Corbin already there. "Is the mess hall open yet?" he asked.

"I think so," Jenkins answered. "Tom Collins said something about the Danes opening up early — especially for us."

A six-pack truck pulled up outside; as he climbed in, Ferguson asked the driver if he had seen any of the helicopter crewmen as yet.

"Yes," the Dane answered, "they are all in the *messen*. I hope you all have good luck today."

"Thank you," Ferguson answered, meaning it.

He was first inside the mess hall, where he was hit by a sudden sharp uplift. The whole of Det. 4 was there; gathered around one long table he saw Major Kimsey and Major Mulder, who would undoubtedly command the two Jollies, and the rest of the flying team: Tiny Heneveld, Bob Seligman, Tom Collins, Ron Cunningham, John Schoen, Sergeant Prevost, and Mike Turner. As he picked up a tray and went for his food, Ferguson felt a vast confidence in Det. 4 and what it could do; he fully realized that they had laid this whole thing on for the sake of the *Penguin*. When he joined them, he made a major concession. "Do you give helicopter lessons?" he asked.

"We're prepared to show you how it's done," Schoen answered.

Major Mulder was more practical. "If you don't mind," he said, "I'd like to have Tiny and Bob fly out with you to the site of the pickup. I want them to look over the debris before we attempt to pick it up."

"Yes, sir," Ferguson responded. He was prepared to give them anything they wanted. His only fear was that somehow, at the last minute, something would go wrong.

140

When he reached the flight line, everything seemed to be in good order. Sergeant Feinberg was on the job, presiding expansively over the preparation of equipment and personnel. This time there were no maintenance stands or tools to be loaded—only the little snow tug that was standing by, with its youthful operator as confident as ever. As soon as Feinberg saw Ferguson, he came over. "I want to bring a lot of hands this time," he said. "There may be quite a bit of muscle work needed to get that nose section loaded. And the whirly boys will want some help with the slings."

"How many?" Ferguson asked.

"Nineteen want to go, sir, and every one of them has earned the trip."

"All right," Ferguson agreed. He felt as though he was walking on egg shells; he didn't dare to do anything that might upset this final, critical stage of the recovery operation.

Feinberg checked with Sergeant Stovers, the loadmaster. "We have a little additional radio gear to load," he announced. "Principally a device to help the Det. Four boys locate us. Sergeant Murphy will handle that end."

"How did you . . .?"

Sergeant Feinberg created a magnificent gesture. "No problem at all; the usually reliable Murphy was guilty of a serious error of judgment concerning a possible outside straight. He is prepared to do penance."

"Did somebody cut the cards?" Stovers asked.

"That insignificant detail escapes me at the moment; I only recall that I was dealing. However, his spirits were lifted shortly after he agreed to cooperate: he held three jacks and they were good." Feinberg turned away, he was much too busy to deal with trivia.

In front of the Det. 4 hangar a turbine engine fired up. Presently two of them were howling and the main rotor of the big Jolly started to turn. As Ferguson watched, he began to understand how men must have felt in Vietnam when they were down and desperate and then saw a Jolly coming after them.

He watched intently as the big HH-3 taxied out to the end of the runway — an absurd thing for a helicopter to do, he thought — and then sat there while more checklists were completed. Then the roar of the twin turbines increased, the rotor spun faster, and with stately dignity the helicopter lifted off the ground. It hovered where it was for almost a full minute while still more checks were made, then it began to move forward and climb with increasing speed. Seconds later it turned southeast toward the ice cap.

"Beautiful, isn't it," Seligman said.

"Damn right it is," Ferguson agreed.

He was in his own cockpit during the pre-engine-start checklist when the second Det. 4 Jolly Green Giant taxied past. He saw Mike Turner in the left-hand seat with Major Mulder on his right. Sergeant Prevost was framed in the open doorway.

Three minutes later the Hercules airlifter was fully alive, hurling its own song of power across the field. The second HH-3 lifted off the end of the runway, poised a few feet off the ground, and then began a stiff climb toward the ice cap, turning as it went.

Ferguson released the brakes and began to taxi. As the C-130 rolled slowly down the ramp, his hands gripping the yoke, he wished that he had the power to tell the *Penguin* that they were all coming.

His own takeoff was a thing of beauty that would have brought joy to the heart of Orville Wright. Then it was up to Lieutenant Jenkins: he had to find what was left of the *Penguin* on the ice cap, and the last phase storm might have completely covered it with loose snow.

Jenkins delivered; he missed his ETA by less than two minutes and his final heading was almost exactly dead on.

Ferguson circled the landing area once to be sure that all was well, then he put the skis down, set up an approach, and watched the snow come closer. The markers had been obliterated, but they were not needed. He raised the nose of the Hercules a few degrees and slid it onto the ice cap at something around a hundred knots with absolute ease.

He was taxiing when Sergeant Feinberg appeared on the bridge. It was a breach of proper discipline, but Ferguson understood that there would be a valid reason.

"Sir," Feinberg made himself heard, "if you could possibly turn her ninety degrees when you're spotted, it will make the loading job a helluva lot easier."

"Right," Ferguson agreed. Two hundred feet farther on he revved up the starboard engines and swung the turboprop around in a quarter circle. When he stopped, the rear loading ramp was facing squarely toward the remains of the derelict bomber. He shut down the power and secured the flight deck. As he climbed into his parka and arctic gloves, he was glad for the moment that he hadn't been chosen as an astronaut after all.

When he reached the main hold, he saw that the rear ramp was already open; the driver of the snow tug was about to start up his machine. For the last time Ferguson went outside and began to walk across the ice cap toward what remained of the old B-17. The forward fuselage section concerned him most; it contained all of the essential controls and was by far the most intricate and essential component of the original airplane. It was its heart and being. It was about to be loaded into his C-130 and he wanted to take part in that operation.

It began almost at once. Sergeant Feinberg, who was in clear command of the first stage, signaled the snow tug into position just in front of the open hole that had been left when the fuselage had been divided into its forward and aft sections. Ropes were run inside and secured to the heavy structural members just above the center section of the wing. The job

143

was made slightly more difficult because a considerable quantity of snow had been blown inside; since the whole forward section was almost half full, it made the entire recovery job look more hopeless than it had at any time in the past.

Even the cockpit had a full foot of snow; when Ferguson went up there to check it out his heart sank — the frigid, frozen controls all but mocked him with their immobility. He understood the terrible toll that three decades of ruthless exposure must have inflicted on delicate instruments and other moving parts.

He recognized the temptation of the Devil and purged it from his mind. The B-17 was a fine, beautiful airplane — the only thing wrong was that it needed some maintenance.

He felt the deck begin to rock gently under his feet; he turned and began to wade through the snow back toward the open end so that he could witness and participate in everything that was going on. The ropes had been attached to the snow tug and were already pulled taut preparatory to movement. As Ferguson came out he saw that some ten men were on each side of the fuselage sections ready to add muscle power as soon as it was needed.

Feinberg checked the ropes and then issued a directive. "Rock it about fifteen degrees each way for half a minute; that'll make sure that it's loose and will form a trough for it to slide in." In response, carefully controlled force was applied first to one side and then to the other; *The Passionate Penguin* stirred in her long sleep.

"Now!" Feinberg shouted and pointed vigorously toward the snow-tug operator. The tracks of the powerful little vehicle bit more deeply into the snow, the ropes came tighter still, and the heavy fuselage section began to slide slowly backwards. When it had built up a speed of two miles an hour, the tug driver began a slow turn.

With massive dignity the nose section of the *Penguin* started

144

to describe a slow arc around the horizon. Ferguson ran forward and joined the long row of men who were helping to push and to guide. Within five minutes the fuselage section was precisely lined up with the rear loading ramp of the C-130. At that moment, without visible sign, the control of the operation passed to Sergeant Stovers, the loadmaster.

He knew precisely what he was going to do. "I need a twenty-degree tilt," he ordered. "It's going to have to go in diagonally to get enough clearance. Otherwise I'll be two inches shy."

In response to his instructions the section was rocked once again until it was sufficiently over on its side. Ferguson reached up and patted the almost obliterated design that had once adorned the bomber's nose. "Hang in there, baby," he said very softly. "You're going home."

The snow tug dropped the lines and pulled to one side. As it did so, Stovers raised the loading ramp of the airlifter until it was in an exactly level position. "Now build me a snow bridge," he told the tug driver. "I'm going to need at least thirty level feet."

The tug operator flipped his gloved hand in the air to indicate how simple it would be and pulled a lever. The blade of his machine scraped up a heavy roll of snow and pushed it into position just under the edge of the raised ramp. Then the driver backed to begin another pass.

Ferguson watched him place one more load and then walked away; it would be at least half an hour before anything else could be done. When he had covered a hundred yards he stopped and let the stillness of the ice cap prevail. The sounds of the working tug were already well in the background. Measured against the immensity of the thing on which he stood the tiny bit of activity he had just left was infinitesimal.

When he had experienced his fill he went slowly back, deliberately letting the minutes pass. The snow tug was still snorting away, but the snow ramp was close to completed.

The driver was running his machine across the top of his forty-foot-long creation, making sure that there were no soft spots that might give way. The snow ramp was precisely lined up with the back of the C-130 and just a little higher than the ramp proper, making it possible to get the long fuselage section straight into the waiting hold of the airlifter that could just barely accommodate it.

Lines were passed inside and through pulleys that Stovers had already rigged close to the forward bulkhead. When they came back out again, they were secured to the tug that was now positioned just beside the snow bridge. To Ferguson the progress after that was agonizingly slow, like watching a great aircraft carrier warp into its dock. Inch by careful inch, the tug backed on signal, tightening the ropes and drawing the nose section of the bomber cautiously forward. It took a full ten minutes to position the section entirely on the snow bridge with its open end less than two feet from the entrance ramp of the C-130.

At that point Stovers stopped everything while he checked still one more time to be sure that no mistake had been made. As he did so, a dozen men spread a snow blanket on the deck of the cargo hold to serve as a sliding base.

What had been slow before now became cautious to the point of exasperation; the tug moved only on signal from Stovers and then only inches at a time. Ferguson could not stand to watch it any longer, and there was nothing he could do. He continued to search the sky and to listen. He glanced at the portable beacon that Sergeant Murphy had put into operation and then focused his eyes toward the distant horizon once more. He saw a tiny black speck approaching in the sky.

He could have yelled for joy, but instead he stood still and watched the speck grow until he could catch the movement of its main rotor. It was approaching rapidly and presently he could detect the sound of its engines. Hardly a minute later the big Sikorsky arrived overhead, hovered for a moment, and then settled down onto the snow.

Major Kimsey emerged in his arctic clothing to find Ferguson waiting to greet him. "We made our fuel drop without incident," the major reported. "How are you making out?"

"This is the hardest load," Ferguson answered, "but we're well along with the job."

"It looks that way. A pretty tight fit."

"We're having to put it in on an angle; we can just make it that way. Stovers knows his business."

"How about a look at those wing sections," the major said. He gathered the rest of his crew and the two Det. 4 pilots who had flown out on the C-130, and then walked over to the nearest of the two massive components. There was no denying its size.

"It looks awfully heavy to us," Lieutenant Seligman ventured.

The major walked around it, peered inside at the open ends, and measured it by visual inspection. "All right," he said finally, "we'll take on some fuel and then give it a try. It's so big it's going to be aerodynamic anyway, so we might as well rig the sling so that the leading edge will be forward. In that way, it can take a good deal of the load off the rotor system. It's a little risky, but the sling will act as a partial spoiler and we can't go very fast with that thing to haul in any event."

"In other words, the wing section will fly itself," Heneveld commented.

"If we do everything right, yes."

There were enough men to spare to help with the rigging of the sling, but it was still rigorous work. It took a full half hour to get it adjusted to the major's satisfaction. They were still hard at it when the second helicopter arrived overhead and settled down close to the C-130.

By the time the fuel had been transferred, the tip of the nose

147

of the still-frozen bomber was disappearing inside the turbo-prop airlifter. The moment of truth was at hand. The crew of Major Kimsey's HH-3 fired up their bird and shortly thereafter lifted off. As its main rotor blasted air downward in a small gale, the rescue Jolly maneuvered over the wing section and two of the Det. 4 men attached the sling from underneath. Ferguson held his breath; this was it and the next few seconds would decide.

The engines of the hovering helicopter surged, the rotor seemed to spin even faster as the lines came tight. For five long seconds there was no visible movement, then, almost as if it were easy, the Jolly Green Giant picked up the cumbersome wing section, turned, and began to move away.

Ferguson watched, hypnotized, as the helicopter climbed some two hundred feet, its massive load dangling below it, and then started to head back toward Thule.

As though it had been a touchdown in a traditional high school football game, there was a spontaneous cheer. At that moment everyone knew that all of the work that had so far gone into the recovery of the ancient four-engined bomber was viable. Ferguson turned to help as much as he could with the refueling of the second helicopter. The tug crossed the snow bridge for the last time and stopped on the loading ramp of the airlifter.

While the fuel was being metered, willing hands rigged the second sling around the remaining wing section under the careful direction of a Det. 4 flight mechanic. In much less time than it had taken previously, Major Mulder found everything ready to his satisfaction. The Jolly he commanded was airborne within five minutes and the second pickup went off perfectly. As the powerful helicopter beat its way higher into the sky, with the last component of the B-17 suspended underneath, Ferguson turned for one last time and surveyed the ice cap where the World War II bomber had stood in deadly isolation for thirty long years. Only the trampled and scraped snow marked the spot where the abandoned airplane had been; there was nothing whatever left. And there was no reason to ever return to this place again.

He turned and almost ran back to his own aircraft. "Let's get the hell out of here!" he shouted.

With a glorious euphoria he stripped off his arctic gloves, his mittens and liners, shed his parka, and climbed into his left-hand seat. Corbin was ready to begin the precise business of the checklist. When he came to "Cabin report," Sergeant Stovers responded on the intercom.

"All pax, cargo, and gear secured. Cabin ready."

Ferguson double-checked the indicator on the panel that showed the rear ramp to be closed and sealed; the confirmation sent a wave of satisfaction through his body.

In sequential order the four engines of the Hercules came to life; the props cut their great discs in the air. Corbin announced, "Checklist complete."

Ferguson altered the pitch and the C-130 responded by sliding forward on its skis. He added more power as he turned onto the marked runway and began his takeoff. He watched the speed grow with primitive delight; the snow rushed backward faster and faster until Corbin called, "Rotate." Ferguson pulled back on the yoke — the nose of the Hercules rose and she came off the ice into the air where she belonged, carrying the massive nose section of the B-17 in her hold.

Within four minutes silence returned to the place the airlifter had left. Within a few days the winds would erase every trace of what had once been there. The only clue that remained was the four runway markers. Perhaps in years to come some pilot might spot them from the air and wonder for what conceivable reason they had been set out in such a totally remote region. And if, perhaps, someone were to guess that the ice cap concealed some sort of frozen buried treasure, and went searching for it with some as yet unimagined sounding device, there would be nothing whatever for him to find.

Ferguson turned to Corbin. "Do you want to bring her home, Red?" he asked.

The long-suffering copilot was more than ready and prepared; he took over the controls without delay. When he was close enough to Thule, he set up an instrument approach in wide-open weather, came down the glide path with ground radar assistance, and flared onto the runway with such precision that he wished he could have saved that landing to frame and hang on the wall of his room.

The tower directed them to Hangar 8 without being asked. As the C-130 taxied onto her designated spot she had company: a mighty C-141 jet airlifter was parked in front of number seven. "More stuff for the Army," Corbin commented as Ferguson slowly turned in response to the signals from the ramp man. When he received the hand across the throat signal, he hit the brakes and then went into the cockpit securing routine. Now if the colonel wanted to order him not to make any more nonessential flights out over the ice cap, he could go right ahead — the job had been done.

All that remained to be sure was the arrival of the wing root sections. He had a foreboding that they actually weighed much more than Holcomb had estimated. Until those sections were in, nothing was certain.

As he got out of his seat, Ferguson visualized a variety of troubles over the ice cap: the sections were too heavy and the choppers, although able to lift them, had not been able to carry them all of the way; fuel supplies had not been adequate for that much weight and bulk; refueling had run into difficulties and the wing sections had had to be jettisoned.

Trying to put potential disasters out of his mind, he left the flight deck and went outside. The rear ramp had been opened and he walked around the back to see for himself. As he did so, a major in flight gear extracted himself from a small group of spectators and came over. He looked inside and said, "Well I'll be damned!" Then he turned to Ferguson. "Is this your airplane?" he asked.

"Which one?"

The major laughed. "We just got here, but we've already heard that you were bringing a B-17 in off the ice cap. I didn't believe it; now I do."

"It isn't all here yet," Ferguson told him. "And if you don't mind, we'd like to keep a low profile on this if we can."

"Got you — we won't say anything stateside. By the way, we're a reserve crew out of McGuire." He held out his hand. "Fred Steinhammer."

"Scott Ferguson." The two men shook hands.

"Now that you've got it, what are you going to do with it?" Steinhammer asked.

"Fly it," Ferguson answered. "It needs a hundred-hour check, of course."

"I'd say a bit more than that. How about the tires? You'll need new ones, I would think."

Despite all of his planning, Ferguson hadn't been able to solve that. Rubber that had been out in all that weather, for that length of time, might be worthless — or seriously dangerous, which was worse.

"We may have to scare up some new ones," he admitted. "Somebody must make them."

"Possibly." The major sounded doubtful. "May I see what else you've got?"

Ferguson waved toward Hangar 8. "Be my guest," he invited. There was no point in being secretive anymore — the colonel had to know. He was badly upset that the acute problem of the tires hadn't been resolved. No one could be expected to be making B-17 tires now. Some might be available somewhere, or possibly there was a current size that could be substituted. But even if they were found, they would cost money and how in hell could he get them shipped all the way up to Thule?

His spirits did not improve even when a motorized crane backed up to lend a helping lift. Bill Stovers was totally involved in preparing to remove the fuselage section, which looked much bigger now than it had on the ice cap. He went into the hangar and again inspected the tires — all three of them. They seemed to be in surprisingly good shape; under the weight of his foot the rubber flexed and appeared to be strong. One thing was clear: they had been all but new when the pilot, whoever he had been, had made his emergency landing on them three decades ago.

He spotted Sergeant Feinberg and walked over to him. "Perry," he said, "I'm concerned about the tires."

"So was I, sir, but we checked them over and they seem to be OK."

"I want a little more than that. See what you can find out. Try calling Akron; one of the big rubber companies there may be able to give us a clue. Their engineers should know something."

Feinberg nodded. "I'll do that, sir, but remember that a lot of airplanes are tied down outside in all kinds of weather for years and the tires seem to be able to take it."

That added a little hope. Ferguson went into Operations and asked if any word had come in from Det. 4. "Both birds are out on a training mission," the duty NCOIC told him. "So far, there's no ETA on either one."

"No trouble reported?"

"No, sir, nothing at all."

"Thank you." He went back to watch the unloading process. The portable crane was making things vastly easier. In less than a third of the time it had taken to get it stowed inside, the long nose section was unloaded. Once it was out, the crane carried it easily into the hangar and set it down gently into a set of cradles that had been built to hold it. Ferguson saw that operation concluded and then went outside with his hands clenched despite his heavy gloves. He was sweating out the helicopters with all his being—everything was so close now! The temperature was well below zero, but he was oblivious to it. In fact he felt warm and he threw back the hood of his parka.

He saw Andy Holcomb squinting toward the southeast; he turned quickly and looked in the same direction. For a moment or two he couldn't be sure, then over the snow heights just visible to him he saw something in the sky.

Standing rock still to aid his vision, he caught the glint of a main rotor, made out the shape of the incoming helicopter, and praise to Almighty God, there was something substantial suspended underneath its fuselage!

He could have yelled out of sheer joy and relief, but he did nothing except stand still and watch the helicopter grow larger as it followed a steady descent path toward the field.

Everyone knew; all remaining hands had come out of the hangar. "Get something out here for them to put it on," he shouted in his excitement. For once, nothing had been prepared.

"Blankets," Bill Stovers called out, and ran for the C-130.

"No!" Sergeant Feinberg shouted after him. "They'll blow away. Rubber life raft!"

Six men hauled one out of the C-130 and inflated it in record time. Meanwhile, disregarding the normal approach patterns, the helicopter crossed over the runway and pulled up into a hover. Holcomb signaled toward the life raft and the airborne crew understood; the aircraft came down very slowly and set the huge wing section squarely on the raft with apparent ease. It's work completed, the HH-3 hover-taxied back to its own hangar and there settled onto the ground.

The crane was summoned and the sling was hooked onto its hanging cable. It lifted the new load easily and rolled into the hangar with two men steadying the wing section to keep it from rotating.

Ferguson was confident then; he knew it could be done.

Det. 4 had proven that they could do it, and all praise to them. But it wasn't over yet.

The ordeal continued for some twenty minutes — then the second of the powerful Sikorsky's came sliding down an invisible sky pathway, bearing the other huge wing root section. The downblast from the main rotor sent snow swirling madly as the helicopter hovered and then set down its load so gently it was difficult to tell the moment that it finally rested on the raft. The sling released and Major Mulder lifted a hand in greeting from the cockpit.

Stage one of his impossible project was all but over; what stage two would bring, Ferguson did not dare to guess.

BOOK TWO

MISSION

CHAPTER ELEVEN

IN THREE WEEKS' time a near miracle took place inside the wide expanse of Hangar 8. Once the rebuilding project got fairly underway, Americans and Danes combined their labors and their skills to bring *The Passionate Penguin* back to respectability, if not to life. The two halves of the fuselage were reunited and bolted securely together. The control surfaces were stripped of their old fabric and expertly recovered with new material — new in the sense that it had never previously been used. Actually it had been occupying shelf space in Supply for some years with very little likelihood of its ever being withdrawn. There was even some aluminum-colored dope on hand so that the job could be properly finished in exactly the original color.

The odor of drying dope produced some fond memories on

the part of those Air Force men who had been associated with aircraft in an earlier day, and a Danish worker who happened to hold an advanced pilot's license in his own country was almost ecstatic. "It can be done," he mumured to himself at frequent intervals. "It can be done!"

Sergeant Holcomb went to Supply to see if he could get some new and unused control cable. The old cables seemed to be perfectly all right, but Lieutenant Ferguson had decreed that they must all be replaced in the interests of maximum safety. At the Supply window, where he was by now the most familiar face on Thule Air Base, he asked if there was any cable available.

"There may be some," the supply man said. "I believe I ran across it the other day. But this we can't declare surplus; if you want any, you'll have to pay for it."

Andy Holcomb stood still while he calculated. All of the control cable systems of the B-17 were in duplicate; by the time that several pairs of cables were run from the cockpit far back to the empennage, and more sets were run all of the way out through the wings, the total length required would be over a thousand feet. "How much is it?" he asked.

"Fifteen cents a foot, as I recall."

Andy winced, but he did not complain — he did not dare to. Already a considerable quantity of materiel had turned up on the diposable list just when it was needed by the workers in Hangar 8. True, all of it had been unquestionably outdated, but control cable was another matter.

"Ten feet ought to do it," the supply man said.

"Why ten feet—" Andy began, and then came to his senses.

"Let me give you ten feet, Sergeant, and then you can come back for however much more you need — if we have it. Just a minute."

When he returned, he was pushing a hand dolly on which a large spool of wire was fastened with a reefer strap. "There ought to be ten feet here," he declared. "I can measure it if you'd like, or you can take it as is."

"Don't bother to measure," Andy answered. "I trust you."

"That's good. A buck fifty, please, and I'll get someone to help you with that dolly. It's pretty heavy."

Andy dug into his pocket. "That's all right, I can manage it. Two guys taking out ten feet of cable would look kind of silly, I think. By the way, how are you fixed for metal polish?"

"We have the right gunk for cleaning up aluminum, a hundred-pound drum's on hand. It's not fresh, because they don't use it on the Jollies."

"We'll take it anyway. I'll be back."

"Bring a couple of bucks — you may need them. We've got to keep people honest around here."

Lieutenant Ferguson, in the best uniform that he could muster for the occasion, presented himself at the colonel's office and checked in with the Executive Officer. A minute or two later he was ushered into Colonel Kleckner's presence, where he observed the formalities. Then he was invited to sit down.

"Lieutenant, I sent for you to pass on some information. The next rotator is bringing up another C-130 crew; the A/C is a Captain Boyd. Do you happen to know him, by any chance?"

"No, sir, I believe not."

"Boyd and his crew will be here while the Army is carrying on its project at Camp Century. They will fly their share of the trips so that you won't have to make them all."

Ferguson was relieved; he had been terribly afraid that he was being replaced and would have to leave Thule and the *Penguin* behind him.

"That's fine, sir," he said.

"I'm not sure that this new crew is ski qualified, so you may have to check them out."

"No problem, sir."

"Fine, speaking of projects, how are you coming along with your B-17?"

It was the first time that the colonel had ever mentioned the subject.

"Better than we had dared to hope, sir. We have her all back here, as I'm sure you know, and the quality of work that's going into her you wouldn't believe. Yesterday they finished the overhaul of the tail-wheel mechanism. The first time that they hooked up a battery and tried it, it worked perfectly."

Colonel Kleckner flashed one of his quick smiles. "That's interesting. I must say, bringing the whole airplane back, one of that size, was quite a feat."

"We couldn't have done it, sir, without Det. Four. This is heresy, sir, but those helicopters are marvelous and the guys that fly them are out of this world. They did the impossible."

The colonel turned his chair a few degrees and made himself more comfortable. "It was valuable training, I'm sure; running back and forth to Kanak isn't too much of a challenge. I suspect that that's why Major Kimsey laid on the exercise, which was, in a way, fortunate for you."

"Extremely fortunate, sir."

Colonel Kleckner waved a hand. "I want all of my units, and every man at this base to improve himself while he's here. The United States Air Force doesn't take a back seat to anyone."

"No, sir, never!"

"How are you financing your reconstruction job?"

"Well, sir, we're going on the assumption that that bird is going to fly again before too long—"

He stopped when he saw a frown cross the colonel's face. But when the base commander said nothing, Ferguson continued. "So we have a little game going. Every rated man, and that includes all ranks that hold a commercial license or better, Danish or American, puts a buck in the kitty, along with his name, whenever he feels like it. When the time comes, we'll have a drawing. The man whose name is pulled gets to fly."

"That sounds logical—and fair. You plan to draw only one name? You said 'the man' whose name comes up."

"Yes, sir, I did. He gets to fly copilot." Ferguson let down his guard; he could not help himself. "That's my airplane, sir, and I'm going to fly it!"

The colonel pushed his lips together for a moment. "Before you set a date, please check with me—just in case."

"Yes, sir, absolutely." Ferguson knew that the interview was over. He stood up, saluted, and exited, in a suitable manner.

It was already much warmer outside, and the days were rapidly getting longer. In a few weeks there would be twenty-four hour summer daylight and the harbor would unfreeze enough to permit waterborne traffic—what there might be of it. Few ships ever dared to venture so far north.

He jumped into a taxi and asked the driver to take him to Hangar 8; it would be more than an hour before mess call and an enormous amount of work remained to be done. As he pushed open the personnel door, he was inspired by the knowledge that the colonel had given the whole project at least a conditional blessing. He had hopefully assumed that; but having it confirmed was the best news he had had since he had seen the second of the wing root sections coming down from off the ice cap.

He walked briskly inside, ready to take on whatever task he would be given to do. He was halfway to the working area before he was suddenly aware that something was seriously wrong. He looked quickly about and saw that although there were several other men in the hangar, they were gathered about one spot and most of them were standing still.

Fighting against the ominous atmosphere that was already surrounding him, he forced himself to walk over to them calmly and then asked, "What is it?"

Corbin, his copilot, answered him. He was a strong, well-controlled young man, but at that moment he fought to keep his voice normal as he answered.

"About an hour ago we started work on the right main landing gear. That's the next thing and it has to be put in shape before we can assemble any further. We were giving all of the components a Class-A inspection when . . . we found that the main structural fitting that holds the gear struts to the wing frame is cracked wide open."

"How badly? Can it be welded?"

Corbin shook his head. "Negative. It's an intricate basic part that has to take high stress on landing. It's got to be in one solid piece and no fix could be acceptable. I wouldn't buy it, and I know you won't either."

Ferguson recognized that his redheaded junior had spoken the truth. "Then we'll have to get another one," he said.

It was a good, bravura speech, but it did not impress the disillusioned men.

In the few seconds of silence that followed his pronouncement, Ferguson saw it all clearly in his mind. The utter remoteness and desolation of Thule was something that seeped into the bones and marrow of the men who served there. The monotony was like a slow poison that took away energy and ambition and left only discouragement in its place. Despite bowling leagues, a good gym, the library, the theater, and all that, nothing could wipe away the ever-present awareness of the High Arctic — its unyielding hostility and the sudden violent death that, at times, was only a few breaths away.

Under such conditions, boredom was all-pervading and the routine nature of the work regularly done was in itself stifling. The *Penguin* project had come like a rescue flare in the Arctic night sky. It had promised something new — a great challenge combined with a massive work commitment, but one that had injected new life throughout every corner of the Thule facility. The *Penguin* herself had become a symbol and she had been blessed by the dedication of the men who labored gladly to restore her. They had chosen to attempt the virtually impossible, and they had found excitement in the process.

Corbin was speaking again. "Even Sergeant Stovers can't suggest any place we can look. God knows where any replacement parts would be now."

Ferguson fought back against the thing that fate had done to him with the desperation of a man facing an avalanche. "Boeing might have one, or even Douglas — they built B-17's too."

"After thirty years?" Corbin shook his head. "You know what the chances are of that. We could advertise, but that would tell the whole world, and the Pentagon, what's going on up here."

Ferguson thought. "I guess this is what I've been afraid of since we began," he admitted. "The time when we'd run into something that we couldn't either fix or replace. And, oh God, a main landing-gear fitting!"

Jenkins came over, still heavy, but almost ten pounds lighter since the work on the airplane had begun. "We're all going to see if we can't come up with something," he offered. "A lot of the guys on this base have got connections."

Ferguson let it all spill out. "Yes, but we need a complicated main structural component, and there haven't been any of those parts available for several aircraft generations."

When no one had anything to say in reply to that, he turned toward the door and went back outside.

That night he was hit by the wild idea that there were at least seven other known B-17's out on the ice cap. One of them might still have the vital part intact, but he knew, at the same moment that that idea crossed his mind, he would never be able to go out and get it. It would take a crane to lift the aircraft up and hold the load while the part was removed. And because of what it was, it would take many hours of labor to get it off under the best of conditions. He would need permission, a satisfactory landing area, and too many other things to make it possible. No dice — and he could not convince himself otherwise.

He turned over in bed and tried once more to get to sleep.

The Thule grapevine was apparently down for maintenance, because it was past 1000 hours the following morning before Chief Master Sergeant Perry Feinberg learned about the disastrous discovery in Hangar 8. At once he knew that it was a matter so grave he would have to give it his fullest personal attention. As he dealt with the pile of work that was part of his daily responsibility, he kept coming back to the problem and exposing it to the searching investigation of his resourceful mind. As soon as he got off at noon, he called a cab and went immediately to see things for himself. When he had done that he repaired to the mess hall where there was now a long table more or less reserved for the B-17 project personnel.

Most of the prime movers were there, including Ferguson, who looked like a man three-quarters of the way through a summer hike across Death Valley. No one was doing very much talking. As Feinberg unloaded his amply filled tray, Andy Holcomb ventured a remark. "I don't know how many of you guys have been in South America, but it is supposed to be a place where every aircraft part ever made can be found. At least it's worth a try."

As soon as he was comfortably installed, Sergeant Feinberg took over. "Gentlemen," he began, "we have certain alternatives and we should know clearly what they are. First, we can try to moonlight-requisition the necessary part from a B-17 somewhere or have it done for us. Forget the ones on the ice cap; the odds are too high against success."

"Agreed," Ferguson said.

"Secondly, we can try to locate a new part on the shelf somewhere in the world; it could still possibly be. We could also try to have one made. Lastly, we can admit that this breaks us and forget the whole thing."

"Over my dead body," Ferguson retorted.

"I didn't propose it," Feinberg replied, "I only stated it as a mathematical possibility. Actually, if we were to stop now, and it became known that I had been associated with the project, my reputation would suffer a massive setback. Therefore we must think of something else."

"Any suggestions?" Corbin asked.

"Just possibly. First, a question: does anybody know the status of Sergeant Murphy, the electronics whiz?"

"He's going out on the next rotator," Tom Collins answered. "You'd have to announce that Jesus was going to preach in person from the summit of Mount Dundas to keep him here."

"Did anyone give him the picture?"

A bearded Dane at the table shook his head. "The picture I have," he announced. "If he saw that, he would not be able to leave — he would be in the coronary care unit at the hospital."

"Another good idea gone down the tube," Feinberg said. "But men are known by the obstacles they overcome."

Ferguson was sitting very still, hardly listening to what was going on. He recognized that he was confronted by defeat, but he refused to accept it. Somehow, some way, they would get out of the predicament. At that moment he had no idea how, but it would have to be done. If only Thule weren't so desperately isolated; stateside he might have a chance.

He caught the fact that he was beginning to think negatively and he determined to correct it. He looked up and for the moment purged the problem from his mind. "Who is the best musician on the base?" he asked.

"Tony Agretti in Supply," Captain Tilton answered. "He plays several instruments and is good at everything."

"Then we've got a job for him," Ferguson continued. "We're going to have to have a suitable celebration when the *Penguin* is finished."

In a flash Tilton understood, and played along. "Of course. We'll make the *Air Force Times*, and have a good shot at *Newsweek* and *Time*. Not to mention *Flying* and all of the other aviation media."

"To do it properly, we'll ask the colonel to give a brief speech. The contribution of Det. Four will have to be stressed. Then the band will play."

"What band?" Stovers asked.

"Tony Agretti's band; he sounds as though he could organize one. Then the wife of the Danish commander, who is the most prominent of the ladies up here, will be introduced. After that we'll push the *Penguin* out of the hangar. Mrs. Kure will rechristen it properly with a bottle of champagne. Frank will have pictures taken; the crowd will cheer.

"Then the crew of the *Penguin* will go on board and start the engines. The Det. Four Jollies will fire up, take off, and hover over each side of the airstrip, far enough back so that they don't create too much air disturbance over the runway. Slowly the *Penguin* will taxi down the ramp while the band plays again."

"Not just any piece of music," Collins interjected. "*The Passionate Penguin March*. Tony can compose it for us; I know him and he will."

"*The Passionate Penguin March*," Ferguson repeated. "A good rousing tune with a cut from the Air Force song sandwiched somewhere in the middle. Meanwhile the B-17 reaches the end of the runway and does the checklists. Then everything stops, the band is quiet, the choppers hover in position. Presently the engines on the B-17 pick up in tempo, the plane begins to roll forward."

Captain Tilton understood perfectly. "The only music the sound of her engines," he continued in Ferguson's place. "Then, directly in front of the grandstand, if we had one, she lifts her nose and takes off once more—the miracle accomplished, the prisoner of the ice cap freed, and a damn good airplane back in operation once more."

"We can use her to give multiengine flight checks," the Dane said. He was an advanced flight instructor in his own country.

"We can run up to visit the guys at Alert, if we can get permission to land," Feinberg contributed. "We can go weekending down in Sondrestrom; they have some women there and there are dances."

"She has over a four-thousand-mile range," Andy Holcomb chimed in. "She can easily go to Iceland, down to McGuire, almost anyplace."

"The gas will cost," the Dane declared, "but we have free hangar space, free maintenance, and no crew costs. We can fly her for peanuts."

"How many will she carry?" Tilton asked of Andy Holcomb.

"Her original crew would be ten, so presumably she could haul twenty warm bodies with no trouble at all. The only limiting factors would be fuselage dimensions and baggage space. We ought to be able to convert the bomb bay into a cargo hold."

"After we get the landing gear fixed," Sergeant Stovers cautioned.

The mood had changed; somehow it was assumed by everyone present that the crushing problem would be resolved one way or another. Ferguson went back to the serving line to get some additional dessert.

That afternoon the C-130 went out to Camp Century and delivered a load. It was all very brisk and businesslike, with

167

the ice cap landing no problem at all. While out there Ferguson and Corbin made a detailed inspection on foot of the landing area and found it to be in good condition for further operations. For once the pilot did not need to concern himself that someone would question why he was there and what he was doing. This was his officially assigned job and he was beyond reproach.

When he returned to Thule, Ferguson found Sergeant Feinberg awaiting him. "It occurred to me that we might have a cup of coffee together if you would like, sir," the big man declared.

"By all means," Ferguson replied. He experienced a little thrill of satisfaction. He felt like a hard-pressed quarterback who has just seen a long desperation pass taken on the run by his tight end. Obviously Perry Feinberg had thought of something.

They sat down together in a corner of the small passenger terminal. "Sir," Feinberg began, "I may have an idea concerning the landing-gear problem. It will require a little maneuvering and a flexibility of outlook concerning the regulations."

"I've bent them out of shape already, Sergeant, so one more time shouldn't matter."

"Hopefully not, but this time it may be necessary to get into another command area. Before undertaking this, I wanted to ask you, in general terms, if you're willing to take a reasonable chance."

"How about yourself?"

Feinberg beamed confidence. "The risk can be minimized; master sergeants do not snitch on one another. But you might be exposed to some criticism if I can't keep the lid on."

"Tell me one thing," Ferguson said. "What are the chances of success?"

Feinberg flexed his shoulder muscles while he framed his reply. "Not too bad, I would say, sir, if everything goes as planned."

"You think we can get the part?"

"Yes, I do."

"How soon?"

"Quite soon, if what I have in mind works."

"Do you want to tell me any more about it?"

"No, sir, because if it comes down to the wire, you will be able to state that you had no personal knowledge of what was going on. And obviously you couldn't have authorized it if you didn't know anything about it."

Ferguson thought. "I see. Boiling it down, you're giving me an out if I need it."

"Precisely, sir. One more thing: I'll have to have that picture of Monica Lee. I trust that it is expendable in a good cause."

"Only for the sake of the *Penguin*," Ferguson declared.

"Obviously, that is what I have in mind."

"Then take it."

"Thank you. On a slightly different matter, sir — you will recall the Danish artist we have here, Viggo Skov?"

"Yes. The colonel thought it would be nice if he would paint a picture of the *Penguin* in flight — to hang in the NCO Club along with a prop."

"The picture, sir, is well underway despite the change in plans. Viggo has now consented to repaint the design on the *Penguin's* nose for us, but a delicate question has arisen. The original is somewhat graphic — you may have noticed."

"Frankly, no, Perry. It's almost obliterated."

"But it can still be made out. Viggo has suggested that he can redo the design with a small modification to make it more acceptable to the middle-class masses, or he can restore it to its original glory, exactly as was — in which case, someone should be standing in front of the nose if any pictures are taken for publication."

"Sergeant Feinberg," Ferguson said formally. "We have undertaken collectively to restore *The Passionate Penguin* to her former proud status *as she was*. I will not kowtow to the Watch and Ward Society. Furthermore, times have changed — as witness Miss Lee's picture."

"Sir, my compliments," the chief master sergeant said "Allow me to inquire if you have an opening in your crew."

"Just get the landing-gear fitting; that's an assignment worthy of your genius."

Feinberg stood up and became immense. "It will be done, sir," he promised.

The road to J Site was displaying its usual spring roughness after the long deep freeze of winter. As Sergeant Feinberg drove the vehicle that he had successfully scrounged for his own use, he took in every aspect of the short but spectacular drive.

Not far from the roadway the base of the ice cap took over command of the terrain. From that point it rose onward and upward toward the incredibly blue sky of the High Arctic. The most extraordinary sight from the roadway was not the beginning of the ice cap, but the four enormous radar antennae of J Site itself. When the region had first been surveyed, the promontory on which they now stood had been designated J Site as a convenient means of reference. After the vast BMEWS installation had been built, the name had stuck. It was J Site to everyone at Thule and was seldom referred to in any other way.

The antennae themselves were each much larger than a football field. They were permanently fixed in position at varying angles to each other, but for practical purposes all of them were aimed toward the most likely source of a possible missile attack against the United States — the Soviet Union. Twenty-four hours of every day, every day of every year, the powerful beams from BMEWS swept the sky and the space far above the atmosphere in a continuing, unbroken watchfulness. Seen from the outside BMEWS was static; a series of covered passageways led from one building to another, offering no protection from the temperatures, but at least keeping most of the frequent snowstorms from interfering with local traffic. There was also a huge radome that housed an eighty-five-foot dish able to turn with high precision and considerable speed toward any target above the horizon, or in outer space. The need to maintain unceasing vigilance was the reason for the existence of J Site and for the presence at that extremely remote location of a staff of several hundred men and two women who worked in unbroken shifts to guard the ramparts of Canada and the United States. The support of J Site was the reason for the existence of Thule Air Base and gave it its principal mission.

Sergeant Feinberg parked his truck and went to one of the few entrances into the BMEWS complex. Despite the utter isolation of the site, an armed guard was stationed immediately inside. Feinberg was required to produce his identification, sign in, and state the exact nature of his business. BMEWS took no chances; the colonel in command was acutely aware of the fact that the construction of the very sophisticated and elaborate facility in the extreme Arctic had been something of an industrial miracle and that the cost had been proportionately high. If for any reason the complex was forced to shut down, a whole flank of the North American continent would be left open without its usual safeguards.

Sergeant Feinberg carried a mailing tube in his hand as he turned down one of the tunnels and by means of it made his way to a large maintenance building that, like everything else at BMEWS, had been built to withstand the worst weather extremes that the Arctic could produce. Equipment and supplies were everywhere — everything likely to be needed at any time had to be kept on hand and at the ready. Most of the vital vehicles were kept inside where they would be protected from the merciless elements outside. Trackmasters were cocked and ready; an ambulance stood directly before the door; a command car with full radio equipment and special tires was poised beside it.

From one end of BMEWS to the other was a considerable distance measured in part by the four immense antennae, but everywhere the spare equipment was stowed in almost perfect order. Sergeant Feinberg paused before a storage room that was rich with the odor of stacked wood. There was a substantial supply in each of the standard sizes, from lath to great timbers, and adjacent to the racks stood all of the woodworking equipment that might be required to make almost anything. Past a fire-alarm point was the entrance to the machine shop.

He went inside without the usual wide smile on his face. His demeanor was serious, as befitted the place where he was. Nothing was ever taken for granted at BMEWS; the whole vast complex had been put there and maintained for years just to catch the one blip that might appear at any moment on one of its scopes. If that were to happen, then data gathered in fractions of a second would be fed to computers and communications established instantly (on an always-open hotline) to NORAD, the North American Air Defense Command inside Cheyenne Mountain near Colorado Springs.

At NORAD the information from BMEWS, plus any supporting information from the other sites — at Clear, Alaska, and in England — would be evaluated as rapidly as trained and whetted human minds could do it. Then, almost at once, the commanding general or his deputy on duty would have to make an awesome decision. He would make it knowing that something was in the air aimed at the United States or Canada, what its trajectory was, its predicted point of impact, and its probable nature. The first incoming shot might be in the form of a salvo, in which case his decision would be easier, but regardless, he would have to commit the nation, notify the President, and do many other things all within the space of a very few minutes. BMEWS could not afford to make even the first mistake.

Inside the machine shop there was an impressive amount of equipment — astonishing to find in northern Greenland. Everything was as well maintained as the rest of the giant facility; even the floor was spotless. As Feinberg came in, a man twice his size came to meet him. He appeared to weigh at least three hundred pounds, but he moved with good coordination and with the air of someone who thoroughly knows his business.

Perry Feinberg was not used to talking to men who were notably larger than himself, but he was entirely comfortable because he knew the quality of the man he had come to see. For once he came right to the point, because that was the way the man he was addressing wanted it. "You've heard about the B-17 that we're rebuilding down the hill."

The huge man spoke in a rich baritone. "Everyone knows about it. There are bets out all over the place."

That was a setback, but Sergeant Feinberg met it squarely. "Are you in on any of them?" he asked.

"Not so you'd notice it. Not yet, anyway."

Feinberg let out a long sigh of relief. "I want to ask a question," he said. "If you had to make a particular part for that airplane here, would you be able to do it?"

His host eyed him. "Bring in the blueprints and we'll make the whole damn thing. We've got all the aluminum here, and the tools. Obviously something's busted — what is it?"

"A main landing-gear fitting."

"Have you got the drawings?"

"No, but out in my truck I've got the part itself. It's cracked."

The huge man rested his weight on a bench. "Bring it in, together with a work order signed by the colonel, and we'll duplicate it for you. Is it heat treated?"

173

"From the general look of it I would say no. Remember that it was originally made more than thirty years ago; they weren't quite as sophisticated then."

"All right, I'll examine it and see which way to go."

"You have the stock on hand?"

"We've got everything; we have to have."

Feinberg waved his hand. "And the equipment," he noted.

"Yes, and one thing you forget: we know what the hell we're doing."

Perry Feinberg looked around before he continued. "Our colonel has given us his tacit blessing so there's no sweat about that. But I don't have a work order."

"Then get one; simple as that."

"Perhaps I have something else."

"There is no something else, Perry, you know that. The boss wants things done right, and so do I."

"Look, I'm not very sure that I can get a work order—a formal one, that is, but Colonel Kleckner carries weight."

"He sure does—get him to ask for it."

"If I have to, I will, but I do have another thought." He unrolled the picture and laid it out on a workbench.

The powerful man bent over and studied it. "That sure in hell is something," he admitted, "but Mike Murphy might not appreciate it. He's pretty square, you know."

"I do, and he's going out on the next rotator. He hasn't seen this; he doesn't know that it exists."

"Is that autograph genuine?"

"I'll cover all bets; a friend of Major Valen's got it in Hollywood for us."

"You probably wanted a radio fixed."

"Right on—but if he saw this, he'd have kittens on the spot."

"He sure would. And he's bound to; these will be out in the millions in a little while. It's a damn good shot and Monica Lee is very popular. He can't miss it."

174

Sergeant Feinberg had the conversation at the critical point and he knew it; everything now depended on how well he presented the next piece of information. "He's going to miss it," he said, "because it's never going to be published. Monica Lee wants to change her image, but her agent will see her dead first. There's a very strict morality clause in her contract because of the type of roles she usually plays. This clearly would violate it, so her agent unleashed the legal eagles and they bought it back. This is an advance proof that got away. It may be the only one that ever will."

The man in overalls was thoughtful. "Next to Diahann Carroll, she's the best-looking woman I've ever seen in my life."

"Damn right," Sergeant Feinberg agreed, slightly altering his choice of words. "I brought it to show you because I know that you're a connoisseur and a major collector of the species."

"There is nothing that equals the beauty of a lovely woman. In this particular instance, there is no vulgarity. No distorted pose, no ultrasuggestive covering-up with a coyly held hand."

"A very significant point," Feinberg agreed. "Now, if you can think of any way to turn out that part for us, say in your spare time, and avoid the embarrassment of having to get a work order for something that we can't prove is a military requirement, it would be an enormous help to us."

"How about the cost of the stock?"

"We'll pay for that."

"I might possibly be able to find a spoiled piece that will do, but don't count on it; we don't spoil very much around here."

"I'm well aware of that. And if you can see your way clear to bend things a little in our direction, then we will express our gratitude with the token gift of this picture for your collection. It *is* autographed, but the salient point is its rarity. In years to come, you may well possess the one-and-only color photograph of Monica Lee's cunt in existence."

It fell silent in the shop. Seconds passed as invisible radar beams of great power noiselessly swept the sky; then the master sergeant in charge of the machine shop made his decision. "It will take some time, perhaps a week."

By means of a delicately sensitive gesture, Sergeant Feinberg indicated that what could not be helped must be endured.

"It depends on how much time I have," the massive machinist relented.

Sergeant Feinberg replied to that by very carefully rolling up the striking photograph. "Here is your picture," he said, with a hairline emphasis on the possessive. "I wouldn't suggest leaving it lying around."

"Nothing lies around in this place — anywhere. I have a vehicle; we can ride back to where your car is."

CHAPTER TWELVE

TO THE MEN of Thule the near gift of a World War II B-17 to rebuild represented almost a godsend — it was something to do, a substantial challenge to be met, and an event unique in their lives. To them the long-derelict bomber was a great deal more than an accumulation of parts that might eventually become a working machine; it was a flying machine with a definite personality, a name, and a soul. To the men of Thule the *Penguin* was a living thing — or would be when they got through with her.

When Chief Master Sergeant Feinberg announced that he had found a source for the broken landing-gear fitting, and that a new one would be forthcoming soon, the restoration work resumed immediately. Wing panels that had withstood weathering for three decades were gone over until they shone like new. Internal structures were inspected and tested until their integrity was proven. New control cables were installed with meticulous care; every pulley over which they passed was examined, serviced, tested, and verified.

When the burly sergeant arrived in his truck, bringing with him the desperately needed new component, he was noticeably reluctant to disclose where and how it had been obtained. It was apparent to everyone who saw it that it was brand-new, but two planes had recently come in with tons of freight and either one could have brought it.

The nose of the B-17 rested on a cradle that held it two feet higher than it would have been if it had been resting on its own landing gear; that made working on the underside easy. Laid out on the floor there was a full-sized pattern of the original name insignia that had once been painted on the nose. Perched on a maintenance stand almost sixteen feet above the floor, Viggo Skov, the Danish artist, was repainting the tail number precisely as it had been. A small crew of men was busy reinstalling the left aileron, which had been fully overhauled, re-covered, and doped the proper aluminum color. When it was finally in place and fastened, they tried the control cables by hand and found that everything worked exactly as it should.

On the long benches two of the power plants had been completely torn down, with hundreds of individual parts laid out in a systematic pattern. Engines number three and four, mounted on stands, were awaiting their turn. On another long bench two of the propellers had been disassembled for overhaul. One set of blades had been reburnished and they were almost brilliant in their apparent newness.

On what had been the flight deck of the bomber so many things had been pulled out that what remained was a skeleton and no more. Not a single instrument was left on the panel, almost all of the control handles were gone, and the switches had been demounted. The pilots' seats had been removed and the bare floor that remained had been prepared for repainting.

178

A forklift bearing a sizable crate came into the hangar from the ramp. The operator ran his machine up to the supply area next to where the main work was being done and asked, "Where do you want this?"

Andy Holcomb, the acknowledged engineer in charge, came over. "What is it?" he asked.

"I don't know, Sergeant, it came up on that last C-141, marked for delivery to Hangar Eight."

"Then leave it right there until we get it open and find out what it is. Are you sure there's no name on it?"

"Nope — just 'Hangar 8' and that's all."

With the help of a Danish worker, Andy pulled the lid open; as he did so, the strong odor of fresh rubber was freed. He worked feverishly to get all of the lumber out of the way and the inner wrappings open. When he had gone far enough to be sure, he let out a shout that brought Ferguson and many of the others almost on the run. The last of the heavy packing paper was torn away to reveal a wooden pallet and on it three brand-new tires — two large ones for the main gear and a much smaller one for the tail wheel.

A calling card was taped to the side of one of the main tires; Ferguson pulled it off and read: *To The Passionate Penguin — happy landings.*

And neatly printed below:

> Goodyear Tire and Rubber Co.
> Frederick L. Steinhammer
> Eastern Sales Manager

It took the still-startled lieutenant several seconds until he remembered the commander of the reserve C-141 crew he had met on the ramp well before the last airlift off the ice cap.

As he stood and looked at the wonderful new tires, and smelled their freshness, he realized that a major uncertainty and been overcome. He had planned to use the thirty-year-old tires because he had no alternative, but he had known in his heart that they might be dangerous. Now that hazard had been swept away.

Sergeant Stovers was not there to share his elation — he was in the mess hall talking with the crew of a Canadian C-130 that was scheduled out to Alert in the morning. "Since you are a communications station," he said, choosing his words carefully, "I presume that you have an electronics maintenance capability."

The very tall captain who headed the crew answered. "Yes, of course we do. Our lads are quite good at it, really."

"Is your bench time fully taken up?"

"I wouldn't say so. Let me put it this way, Sergeant: we'd be delighted to overhaul the B-17's radios for you if you'd like. In fact, we've already talked about it. But we didn't want to be forward, particularly since its your project. So we were rather waiting to see if our assistance would be welcome."

Sergeant Stovers raised his coffee cup. "At this point, sir, I'd say that it's close to essential. The only man we had who was really qualified to do the job just left on the rotator.

The captain smiled. "Actually, we'd be quite proud to be part of the program. If we can have the sets to take with us, we may be able to get some of them back down to you within the next two weeks or so."

"We have a lot of good parts in Supply," Stovers said.

"So have we, and the commander is a noble citizen; he'll be for it, I'm sure. Any chance of getting a ride later on?"

"You're a cinch," Stovers declared. "Get an approval from your CO and we'll fly her up and visit you. Then we'll hop everybody that wants to go."

His Canadian counterpart lifted a hand. "Let's finish our coffee first," he said.

In two weeks' time *The Passionate Penguin* stood in Hangar 8 on her own landing gear, her three brand-new tires filling the whole area with an aroma of freshness. Once more her wings reached out over a hundred feet in span and it is doubtful that they ever shone as brilliantly as they did then. On the flight bridge the overhauled control yokes had been reinstalled. They moved easily with the precision of fine machinery, and as they did, the control surfaces responded with microscopic accuracy.

Colonel Kleckner himself tried them out personally and could not restrain a wide smile. "That's a remarkable job," he declared. "It would pass any inspection anywhere."

Lieutenant Ferguson, who was his guide at that moment, responded. "We know it, sir. We want you to be fully aware that nothing is being done casually. Everything is being checked three times, at least, and the final inspection team is demanding perfection. This is going to be the best B-17 that ever took to the air."

"You aren't writing home about this are you?" the colonel asked.

"No, sir!"

"Well don't; it might be better to keep this entirely to ourselves. In fact, Captain Tilton got an inquiry through the PR office in the head shed asking about the B-17 we were building up here."

Ferguson felt a sudden taste of shock. "How did he handle that, sir?"

"I believe that he reported something about a model building project that someone had dreamed up. The size of the model was not specified."

"Sir, he's a helluva good man."

"I'm fully aware of that, Scotty. How about the instruments? If they can be salvaged, they'll need complete overhauls."

"The guys up at J Site offered to do that for us, sir; they have full facilities. In fact, the artificial horizon's back already. The vacuum system hasn't been overhauled yet, so it's still out on the bench — under cover, of course."

"Batteries?"

"Supply has them."

"How about the wiring?"

"Every bit of it is being replaced, sir, and we have new bulbs for all of the lights. Using an outside power cart, we've cycled the landing gear more than fifty times without any trace of a malfunction."

The colonel looked around him. "You're going to end up with a virtually new airplane."

"That's exactly what we have in mind, sir. She will have zero time on everything."

"I'll drop in again," the colonel promised.

"Do that, sir — we'd like to have you." He would have said more, but his mind was fully occupied with the fuel-cell tests that were the next thing on the program.

For the next three weeks the normal work of Thule Air Base went forward. Ferguson made several trips out to Camp Century, both with his own crew and with Boyd's to be sure that everyone was fully checked out on ice cap operations. Otherwise, he spent each spare minute in Hangar 8, following every step of the operation and doing as much himself as he could possibly manage to fit in.

The biggest single event, at the end of that time, was the remounting of the number three engine. The crane lifted it easily into position and the actual installation work, in the relative comfort of the hangar, was comparatively simple. All of the controls were hooked up and all of the plumbing was meticulously recoupled. By all reasonable theory, the engine should run. It would have been well to try it out on a test stand first, but that had presented too many problems and the decision had been made to run it in, if possible, in position on the airframe.

The propeller that went onto the end of the shaft appeared to be brand-new. It was far from an easy job to reinstall all of the prop controls, but the work was done with the same

182

enthusiasm and care that had characterized every ac-
complishment along the way. When at last the job was
finished, it was past 2400 hours and everyone was exhausted.

The following morning was Saturday, which meant that
most of the personnel would be off work; by 1000 hours the
grapevine had produced an audience of more than two
hundred gathered around the closed door of Hangar 8. At
1012 hours the main door was opened and the *Penguin* was
pushed out. With her single restored engine once more facing
a point somewhere above the horizon, she was grotesquely
incomplete, but to the men who had been working on her for
so many weeks, she was the most beautiful aircraft that had
ever challenged the sky.

His palms wet with perspiration, Ferguson sat in the
left-hand seat, using the original cushion that had been the
first thing he had personally recovered from the hopeless
wreck on the ice cap. When the twenty-man ground crew had
pushed the plane into the position that he wanted, he pushed
against the brakes and got an immediate response. He tested
the controls for the hundredth time, just for the joy of feeling
them move so smoothly. Then he sat still while the battery
cart was wheeled up and plugged in.

Andy Holcomb appeared on the ramp in front of the nose.
"Anytime," he called up.

Ferguson heard him through the open window. In response
he checked visually and then called out, "Clear!"

He pumped the prime and then activated the starter. The
freshly rebuilt unit responded immediately; for the first time
in three decades the heavy propeller began to turn. The crowd
on the ground was still — waiting to see what, if anything, was
going to happen. When he judged that the time was right,
Ferguson turned the ignition switch to BOTH and held a deep
breath in his lungs.

The propeller continued to turn slowly under the impetus
of the starter; the engine remained dead and still. Then there

was a sharp retort — almost like a pistol shot — and a burst of smoke came out of the exhaust. In four seconds there was another, then several. Ferguson cut off the starter, but after a few more erratic bursts, the engine came to a halt.

"Again!" he shouted to the ground crew. In response, Holcomb drew a circle in the air with his right hand. Ferguson reengaged the starter, counted six passes of a propeller blade through the copilot's window, and then turned on the ignition once again.

He was answered almost at once by a staccato burst of sound. There were sharp gaps, but the propeller began to spin far faster. With his hand holding the throttle from underneath, which he had found to be the only feasible position, he nursed fuel to the struggling power plant, giving it more when it needed it, cutting back at once when it threatened to flood. He was more used to turbine engines, but he understood this one and he had put in long hours of work helping to clean every component and put it all back together in correct sequence.

The roughness peaked and then fell away; through the open window there came the almost steady beat of the 1,200-horsepower power plant that was spinning its propeller into a silver disc. Ferguson felt the airframe vibrate and knew that life had returned to it. He mind-vaulted back to the bitterly cold morning when he had first explored the flight deck of *The Passionate Penguin* and had found the controls as cold and rigid as stone monuments in the dead of winter.

Now they moved.

He heard the cheer outside, but it meant little to him. It was the engine that he heard as it settled down into smoothness. He let it run for five minutes before he tried the propeller pitch control. The blades responded — he could feel it. By gradual stages he tested the propeller all of the way up to full feather and back; as far as he could tell, everything was perfect. He ran the engine in for a full hour at slow speed; during that time almost everyone at Thule came by to have a look. A number of vehicles came down from J Site and one from the incredibly isolated P Mountain station. Several times more Ferguson cycled the propeller and each time it responded — apparently flawlessly.

Corbin came up and took over the copilot's seat. In response Ferguson relinquished the run-in test to his partner. Corbin had a good deal of time on small piston-engined aircraft and held a civilian flight instructor's rating. Also, he had worked like a beaver on the engine rebuilding.

After an hour and a half, Corbin shut down the engine and secured the proper controls. When he came off the flight deck there was a grin on his face that ran almost from ear to ear.

In the NCO Club that evening, Tom Collins called a meeting to which ten key invitees responded. Ferguson was there of course, and his whole crew; some of Det. 4 sat in, along with Collins, the indispensable Sergeant Feinberg, and a powerful Dane named Karsten Thorlund, who was the acknowledged head of the civilians engaged in the rebuilding project.

When the drinks had been served and everything was ready, Collins took the floor. "Gentlemen," he began, "from the very start of this thing, we've been going on the very sound premise that we were going to restore the *Penguin* to all of her former glory, just as she was."

"Amen," Sergeant Stovers said over his beer.

"Now," Tom went on, "I want to propose an exception — if we can do it. You all know how much we're indebted to the Canadians up at Alert for overhauling the electronics for us. But there's a big problem; the frequencies have all changed and so has the whole system of radio navigation. Everything that the *Penguin* has is low frequency; she can tune in all of the range legs, but there aren't any more left."

He waited for some response to that, but everyone else chose to remain quiet. He was right and they all knew it; a new

185

electronic age had been born since the bomber had been abandoned on the ice cap.

Tom continued. "We're going to fly her, of course, and when the story gets out about what's been done here, I suspect that the *Penguin* is going to be one of the most famous planes in the world. She's going to have to go to a lot of different places and make personal appearances; you guys all remember the Navy's *Truculent Turtle* and how much mileage they got out of her."

"Definitely," Sergeant Feinberg said.

"So baby is going to have to have some modern electronics; without them she won't be able to communicate."

"Looking at it that way," Ferguson said, thinking aloud, "she's going to need, at the very least, dual OMNI, TACAN with DME, in all probability single sideband since she's long-legged with more than a four-thousand-mile range, and at least one transponder: she's got to be able to squawk."

"All of which adds up to about thirty grand even without the VORTAC," Corbin declared. "And none of that gear is surplus."

"First," Thorlund interjected in a rich baritone, "we have to decide if we want to install modern electronics or not."

There was some discussion in response, but even the diehard traditionalists had to concede that a four-engined aircraft equipped with radios that no one could hear and that were unable to receive any current communications would be hopelessly handicapped. "She'd never be able to file IFR," Collins summed up, "and that's grossly beneath her dignity, if nothing else."

"We have to do it," Corbin said. "I've been thinking the same thing, but I didn't want to rock the boat."

"How about the radios we have?" Stovers asked.

Ferguson answered him. "Anything she can use she keeps. Otherwise . . ."

"Has anybody got any ideas?" Holcomb asked.

186

In the thick silence that followed not even Sergeant Perry Feinberg was able to come up with a suggestion. He was, however, thinking. "Since she's out of the Air Force inventory," he said, "we can't draw the gear in the usual way."

"Isn't there a crashed airplane somewhere between here and Alert?" Tiny Heneveld of Det. 4 asked.

"Yes," Corbin answered. "I've heard about it. But that stuff has been through an honest-to-gosh crash and it won't be worth an empty pea pod. You can throw it into the chop suey, and that's all."

"Not quite," Mike Turner said.

"Expound," Perry Feinberg invited.

"Simple: when you've got a piece of radio gear that doesn't work, you turn it in to be fixed. If they can't fix it, they issue you a new one."

Chief Master Sergeant Feinberg sat stock still while a dawning light crossed his broad face, then he turned slowly and looked at the young helicopter pilot with new respect and possibly a certain amount of awe. "Do you realize what you have just done?" he asked. "You have forever settled a question that has confronted the Air Force since its inception. You have, at this sacred moment, proven for all time the indisputable worth and value of second lieutenants. It is a monumental event — and to think that I am present here to witness it!"

"How will we get the sets?" Corbin asked.

"Difficult, but possible," Feinberg answered. "If all else fails, I have Eskimo friends and they, in turn, have dog teams. Something will be worked out."

On the first day that the sun remained above the horizon long enough to give adequate daylight at midnight, the number two engine was successfully tested. With two power plants available, Ferguson made a ground phone call to the tower and then, armed with the necessary permission, he taxied the *Penguin* to the end of the runway and ran up. When he was satisfied, he turned as if for takeoff, started down the 10,000-foot strip and ran for over a mile at fifty knots with the tail lifted into flying position. It was the most exciting ride he had ever had; only by the exercise of great willpower did he keep himself from pushing the throttles all the way forward to see if she would come off the ground. She was empty of any payload and while she was shy some 2,400 horsepower, she was also relieved of some 5,000 pounds of engine weight. Probably she would have been able to do it, but the time was not yet.

When he went to bed that night, Ferguson lay on his back and looked up at the ceiling, his mind churning and his body actively resisting any approach of sleep. He was, at that moment, in love, and the object of his affections was not a young woman, but a machine.

Even at minimum wage scales, the amount of work that had already gone into the rebuilding of the *Penguin* represented far more than the aircraft itself could possibly be worth — that is, if she were to be considered as so much aluminum, so many thousands of rivets, so many miles of wiring, so many pounds of various fluids, so much rubber, and so many other ingredients. But it was impossible for him to think of her that way. Skilled pilot that he was, he had never known any airplane as well as he knew that B-17 and the whole, to him, was vastly greater than the sum of the parts.

He recalled reading about a railroad engineer who, upon his retirement, had asked to buy the locomotive that had been his constant working partner for thirty years. Because steam power was going out anyway, the railroad had given him the engine. Together with his friends, the engineer had laid two miles of temporary track, from the railroad yards to his home. On a great day in his life he had driven the engine for the last time, over the impromptu rails and onto the side yard of his property. During his retirement his familiar iron friend was his faithful companion. It, too, took up a new career and became an enormous attraction for all of the neighborhood children.

A week later the original nose insignia of *The Passionate Penguin* had been repainted in brilliant fresh colors. The third engine was ready to be reinstalled and tested and most of the instruments were entirely overhauled and certified accurate. The C-130 Hercules made a trip to Anchorage, Alaska, for some essential maintenance; Captain Boyd and his crew took her almost literally across the pole on a long nonstop flight plan that covered some of the most desolate parts of the globe. In order to at least give the appearance of doing something officially useful, Scott Ferguson spent considerable time in the Det. 4 hangar familiarizing himself with the HH-3 helicopter. He made two trips to the Eskimo village of Kanak and enjoyed every moment of both experiences.

The number one engine ran like a dream. When it had been carefully tested, and when the crew working on number four reported no problems with their rebuilding chore, Ferguson went to see the colonel. At the request of both men, Captain Tilton, the Information Officer, was also present.

"Sir," Ferguson began. "The *Penguin* is on schedule — a little ahead of it, in fact. All of the instruments check out, three of the four engines are running like Swiss watches, and the structure of the airframe couldn't possibly be better. You know the quality of the work that's gone into her."

"I certainly do," the colonel agreed, "and that brings up a point I was going to ask you: are you going to paint *United States Air Force* down her side?"

Ferguson hesitated. "I would appreciate some guidance from you on that, sir," he said.

"Well, this is unofficial, of course, but if she did have the Air Force name on her, it might simplify getting fuel when you need it and so on. Avionics, for instance."

"She is a war bird," Tilton said. "The C-47's that were her contemporaries are still flying, in many instances, and they carry the Air Force name."

"Did you say avionics, sir?" Ferguson asked.

"Well, I can't have an aircraft flying around up here without suitable communications equipment and navigational gear. But I also can't have any equipment issued to what might be considered a civilian bird."

Ferguson saw the light. "Sir, the *Penguin* originally joined the Air Force when it was the Army Air Corps and she never quit. The name goes on."

"That's very good, because I called over to Anchorage to have them send some gear back on the C-130. I couldn't very well report that it was for a bomber, so I told them that she was a rescue vehicle. Do you recall the Dumbo B-17's that carried lifeboats underneath them during the final stages of World War II?"

"Come to think of it, sir — yes!"

Captain Tilton recognized his moment. "We have the celebration laid out, sir, and it looks very good, if I may say so. The painting of the B-17 in flight has been completed; we want to start the festivities with a special breakfast for all hands who took part in the work; a few have left, but we can't help that. At the conclusion of the meal, we'd like to have you unveil the painting. This will be at the NCO Club. Champagne will be served — to all but the flight crew.

"The formal ceremonies will start at 1400 hours at the flight line. Chaplain Valen will open with prayer, then Det. Four will be given a plaque for their part in bringing in the wing roots. Sergeant Feinberg will speak briefly on the project, how it came about, and pay tribute to Lieutenant Ferguson for having inspired the whole thing. Lieutenant Jane Miles at J Site will be Miss B-17 for the day. You know her?"

"I do," the colonel said.

"Then, sir, you, on behalf of the base, and Commander

Kure, representing Denmark, will escort Mrs. Kure to the hangar. The doors will be opened and the aircraft will be rolled out onto the ramp. With the photographers on the job, Mrs. Kure will rechristen the *Penguin*."

"Wait a minute," the colonel interjected. "Mrs. Kure is a very refined lady — have you forgotten the design on the nose of the plane?"

"Sir, we discussed that with the commander and he assured us that it would be all right."

"OK, then. Continue."

Tilton consulted his notes. "After Mrs. Kure has done the honors, the band will play the Air Force song. As soon as that is over, the crew will march out in formation and stand beside the B-17 while the national anthem is played. This will all be filmed, of course. After the anthem, the crew will board the aircraft and start engines. The tower will give clearance. As the plane taxies to the end of the runway, the band will play *The Passionate Penguin March*. Tony did a wonderful job on that — it's a little suggestive of the 'Grand March' in *Aida*."

Tilton paused for effect and discovered that he had the colonel's complete attention. "Then, sir, everything will be quiet while the *Penguin* runs up, clears the tower, and moves into position. We'll have the tower show her a green light, so that everyone can see it."

"You might want to hook up the communications into the PA system," the colonel suggested.

"Excellent, sir! We should have thought of that." Tilton made a note. "Then, after the green light the tower will also voice clear the *Penguin* for takeoff. That will be the most dramatic moment: she will start down the runway and time her takeoff so that she will be just opposite the spectators when she lifts into the air. After she lands, the final event planned is a gala dinner for all hands. And we would like very much to have you sign an order, sir, restoring the *Penguin* to operational status. The rescue-craft idea is outstanding: if

191

someone is taken sick at Alert, she can go up and get him. They don't have a hospital, and we do."

"When is this to be?" the colonel asked.

Ferguson was alertly proud. "Anytime after twenty days, sir. We want to run all of the final tests to be absolutely sure that she's one hundred percent."

"So ordered," the colonel declared.

Airman Robert Elliott did not want to leave Thule. His tour would be over in two more days, but missing the rollout and flight of the B-17 represented a material disappointment. He asked for, and was denied, a thirty-day extension of his tour. As a consequence, he departed as scheduled on the rotator and duly arrived at McGuire Air Force Base some hours later.

Since he was automatically on furlough, he did not wait for a military ride; he took ground transportation to Philadelphia International Airport and from there caught a 707 bound for Los Angeles. As he sat on the cushions, admiring the stewardesses and reflecting on civilian life, Airman Elliott began to think of the many things he was going to tell his family when he got off the plane. When his lunch was served he tied in with a willing appetite, but he could not forget the many hours of work he had so gladly put in helping to clean and polish the fuselage of the noble B-17.

There was a civilian, a man in his fifties, seated with him. The middle seat was empty and had been folded down to make a common table. That invited conversation and Elliott was more than willing. He exchanged the usual pleasantries with his companion and then, in answer to a question, told him that he was returning home from Thule.

"I understand that that is a very tough tour," the civilian said.

"Not so bad, sir. The food is all right, and you get used to it after a while."

"But it still must be awfully boring."

Elliott dropped his voice. "Not this time, sir. You see, we had something going."

"A sports tournament?"

"Oh no, something much better than that." He stopped, remembering the agreement that nothing would be said or written stateside until the rebuilding was an accomplished fact, but it was all but done now and he had already, to a degree at least, committed himself. "We got into an airplane rebuilding project," he added, and then wished that he hadn't.

"Hey, that sounds like fun!"

Obviously the civilian was all right. "It was, sir, a lot. It was really something to do."

"Tell me about it."

Elliott thought quickly, but it was a friendly inquiry and nothing more. And the story was a wonderful one. He told it, not in detail, but with enough particulars to convey the basic idea.

The civilian displayed considerable interest. "They aren't going to try and fly it again, are they?" he asked. The tone of his voice betrayed a concern that was an immediate warning.

Elliott all but wished himself dead. "I don't think so," he almost lied, "at least not for some time." He turned his full attention back to his food tray. When the man he had been talking to had nothing more to say, and appeared to be thinking deeply, Elliott held his lips hard together, shut his eyes, and prayed fervently. Every bit of joy had gone out of his life and he was almost afraid to face his parents. He would not dare tell them one thing about the B-17.

TO COMMANDER THULE AIR BASE PRIORITY INFORMATION RECEIVED THIS HEADQUARTERS INDICATES PROJECT WITHIN YOUR COMMAND REBUILDING DERELICT B-17 BOMBER RETRIEVED FROM ICE CAP. AS RECREATIONAL ACTIVITY, PROJECT IS APPROVED PROVIDING COMPLETED

AIRCRAFT, IF FINISHED, IS USED FOR DISPLAY PURPOSES ONLY. SINCE AIRFRAME EXPOSED TO EXTREME WEATHER CONDITIONS FOR MORE THAN THIRTY YEARS, IT IS POSTED UNSAFE AND MAY NOT BE FLOWN UNDER ANY CIRCUMSTANCES REPEAT UNDER ANY CIRCUMSTANCES. ADVISE ALL CONCERNED PERSONNEL THIS DIRECTIVE IMMEDIATELY. END.

RECORDS AND REFUSAL BRANCH
DIRECTOR OF AEROSPACE SAFETY
NORTON AIR FORCE BASE, CALIFORNIA

OFFICIAL

CHAPTER THIRTEEN

IN STUNNED, silent shock, Thule Air Base carried on with its assigned mission. The door to Hangar 8 remained closed; for several days no one entered it unless he was required to do so.

The reenlistment office reported that no one had been in, not even the career personnel who had chosen the Air Force as their life's work.

When the base theater had a flying film booked, almost no one showed up to see the picture.

The consumption of alcoholic beverages at the clubs increased to the point where the medical officers recommended to the commander that some counteraction should be taken. There were three traffic accidents during a period when such incidents were all but unknown.

The personnel officer received so many applications for

transfer, and so many sets of early retirement papers, he went in some haste to see the base commander.

"Colonel," he reported, "as long as I've been in the Air Force, I've never seen morale go to pieces like this. Look here, sir." He handed over a formal document.

Colonel Kleckner glanced at it and registered genuine surprise. "I can't believe it," he said.

"Well, there it is: Sergeant Perry S. Feinberg putting in to leave the service."

It was a stunning shock. "I've been under the impression that the Air Force was his whole life," the colonel said quietly.

"I agree with you, sir, I'm sure that it was. But if this thing has gotten so bad that even Sergeant Feinberg can't stand up under it, then Thule Air Base is falling apart. No reflection on you, sir. We all know that it wasn't your fault in any way."

"I never would have believed it of Feinberg," the colonel said, half to himself.

"It's a clincher, sir, I admit. Is there anything we can do about it?"

The colonel sat very still and thought hard for several more seconds, then he issued an order. "Send Sergeant Feinberg to see me," he directed.

When the sergeant reported, he snapped to attention before the colonel's desk, saluted, and said crisply, "Sergeant Feinberg reporting to the colonel as ordered, sir."

The colonel returned the salute. "At ease, Sergeant, sit down."

"Yes, sir." Sergeant Feinberg sat with strict protocol and remained straight in his chair. Colonel Kleckner ordered two coffees to be brought in, and then closed the door to his office.

"Sergeant," the colonel continued when he was behind his desk once more, "this is a strictly confidential meeting; you will not repeat one word of it, in any form, outside this office."

"Understood, sir."

"At any time, or under any circumstances."

"No, sir — under no circumstances whatsoever."

The colonel remained silent until a tap on the door announced the arrival of the coffee. After it had been delivered, and the door was again shut, the colonel continued. "I am aware that the morale at Thule is in bad condition."

"It's gone straight to hell in a bucket, sir. Beyond the point of retrievability I would say, sir."

"And it has hit you personally."

"I'm terminating my career, sir."

"Drop the formality, Perry — this is on a man-to-man basis."

"In that case, sir, I'm going to get my ass out of here as soon as the Lord will let me."

The colonel drank some of his coffee. "I don't blame you one damn bit; I wish I could do the same. But you know that I can't. However, there are some things that I can do; a base commander does enjoy certain privileges."

"Such as, sir?"

"Up to a point, I can make waves. I have a few friends who sit higher on the totem pole than I do."

"Colonel, do I understand correctly that you're prepared to go to bat for us?"

"The United States Air Force," Colonel Keckner said distinctly, "is made up of fighting men; that's what we're trained to do."

"Sir, I'm listening intently."

"Then hear this: I have been following closely every step of the work you have been doing on that B-17, ever since you came back with the first engine. A prop I could understand, but when you brought in an engine, with all of the work that that must have involved out on the ice cap under severe conditions, I understood what was up. Frankly, I didn't think you could do it or even come close — I'll admit privately that you took me on that one."

He paused, but Feinberg said nothing.

"Perry, I've personally inspected the work as it's gone forward and I know the records of the men who have been handling the technical requirements. The reconstruction job has been uncompromising and that airplane, in my opinion, is going to be entirely airworthy and safe."

"Thank you, sir."

"Now all I have to do is to convince certain other people of that fact. So here's what I want you to do: you may leak the fact, very cautiously, that all may not be lost as yet. Then I want you to withdraw your retirement papers. I'm not ordering you to do that—I can't—but I'm requesting it. I need a con artist now of unqualified capability and I don't have to look very far to find him."

"And then, sir?"

"I want you to do your best to get the troops to complete the job they started. There's one more engine to be installed and run in, new avionics to be installed and tested, and some instrument work to be gone over. How about the wiring and other connections behind the instrument panel?"

"Every bit of it has been overhauled, Colonel, and replaced if the slightest doubt existed."

"Did you complete the fuel-cell tests?"

"Yes, sir, they checked out one hundred percent. It was a new airplane, you know, when it was ditched on the ice cap. She had only a few hours on her."

"I want the job finished—and I'm not going to look too critically at the work records for the next two or three weeks, in case someone happens to be in Hangar Eight instead of somewhere else."

"That won't be necessary, sir."

"Can you con them into doing it?"

"With your assurance, sir, that I'm not selling them down the river, I can."

"Then do it. You are at liberty to make it known, discreetly, that I am taking a personal interest and plan to do what I can to have the curse lifted. I have a leave coming up; I may take part of it paying a visit to Norton."

Eleven days later, at 2035 hours, Lieutenant Scott Ferguson stood alone in Hangar 8. The overhead lights were reflected brilliantly by the surfaces of the apparently brand-new B-17 that stood in proud glory on the concrete flooring. She was no longer consigned to the depressed area, she occupied the best spot the hangar had to offer. That afternoon Ferguson had had the airplane out on the ramp and, with the help of Corbin, Holcomb, Jenkins, and Stovers, he had checked her out completely. All of the engines had been run, all of the instruments had been tested, all of the avionics had been verified as far as had been possible on the ground. He had taxied her up and down the field several times and twice he had had her on the runway, trying her out just under flying speed. She hadn't had the power and the sophistication of the C-130 Hercules, of course, but she had proven one thing to his satisfaction: she was an airplane worthy of any sky that the world had to offer.

He looked at her now, rested his hand against the side of her fuselage, and then looked up at the brilliantly repainted insignia. "And fuck the whole goddamn air-safety branch too," he said aloud. "Until they get their thumbs out of their asses and learn what the score is."

He felt better after that. He did not yet know that Colonel Kleckner had, within the past hour, had a final answer to his well-supported request for reconsideration of the decision concerning the B-17. Norton had said "No" with force and clarity. Furthermore, it was made completely clear that the subject was closed. It was suggested that the revived bomber be shipped out on a convenient vessel to a supply depot. There it would be considered as a possible exhibit for the Air Force museum at Wright-Patterson Air Force Base. Disassembly was recommended.

Colonel Kleckner sat in his office with his counterpart, Colonel Jason of the United States Army. The door was again closed and the discussion was private. "Now that's the situation," Colonel Kleckner said. "For the moment I'm sitting on Norton's final decision; if I let that one out of the bag, then morale all over this base is going to hit rock bottom — which is about where I am right now on this whole thing."

"How can I help?" Jason asked.

"By creating a diversion. You see, Jack, within the next sixty days a good forty percent of the personnel who worked on restoring the B-17 will be rotated back stateside to other assignments. Once they are out of here, and replaced with new people who had no stake in the job, the tension will be proportionately less. So every week that goes by without an explosion is an added period of grace."

"Who know about this?"

"The two or three communications people who handled the message from Norton; I have the lid on them. I also notified the chaplains for obvious reasons. Now, it would help immensely if you and your crew at Camp Century could manage to kick up a storm — to require a lot of support and keep my hands fully occupied."

"As a matter of fact, Jim, I've been deliberately going the other route — keeping a low profile so as not to upset you and your operation too much. There is a great deal we could ask for, and to our benefit."

"Then start asking. Bring people in and out; create some action. If anyone has so much as a sore throat, call for a medevac. How do you read me?"

"I read you five-square, Jim, on the same frequency. To start with, I would like to rotate my people back here for R and R — for a good base exchange, for some different food, for a chance to see some daylight. Perhaps you could lay on some recreational trips in the vicinity and delegate people to take our guys out to see the sights."

"Rest and recreation at Thule is something new, I must admit—but we can do it, as of now. Just give my people something to do, and something else to think about."

"We will: I'll have my PE officer get up some teams to challenge Thule in every sport we can think of."

"Excellent! That's what I need, Jack. I can't sit on this forever, but I want the blow to be as easy as I can make it."

"Is there any chance of your air-safety people changing their minds?"

"None whatever—I asked to have a senior engineering officer come up here to inspect the B-17 himself and see what a phenomenal job our people did on it, but they wouldn't go along."

Jason got up. "We'll start making waves as of tomorrow," he promised. "I'll keep it up until you say 'when.' "

"God bless you," Colonel Kleckner concluded.

In a matter of days the activity at Thule was redoubled. The base swarmed with Army men who were there on a variety of different assignments. An Army chaplain preached the morning Protestant sermon to an increased congregation. Several hiking parties were organized to go up Mount Dundas. Captain Tilton, who did not directly know the reason for all this, but who could make a shrewd guess, increased the publication frequency of *Thule Times* to weekly and added more pages to cover the Army activities. An interservice sports tournament drew a good number of participants. While all of this was going on, each week the rotator brought fresh personnel and took back some of the old hands who had been engaged in Operation Penguin.

During this time the days began to grow darker at midnight and the temperatures that had been reaching the mid-fifties were sinking steadily. A mild Phase Alert occurred, giving warning that before long Thule would again be in the fierce grip of the Arctic, with its bitter, savage winds and the blackness of unrelieved night.

Colonel Kleckner had slightly less than two months to go on his own tour, but he still had not released the information that the B-17 had been permanently grounded. His playing for time had been at least partially successful; more than thirty percent of the rebuilders had left the base and those who remained had probably drawn their own conclusions. When he checked his personnel charts, the colonel saw that in another three weeks he would lose four of his best NCO's, all of whom had elected to return to civilian life. They were experienced and valuable career men, but they had had it with the Air Force and they did not mind saying so.

In six weeks a major segment of Det. 4 would be replaced *en masse;* one week after that Sergeant Feinberg would be on the outbound list. The two C-130 crews were intact and no orders had been cut to relieve them; the Army was still busy at Camp Century and some colder-weather experiments had been scheduled.

At 1535 hours on Thursday afternoon, Angelo in Base Weather put out a notification of a probable incoming phase. New personnel were immediately rebriefed on the exact meaning of Arctic storms and of the acute danger that they represented. Once again the story was told of the cook who had attempted to run from one building to another ninety feet distant during a Phase Two without bothering to put on his arctic clothing. His frozen body had been recovered by rescue crews a few hours later.

Phase Alert was declared at 2120 hours. The temperature was plummeting and the winds were growing rapidly into howling intensity. Announcement of Phase One conditions followed eighteen minutes later. The base movie at once shut down, the library closed, and all personnel were advised to return to their quarters without delay. The base taxi service went into high gear to get everyone delivered in minimum time.

At 2210 hours conditions had deteriorated drastically and the weather section declared Phase Two. In Building 708 the command post was opened and the head count of all persons at Thule was activated. By that time the raging storm outside was hammering against the well-protected windows, and the more experienced hands knew that a full-flung Phase Three was a definite possibility. The Trackmaster crews were already with their vehicles, ready to respond to any calls for rescue assistance.

Four men who had been in a six-pack truck en route from J Site were the cause of concern until they phoned in that they had, per regulations, taken shelter in one of the phase shacks along the road. After a check with Weather, the colonel dispatched a Trackmaster to recover them and bring them back to base.

The head count was completed in thirty-nine minutes; everyone had been accounted for. Lieutenant Kane, the Transportation Officer, shut down the last of the taxi service and ordered all vehicles off the roads until further notice — rescue equipment excepted.

At two minutes after midnight the PA system came on with the expected announcement that Phase Three was in effect. The rage of the Arctic weather took complete command of Thule and no one dared to venture outside for any reason whatsoever. The Army detachment reported from Camp Century that everything had been secured as far as possible and that all personnel were safe in their barracks under the ice.

In his own quarters, the colonel found it hard to sit still. He had a pile of work with him, but none of it was urgent. Thule was his command and he was responsible for it in every respect that dealt with the United States Air Force, but he was still grateful that he would not have to go through another year facing the grimness and the isolation of the extreme Arctic.

He thought about the immense amount of work that had gone into Operation Penguin and the acute disappointment that had been handed down to the men who had given so much of themselves to accomplish the near impossible. He would have enjoyed his tour a great deal more if it had not been for that.

He called Weather and asked Angelo for an indication as to the duration of the storm. The reply he got was not encouraging: Phase Three would be in effect for at least another eight hours and very likely much longer than that. It was highly doubtful that the rotator would be able to come in on time or take out the relieved personnel on schedule. Thule, J Site, P Mountain, and certainly Alert, more than four hundred miles still farther north, were all catching hell and the end was not in sight.

In the morning the phase rations were broken out. In Building 708 the food was not too bad since most of the men had refrigerators in their rooms and usually a hot plate or small grill of some kind. Coffee, hot cocoa, fried-ham sandwiches, and a good many other things were to be had. Everything was shared and the enforced day off was made as livable as possible. Det. 4 had its usual poker game going; Frank Tilton was busy at the typewriter putting together something he did not choose to discuss; Major Valen was preparing his sermon for the following Sunday. After an impromptu meal of phase rations was finished, the evening broke down into an assortment of minor personal activities. Most of the men went to bed early and thought about home.

Shortly before 1200 hours the following day, five of the men of Det. 4 tapped on the door of the colonel's quarters. Invited to enter and sit down, they made themselves as comfortable as possible on what chairs there were, and on the edges of the few pieces of furniture.

"Colonel," Tom Collins began. "We've been waiting a

helluva long time to hear some further news about the *Penguin*. Norton turned us down again, is that right?"

"Yes," Colonel Kleckner admitted, "and they won't reconsider the matter. I tried everything I could think of, and got in touch with some pretty good personal friends, but I couldn't move them. The bird is grounded."

"Permanently, we take it."

"I'm afraid so. They've recommended that we disassemble her and ship her out by sea to Wright-Pat for inclusion in the Air Force museum."

"How long ago, sir?"

"Actually, quite some time. But no convenient vessel seemed to put into port when the water was open. At least not after I got the final message."

"Then we're busted."

"Yes."

"Does Scotty Ferguson know this?" Ron Cunningham asked.

The colonel shook his head. "I haven't told him so directly."

John Schoen was grim. "It's going to tear him up," he said. "I'm sure he's guessed, but . . . damn it to hell."

"I agree," the colonel responded. "It's like that sometimes."

Bob Seligman spoke up. "Colonel, we pretty much concluded that this was the case. When this storm is over, we're going to throw one hell of a party in honor of the *Penguin* anyway. At the club. Will you come?"

"Positively. At least we can unveil the painting and hang it properly."

"That's what we had in mind," Seligman said.

By mid-afternoon of the following day the storm was stepped down to Phase Two. That in itself offered very little additional liberty, but it was an indication that the mess hall might be open that night. The colonel called Weather once more and was told that he could expect a downgrade to Phase One sometime around 1800 hours. As soon as he had that information, he called Commander Kure and relayed it; the commander in turn advised that if the forecast held up, a hot meal would be prepared for all hands as soon as the storm had abated to Phase One intensity.

The forecast was good; Phase One was declared at 1815 and very shortly thereafter Thule once more began to show signs of external life. The storm was still powerful, but vehicles were able to crawl cautiously down the roads and the mess hall was ablaze with bright lights.

Because time was getting short for many of the people concerned, the junior officers' party at the NCO Club in honor of *The Passionate Penguin* was laid on without delay. It was announced that the theme would be the Fifties, with all appropriate costumes, music, and song. Obviously the resources for any kind of special dress were extremely limited at Thule, but there was a faint air of desperation about the whole thing that simply ignored any restrictions. By the end of the week everything had been prepared and the long, narrow private dining room at the club had been set up with the best that the facility had to offer. At one end of the room the painting of the *Penguin* had been placed on a easel and then covered with an appropriate drape. Red napkins carefully folded into cylinders stood at each place; the silverware was sparkling clean. For a dinner arrangement several hundred miles north of the Arctic Circle, it was an impressive display.

The participants and guests began to arrive a little after 1800 hours and took their ease at the bar. Uniforms were conspicuously absent; striped shirts had been broken out, loud ties had been unearthed, and work pants had been used to create a costume effect. The PA system poured out the music of Chuck Berry and the two bartenders produced concoctions to suit the rapidly growing trade. A new cocktail named "the Penguin's Playmate" had been created for the occasion and was tried out with ironic frequency. By 1900 hours the mood of most of those present had been softened somewhat, but Det. 4 had not yet put in an appearance.

Dinner was announced and the men filed in. The carefully prepared room was admired as the place cards were read. As the men began to seat themselves, sounds were heard from the lobby; presently Det. 4 came streaming in, loudly and boisterously, almost the perfect epitome of a street gang. They had all turned their flying jackets inside out so that the international orange liners became flashy jackets. On the back of each was a bold patch that read PHARAOHS. Their pants were as outlandish an assortment as the Far Arctic could produce; their hair was slicked back and their faces were smeared with grime. They shouted and pushed, they snarled at each other and anyone who got in their way, they upset chairs as they went.

One man grabbed a bottle of wine and spilled it as others tried to take it away amid curses and shouts. An unattended drink was snatched up and consumed. Someone shouted from the lobby and a moment later two more gang members burst into the room and tossed onto the table the four hubcaps from the colonel's staff car.

The entrance was a smashing success; laughs came tumbling on top of one another — jeers were thrown across the table and feigned insults brought pretended threats of instant violence. The tensions that had been building for weeks spilled out into the open and the accumulated bitterness was let loose. Toasts to all sorts of fanciful subjects were raised and downed. Steaks and salads were brought in, but little attention was paid to the food. It was an uninhibited bash, and every man present threw himself into the mood of abandonment.

They ate when they were able, but the noise level remained high and unrestrained. "Get some women up here!" someone shouted. "Get some go-go girls to take off their pants and dance!" That brought a fresh spasm of loud clapping and cheers. There were no go-go dancers, but that mattered little—they created them. Someone raised a glass and proposed a toast to the health of the Director of Air Safety — he was shouted down in a chorus of boos. The Pharaohs rose to attack; someone emptied a half-filled glass of beer over the toaster's head. The colonel laughed until there were tears in his eyes.

Above the noise in the room the PA system came on. Enough quiet fell to hear what was said: another Phase Alert had been declared.

No one heeded it; more beer was called for. The waiters tried to clear away the plates and succeeded in part; as one of them bent across the table he was solidly goosed by a leering street character who roared at his discomfort. The waiter acted out his indignation, playing his part in the grand farce. The dessert was on a cart, ready to be brought in, but first attention was given to keeping the wine glasses full. Hardly anyone sat still in his chair; the abandonment seized hold of everyone and wild shouting again filled the room. Then one of the men picked up a hubcap, banged on it to be heard over the din, and when he had attracted everyone's attention, he called on the colonel to unveil the portrait.

"Come on," the speaker urged, "let's see the best god-damned airplane that ever was! One of them brought my father back with six dead men along with him."

"Was he alive?" someone shouted back.

"Well what the hell, *I'm* here!"

The club manager came in as the colonel rose to make his speech. The manager located Major Kimsey with some difficulty and bent over him for a few moments. Kimsey got up and left the room.

The colonel fought his way up to the end of the room, prepared to do his duty. At last he stood by the painting and waited for the room to quiet down enough so that he could speak. He had some quips that were well suited to the moment; as he stood by the covered picture he did so in anything but a military manner. A glass of wine was in his left hand.

"Gentlemen," he shouted, "—if there's anyone here who answers that description . . ."

A loud laugh echoed him; the Pharaohs jumped to their feet—insulted and outraged. The hubcap was banged again to restore order.

Major Kimsey came back into the room and, putting his fingers to his lips, gave a loud whistle. It cut through the other noise of the party and commanded attention. When he got it, he had dropped his role and was suddenly a field-grade officer. There was an abrupt silence.

"We have an emergency medevac," he said. "Dr. Pedersen radioed from Kanak. He has a Greenlander girl who's been attacked by dogs and needs hospitalization immediately. It's marginal because we've got a Phase Alert on. Our only chance is to go now."

With the abruptness of a thunderclap the party was over. The Pharaohs vanished and the pilots of Det. 4 hurried as quickly as they could from the room. Major Valen was with them; the medical officers were immediately behind.

In less than a minute the room was empty—the painting still covered on its easel, the desserts unserved.

Major Mulder was on the telephone, calling for transportation. Captain Bowditch, the surgeon, was on another line to the hospital. A wild idea hit Scott Ferguson; he grabbed Mike Turner and asked, "What kind of a landing strip do they have up there?"

"A helipad, that's all. No runway."

"The C-130 won't help?"

"Can't use it."

In the lobby the flying jackets were being quickly reversed.

A six-pack pulled up outside and it was filled almost immediately. Another was directly behind it. In a matter of seconds all of Det. 4 was gone; in the second truck, Scott Ferguson rode along, hoping that in some possible way he could help. The colonel offered to drop Captain Markley, the internist, and the surgeon at the hospital.

As the first of the six-packs unloaded at the Det. 4 hangar, another pulled up with a contingent of the NCO's. No time was wasted in unnecessary conversation; Major Mulder went inside immediately and phoned Weather. "How bad is it now and how much time do we have?" he asked.

A staff car taxi pulled up and Major Linda Dashner, one of the three nurses at Thule, unloaded her flight gear and a medical kit. "I didn't have time to dress," she explained as soon as she was inside. "I'll do it here."

Woody Kimsey gave her a few seconds. "No dice. This is going to be very tough and we may not be able to get there at all if it gets any worse."

The major shed her parka. "I'm coming," she declared, and began to get into her flying suit.

Kimsey went quickly into the main hangar bay where Tiny Heneveld met him at the number one aircraft. "Are we going?" Heneveld asked. It was less a question than an urging.

"We're going to try," Kimsey answered.

Det. 4 was at full strength within five minutes. Then Kimsey spoke quickly and precisely to the other officers of his command. "Here it is: Jolly One will depart ASAP. Dick, you cock number two and keep in communication. Be ready to pick up the mission, if you can, if we run into trouble. The weather is right on edge—we may not be able to make it."

"The chances will be better if we both go," Mulder countered.

Kimsey shook his head. "You might have to come and get us—we don't want to have to divert to get you. But give us full back up, please." He saw over his shoulder that the number one helicopter was being pushed forward as the main hangar door began to open. "Any more information?" he asked.

An NCO was there with the answer. "Yes, sir. The girl is eight years old. She was out with her father feeding the dogs when she apparently tripped and fell down. As soon as she was prone the dogs jumped her. She's been bitten and lacerated. Dr. Pedersen says that her only chance is to get her into the hospital as quickly as possible."

"Any weather from Kanak?"

"Yes, sir—very tough. Ole, the Dane in charge there, advises extreme care. He didn't tell us not to come."

"He couldn't," the major answered. "All right, let's go."

CHAPTER FOURTEEN

ALTHOUGH WINTER was yet to come, the Arctic was already showing its strength in the winds that whipped across the ramp and in the whirling mists of early snow that cut visibility to a few yards. It was fully dark as Forest Kimsey, seated behind the controls of Jolly One, began the complicated checklist.

He was interrupted briefly once by the flight mechanic, who reported that Lieutenant Ferguson was ready in flight gear and asking to come along. "Why?" Kimsey asked.

Ferguson, who already had a headset on, answered for himself. "I can make a hand, and help the flight nurse. On this one it might be useful."

That was true and Ferguson knew the risks; he was an experienced pilot fully familiar with Arctic conditions. "All right," Kimsey said and then returned to checking out his own aircraft. He had firm doubts that he would be able to make it to Kanak, but he was determined to try. In the rescue business the safety of aircraft and their crews was always secondary to the mission of saving human life — the ARRS PJ's were living proof of that. He himself had often been moved by those men and the work that they did. Expert parachutists and scuba divers, they were prepared at any time to jump under any conditions whatsoever to save anyone. Their heroism was legendary.

"Checklist complete," Seligman reported.

Seconds later the first of the big Sikorsky's turbines began to come to life. As it caught hold, ground personnel on signal pushed the aircraft out onto the ramp and into the blast of the wind. The second turbine fired up, then the overhead main rotor began to turn. As it picked up speed the helicopter rocked on its gear, resisting the wind that challenged its right to even attempt to fly. As soon as the hangar door closed behind it, it was black in every direction; the field lights were on, but they were all but invisible.

Major Kimsey made an immediate decision not to follow usual procedure and go to the end of the runway for takeoff — the ground gusts were much too strong for that. He nodded to Seligman, who called the tower and asked for immediate takeoff from where they were. It was a useless formality; nothing else would be in the air for hundreds of miles in any direction. The tower gave permission, but warned that Phase One might be declared at any moment.

Seligman acknowledged and broke off. The main rotor whirled faster, the Sikorsky rolled forward a few feet and lifted off.

As soon as he was safely airborne, Kimsey set up a long climbing turn toward the north. His aircraft bucked underneath him and swayed dangerously as sharp gusts hit it, but he had expected that. It was an insane night to be flying, but that consideration had to be ignored. At 3,000 feet he leveled off and set up the best cruising speed that he dared under those weather conditions. He pushed the transmit button. "Thule from Jolly One," he said. "Tell Kanak we're on our way."

As the helicopter continued to fight her way through the violent Arctic night, Major Dashner checked the contents of her medical kit and chose the location where she wanted the litter rigged. Around her the men on board were firmly strapped in, riding out the storm quietly, although each one of them knew that the hazard level was high.

Thule called to report Phase One. Seligman acknowledged and asked if there was any further information from Kanak, especially weather data. Nothing more had been received, which meant little; all of the men on board the HH-3, including Ferguson, knew that putting down on the helipad at Kanak, in the face of the winds that would be tearing across the ground there, would be a risky business.

The howling of the turbines remained constant; the main rotor absorbing the shocks and the gusts as the mission continued. At times the aircraft skidded sideways or bounded upward in response to a vertical gust, but the pilots held control and kept a steady heading. "Half way," Seligman reported sometime later from the cockpit.

As if in reply, the aircraft caught a particularly bad gust that shook her from stem to stern, but the rotor settled in and held steady. Off toward the east a rising watery moon provided a limited, ghostlike light that barely showed the massive whiteness of the ice cap. Navigation was a problem under those conditions, but both of the pilots had made the trip many times before and what landmarks they could detect told them that they were substantially on course.

Ten minutes later the gusts seemed to become sharper and more violent. Controlling the helicopter became a more acute problem as a consequence; Major Kimsey began a letdown in the hope of finding less violent air. If that helped at all he could not detect it; the aircraft bucked and yawed as it churned its way through the sky. Thule called for a report; Seligman answered that they had descended to 2,000 feet and that the ETA at Kanak was approximately twenty minutes. There was no fresh news from the Eskimo village.

In the cabin, Ferguson almost regretted that he had asked to come. The constant bucking of the aircraft was beginning to disturb him a little despite his nearly 3,000 hours of flight time. It was one thing to be sitting up front doing the flying; it was quite another to be sitting in back, helpless to do anything but ride out the bumps as best he could.

In the cockpit Bob Seligman took over the flying while the major peered ahead, looking for the lights of Kanak. Sometimes, even in fairly heavy snow, they could be seen at a distance, but the blackness of the night was virtually unrelieved and it was no longer possible to fix the position of the helicopter by landmarks or radio aids. As she continued to buck and skid in the insatiable gusts, the Arctic closed in around her, waiting for her to falter in her struggles, or for either of the pilots to make a single serious mistake. But the HH-3 flew on. The pressurized blades continued to whirl overhead; the highly intricate rotor head responded to the commands it was given as the Sikorsky fought onward through the violently unstable air.

Three minutes short of the ETA the lights of Kanak had not been sighted, but that could be due to the greatly reduced visibility. Then the small transmitter at the village came on the air and within a few seconds the ADF needle pointed the way ten degrees to the left. Kimsey took back the aircraft, made the correction, and began to descend; ninety seconds later Seligman pointed dead ahead. A tiny pattern of faint lights appeared to flash off and on through the swirling snow. Seligman began to read off the before-landing checklist.

When everything was properly set, the major turned on the landing lights and lowered the gear. At 400 feet he crossed the tiny village and set up final approach to the helipad that was a scant quarter-mile away. The HH-3 settled, holding her course directly toward touchdown. The ground wind was very strong, but it held steady for four or five seconds and that was all the major needed to fly the Jolly directly onto the ground.

The side door was already open with the safety bar in place. Sergeant Prevost looked back toward the village, and saw the advancing lights of some kind of vehicle. In his judgment it was at least Phase One, but the flight out was over and it was always shorter going home.

Less than a minute later Major Kimsey jumped to the ground in time to meet Dr. Henrik Pedersen, whose long lean frame was partially encased in a well-worn parka. "My prayers are answered," the physician said. "I have her here in the truck. She is sedated, but I very much fear that she is in serious danger. From rabies; Dr. Markley will know that already."

"Have you talked with him?"

"Not from tonight, but he understands the great danger of that virus up here. Almost always it is fatal, but if she can be saved, he has the facilities and the knowledge."

The nurse came out of the opened rear ramp and joined the men.

"Are you coming back with us, doctor?" Major Dashner asked.

"With you to care for the patient, I can stay here, and I am needed. In just a few hours, I have a delivery. It will have to be Caesarean and there are some complications."

Two fur-clad Eskimo men slid a litter out of the truck and carried it to the helicopter. Sergeant Prevost directed them and with another crewman rigged it into position.

"What is the patient's name?" Linda Dashner asked above the noise of the turbines.

"She is called Bebiane Jeremiassen. She is eight years of age. Three bites, several lacerations. I have given Demerol. If she needs anything further during the flight back, you have my permission to administer it."

"Very well, doctor."

The Danish physician produced an envelope from one of the pockets of his parka. "I have here written everything I can for Doctor Markley, and it is for you to read also. Now hurry, please, for her condition is not good."

"Good night, doctor, thank you," Major Kimsey said and went back into his aircraft. The rear ramp had already been closed and the main rotor was still turning. He checked to be sure that the patient had been properly secured and then climbed quickly into his own seat. The girl looked so tiny and pathetic underneath the blankets that had been wrapped around her, he wondered how much the hospital could do for her. But his part came first. "Checklist," he ordered while he was still fastening his harness.

Within a minute the main rotor was whirling powerfully, the twin turbines splitting the blackness of the night with their blast of sound. Then the helicopter rose into the air, turned quickly almost in a hover, and began to climb rapidly toward the south. "Gear up," Seligman reported. A gust jolted him so hard his teeth collided, but they were high enough now so that they could not be flung back down against the ground.

As soon as he had 2,000 feet, Major Kimsey called Thule and advised that he was on the way back. Thule acknowledged and warned that conditions had deteriorated since the flight had departed.

"How do you read me?" the major asked.

"Three-by-three, proceed with your message."

"Advise Major Mulder to have the hangar open as soon as we touch down. Have the ambulance inside. We will taxi directly in after landing; ear protection will be necessary in the area."

"Understood. Wilco. Over."

"No further message. Out."

Major Linda Dashner was pale and perspiring — the beginning symptoms of airsickness — but she was making a determined effort to take care of her patient. The frequently violent movements of the aircraft made it almost impossible for her to keep her footing beside the litter. Ferguson saw her problem and responded; he braced himself as securely as he could and then held her around the waist. It was less than entirely satisfactory, but it worked well enough. The fact that he had not been that close to a woman in months might have affected him, but the incessant gyrations of the helicopter wiped every other circumstance out of his mind. When he could, he looked at his wristwatch and counted off the agonizingly slow minutes that were passing.

The little girl lay on her back with her eyes closed. Despite the injection she had been given, she stirred quite a bit and once her eyes opened for a brief moment. They would have been attractive, almond-shaped eyes if they had not been clouded by pain, bewilderment, and shock. Emergency dressings had been applied to several places on her small body; the nurse checked them and replaced two that were blood-soaked. There were clear tooth marks on one side of her jaw; when Major Dashner saw them she pressed her lips together, looked at Ferguson, and shook her head. "That's very bad," she said.

"If she needs blood —" Ferguson began.

The nurse interrupted him. "I wouldn't dare to rig it, not in this turbulence. Only as a last resort." She checked in her kit and prepared a fresh injection of Demerol in case it would be needed. "If something happens," she explained, "I want to have that ready."

"I'm sure we'll make it," Ferguson said. He looked once more at his watch and was immensely grateful that eleven minutes had been ticked off; every additional minute that they flew on reduced the risk and brought their arrival back at Thule closer. Although he was not qualified in rotary-wing

218

aircraft, he had to admire the technique of the pilots who were successfully battling the worst flying weather he had ever experienced. Every few seconds the cabin would pitch with alarming suddenness in one direction or another, but the men up front recovered each time. They couldn't rely on the automatic flight control system; the weather was far too bad for that. They had to be flying by hand—and under instrument conditions that were close to intolerable.

To keep his mind occupied, he concentrated his attention on the thin little patient who had been so savagely mauled. He tried to evaluate her chances of recovery; as far as he could see she should be all right if they got her into the hospital within the next hour. He focused his mind on the toughness of the Eskimo people; they were continuously exposed to severe conditions and their physical stamina was remarkable. Young and little as Bebiane was, that heritage could help her.

When he realized that Linda Dashner was beginning to have stomach convulsions, he handed a wax-lined bag to her just in time. She seized the bag, thrust her face into it, and allowed the contents of her stomach to discharge. After a few seconds she coughed and then vomited again; the bag was already full. Sergeant Prevost provided another while Ferguson, whose own stomach was giving him considerable trouble, disposed of the full one in the aircraft's trash container.

"Feel better now?" he asked.

The unhappy young woman nodded her head enough to answer him as she fought to regain her self-control. Every motion of the aircraft was agony to her; she bent over and made use of the fresh bag, gasping for air as she did so. With Prevost's help, Ferguson got her to sit down and strapped her in. The little Eskimo girl was quiet, mercifully unaware of the stormy ride she was enduring. As the flight nurse sat with her head almost between her knees, the helicopter changed attitude and Ferguson realized that they were beginning to descend.

Major Kimsey called the tower to report himself eight minutes out. This time the communications were distinct and clear; he was told that the hangar would be opened as soon as he was down and that the ambulance, with Dr. Markley, was waiting inside. The base was approaching Phase Two status. The controller gave him clearance direct to the hangar, then he alerted the fire and crash equipment, telling them the approach the helicopter was going to take.

At four minutes before the ETA, the emergency equipment rolled into position on each side of the hangar doors, out of the way but ready to respond immediately if necessary. Eighty seconds later the landing lights of the incoming aircraft could be seen.

It was almost over then, but the very last part could be the worst. Major Kimsey flew directly across the field at two hundred feet, slowed, and began to let down. For a moment the helicopter almost broke out of control, then it straightened and kept up its angle of descent. Six feet above the ramp it went into hover; fighting the heavy wind, it eased down, and then dropped onto the ramp. As soon as the wheels had hit the concrete, a dozen parka-clad men ran to help control it on the ground. The aircraft turned and then headed toward the bright welcoming lights less than a hundred and fifty feet away. The major cut the turbines to idle and let the rotors slow down as the ground crew pushed his aircraft forward. As the wheels crossed the threshold of the hangar, he shut the turbines down and applied the main rotor brake.

Sergeant Prevost dropped the rear ramp and the doctor came aboard. Under his direction the litter was moved to the ambulance; the patient was on her way to the hospital very shortly thereafter.

Since their part was now over, the men of Det. 4 took time to catch up with themselves. Major Dashner was installed in a deep, comfortable chair where she could remain perfectly still—the most effective relief she could have. Ferguson followed her example; it had been a very rough ride and he was ready for a little peace and quiet himself.

Dick Mulder met Kimsey as he came off the aircraft. "How was it?" he asked.

"We went and we came back — that's about it."

Bob Seligman deplaned and headed for the latrine. He had taken a considerable beating too; it had not been easy in the cockpit.

In the hospital, little Bebiane Jeremiassen, undergoing careful examination, lay very still on the table in one of the two operating rooms. Captain Markley, the internist, was working over her while Captain Bowditch, the surgeon, stood by to suture her wounds. Both available nurses were on hand to assist.

"I don't like this," Markley said. "I understood that she had been attacked early this evening in Kanak. Apparently that isn't the case. I think we should try to raise Dr. Pedersen and get a fuller history."

At that moment there was a tap on the door. That was most unusual; the operating areas were kept immaculately clean and no outside personnel were admitted. One of the nurses responded and came back with an envelope. "Sergeant Prevost brought this," she said. "It's from Dr. Pedersen; they forgot to give it to you in the hangar."

Markley tore it open quickly and began to read. As he did so, added evidence of concern shadowed his smooth, youthful face. "Here's the answer," he said. "She was hurt more than three days ago when she was out with her family at a hunting camp. They brought her in the best way they could, but Pedersen didn't see her until earlier tonight. Apparently she also had some sort of mishap on the way — that would account for the fresh bleeding."

He read on before he continued. "Pedersen is very concerned about rabies, of course. Besides the face, she was bitten in two other places."

"Did he give her a Pasteur shot?"

Markley nodded. "Yes, and we'll continue the series, of course, but that three-day interval before she was treated has got me scared."

Bowditch saw no reason not to state it plainly. "With a bite on the face, that close to the brain, the incubation could be fairly rapid, too. And I don't see any way to get the head of the dog for lab work. They may not know which one it was that actually bit her."

"There may have been more than one, since there was a pack. Bob, I think we'll have to assume that the animal was rabid, since sixty percent of them are. Go ahead and get those lacerations cleaned up, irrigated, and sutured. Meanwhile, I'll try to get her stabilized."

"Right." Bowditch began his careful, skilled work while his patient was still well under the merciful influence of the Demerol. For close to an hour he repaired the damage as continuous information on her vital signs was supplied to him. When he had done everything that he could at that stage, he emerged from the operating room to find Colonel Kleckner waiting outside. Scott Ferguson was there too, and three of the men from Det. 4.

Bowditch dropped into a chair and removed his surgeon's mask so that he could talk more easily. Like Ferguson, he was also a very young man, slender almost to the point of being lean, but he knew his profession and he had the hands to practice it. "I'm damn glad that you got her in here tonight," he said. "If you hadn't, it might have been a lot worse. I've just cleaned up all of the lacerations. At her age, and in her general physical condition, they shouldn't cause too many problems."

"How about rabies?" the colonel asked.

"The question is whether Dr. Pedersen saw her in time. She was bitten on the face more than three days ago, which may have injected the virus very close to the brain. Frankly, Herb and I are very worried about that."

"If she has it, what are her chances?" Ferguson asked.

"To be honest, very poor. Rabies in humans has always been considered to be a hundred percent fatal, but there is a treatment now and a recovery was reported in 1971. We're going to give it everything we've got."

The colonel was visibly concerned. "How about it, Bob, are we equipped to use that procedure here if it becomes necessary? If not, the moment the weather permits I'll have her transported in the C-130 to any facility you specify."

Ferguson didn't wait to let the surgeon answer. "If it's critical, we can get out of here tonight. We have the range to clear this storm and lift her directly to Walter Reed or wherever you say. Shall we get ready?"

Bowditch quickly shook his head. "I don't think she should be moved, and we have almost everything here. We're going to watch her on a minute-by-minute basis; if she shows any signs of going into fasciculation, then I'm sure that Herb will immobilize her. If it gets that far, then our respirator won't be adequate; we'll have to have a Bennett MA-1. They've got one at Dronning Ingrid's Hospital in Godthaab. We can ask for it along with a catastrophic team; there'll be time enough for that."

"Will they respond?" the colonel asked.

"Absolutely. The patient is a Greenlander, which means a lot to them. But they would come anyway."

Throughout the rest of the night an intense watch was kept over the tiny Eskimo girl; Markley broke his sleep three times to check on her condition and to instruct Captain Debra Lyons, who was continuously at her bedside. Fortunately, the only other patient in the hospital was an Army man recuperating from a cracked rib, and his condition imposed no problems.

At 1100 hours the following morning Linda Dashner, who had taken over from the night nurse, noticed that her patient coughed twice within five minutes. Normally that would not have unduly concerned her, but because she knew exactly what to watch for, she called the doctor.

Markley responded quickly and examined Bebiane's throat for visible evidence of soreness. "I've got to talk to her," he said. "Some of the Danes here can speak Eskimo; I need one as soon as possible. Commander Kure will know."

Linda left quickly and picked up the nearest phone. Fifteen minutes later Karsten Thorlund appeared at the door of the sickroom. "You speak Eskimo?" Markley asked.

The Dane nodded. "That I do."

"Good. Introduce yourself and explain that I want her to answer some questions."

The internist could not understand a word that was spoken, but he saw that communications had been established. "Does your throat feel sore?" he asked through the interpreter.

His little patient slowly nodded her head.

He smiled at her. "How about something to eat? We have good food here."

After that had been translated, the child rolled her head a minimum amount on the pillow. Markley looked at Linda. "Note loss of appetite." Then he turned back to Bebiane. "Do you have a headache?" he asked.

This time the answer came verbally. "She says a little," Thorlund translated.

"Ask her if she has any feeling of nausea."

"Doctor, she may not know what that means."

"Then ask her if her stomach feels all right."

Thorlund took longer to get the answer to that. "She does not feel good, but she says that is because she hurts all over. She asks that her father not kill the dogs because they will be needed this winter."

Markley drew Linda aside. "Watch for any indications that she is unduly sensitive to either noise or light. Also, I want you to offer her a drink of water, milk, or whatever at least every half hour. I want to know if she accepts any liquids, or if she displays definite rejection. And if you note any excess salivation, notify me at once."

"Yes, doctor."

"I will stay," Thorlund volunteered. "It may help her to talk to someone. And if she wishes to say something to the nurse, I can translate."

"Thank you — I much appreciate it."

"I do not mind, doctor; there is no place to go."

When the lunch tray arrived, the child perked up and ate a little. After that she rested quietly until shortly after 1500 hours; then she motioned to the man who could understand her and made a request. Thorlund translated for the nurse. "She says that the light in the ceiling is hurting her eyes. She asks that you turn it off."

Linda stepped to the switch and obliged. She checked her patient to be sure that she was all right, then she stepped out and called Markley at once. As soon as the internist had that fresh bit of news, he picked up his phone and dialed Weather. "What are the chances of getting a flight in here tomorrow if we have to?" he asked.

"Tomorrow should be all right," the duty forecaster told him. "We expect diminished winds, well below Phase Alert. However, we have another storm coming in, probably in a day or two."

"Thank you." That much, at least, had been good news. The doctor hung up for a moment and then called the base operator. "I want to talk to Dronning Ingrid's Hospital at Godthaab," he said. "Medical priority."

"Right. Call you back, sir."

Markley crossed to Bowditch's office to fill his colleague in. "Right now it doesn't look too good," he said. "She's got a slight sore throat, very little appetite, and she just asked to have the ceiling light in her room turned off."

Bowditch considered that. "Indicative," he agreed, "but fortunately not conclusive. She was pretty badly mauled and she had a rough time of it until Pedersen was able to give her that Demerol. Then she had a Pasteur shot, and I did quite a bit of work on her. All that could cause a loss of appetite and contribute to a sore throat. And she may simply have gotten tired of staring up at that light."

"Is that your honest medical opinion?" Markley asked calmly.

"It's one way of looking at it."

The young internist took a deep breath and let it out again. "All right, but I've got a call in to Godthaab to alert them that we have at least a fifty-percent chance of a case of human rabies here. If the symptoms persist, or if I get any new indications, I'm going to ask them to send their Bennett up here."

"With a team?"

"Yes. The moment that she shows the first sign of muscle spasms, if she does, I'm going to immobilize her."

"Tough on the patient."

"I know it, but not as tough as losing her young life. And that's what I'm facing now." He heard the phone ring on his desk and he hurried to answer it. While he was talking, Bowditch pushed a cart of supplies down the corridor himself on his way to check on the lacerations that he had repaired the night before. There was visible reddening around one of the spots where the girl had been bitten; as soon as he discovered it, he sent word to Markley.

Less than an hour later the hospital at Godthaab called back; the chief of staff there asked for the latest report. Markley confirmed that his patient was already showing many of the classical symptoms of rabies. She had been given her second Pasteur shot, but the indicated treatment probably had been started too late.

As Markley finished reporting, Bowditch was back and touched him on the arm. "She refused water, and when the nurse set it on the table beside her, she deliberately knocked it away."

For a second Markely looked ashen, then with his voice a little tighter than usual, he reported the new information over the telephone.

"We will set up a team immediately," the chief of staff at Godthaab advised. "They will start up in the morning and will bring our Bennett with them. When do you plan to immobilize?"

"At the first sign of muscle spasms."

"Good—I concur. Look for our people tomorrow afternoon. Will you need them sooner?"

"No, doctor—we have a small respirator here that is good for several hours."

"You have enough curare? I can send some."

"We have the curare. Doctor, thank you for this help; if I have to immobilize her, then your team will be essential as well as your respirator. How are they coming?"

"Helicopter to Sondrestrom; there we have a Twin Otter, ski-equipped, to make the flight. Please keep us advised on your patient's condition."

Markley promised that he would and broke the connection. He looked up to see Major Valen waiting in front of his desk. "May I see your patient?" the chaplain asked.

The young internist knew better than to refuse that; he took the major down the hall and ushered him into the room. Valen bent over the bed where the little girl lay, offering her a confident smile as he did so. She was clearly a plucky little thing and without the disfigurement of the bite, her small, Oriental-type face was appealingly attractive. When he began to talk with her through Thorlund, she asked if her family was all right and how the hunt was going.

Valen stayed only briefly; then he announced, "I'm going to the chapel." Markley understood and nodded his appreciation; then he went back to work.

The watch was kept, uninterrupted throughout the night, as Bebiane slept. In the early morning she appeared somewhat

227

better: she no longer had a headache and she ate moderately well, though for only a short time.

At almost the same time, a Sikorsky S-61 sitting on the helipad at Godthaab was loaded with the Bennett respirator bound for Thule. As soon as that vital piece of equipment had been stowed, Dr. Rasmus Lindegaard, the thoracic surgeon on the staff of the Dronning Ingrid's Hospital, boarded the helicopter together with the three chosen nurses: Grethe Morgensen, Vibeke Toft, and Helle Nielsen, all of whom were specially qualified in the use of the Bennett.

As soon as the passengers had been seated and secured, the pilot increased the power, made a final check, and then lifted off the ground. In less than five minutes he was at his cruising altitude and headed north toward Sondrestrom.

During most of the morning there was no significant change detected in the condition of Bebiane Jeremiassen. Four of the men from Det. 4 came to see her and brought some little gifts they had bought for her in the BX. J Site phoned down for a bulletin. Scott Ferguson put in an appearance with a bag of candy. Since children were rare exceptions at Thule, there had been nothing available that was any more suitable. He sat with her a little while, but she did not know him and they could not converse in any common language. He left when he saw that the child was restless and that he was contributing nothing to her welfare.

A call came in that the helicopter from Godthaab had arrived at Sondrestrom and that the transfer was being made to the Twin Otter. Dr. Pedersen at Kanak was brought up to date. Major Kimsey checked with the hospital as to the advisability of laying on a trip to the Eskimo village to bring back Bebiane's parents and possibly some other members of her family. Dr. Markley gave a qualified response, saying that her family could see her as long as her condition remained relatively stable. Invisibly, but powerfully, much of the life at Thule began to revolve around that one hospital room where a

228

small Greenlander girl might or might not be critically ill. There were many fathers on the base, Danish and American.

Then, with abrupt suddenness, the issue was decided not long after 1200 hours. Since his patient had been resting as comfortably as could be expected, and no immediate developments were expected, Captain Markley had left the hospital for the mess hall and a hot meal that he badly needed — he had been exceedingly hard pressed for the past thirty hours. But he had only been eating for a minute or two when he was urgently summoned. He rushed out, jumped into his vehicle, and was back with his patient in hardly more than five minutes. In the sickroom he found Bowditch with two of the nurses. Muscular spasms had begun. That deadly symptom wiped out the last remaining doubt; he knew then that his patient did have rabies and, despite the courage that still showed in her frightened little face, she was almost certainly doomed.

Thrusting that fact out of his mind, he went to work without a wasted motion. As he checked the patient rapidly yet carefully, he was brought up to the minute on the little girl's vital signs and condition. She was squinting her eyes against the overhead light and it was evident that a savage new kind of pain had entered into her slim body.

Markley gave swift orders. "Linda, get that light off and rig an IV. Bob, please check on the respirator and get it in here as soon as you can. Debra, I'll need the curare. And tell Thorlund that I want him immediately."

Bowditch opened the closet where the small respirator was ready and waiting. "I've already checked it out," he reported. "And the curare is right here."

He had just finished speaking when Thorlund appeared. "Listen," Markley said to him. "I want you to explain to her that we are going to stop the pain and the spasms. To do that, we're going to put her almost to sleep. She won't be able to move — not a muscle of her body. She won't even be able to breathe for herself; the machine will have to do it. But try to convince her not to be frightened or to worry. I'm sorry, but it's the only way I can treat her now."

The Dane bent down over the small, prone figure and spoke to her for half a minute in her own language. As he did so, her eyes came wider and there was fright in them; Markley had foreseen that, but there was nothing whatever he could do. She had to be told, otherwise she might become so terrified that she would lose her reason. Finally, through her growing agony, she said something in reply.

Thorlund straightened up to translate it. "Doctor, she says that she understands. She knows about the dog bite disease and despite what I explained to her, as you said, she accepts that she is going to die."

Markley clamped his teeth hard together. "Tell her that isn't so, God willing. Not if I can help it."

For a moment the protracted tension he had been under, and the extreme gravity of the situation he now faced, very nearly got to him. He hung on by the force of his will augmented by the full knowledge of the responsibility that he would now have to assume. Then the strength of his temperament and the discipline of his profession restored him and he was ready to do battle. He did not even hear the subdued PA system when it came on, and the announcement of Phase Alert was blocked out of his brain.

CHAPTER FIFTEEN

ON THE POSTING board at Thule Operations the Twin Otter was shown inbound with the tail number, the pilot's name, and the estimated time of arrival. The ETA was an intelligent guess that would be corrected with the swipe of an eraser as soon as the aircraft made its first contact and reported. In the remarks column, MEDICAL EMERGENCY was lettered in colored chalk. Everyone knew that already, but the Thule Ops people did things right and according to the book.

When the Phase Alert was called, Operations immediately got in touch with Sondrestrom and asked for a report from there. It was not encouraging: another storm was moving in and conditions were deteriorating rapidly. Sondrestrom Operations promised to advise Thule at once of any changes.

Thule also asked for immediate reports on any contacts made with the Twin Otter.

As soon as that call had been completed, the duty NCOIC called Major Eastcott and advised him of the circumstances. The operations officer asked to be kept up to date on a minute-by-minute basis. Then he called and got a status report on the C-130. It was just out of a periodic inspection, fully operational, and ready to go.

His next call was to Det. 4, where he talked with Major Mulder for several minutes. The two field-grade officers agreed completely on the developing situation: the Twin Otter was a very rugged bird, the pilot was widely known as an Arctic expert, and there was no reason for undue concern.

Eastcott called Weather and got the latest word from there. Nothing new had come in within the past twenty minutes and the Phase Alert stood. Meanwhile, Base Operations notified the tower and then called the hospital.

One of the nurses took the call. She advised that both doctors were unavailable and that the dental surgeon was tied up with a patient. Operations asked that the physicians be notified, when possible, that a weather situation had developed. Word from the Twin Otter was expected shortly — as soon as it came in, the information would be passed along.

While this was going on, Dr. Markley was fully engaged with his patient — he didn't have a minute for anything else. When he, Bowditch, and the nurses had her ready, the internist took the syringe of curare and, turning the little girl over, he made a careful, expert injection into the upper right quadrant of her right buttock. As soon as he had done that he turned the child back over and then smiled at her to give her the confidence she would so desperately need to have within the next few minutes. He spoke to Thorlund, who, in turn, translated his words for Bebiane. Through the Dane he told her that she would feel her body begin to become stiff, that she would not be able to use her muscles, and then very soon she would find that she was falling asleep. He hoped to Almighty God that this last statement was true, because if she remained conscious she might be confronted by stark terror. He had already resolved that if he detected any evidence of consciousness in her, he would put her under and keep her there. When Bebiane slowly nodded that she understood, Debra bent over and fitted the respirator hose over her face. After that had been done, the girl looked up with frightened eyes. Markley countered that by laying his strong hand on top of hers to loan her some of his courage and understanding. He continued to offer his comfort until the powerful drug began to take hold. Then he withdrew and let the nurses carry on.

He stepped out into the corridor and motioned Thorlund to follow him. "Karsten," he said, "thank you for all you've done. You can take it easy now, for a while. During the time that she's immoblized she won't be able to speak and probably she won't be able to hear either."

"I heard you say curare, doctor — is that not a poison?"

Markley nodded. "Yes, it's the same stuff they use on arrows in South America. But it has a very important medical use — it can paralyze a person so that he cannot make the slightest movement. That is what I have just done to her. By keeping her totally still, it stops the spasms and prevents the disease from literally tearing her apart. If we are very lucky, the disease may burn itself out. If that happens, she can recover."

"For how long must she lie so still?"

"Possibly two weeks — or three."

"Can she endure that?"

Markley hesitated to answer the question despite the fact that it was a reasonable one. But it was sure to arise again. "I think so. Essentially the same technique has saved patients with tetanus, and the spasms produced by that disease are unendurable. Most of the time she should be unconscious, which will help immensely. The only alternative, according to present knowledge, is to let her die."

Thorlund nodded slowly. "Then I say that you have done the right thing. I go now to pray for her."

"We all will," Markley said. He went back to his desk, knowing beyond any question that he had taken the only step that he possibly could, but he would nevertheless worry every minute until his little patient had been put on the Bennett and it had taken over the essential job of respirating her body. The small portable machine that was already at work would be able to do the job for a little while, but it had been designed for short use only and its capability was limited to a few hours.

He could safely go and get his interrupted lunch now, but he had lost his appetite. Bowditch was looking at him. "I prescribe some medicinal spirits," the surgeon said.

"I'll think about it," Markley answered.

Frank Tilton, the Information Officer, was keeping up to date on everything, which was his job. Consequently, he happened to be the one who put a call in to Weather just in time to receive a considerable jolt. Angelo, the forecaster, spoke to him only briefly; he was intensely busy. "It looked all right until above five minutes ago," he said. "New data has come in and I'm drawing a fresh map right now."

"Which means what?"

"We have a strong storm inbound; it came out of nowhere and it's gaining rapidly. We'll probably have a Phase One shortly."

"Can a Twin Otter fly through that?"

"Probably, if it doesn't get any worse. No guarantees right now on anything. That's it. Good-bye."

Tilton hung up, crossed the hallway, and asked to see the colonel. Seconds later he was in the commander's office, where he passed on the fresh information he had just been

234

given. Colonel Kleckner listened and then immediately called Det. 4. "It's a new ball game," he said. "There's an inbound storm that's picking up speed and it could be severe. Sondrestrom is also in bad shape. I suggest that you put your unit on alert status, just in case."

"Yes, sir—immediately."

"Thank you." The colonel hung up. "Get me Mike Kane," he directed. The Transportation Officer answered that summons promptly and stood waiting for orders. "Has transportation been laid on for the incoming medical people and their equipment?" Kleckner asked.

"Yes, sir, it has."

"Good. I understand that the Otter is bringing a respirator that's urgently needed. Find out from Captain Markley how big it is and have enough people there to handle it."

"That's been done, sir. Everything is set up to be in position forty-five minutes before the final ETA. I'll be there myself to see that there aren't any hitches."

"Very good," the colonel said. "Notify me immediately of any changes."

"Yes, sir."

Base Operations called to advise that Jolly Two had returned from Kanak with the parents and family of Bebiane Jeremiassen. It had been another rough trip, but not as bad as last time. The Eskimos had accepted the helicopters as part of their cultural environment; with stoic immobility the Jeremiassens had ridden in it toward the military hospital where their daughter lay. Thorlund was there to meet them, and he surprised them with the news that the girl was still alive—they had known about the consequences of rabies long before the air base had been built. When he explained that special people and equipment were en route from Godthaab solely to help her, they were stunned and grateful. They had not dared to hope for so much. Dr. Pedersen, who spoke their language fluently, had prepared them for the worst.

In Operations, word came in from Sondrestrom: despite repeated calls on several frequencies, they had not been able to raise the Otter. Undoubtedly, due to weather conditions the plane had been flying close to the surface of the ice cap, consequently there was no radar contact. Sondrestrom further advised that weather there was in phase condition and the field had been closed to anything but emergency landings. Blind broadcasts with that information had been put out to the Otter on all frequencies that the aircraft would be likely to be guarding. It had been assumed that the pilot had experienced transmitter failure, something that usually managed to happen at the most inconvenient times possible.

Thule went on-the-air directly. There had been no contact with the Otter, but that had not been a cause of concern. A number of calls went out on all likely frequencies, including 121.5, which is internationally reserved for emergency use. There was no response whatever. When it had been determined that two-way communications could not be established, a special blind weather broadcast was put out and repeated several times. The pilot was also asked to climb to a higher altitude, if possible, so that the 360-degree radar at J site could obtain a fix.

The door to the operations room opened and Colonel Kleckner came in. "What have you got?" he asked. Before the NCOIC could answer him, the PA system called for attention. Phase One was declared. The colonel picked up a phone and called Weather. Because he was the colonel, he got through immediately. "Exactly how bad is it?" he asked.

"Definitely Phase Two is coming, sir. Right now we're damn glad that the Jolly is back in the barn. It looks bad for the Otter."

"Any chance of it letting up in the next hour or so?"

"Sir, I doubt it very much. This whole system came up right out of nowhere and we still don't know its extent. Sondrestrom is socked in; Alert is still open."

236

"I don't think the Otter could make it that far," the colonel said. "What's the latest map that you have?"

"Fifteen minutes old."

"I'm coming in to see it."

In the weather section the colonel studied the fresh weather map and then all of the available sequences. When he had done so, he was in full agreement with the forecasting staff. He went back into the operations section, called his headquarters, and declared an emergency alert. All personnel and equipment with rescue assignments or capability were ordered on standby.

The word was immediately passed to J Site; the radar center responded by putting its own Trackmasters and crews on alert status. The huge antenna that normally patrolled the hundreds of objects known to be in space, both artificial satellites and space debris, abandoned that vital duty and, dropping low, sent its powerful beam out over the ice cap. It swept across and back over a considerable arc, but no target return showed on any of the scopes.

The terminal was comfortably filled by the men who had been summoned to transport the medical personnel and the respirator to the hospital. Lieutenant Kane kept them there, awaiting some word that would allow him to make an intelligent decision. The ETA that was posted on the board crept closer. When it passed, the NCO on duty erased it and carefully printed in the word OPEN.

The minutes passed and slowly chained themselves into a half hour. The radio calls continued without response. Weather data was put out blind, together with all other available information. By now transmitter failure was almost a certainty, but it was entirely possible that the Twin Otter could still receive. At literally any moment the missing aircraft could appear over the edge of the ice cap. The field lights were turned on at maximum intensity.

At fifty minutes past the estimated arrival time, Colonel

Kleckner spoke to the operations NCOIC. "Raise Sondre-strom. Get the fuel load on the Otter, the cruising speed, and the rate of consumption if they have it."

"Yes, sir."

Sondrestrom had most of the figures readily available; another Otter pilot was keeping a news watch on their operations and he, of course, was fully familiar with the aircraft. He reported that the pilot had left with full tanks and that he had already computed the maximum duration time in the air: at 1827 hours the Twin Otter would be out of fuel.

The radio calls continued. J Site reported that still no radar echo had been received. No one thought of dinner. It was very quiet until the phone broke the silence. Dr. Markley was on the line. He was extremely anxious; he had his patient immobilized, and she could not stay alive without the Bennett respirator for many more hours.

The colonel checked once more with Weather. There were no new data to report.

Many times before in his career the colonel had stood by, awaiting an incoming aircraft that was long overdue. In combat situations that happened all the time, and to a degree he was hardened to it. This was a different matter, and fighting men who took their chances by choice were not involved. He walked up and down, thinking his own thoughts, until someone put a cup of coffee into his hand. He drank it without being aware of what he was doing.

At 1800 hours the quiet was like a thick, inert gas that filled the room. The transportation people were still standing by; Lieutenant Kane remained in the chair where he had been waiting for the past two hours. A new crew came on duty at the operations desk, but the men who had been relieved chose to remain. The colonel picked up the phone to communicate with J Site and put it down again; he knew perfectly well that they would call within seconds if they had anything at all.

The PA system came on with the announcement that Phase

Two was in effect. The colonel was notified that all persons on the base had been accounted for. Two Trackmasters were standing by the Det. 4 hangar for possible airlift onto the ice cap.

Silently, the colonel watched the clock, as did every man in the crowded terminal building; 1827 hours occurred when the sweep second hand reached the top of the dial and continued inexorably onward. It took no notice whatever — its function was to measure off the astronomical units called minutes and it did so tirelessly and without emotion.

The colonel knew that it was up to him to say what everyone knew. He gave it another five minutes and then made the announcement. "It can only be one thing," he said into the heavy silence. "Somewhere they're down on the ice cap."

There appeared to be nothing that could be effectively done at that moment except to maintain a listening watch on all likely channels. The weather was all but unflyable, even under emergency conditions. The colonel actually considered the possibility of an immediate search; nothing would be visible on the ice cap in the all-but-total darkness, but it might be possible to sight a flare — if someone was lucky enough to be fairly close to where the Twin Otter was down — or to pick up a radio signal too weak to have been heard at either Thule or Sondrestrom.

Colonel Kleckner — allowed to do so because he was the commander — donned his parka and stepped outside for a minute or two to survey the weather personally, with the eyes of a long-experienced pilot. He came back in, went to the operations counter, and said, "Get some Trackmasters down here to move these men to their quarters. There's enough visibility for that."

The NCOIC picked up a phone and passed the word. As he did so, the colonel was considering another possibility. The

Otter was ski-equipped and the pilot was widely known for his ability. In the face of severe weather warnings, he could very well have elected an intentional landing on the ice cap to wait for better conditions. As soon as they came, he would take off once more and complete the remainder of his flight to Thule. So it was entirely possible that once the weather lifted, the Otter might be inbound any time thereafter.

He very much hoped that was the case, for the sake of the little Eskimo girl more than anything else.

He called the tower and gave instructions to keep up a constant alert watch. The man on duty advised the colonel that he was doing just that. The phone rang and Major Mulder was on the line. He reported that Det. 4 was standing by on alert-status, ready to fly. Both birds were fully gassed and cocked; they could be off the ground minutes after the bell rang.

Angelo came in from Weather holding a fresh map he had just finished. Without unnecessary comment, he spread it out for the colonel to read. "It's too early to tell anything definite," he said, "but there's a possibility of an improvement by zero-six-hundred. Not too much of a one."

"When might we be down below Phase Alert?"

Angelo ran powerful fingers through his black hair. "I'd hate to say, sir, it might be twenty-four hours — or even more. Possibily less. I know I'm not being definite, but I honestly don't know."

The colonel respected him for that answer. "Are you going to stay on watch?"

"Yes, sir, I'm not going anyplace."

"Good. If I'm not here, raise me at my quarters the moment you have anything more to go on."

"Understood, sir. From this minute on."

The colonel went back to the operations counter. "Get me the commander at Sondrestrom," he directed. "Colonel Olsen."

240

The man on the communications desk raised a hand in the air. He continued to listen for almost a full minute, then he turned to speak. "Colonel Olsen was just on the horn to the Pentagon, sir; their operator patched me in so we would know what was going on. Sondrestrom reported that they had lost contact with the Otter, what its mission was, and that it was down on the ice cap. Colonel Olsen advised that they are going to mount a full blower search beginning at daybreak, or as soon after that as the weather allows. At present the field is closed and conditions are totally unflyable. None of the weather stations in the area saw this one coming—it just popped up out of nowhere."

"Cancel my request," the colonel answered, "that's all I need to know."

A Trackmaster rumbled up outside and the driver gave a blast on the horn. In response the colonel donned his parka once more and this time drew on his gloves. "I'll be at the hospital," he advised.

Shortly after 0700 hours the following morning, weather was downgraded to Phase One. Major Eastcott, who had been keeping very close watch, decided to his own satisfaction that the change had not been fully justified; it probably had been done to make the mess hall once more available. The major went down the hall and picked up Captain Boyd. "Let's go," he said.

"Right." The two men left together, unplugged the major's vehicle, and set out for a hearty breakfast. They might well need it before the day was over. The weather on the way to the mess hall was fierce and the winds rocked even the pickup truck as it made its way slowly down the partly obscured roadway.

Det. 4 was gathered around one of the long tables when they went inside, but Eastcott spotted Bowditch attacking a plate of ham and eggs and went to him immediately. "How's your patient, Bob?" he asked.

Bowditch stopped eating to reply. "She's Herb's patient; he's with her now. She's immobilized, probably unconscious, and no significant change. So far the small respirator is doing the job, but it can't hold out indefinitely."

"If it goes, what then?"

"Then Herb will have to bring her out of it fast. That will allow the spasms to start in again; after that it's only a question of time."

"Terminal, then."

Bowditch nodded. "If that happens, no way. It would be kinder to keep her under and just let her stop breathing. I can't suggest that, of course . . ."

"I understand." Eastcott went to the serving line and got his own food. Twenty minutes later, when both he and Boyd had finished eating, they took the truck to the flight line and entered the hangar where the C-130 was kept. There they found Ferguson and his whole crew busy getting everything ready. They had food packs and survival equipment to be dropped, portable radios, an extra load of blankets, a heater unit, and everything else that both Sergeant Stovers and Sergeant Holcomb had been able to think of that might be needed.

"I see you guys got here first," Eastcott said.

"We've been here since daybreak," Ferguson answered. "We mapped it all out last night. But you guys are welcome; we're going to need all the eyes we can carry, and relief pilots. That's you. We've already got full tanks and the bird is cocked."

"How about the rest of my crew?" Boyd asked. "They're coming down."

"We can probably use them, but we're going the moment that Ops gives the green light. Jenkins is down there now sitting on their necks."

The phone rang and Ferguson picked it up. "Get your ass down here on the double," Jenkins almost shouted. "Now!"

Ferguson grabbed the nearest parka, not caring whose it was, and dashed out the door. He had never heard Jenkins talk like that before and it put fire into his bloodstream. He almost burst into Operations to find his navigator holding a teletype in his shaking fingers. "From the Pentagon. Immediate orders to mount a maximum search with all available aircraft the moment the weather permits takeoffs. Scotty, *all available aircraft!*"

It took Scott Ferguson a second or two; he had painstakingly built a solid wall in his mind and he had to crash through it. "*The colonel*," he said.

"I've got a vehicle."

"Go."

Ferguson jumped into the pickup while Jenkins, moving with amazing speed for his weight, hopped into the driver's seat and hit the starter. Despite the hostility of the still savage weather, they made it to the administration building with total disregard of the high hazard on the roadways. Once inside, both men shucked their parkas and then consumed minimum seconds in presenting themselves at the outer office of the commander's suite. "Lieutenants Ferguson and Jenkins to see the colonel," Scott said to the duty sergeant. "Urgent."

"How urgent, sir? He's on the telephone."

"ASAP."

The sergeant disappeared inside and was back in fifteen seconds. He gestured them in. Ferguson forced himself to enter the inner office with decorum; Jenkins was so close behind him they almost collided. Colonel Kleckner, who was still on the line, smiled and waved them to chairs. Ferguson sat down on the edge of his.

For more than another full minute the colonel talked on. Neither of his visitors wanted to listen, but they got the gist of it anyway. McGuire had no better weather information to offer and all flights into northeastern Canada had been cancelled. McGuire had located another Bennett, but it was in use and could not possibly be spared. The search for an available unit was continuing. At last the colonel hung up.

"What's happened, gentlemen?" he asked.

Ferguson could not help himself; the forced delay had caused emotions to boil up within him that were beyond control. They had been too long suppressed and they almost erupted through his brain. "Sir," he said. "Read this!" He handed over the message.

Colonel Kleckner scanned it quickly. "I've already seen it," he responded. "I also know you've got your aircraft cocked and ready. And Det. Four is all set too."

"That isn't it, sir. Look again. It says *all available aircraft!*"

The colonel made his decision within three seconds. "Sorry, Scotty, I can't let you do it. You understand . . ."

Ferguson's eyes blazed. "God dammit, sir, we've got to! You know the score: you've got five people at least stranded somewhere out on the ice cap and one more here dying in the hospital if she doesn't get that respirator. The B-17 is low and slow if she wants to be and she's got the range — more than four thousand miles. That's twenty hours plus! Det. Four can't touch that. Sir, you can bust my ass if you want to, *but you've got to let us go!*"

The colonel didn't answer; instead he got to his feet. He led the way out of his office, said "Operations" to his sergeant, and paused in the lobby to get into his parka. "Have you got anything new from Weather?" he asked.

"Not yet, sir, any minute — we hope."

The colonel led the way to his staff car. There was no conversation as the three men got in and none as the colonel made the short drive to the operations building. He parked directly next to the door in the slot that was permanently reserved for him, then went inside.

Fortunately Angelo was bent over the operations counter.

244

The colonel tapped him on the back. "How soon?" he asked.

"Still not good, but substantial improvement in two to three hours, sir — possibly even less. Det. Four wants to go now."

"Negative. Where's Major Eastcott?"

"In the C-130 hangar, sir."

"I'll be there."

It still being officially Phase One, the colonel elected to walk the short distance. He entered the hangar and satisfied himself within one minute that every possible preparation had been made. Then he turned to Ferguson. "How long ago since you were in Hangar Eight?" he asked.

That was the fearful question that Ferguson had anticipated — because no one had been in the hangar for weeks, except for a few of the new people who had gone out of curiosity. He stretched the truth as far as he dared. "Not too long ago," he answered.

Colonel Kleckner gave him a careful look; then he said, "Let's go and see."

The three men went outside once more and battled the very stiff wind that was almost roaring down the flight line. Ferguson reached the personnel door of the hangar first and held it open. The colonel stepped inside, closely followed by Jenkins and Ferguson.

The overhead lights were on. In stately dignity the silent form of *The Passionate Penguin* stood with her wings widespread in the center of the concrete floor. Surrounding her there were at least a dozen men hard at work. One, with a flashlight, was checking the landing-gear wells. Four more were up on the wing checking gas caps and the upper cowl fasteners. As Colonel Kleckner approached the busy scene, Sergeant Feinberg, a confident smile on his massive face, came to meet him.

"Good morning, sir! The emergency supplies are en route; we'll be loading them within the next five minutes." He called loudly over his shoulder. "How's the cockpit check coming?"

"AOK," someone shouted in reply.

In the long, sometimes brilliant, military career of Colonel James Kleckner there had been many memorable moments, some happy, some not. He had them all impressed on his memory, but none of them had ever matched what confronted him then. He stood still, and he thought.

Sergeant Feinberg caught it and motioned to Ferguson. "May I see you a moment, sir?" he asked. He led the way over to the B-17 and stood under the wing. "My God," he said, "why didn't you tip me off! I didn't get the word until you were practically in the HQ building, and I had to set this up faster than anything I've ever done in my life. Actually four of the troops aren't even mechanics. We had the show going for all of fifteen seconds before the colonel came through the door."

"Is any of it real?" Ferguson asked.

"Of course it's real — all but the deadheads. I told them to go up and inspect the gas caps. We'll redo that, of course."

"You saw the message?"

"Sir, let's not waste time with childish questions. The colonel looks about ripe, let's hit him now." He strode across the floor. "Sir," he said to the colonel, "the moment we saw that message ordering all available aircraft to respond, we knew what that meant. Here are the emergency supplies now." Several more men came in as the door opened enough to admit a pickup truck piled with blankets and other equipment.

The colonel was not impressed; instead he walked over to the B-17 and began to make his own detailed inspection. He spent a full ten minutes. He smelled the fresh oil, checked the inflation of the tires by visual examination, and went over the flying surfaces in detail. By the time that he had finished, a small group of some ten or twelve qualified pilots, three of them civilian Danes, were gathered — watching.

246

Colonel Kleckner asked for a rag and wiped his hands. Then, quite calmly and in a normal voice, he addressed the men who were waiting breathlessly. "All right," he said. "In view of the all-important fact that a number of lives are on the line, it's my opinion that the new order we have received supersedes the old one from Norton. If it doesn't, they can argue about if afterwards."

He stopped and looked again at the venerable, yet new, bomber that had been so miraculously resurrected despite its thirty desolate years on the pitiless ice cap. "I see that you have added *United States Air Force* properly on the sides. That's important, because I'm sticking my neck out a mile and I know it. Ferguson, can you handle her all right?"

"Yes, sir!"

"Then Boyd will fly the C-130; he and his crew are down there now with Major Eastcott."

"Yes, sir — we know."

Sergeant Feinberg cleared his throat. "Captain Boyd is already aware, sir, that he will be taking out the C-130. I understand that Major Eastcott is going with him, as copilot."

"Speaking of copilots," Jenkins said, "we're honor bound to have a drawing. A lot of guys threw dollars into the pot when we needed the money for supplies. Some of them aren't here any more, but about ten of them are on hand right now."

"I'm more interested in who's qualified," the colonel said.

"Nobody was allowed to contribute who wasn't," Jenkins told him. "They wouldn't take my money, although I have a private license. It had to be commercial or better, with an absolute minimum of six hundred hours. And every man knows the airplane down to the last rivet."

Although he didn't say so, the colonel was perfectly aware that the B-17 had been designed with the knowledge that most of the pilots destined to fly it would be green and inexperienced. It had been made as simple as possible as a result. Few of the aircraft commanders who were assigned to them had a total of 600 hours when they first took over in the left-hand seat. "Go ahead and draw," he said.

Sergeant Feinberg did the honors. He produced the cardboard box that held the names and shook it vigorously. "Gentlemen," he declared, "it is now time for me to reveal that I happen to hold an FAA commercial pilot's license and I have well in excess of a thousand hours. So my name is in here a good many times." He beamed at the colonel. "Sir," he asked, "will you do the honors?"

"I would prefer to be kept out of it," the colonel said.

Sergeant Feinberg caught sight of Bill Stovers, who was just coming out of the fuselage after having checked everything there. "Pull a name, Bill," he invited.

Sergeant Stovers reached in an extracted a piece of paper. Since no one seemed anxious to take it from him, he opened it and read aloud. "Colonel James Kleckner," he announced.

CHAPTER SIXTEEN

WHILE WAITING FOR weather clearance, Major Eastcott laid out the search patterns to be followed the moment that conditions permitted takeoffs. Sondrestrom, at least for some time, would not be able to help; the field there was firmly closed down and the weather section at the scene held out no hope of improved conditions for at least twelve hours. With luck, the Thule rescue craft would be airborne long before that.

Of the four aircraft available, three could actually land on the ice cap: both of the helicopters and the ski-equipped C-130. The major was not at all sure that the B-17 would be permitted to fly, but he entertained no doubt that it could. In laying out the search patterns, he plotted the relatively short-ranged Sikorskys to cover the nearby areas. They were high probability sectors on his layout and if either helicopter made the find, it could set down and pick up the survivors immediately. He had plotted rescue efforts many times before, so the word "survivors" came automatically into his mind. But he did not for a moment forget the vital Bennett respirator.

The C-130 he scheduled to fly at a higher altitude, searching for a possible flare and keeping a constant listening watch in the hope of picking up even a very faint radio signal.

The B-17 — which had long-range capability and could maintain a safe slow speed — he assigned to an advancing line search back and forth across the ice cap at low altitude. That would be almost entirely a visual operation. He was glad that he had the old bomber to put to work; it was vitally needed. He knew without checking that there was nothing up at Alert that could come down to help out.

When he had his charts completed, the major called for a conference of the aircraft commanders. In response majors Kimsey and Mulder came up from Det. 4, Captain Boyd checked in for the C-130 crew, and Scott Ferguson came with Colonel Kleckner. In ten minutes Major Eastcott laid the whole picture out and made certain that each crew commander understood his individual responsibilities. Although the tensions inherent in combat situations are great, a coordinated rescue effort can reach even higher levels of emotion, and the air was charged with it. When Eastcott finished, he asked for a final status check. As he had expected, every man and every aircraft was ready and waiting; only the weather was holding things back.

A six-pack arrived from the mess hall with hot food for everyone. That was a welcome interruption, particularly since none of the aircraft commanders or crewmen had even contemplated leaving their duty stations to eat. The word also came that a supply of box lunches was being prepared and would be delivered to the flight line shortly.

By the time that the meal was over, it seemed to Colonel

Kleckner that the weather had definitely abated a little. Everyone else was constantly checking too, anxiously awaiting wind conditions that would be down enough to permit safe takeoffs. Det. 4 once more wanted to go immediately and once more the colonel refused permission. He had one urgent rescue situation on his hands and he most emphatically didn't want any more.

At 1350 Weather called to say that operations might be possible in another one to two hours. That was regarded as definite and the tension in the terminal increased even more. Major Eastcott called the hospital and assured Captain Bowditch, who answered, that the air search would be launched shortly, and at the earliest possible moment.

Twenty minutes later, after his fifth trip outside since the weather announcement, Major Ramsey declared that the winds were off enough to permit helicopter takeoffs. Colonel Kleckner went outside with him to verify that, came back in, and said without dramatics, "I think we can get ready now."

The Thule flight line erupted into action. The Det. 4 hangar was the first one open; within two minutes after that the howl of turbines began to override the constant noise of the wind. From a little farther up the field, the blast of the APU on the C-130 Hercules added a fresh voice. And the main door to Hangar 8 was activated to permit *The Passionate Penguin* to be pushed out onto the ramp.

As the four mighty turbine engines of the C-130 began to add their full-throated roar to the cacophony of sound, for just a moment or two Scott Ferguson wished that he had power like that at his command. He was used to it and he knew what it could do. Then he purged that sinful thought out of his mind the way that a Puritan would have condemned adultery, and remembered that almost 5,000 horsepower was all that he could possibly want or need.

Andy Holcomb was busy making a totally unnecessary final exterior inspection of the B-17; it was in perfect condition

251

and he knew it. As he had many times before, particularly for the taxi tests he had made, Ferguson climbed up the crew ladder into the Boeing bomber, planted himself firmly in the left-hand seat, and secured the newly installed harness. It was familiar to him now, the whole flight bridge and cockpit: every control, every gauge, and every instrument. He moved the yoke backwards and forwards; then he turned the wheel and felt the balance of the movable surfaces.

Sergeant Stovers tapped him on the shoulder. "All set in the back," he said. It was odd seeing his familiar face in a strange setting; then he forced himself to remember that Stovers, his loadmaster on the C-130, was just as fully qualified on this older, smaller, slower, but dependable piston-powered aircraft. Jenkins came up the ladder with a grin on his face. "Dammit, she's beautiful!" he said.

A full sense of shame punished Ferguson for his heresy; he had asked for this, he had pleaded for it, and he had relinquished the C-130 to get it. He did not understand himself; he had wanted to fly this aircraft so badly. Then it came to him: the rescue was the thing — the all-important mission of saving human life. He had known too well that the Hercules was far better equipped, and that hammering thought had been plaguing the back of his mind. He wanted to make his utmost effort for the sake of the people somewhere out on the ice cap and for the helpless child he had last seen lying rigid in a coma in the hospital with an inadequate temporary respirator keeping her alive minute by minute. Out there somewhere there was a machine that might possibly be able to give her back her life.

God damn it, he had an airplane to fly, get on with it! Boyd and his crew would milk the C-130 for everything she could give and they knew their business. He felt the airframe move and moments later Colonel Kleckner came into the cockpit. "The winds are definitely down," he said quite cheerfully.

"They've fallen off noticeably during the last fifteen minutes. How does she look?"

"Full tanks and ready to go," Ferguson answered. "Andy Holcomb is making the final pre-flight; he'll be through any minute."

"Are there any checklists?"

"Yes, sir. We prepared a full set; you'll find them on cards right there." He pointed.

Ferguson looked out and saw Holcomb standing motionless, in front of the nose and a little to the left. Suddenly his whole world became the B-17 and he wanted to fly her more than any aircraft that had ever been launched.

"Pre-engine-start checklist," he ordered.

In response Colonel Kleckner began to read off the neatly typed items, Ferguson responding to each one.

"Checklist complete," the colonel said.

Ferguson showed Holcomb a thumbs-up sign through the windshield. In response the flight engineer looked quickly each way, then he whirled a hand in the "start-engines" signal. As he was replaced by Sergeant Feinberg, he ran around the wing, well out of range of the propellers, and climbed up the crew ladder. Moments later the first of the four piston engines barked into action. When it had blown back its thick burst of smoke and then settled down, Ferguson started number two. The power plant caught quickly and evenly.

Number three joined its voice to the mounting chorus. He started number four and the *Penguin* vibrated with life. "Pre-taxi checklist," he directed.

The colonel read off the few items and then said, "Checklist complete."

Ferguson fitted on his modern headset, adjusted the microphone in front of his lips, and called ground control. "Air Force three-six-zero, ready to taxi," he reported.

"Air Force three-six-zero, follow the Herc, please."

Ferguson chafed, but the instruction was right and he knew it; the C-130 would climb out at more than twice the speed of the B-17 and the big, turbine-powered airlifter had no need to run up and check the mags, propeller controls, and all that. He bent over to verify the mixture on number three and when he looked up again, one of the HH-3's was taxiing past. Since it wouldn't have to fly the pattern at all, it would probably be the first aircraft off the ground.

On the airframe a door opened for a few seconds and then closed. Ferguson pressed the intercom. "What was that?" he asked.

Stovers answered in a surprisingly crisp manner for him. "Sergeant Feinberg coming aboard, sir."

"Negative," Ferguson said. "No riders."

He expected Stovers to respond to that, but he didn't. A few seconds later Sergeant Feinberg himself appeared behind Ferguson's chair. The A/C moved one of his headphones so he could converse. "We didn't provide for you," he said. The moment the words were out he knew he had made a mistake.

"Yes, sir, you did — I saw to it myself." Feinberg read the expression on Ferguson's face and suddenly became forceful. "Look, sir, I can con you into it, but we don't have the time. Please!"

At that moment Stovers's voice came over the intercom again. "Feinberg is a scanner, sir — we need him."

The thunder of the C-130 taxiing past, its great turbines howling, cut out further conversation and relieved Ferguson from having to make a decision. Then ground control was calling. "Three-six-zero."

"Three-six-zero."

" 'Six-zero, Jolly Two will follow you. You are cleared to taxi behind the C-130. Runway three-four. Wind still gusting to forty knots, observe caution."

"Wilco, 'six-zero."

Ferguson pushed the throttles slowly forward and felt the

engines respond. The *Penguin* began to roll and with her forward movement came a certain stately dignity.

Colonel Kleckner was watching out of the side window, performing the copilot's duty. It had been a long time since he had occupied that position, but he knew every aspect of the flying business.

At the run-up area he had used before, Ferguson stopped, set the parking brake, and began his systematic check of the engines. He had no analyzers, so he did without them. He ran each engine individually up to 1,800 rpm and then checked the mags: left, both; right, both. After each runup he cycled the propeller and took great delight in the fact that every response was close to perfect; he knew that the colonel would miss none of it. The biggest mag drop he got was 75 rpm, which was well within limits. Not bad after thirty years on the ice cap!

He switched the VHF transceiver to 126.2 and called the tower. He was told to stand by. "Jolly One, cleared for takeoff."

"Jolly One." He watched and saw the Sikorsky lift off and then climb upward, doing what would have been considered impossible when the first B-17 had been rolled out.

As soon as the helicopter was clear of the pattern, the C-130 called in. "Thule tower, Herc ready to go."

"Herc cleared for takeoff, procedure departure."

The turbines of the C-130 hurled shock waves of power across the field as the airlifter moved forward, gained speed, held its heading on the runway, and then rotated. It came off like the great bird that it was, climbing up into the sky with mighty authority.

The colonel used his microphone. "Thule tower, *Penguin* ready for takeoff."

That was like an electric shock to Ferguson: *Penguin ready for takeoff!*

"*Penguin* cleared to position and hold."

In reply Ferguson released the brake, added power, and

taxied onto the end of the runway. He looked down 10,000 feet of 150-foot-wide white pavement and knew that the moment of truth was at hand.

"*Penguin*, cleared for takeoff."

Ferguson nodded his head, fitted his hand underneath the throttle handles and pushed. As the bomber began to move, he continued to push until all four engines were wide open. The power plants roared and the propellers bit into the air.

The speed began to build; Ferguson held the yoke forward with his left hand and the tail lifted off the ground. The plane rode on her main landing gear as she accelerated, not as fast as the C-130, but fast enough. He felt her begin to lighten, the tires skipped slightly on the uneven surface of the runway.

Then, by that wonderful empathy that can exist between man and machine, he knew that she was ready. With both hands he eased back on the yoke and with magnificent smoothness, despite the gusting air, *The Passionate Penguin* lifted off the ground.

The runway fell away. She caught a bump but it did not disconcert her — she climbed steadily, boring upward. Ferguson's hands locked around the yoke and in an instantaneous flashback he remember the time he had stood on the ice cap, had looked at her in her frozen, lifeless immobility, and had dreamed that he was flying her out of her prison. Now, in a sense, he was. As a machine, the *Penguin* was working beautifully, like a brand-new piece of equipment fresh from the factory test-pilot's hands. The impact of the whole thing generated a powerful emotion in him — a feeling of strangeness combined with profound triumph. His spirit soared, and he knew that the all-but-impossible had been done and that now he was holding the yoke in his hands and living through an experience that no man had ever known before. The power of the engines accompanied his thoughts. Neil Armstrong could not have felt more exhilaration when he first set foot on the surface of the moon.

When he reached the nondirectional beacon, he checked his altitude and then turned her left, toward the ice cap that now held another aircraft that might or might not be in desperate need of help. The *Passionate Penguin* climbed higher into the troubled sky, responding to — but ignoring — the gusts that forced her to deviate from her established course. Ferguson flew her carefully, feeling her out, experiencing the solidness with which she pulled herself through the air.

He looked down at the immense ocean of ice that lay below him and then pressed the intercom. "Start visual scanning search," he ordered. "I want both sides covered at all times, from now on."

"Yes, sir." Stovers responded.

Against the stark blue of the Arctic sky, where it became visible, *The Passionate Penguin* flew on, a magnificent machine that responded to every command from her pilot.

With a nod Ferguson turned her over to Colonel Kleckner and then sat back, searching the immense ice cap, and letting the richness of life fill him. On the surface below, the winds were still treacherous, but here in the sky aboard his fine and wonderful aircraft, he heard the song of the angels.

CHAPTER SEVENTEEN

BRIGADIER GENERAL EVERETT PRITCHARD carried out his Pentagon assignment with distinction, but much of the time he wished strongly that he was back out in a field command. Technically he was no longer on flying status, but he still wore his command-pilot's wings atop the impressive display of ribbons on his uniform. Having made it his business to visit the various units over which he had jurisdiction as often as he was reasonably able, he had scheduled himself up to Thule and was planning his departure when he received word that that whole area was socked in by a more or less unexpected Arctic storm.

Armed with that information, he put in a call to his old friend Colonel James Kleckner to set up a new time for his visit. At Thule the call was transferred to Operations, where the NCOIC answered the telephone. He told the general's aide that a full-scale rescue effort was underway and that the colonel was personally taking part.

The line was held open while the general was informed. Immediately thereafter, the general picked up the phone himself to learn the details. When he had been given the story, he asked without hesitating, "Is there anything we can do from here to help?"

"I doubt it, sir," the Thule operations man answered. "Sondrestrom is closed and they report the whole area as unflyable. Hopefully, before any additional equipment could get up here, we'll have the job done."

"How many aircraft do you have out on search, Sergeant?"

"Four, sir."

"And what are they?"

The man at Thule had anticipated that possible question. "Two Jollies, sir, from Det. Four, a Hercules, and the *Penguin*."

"Thank you very much, Sergeant. I would like to be notified personally as soon as there is definite news."

"I'll pass that word, sir."

"Good-bye." The general hung up. A few seconds after he had done so, he turned to his aide, a resourceful young captain who had caught his eye some months before. "Sam," the general asked, "what is a penguin?"

"A penguin, sir?"

"A penguin."

The captain flushed slightly. "It's the Antarctic bird, of course, but could you give me a clue as to what kind of penguin we're talking about?"

"It's something that flies — military I presume, but it could be civilian."

"I'll check, sir, immediately." The captain left the office. He was back a few minutes later. "Sir, the Penguin is a

Norwegian ship-to-ship tactical missile. Do you need the specs?"

General Pritchard thought briefly. "That was pretty quick," he said. "Where did you get that information?"

"From the *Defense/Aerospace Code Name Handbook.* It's also listed in Taylor's *Missiles of the World*; I double-checked, sir."

"Nice work, but that isn't the penguin that I mean. There's another one, an airplane. The most likely bets are either Canadian or Danish, but I admit that I haven't heard of it — not that I recall."

"That's two of us, sir, but I'll see what I can find out."

The captain was gone for some time. When he did return he was slightly flustered. "Were you able to find it?" the general asked.

"Yes, sir, the library was able to dig it out. It took a little time because it's very obscure."

"I know, otherwise I would probably know of it. Anyhow, that's what's flying over the Greenland Ice Cap right now."

The captain shook his head. "No, sir, it isn't."

"Why not?"

"Because it couldn't fly."

The general looked at him. "Didn't you say that it's an airplane?" he asked. "Or imply it?"

"Yes, sir, I did."

"Are you trying to tell me that there's an airplane that can't fly?"

The captain swallowed. "Yes, sir, I am."

Then the general understood. "It was never operational — is that what you mean?"

"No, sir, it was fully operational. But it couldn't fly."

"Sam, has it occurred to you that you're not making sense?"

"Sir, let me explain. The Penguin was built by Bleriot during World War One."

"You mean 'Two.' "

"No, sir, 'One.' It definitely was an airplane, but its wings

260

were intentionally clipped so that it couldn't get off the ground. It was used to teach student pilots the feel of the controls at high speed. By that they meant forty-five miles per hour. So, sir, I doubt like hell if that kind of penguin is flying over the Greenland Ice Cap, and according to the best that the library has, that's positively the only airplane called 'a penguin' that was ever built."

General Pritchard thought briefly once more. "Get me Thule Ops," he said.

When the call came through it was a little hard to hear at the northern end because one of the Det. 4 Jollies was back for fuel and was making a considerable noise just outside on the ramp. "This is General Pritchard."

"Yes, sir!"

"First, is there any news concerning your rescue effort?"

"Not yet, sir, but everyone is going forward full bore. Everything possible has been laid on, sir."

"Good. Now you reported that one of the aircraft on the mission is 'a penguin,' is that correct?"

"Yes, sir."

"We don't seem to have a record of that aircraft here. First of all, who's flying it?"

"Lieutenant Ferguson and Colonel Kleckner, sir, and there's a relief pilot on board also — Lieutenant Corbin."

"And precisely what is it?"

That was it and the NCOIC was cornered. "The *Penguin*, sir, is a Boeing B-17E. She has more than a four-thousand-mile range and departed here on the mission with full tanks."

"Sergeant, did you say a *B-17?*"

"That is affirmative, sir."

"Where in hell did they get that?"

"It was in Hangar Eight, sir."

"In what kind of condition?"

"In perfect condition, sir. Zero time on everything when she took off, just out of a complete overhaul."

"And you said that Colonel Kleckner is flying her?"

"He's definitely on board, yes, sir."

"Thank you very much, Sergeant."

"You're welcome, sir."

As he leaned back in his chair, General Everett Pritchard was a little puzzled while he ran things quickly through his mind. The picture made no sense whatever, because if there had been a B-17 parked somewhere up at Thule for a period of years, he couldn't possibly have failed to be aware of it.

He picked up a telephone. "Get me General Miller," he directed.

Within a few moments his colleague was on the line. "Bill," Pritchard said, "I've got an odd one I'd like to ask you about." He sketched the situation at Thule and explained the emergency rescue attempt. "Now comes the strange part," he concluded. "When I asked them for a fuller ID on that 'penguin,' they reported back that it was a B-17. Repeat, a B-17, apparently named *'Penguin.'* Just as a starter, to the best of my knowledge no B-17's were ever at Thule. Do you know anything about this?"

It was quiet on the line for several seconds before General Miller answered. When he did, his words came slowly and carefully. "I might, except for one thing — which makes what I have in mind utterly impossible."

What remained of the Arctic daylight was rapidly fading from the sky. Now well south of Thule, maintaining her systematic advancing line search of the ice cap, *The Passionate Penguin* was flying through increasingly rough air. Although his own mind was already made up, Ferguson called a council of war via the intercom. "We have a choice," he said. "We can return home and resume at daybreak, presumably in better weather. Or we can keep on going; there's plenty of fuel and we have the box lunches. However, at night the flying will be

262

more hazardous and we won't have enough visibility to pick up anything on the ice cap."

"Sir." Ferguson recognized the voice of Sergeant Feinberg. "Go ahead."

"We've already discussed that back here, and we're unanimous to continue. In the morning could be too late."

Ferguson looked at the colonel. "You, sir?"

"You're the A/C."

Ferguson raised Thule on the VHF. "Air Force three-six-zero," he reported. "Results negative to date. We will continue mission. Over."

"Three-six-zero, roger. All others continuing also."

"Any report from the hospital?"

"Nothing encouraging, sir."

"Thank you."

Ferguson got up and Corbin replaced him. He went back into the surprisingly small fuselage and used a relief tube. The heater was working full blast, but it was still cold inside the aircraft. There was no insulation of any kind and the temperature outside at more than 10,000 feet was frigid. The men who had been keeping a continuous lookout were uncomfortable, but were not complaining. Sergeant Stovers was posted on the port side, looking out the large window that had been intended to be replaced by a gun position. Opposite him there was a crew member Ferguson hadn't realized was on board—Atwater from Supply. "How about some coffee?" Ferguson inquired.

Andy Holcomb answered him. "I'm afraid it's all gone, sir, but we have drinking water. We brought plenty of that. Actually, there is some hot coffee, but we're saving it."

"I understand."

Ferguson broke open a lunch box, wrote his name on the cover, and extracted a piece of fried chicken. The cold food tasted good; he hadn't realized how hungry he was.

"Sir," Holcomb said. "She flies better than I had thought possible. She's a great airplane."

"Damn right," Ferguson responded. He looked out of the window, down onto the darkening ice cap, and tried to estimate their chances. "It's a helluva big area," he said, half to himself. "Immense. The *Penguin* was out in plain sight for thirty years and no one that we know of saw her."

They all knew that and no one commented. The wings began to bank as another systematic line search was concluded; slowly the aircraft turned ninety degrees, went further south for two minutes, then turned again another ninety degrees to resume the search pattern. The two lookouts got up and were immediately replaced. To keep outside vision as clear as possible, no lights were being used inside the plane except for the concentrated one above the navigator's desk. With his chart spread out before him, Jenkins kept careful, minute-by-minute track of the *Penguin*'s position. He had no LORAN receiver, but he did not need it; the newly installed TACAN was enough.

Ferguson looked over the shoulder of Sergeant Feinberg, who had taken up the watch on the starboard side. "Thanks for all you're doing," he said, making it a general comment.

"This is nothing," Feinberg answered him. "Think of J Site; if they can keep going on five different scopes more than eight thousand hours a year, who are we to complain?"

There was nothing to be added to that. Ferguson found a sandwich in his lunch box and bit into it. It was thickly cut ham. As he chewed, he wondered if the people stranded on the ice cap had any rations at all.

When he had eaten all that he wanted, and had drunk some water, he returned to the flight deck and relieved the colonel. He sat on the right-hand side, letting Corbin keep the command seat. The four engines were running smoothly, their combined thunder subdued because they had been pulled back into long-range cruise. The propellers were synchronized and despite the frequent moderate turbulence, they stayed that way. Idly, Ferguson wondered if they had crossed the spot where the B-17 had first been rediscovered. He could have found out by asking Jenkins, but he preferred not to know.

When it was completely dark he made a decision not to use the navigation lights; they might hamper the scanners. He looked out and saw that Corbin had them on. He was about to order them off when he changed his mind — it occurred to him that the people on the ice cap might be able to see a light when they couldn't hear the engines. They would be frozen, probably hungry, and completely miserable. He had no idea of the condition of the Otter, but any hope that it might have come in under its own power had long ago been abandoned. The B-17 reached the end of the search leg; Corbin let it go on for another five minutes on the odd chance that there might be something out there; then he turned. "Did you get that leg extension?" he asked Jenkins over the intercom.

"Yes, I did."

As he established the new heading, Ferguson called Thule once more. "Any news?" he asked.

"Negative, except for a call from the Pentagon."

"Have we a problem?"

"I don't think so. One of the Det. 4 birds is in for gas and a relief crew; it's going right out again."

"How about the C-130?"

"Still flying higher altitude patterns, west of you."

"Anything from the hospital?"

"No, but they keep calling, asking for news from us. I gather it's not good."

"Thank you."

The Passionate Penguin flew on. The night folded in around her, shrouding the ice cap and leaving her isolated in a black void. At hardly more than 160 miles per hour she absorbed the endless small bumps and continued on her heading.

Ferguson wondered how Jenkins was possibly able to plot her position; they were well out of the effective range of the DME and he had not done any celestial work; apparently he wasn't equipped for it. He pressed a button for the intercom. "Do you know where we are?" he asked.

"Yes." Then the navigator added a little heavily: "Over the ice cap."

The colonel reappeared on the flight deck. "How about a relief?" he asked.

Corbin answered him. "Take it easy, sir, for a while. We're all right."

Ferguson looked down and tried to see if he could distinguish anything. There were some slightly colored shadows, but he knew that if there was an aircraft sitting on the ice directly in his range of vision, he would not be able to see it. Number four engine fell slightly out of step and he made a minute throttle adjustment.

The intercom came on; Bill Stovers's voice was abruptly tense. "I have a flare, or what looked like one. Four o'clock, range two to three miles."

The ennui that had permeated the cold, narrow aircraft burst apart and surging excitement began to replace it. Ferguson repeated, "Flare at four o'clock, range two to three miles." He looked at Corbin, who lifted his hands off the yoke. Ferguson seized hold, banked into a precision turn, and counted off the seconds until he had completed 115 degrees; then he rolled her out almost exactly on the heading he wanted. He bent forward over the yoke, straining his eyes, and silently praying that it hadn't been a meteor. "We can signal with the landing light," he told Corbin. His copilot hit the switch; the powerful beam split the night sky, off and on several times.

In answer an unmistakable flare came up off the ice cap and hung in the air a little to the port side. Forcing himself to keep calm, and aware that the colonel was positioned directly behind him, he hit the transmit button. "Thule radio, this is Air Force three-six-zero."

"Three-six-zero."

"We have a flare off the ice cap, positive ID. Our position follows."

"Penguin 'six-zero, please confirm you have a find."

"That is affirmative, Penguin 'six-zero." He stopped and let Jenkins relay their position. Then he checked his altimeter, banked, and began a spiral descent as close as he could to the spot where the flare had appeared. The landing light cut a narrow cone as he reset the transceiver to 121.5 and called: "Otter on the ice cap, do you read? Otter, do you read?"

There was no reply. Holcomb came on the intercom. "He's probably got complete electrical failure, sir, and that would put him down at night — no instruments. And he wouldn't be able to start up again."

It all made sense then. Every man on board the *Penguin* was looking out, trying to see the unseeable. Ferguson leveled off as close to the invisible top of the ice cap as he dared; as he did so, Sergeant Stovers released a parachute flare. The brilliant light rebounded from the snow-covered ice mass, and Atwater, at the port-side scanning window, let out a yell, "There she is!"

Ferguson racked the *Penguin* around until he had the Otter in front of the nose, where he could see it clearly. One person was standing beside it; he presumed that would be the pilot who had fired the Very pistol. The aircraft, he noted, had a damaged wingtip.

He had no idea how that had happened, and he didn't care. As he flew directly over, he rocked his wings as an added reassurance. It never occurred to him to wonder what the pilot on the ground would think when he saw a B-17 overhead; far more pressing matters were on his mind.

Sergeant Holcomb's voice came into his headset. "On the next pass, we'll drop some supplies, through the bomb-bay door."

"Don't fall out."

"We won't."

He used the radio once more. "Thule, this is Penguin three-six-zero. The Otter has been sighted on the ice cap; there is at least one survivor."

He got a direct answer to that. "Penguin 'six-zero, this is Jolly Two. We are en route to your position. ETA thirty-six minutes."

Ferguson acknowledged. "Jolly Two, we will orbit this location at eleven thousand feet true altitude; please advise your altitude."

"Jolly Two to Penguin, we will approach at twelve thousand with landing light on. Advise when visual contact made. Over."

Another voice cut in and Ferguson recognized Boyd's crisp tone. "Penguin, this is C-130. How can we assist? Over."

Colonel Kleckner tapped Ferguson on the shoulder and took over the right-hand seat. As soon as the colonel was fastened in, Corbin yielded his place so that the aircraft commander could return to where he belonged. As Scott was getting his own harness on, the colonel answered the radio call. "Herc niner-four, if your fuel allows, you might come over at thirteen thousand and stand by in case we need you."

"Herc to Penguin, wilco. ETA twenty-eight minutes. Out."

Thule came in again. "Air Force 'six-zero, Godthaab asks if you have any indication that their medical people aboard the Otter are all right. Over."

Ferguson responded. " 'Six-zero to Thule, no data either way as yet, but Otter appears to have only slight damage. More later. Out."

With both the gear and the flaps down, he slowed the

Penguin to what he considered a minimum safe flying speed in the very gusty air. By the last light from the flare he positioned her so that she would pass the Otter seventy or eighty feet off its wingtip. "Ready for drop?" he asked.

"Ready."

"Stand by." He let the *Penguin* descend with her landing lights on until she was barely skimming the ice cap. "Three, two, one — go," he directed.

Five seconds later Holcomb reported. "Bombs away. It looked good from here."

"What went?"

"Blankets, hot coffee, food, and a medical kit."

"Good. That should hold them until the Jolly gets here. Jenk, can you make a good guess as to the surface wind?"

The navigator came back promptly. "I can give you the exact wind. I've got a driftmeter and I took a double drift when I had the chance. Zero-six-zero at thirty-three knots."

Ferguson climbed back up to 11,000 feet and then held steady, swinging in a fixed orbit around the downed Otter. He would have liked to have radioed back more information concerning the people it was carrying, but the HH-3 was due shortly. Less than five minutes later he picked up an approaching landing light in the sky.

He pressed to transmit. "Jolly Two, we have you in sight. Surface wind is zero-six-zero at thirty-three, heavy gusts. Advise if you want flare." That done, he returned to 121.5 and transmitted. "Otter, if you read, Jolly Green Giant is in sight and will pick you up shortly. Set out a flare or something for her if you can."

He listened for an acknowledgment, but he did not expect one and none came. He looked again at the incoming helicopter and saw that it was descending rapidly. In less than a minute it passed underneath, aiming for the center of his orbit. Apparently the Otter pilot heard enough of the sound to identify it as a helicopter; a red flare appeared on the surface of

269

the snow and, a few seconds later, another one, a hundred feet from the first.

When he knew that it was safe to do so, Ferguson, descended a little and flew just to the right of the twin flares. By the landing lights of the helicopter he saw the swirling snow whipped up by its main rotor; as he flew past, Tom Collins's voice came in with sharp clarity. "On the ground, no sweat. Stand by."

For three minutes Ferguson flew *The Passionate Penguin* in a close spiral around the marking flares while he waited for further word. He did not realize that the C-130 had arrived overhead until he was almost blinded by the brilliant flare that it released in the sky. Then the whole thing was laid out with photographic clarity: the Otter with a crumpled wingtip, the big Sikorsky close by with its rotor still turning, and three people on the ice cap moving from the Otter toward the helicopter.

The C-130 called. "Jolly, do you have enough hands to move the respirator? If not, we can make a ski landing and assist."

Major Mulder's voice answered. "No problem; we have six aboard and it can't be that big. But please stand by."

"Will do."

By the light of the flare Ferguson saw that there were now more people on the ice cap, but he could not distinguish much about them. Arctic gear was arctic gear on man or woman, and none of it was designed for style.

Presently Collins came on again. "Report on Otter crew and pax. Everyone OK. Pilot had complete electrical failure and instrument vacuum system went out. He put down blind to wait for weather lift and ground looped. The Otter was damaged enough to make it unflyable. We're transferring the respirator and will be homeward bound in about ten minutes. You can start back anytime."

"Thank you, Jolly, but we'll stay right here until you're airborne and on you way," Ferguson responded.

"Damn right," the colonel said over the intercom.

Twelve minutes later the twin-turbine Sikorsky rescue helicopter lifted off the ice cap, swung around, and set a course for Thule. Overhead the C-130 Hercules broke station and flew rapidly northward. Scott Ferguson turned *The Passionate Penguin* toward home and began a steady climb to a respectable altitude. He had been airborne for a good many hours and he was more than ready to call it a day. By now flying the B-17 was almost automatic with him and he felt as though he had been handling her for years.

He pressed the transmit button one more time and spoke to the helicopter that was now well below him. "Penguin to Jolly Two," he said. "A nice pickup off the ice cap. Congratulations."

Major Mulder replied. "Thank you, Penguin. We've had some valuable practice."

The C-130, with its much greater speed, was the first to arrive back and swing into the Thule landing pattern. The weather situation had improved materially and phase conditions had passed. Jolly One put in an appearance five minutes later and settled down on the runway. Both aircraft received the same piece of news; it was at that moment touch and go at the hospital where the Bennett respirator was desperately needed; only the knowledge that that vital piece of equipment was being brought in as fast as the HH-3 could fly offered any encouragement at all. Lieutenant Kane had positioned the necessary ground vehicles well in advance of the ETA and Sergeant Ragan, of the Air Police, had provided an escort in the hope that it might save an additional two or three minutes.

As the HH-3 flew in with the medical personnel and the Bennett on board, Ferguson kept *The Passionate Penguin* above and behind her so that he could keep the lights of the helicopter constantly in view. If anything were to happen — which was extremely unlikely, but possible — he did not want to have to waste two minutes in reporting that fact and beginning another orbit.

Fortunately, the precaution was unnecessary. Jenkins did not quarrel with the heading being held, although he kept up his chart work like the professional that he was. The Thule beacon came in loud and clear and the ADF told him that he was on the right flight path. When the edge of the ice cap finally came, he could see the lights of Thule ahead and below.

Ferguson held his altitude to allow the Jolly to land first. It did so, cutting straight in across the field and setting down almost directly in front of the operations building. The moment that the aircraft was firmly on the ground it was surrounded by people. The ambulance backed up, and there was frenzied activity.

Bringing up the rear, Ferguson flew toward the beacon and set up a proper instrument approach. He didn't require the glide slope or any radar assistance; the runway was in plain sight, but he did everything according to the book. Gear and flaps down, he came in over the boundary lights, reminded himself once more that he was flying a tail-dragger, not a tricycle-geared aircraft, and held the *Penguin* off the runway as he slowed her down and let the tail sink into landing position. When she finally settled on, it was a picture-book landing and he knew it. After contacting ground control, he taxied up in front of Hangar 8, and at long last cut the switches. *The Passionate Penguin* came to rest and stood with stately dignity.

Colonel Kleckner got up a little stiffly. "I may catch hell," he admitted. "If I do, it won't hurt that we made the discovery. If we hadn't . . ." He had no need to finish the sentence.

"Also, sir," Ferguson added, "they might have some

272

trouble proving that the *Penguin* can't get off the ground. She flew through some pretty rough air today."

"I've got a lot to do now," the colonel said, and left the flight deck. The crew doorway was already open; through it he climbed down onto the ground.

At the hospital, the Bennett respirator was at that moment being delivered to the room where little Bebiane Jeremiassen lay immobilized, as still and silent as death itself. Ignoring his ordeal on the ice cap, Dr. Lindegaard connected the machine and checked it out. He had it ready in less than a minute. He wheeled it to the bedside and, with Markley's help, switched the tiny patient onto the new and vastly more efficient machine. "How much longer would your portable unit have lasted?" the Danish doctor asked.

"We thought we were losing her twice within the hour before you got here. It was a matter of minutes."

"I understand. Doctor, I wish to have you meet our nurses. They have been through quite a bit in the last many hours, but they are ready to begin work. Mrs. Toft will take the first shift. She is, I think, in a little better shape than Miss Morgensen or Mrs. Nielsen."

"If Mrs. Toft can, it would be a great help. Captain Lyons will stay on watch; if anything is needed, she will know where it is."

For five minutes the two doctors conferred on the condition of the little Eskimo girl. Dr. Lindegaard made a personal examination of her and then read the chart in detail. "There is no question whatever," he said. "Your treatment was the only procedure to be followed. If she lives, it will be because of you."

Markley shook his head, then he pointed to the Bennett. "Without that . . ." he began and then stopped.

"I wish to ask one question," Dr. Lindegaard said. "We were discovered on the ice cap by a plane of your Air

Force—by the flare light I read it. But, doctor, I cannot understand; I would swear that it was a B-17! I do not know much about airplanes, but that one is so famous."

"So they flew it, did they? I hadn't heard."

Nurse Vibeke Toft, fresh in a starched uniform, came down the hall ready for duty. "Are you all right?" Markley asked.

The nurse answered in excellent English. "I am fine, doctor. It is agreed that I will watch for two hours, then Miss Morgensen will take over. That will give her and Helle time to eat and rest a little. Helle, Mrs. Nielsen, will take over four hours later, after a little sleep."

As Debra Lyons began to brief her Danish colleague, Markley leaned against the wall, giving way for a moment to the fatigue that the strain he had been under had intensified. "Doctor," he said, "when you feel up to it . . ."

Lindegaard put a hand on his shoulder. "Go, please, doctor, and get some rest. I will guard your patient. If an emergency comes, I will call you."

Quite suddenly Markley felt that most of his remaining energy had drained out of his body. "I think that I will," he said. "Thank you for coming. And thank God for the Bennett. Now that she's on it, I feel a little better."

Lindegaard nodded. "I think that you should. She is young and these Greenlander children are very sturdy and strong, even when little. She now has the best chance that it is possible to give her with what we know."

Utterly weary, but hopeful, Dr. Herbert Markley walked up the corridor toward the place where he could lie down and rest.

CHAPTER EIGHTEEN

IN THE CENTER of the huge floor of Hangar 8, *The Passionate Penguin* stood in the position of honor. She had been wiped down, and the slight amount of soil that she had picked up on her underside had been washed away. Her fuel tanks had been topped, her oil had been checked and replenished, and she awaited the signal for further action. Only one noticeable change had taken place—a rescue "find" symbol had been proudly painted on her nose. It was her first earned decoration.

Outside, Thule Approach Control cleared a C-141 from McGuire to the tower frequency. The big jet airlifter came down the glide path, flared, greased on, and began a dignified taxi toward the place where a waiting signalman stood positioned on the ramp. When it had been spotted, the pilot cut the engines and a small reception committee of Thule personnel came forward. Colonel Kleckner was in the lead. He did not need to look at the two-starred plate displayed in the window to know that a major general was on board. Two staff cars rolled out and took positions just off the port wingtip.

The side door opened, there were a few seconds of delay, and then General William H. Miller deplaned briskly. He returned Colonel Kleckner's salute and then shook hands cordially. "Good to see you, Jim," the general said.

"Welcome to Thule, sir. It's good to have you back."

The general paused and looked around him. "You know, you can call me crazy if you want to, but I like this place. Colonel Lancaster, who served a tour up here, told me that it was the most exotic spot on earth, and I'm inclined to agree with him."

The general greeted the other officers who had come to meet him, and shook hands with the First Sergeant. Then, with his aide behind him, he walked to the forward staff car. As the aide got into the front seat next to the driver, Colonel Kleckner and the general sat together in back. "Not too cold today," the general remarked.

"No, sir, by Thule standards we're having a heat wave. It's barely below zero."

Presently the staff car pulled up before Building 708. "Your quarters are here, sir," Colonel Kleckner said. "We have a small dinner laid on for you and your staff at 1900 hours at the club. That will give you an opportunity to get some rest."

The general got out of the car. "Let me change out of flight gear," he said, "then, if you don't mind, I'd very much like to visit the hospital."

"Certainly, sir, no problem at all."

In his room the general became more informal. "Jim, how are things going up here?"

"Smoothly and well. J Site has no problems that I'm aware

276

of and our own operations are in good shape. The staff up here right now is all I could ask for. Off the record, Bill, we're in better shape now than we have been for some time."

The general sat on the edge of a chair while he stripped off his flight suit. "Jim, while we have a few minutes together, I want to tell you that I had to throw my weight around a little and smooth down some feathers at Norton. But I want to add something to that: if I had been here, and in command at the time, I would have done precisely what you did, and I told them that flat out. There was a minor rhubarb, but I got them calmed down. I very clearly pointed out that all available aircraft had been ordered to fly and what the hell . . ." He dropped a heavy shoe onto the floor. "What have you done with that B-17 since then?"

"I ordered it back into the hangar, to remain there until the question of its airworthiness is finally cleared up. Between you and me, it's in as good shape as anything in the inventory. You won't believe it when you see it."

"I intend to see it." The general disposed of the other shoe and went to the washbasin. Conversation stopped while he refreshed himself there and used the bathroom. As he came out his aide tapped on the bedroom door and handed in a freshly pressed dress uniform. The general accepted it and began to put it on. He touched on two or three classified matters, knowing that the quarters were secure, and finally was ready to leave. He picked up the parka that had been provided for him and selected from the array of arctic-type gloves. "All right, let's go," he said.

At the hospital, the entire staff, minus one nurse, was on hand to provide a formal welcome. Once more the general shook hands all around; then he addressed himself to Dr. Markley. "Captain, is it permissible for me to see your patient?"

"Certainly, sir. I would also like to have you meet the Danish catastrophic team that responded to our urgent need.

They are top people—I can say that without reservation."

He led the way down the corridor and paused before showing the general into the sickroom. "You understand that she is still immobilized," he said.

"Yes, I do. I consider it remarkable that she is still alive. According to the medical officer who briefed me, at my request, her chances were almost nil."

"Almost, sir, but not absolutely. Come in, please."

As the general stood and looked down at the small body lying on the hospital bed, an almost visible shadow seemed to pass across his face.

"Sir," Colonel Kleckner said, "I'd like to have you meet the others. Major Dashner is the nurse who went with the flight up to Kanak under Phase Two conditions to bring the patient back. Miss Morgensen is a member of the Danish team. Dr. Lindegaard is at Kanak now to see Dr. Pedersen, but he will be back in time for the dinner party."

"Good." The reply was mechanical; the general was still looking down at the thin little form lying on the bed. "Is she awake at all?" he asked.

"No," Markley answered. "We made certain of that. If she makes it, this period will just be a gap in her life."

The general continued to look at the little girl. "I know that she is still alive—obviously. But what is the honest prognosis—has she any chance at all to recover?"

Markley was extremely cautious. "I'll put it this way, sir: by all of the odds, even with normally good fortune on her side, she would be dead by now. But, as you can see, she isn't. It is Dr. Lindegaard's opinion that the disease has been arrested. We have the full details on the first reported case of human recovery from rabies. Up to this point, her history is paralleling that one."

Miss Morgensen spoke up for the first time. "If you will allow me, General, I wish to say that if she lives, it will be because of Dr. Markley, and Dr. Bowditch, and what they did before we got here."

The general looked at her and liked what he saw. "Thank you," he said. "I would like to ask you a question, if the doctor doesn't mind."

Markley nodded his consent.

"Based on your own experience, Miss Morgensen, would you give this patient one chance, in say fifty, to survive?"

The Danish nurse met his inquiring eyes evenly and squarely. "Sir, since she has now come this far, I would give her better than that. I am a believer, sir; I expect her to recover."

"Major Dashner?" the general asked.

"I believe, sir, that Dr. Markley is being very cautious, and very modest."

The general lingered. "I presume that the chaplain has been in," he said.

Grethe Morgensen answered that. "Every day, sir, usually at least twice. Both chaplains, as a matter of fact. The Catholic chaplain has said masses for her, and Major Valen has conducted special services in the chapel."

"Well," the general said after thinking for a moment, "if she's got God on her side she'll make it, and it looks as if she does." He turned and left the room.

Outside Colonel Kleckner glanced at his watch, saw that there was plenty of time available, and asked: "What now, sir? Would you care to come over to headquarters?"

"Is there something pressing on hand?"

"No, sir, not to my knowledge."

"Then perhaps we could go down to the flight line."

The colonel's staff car, with the warning light on top, pulled away from the hospital as a small blue flag bearing two stars fluttered in a socket next to the front bumper. The driver pulled up smoothly beside the personnel door to Hangar 8 and then, as he got out to open the car door, accidently touched the horn for a bare moment.

The general got to his feet and waited for his host to join him. Then, as his aide held the door open, he went inside.

The overhead lights were already on. In the center of the floor *The Passionate Penguin* gleamed with newness; not a single spot disfigured her shining surfaces. UNITED STATES AIR FORCE was lettered perfectly on the side of her fuselage. In front of her nose, in immaculate class-A uniform, her crew stood at attention in a dead-straight line. Every man's hands were precisely at his sides, every man's eyes were straight forward and unblinking, every man's shoes had been spit-shined to perfection.

The general approached the very tall, quite slender, rather good-looking young lieutenant who was at the end of the line closest to the nose of the aircraft. As the general stopped before him, Ferguson snapped a salute on behalf of the crew. "Air Force B-17 three-six-zero ready for inspection, sir," he reported in crisp military tones.

The general walked slowly down the line of men and examined each one. Lieutenant Corbin, whose wings identified him as the copilot, as did his position in line, was textbook perfect. Lieutenant Jenkins, knowing that he was somewhat overweight, held his stomach in and his shoulders back.

Sergeant Holcomb had creases in his trousers that would have served to cut the grass, had there been any at Thule. Sergeant Stovers stood with the pride of a professional. Sergeant Perry Feinberg, who had three days to go on his Thule tour, was massive; his usually mobile face was like granite. Atwater was crisp and self-conscious, trying to look at least a bit larger than his essentially small frame would permit.

The general came down the back of the line and, as he looked with an experienced eye, he could detect no flaw.

When he had finished, he turned to Ferguson once more. "At ease, gentlemen," he said. "Most satisfactory. Your name, Lieutenant?"

"Scott Ferguson, sir."

"I'd like to meet the rest of your crew."

"My honor, sir." Ferguson stepped out of the rank. "Sir, may I present Lieutenant Corbin, copilot; Lieutenant Jenkins, navigator; Sergeant Holcomb, flight engineer; Sergeant Stovers, loadmaster —"

"Hell, Bill," the general said.

"Good afternoon, sir."

"Since you are the most careful and meticulous man around an airplane I have ever known, tell me," the general said. "How good is this B-17?"

"The best goddamned airplane in the United States Air Force, sir."

Ferguson presented Feinberg and Atwater, who shook hands a little formally.

"I'd like to go on board," the general said.

"Yes, sir," Ferguson responded. He glanced at the general's wings, then led the way to the crew entrance ladder and stepped aside. The general went up the ladder and turned right into the bomb-bay area. He went slowly, making an intensive inspection of everything that he saw. He went back as far as he was able, checking the control-cable pulleys, the rear-door latch, every detail within his reach. "It could be that Sergeant Stovers was right," he said.

"He spoke for the entire crew, sir."

The general turned around and made his way up toward the flight deck. He checked the navigator's station and noted the Bendix octant that was properly positioned under the deck. "Is that the original Mixmaster?" he asked.

"Yes, sir, it is."

"Does it work?"

"Perfectly, sir. Everything on board this aircraft, and every part of it, has been completely gone over and brought up to the highest standards."

"I see." The general went forward and looked down at the console. He remained there for over half a minute without moving, then he sat down in the left-hand seat. Since he was a command pilot, that was his prerogative. He surveyed the instrument panel in detail; then he studied the bank of switches above his head. Finally he gave his attention to the console. "I see that you've put in all modern avionics," he said.

"Yes, sir. There is one original radio on board, and fully operational of course, but it was Colonel Kleckner's opinion that she should be fitted with all necessary modern communications and navaids."

"There isn't any single sideband," the general noted.

"No, sir, but it will go right here when we can get hold of a set to install. Otherwise, as you see, sir, she has dual OMNI, TACAN, DME, glide-slope readout and full ILS equipment."

"What else would you like to install?"

"Weather radar, sir."

"Would you be able to fit it if you had it—without a radome?"

"Yes, sir, that problem has already been solved. All we need is the set."

"How about the tires?"

"Brand-new ones, sir; Goodyear sent them to us. More accurately, sir, they were sent to the aircraft herself. She accepted gratefully."

The general felt the controls. "I can't find anything wrong here," he said.

"You won't, sir.

"You seem proud of her."

"I am, sir. She's my airplane and I love every rivet in her."

"No, Lieutenant—she's mine."

"I don't follow you, sir."

"All right, Lieutenant, I'll spell it out for you. When you first spotted the *Penguin* on the ice cap, she was facing more or less west. And she was resting on her gear — the wheels had been put down."

"That's correct, sir."

"You might like to know about those last few moments, Lieutenant. I can tell you, because I was flying her. I knew that the rule book said in all emergency crash landings the wheels are to be kept retracted and the aircraft is to be bellied in. That's the safest way, but it kills the bird — finally and completely in most instances. I couldn't do that to her, and furthermore, I held on to the hope that the Arctic storm that had us hopelessly iced up would pass and that we would somehow get airborne again. We had crates on board and plenty of gasoline, so we might have been able to thaw her out in some way. You know that I was carrying a vital piece of cargo, and I wasn't going to abandon it, no matter what. We did try to start fires, until we discovered that no one had any matches."

"My respects, sir, and my admiration." Ferguson had thought so many times about the pilot of the B-17, but it had never occurred to him that he might have been a career professional. Now he knew.

He looked out and saw that Sergeant Feinberg was standing beside the controls that operated the main hangar door — the man was a mind reader. Without invitation, Ferguson sat down next to the general, fastened his harness, and then reached for the set of checklist cards. Before him the huge door began to yawn open. Sergeant Holcomb stood in front of the nose, caught his attention, and gestured that the brakes were to be released.

Ferguson read from the top card in his hand. "Pre-engine-start checklist."

The general reached over and fitted his hand on the throttles from the underside. "Dammit, I'd sure like to," he said.

"Sir, correct me if I'm wrong, but aren't those two stars I see on your shoulder?"

"Three actually — I've just been confirmed for another one."

"Then why are we sitting here?"

Holcomb motioned forward; from somewhere there were enough people to roll the *Penguin* toward the opening that led to the ramp. As the aircraft moved, Ferguson read off the first item on the list. The general checked and responded. He was well aware that rank has its privileges. Sergeant Stovers came aboard as Sergeant Holcomb continued to supervise the rolling of the stately bomber out onto the ramp.

Seventeen minutes later *The Passionate Penguin* lifted off the Thule runway, Major General William Miller at the controls. He flew her for almost an hour and during that time Ferguson sat still and kept his mouth shut. When the general finally elected to come in he made an instrument approach that was perfection itself. When the new tires had touched down so gently it could hardly be felt, and the *Penguin* had rolled to a halt, her engines idling, the general finally spoke across the console that separated the two pilots' seats. "Thank you, Lieutenant," he said.

"Thank you, sir. It's your airplane. Sir, may I ask a question?"

"Go ahead."

"Can you tell me what was in the crate we recovered?"

The general thought for a moment before he answered that. "I guess that I can — now. It was a highly classified new type of coding machine; fortunately there was a second prototype that got over there OK. It's totally outdated now, of course, but there were certain components in it that are still being used."

"I understand, sir. I won't say a word."

"Don't." The general taxied as though he was reluctant to see the flight end. "I haven't decided," he said. "The Air Force

284

museum will want her, but that's a graveyard. Now her promotional value should be enormous. We could send her everywhere."

"Sergeant Feinberg has some ideas about that, sir. He feels that she could star in a motion picture. She could join the recruiting service. Rebuilding classic cars and airplanes is very big right now, all over the country and the world."

The general turned the beautiful bomber — and she was beautiful — onto the spot that the ground man was indicating, and then cut the switches. He sat still, showing no inclination to get up. Ferguson stayed where he was, remaining silent.

Finally the general spoke. "Lieutenant, a thought has occurred to me. I think that the *Penguin* has a considerable future in the various areas we've just mentioned. And she's airworthy, no doubt of that. We can let the maintenance types look her over if they feel that they must."

"Yes, sir, why not."

"A general officer under most circumstances is entitled to his own aircraft. And if he is fortunate enough to be chosen for three-star rank, then he can pretty much have the one he wants."

"I hope that he can also select the crew."

"Oh, yes. Which brings up a little matter that I had almost forgotten." The general reached into his pocket and extracted a small blue box. "At the time I put the *Penguin* onto the ice cap, I was a captain. These are the original insignia I was wearing during the flight." He opened the box to display the sets of twin bars. You're due pretty soon, aren't you?"

"Within the next two or three months I believe, sir."

"Then when the time comes, I'd like to have you wear these. They go with the airplane."

"I'll treasure them, sir. When it's appropriate, I'd be very proud if you'd put them on for me."

"I'd be honored. Now let's get out of here."

Five minutes later the two men stood looking up at the

insignia on the nose of *The Passionate Penguin*. "I'm glad that you didn't change it," the general said.

"Certainly not, sir. It was suggested, but immediately voted down."

"Are you coming to the party tonight, Lieutenant?"

"Sir, only an emergency call to fly the *Penguin* could keep me away."

The general took his departure. The remainder of the *Penguin*'s crew, with an instinctive understanding of the situation, had kept away from the airplane. The men were gathered, talking quietly together, in a corner of the hangar. As Ferguson walked over to join them, Sergeant Feinberg drew him aside. "May I suggest a little man-to-man discussion," he proposed.

"Go ahead, Perry."

"Several of us have noticed that the general is in a very warm and mellow mood. Also he seems very much attached to the *Penguin*. Now I seem to recall that the pilot who originally landed her on the ice cap was also named Miller. Of course that's a very common name."

"But an uncommon man, Perry. Your guess is right; he's the one."

Across Perry Feinberg's wide face a cunning grin began to form. "Then certainly we should take advantage of the situation. I approve of generals, particularly when they can be useful. Considering all things, now might be the ideal time to hit him for some single sideband equipment and the weather radar. The Air Force can well afford it."

Ferguson nodded. "Perry, maybe it's being around you so much lately that's done it, but I am beginning to acquire the technique. The same thought came to me. There is to be a small party this evening. I shall choose the right moment."

"Then I consider that the matter is settled. I only regret that I won't be here personally to supervise the installation."

"While we're on this general subject," Ferguson said, "I

286

have a question to ask you. Just before we took off in the *Penguin*, you said to me, 'I can con you into it, but I don't have the time.' Do you recall that phrase?"

"Yes, Lieutenant, I do." A slight touch of discomfort tinged his words.

"How did you propose to con me?"

Sergeant Feinberg very nearly blushed. "Well, sir, you know how it is; an artist doesn't always like to talk about his work."

"I want to know."

"Very well, if that's an order. Precisely the way I did do it: wait until the last moment and then protest that there isn't time to engage in any discussions. That was how I had it planned from the beginning."

Ferguson nodded. "That's a good point to know," he said.

The colonel raised a toast. "Although some of the junior officers may not agree, I have for a long time maintained that a woman never attains her maximum charm until she has reached thirty. With that thought in mind, I give you one who fits that description, *The Passionate Penguin*."

After the toast had been drunk, Tom Collins rose. "I now give you the Twin Otter," he said. "That will be a vastly easier job, of course. Then, I have noted from the charts, there is an Aero Commander on the ice cap, quite nearby, that is reported to be intact."

"There's also a B-29," Captain Tilton contributed.

"Forget it," the general advised. "It burns too much gas."

"How many planes are actually out there?" Major Valen asked.

"Over forty," Major Mulder answered, "but about half of them were destroyed on impact. Ten or twelve, of various types and kinds, are known to be substantially undamaged."

That called for another round and it was drunk with enthusiasm.

In the morning, General Miller made a call to the Pentagon from Colonel Kleckner's office. He asked for, and got, the general who headed the Air Force Office of Information, a sometimes harrowing assignment that carried more weight than is generally appreciated.

"Charlie," Miller said. "You know about the B-17 they've rebuilt up here."

"Of course. As a matter of fact, it's your old airplane, isn't it?"

"Precisely, so I've got an idea. What if I were to fly her back after all these years — could you get any mileage out of that?"

"*Hell, yes* — the visual appeal would be great. The TV networks will love it. What's the bird's actual status?"

"She's officially back in commission. All the maintenance requirements have been met, and by the book, that's all it took."

"Great. Send me a crew list as soon as you can. I'll have bios ready for the press, pictures, all that. Is Tilton in on this?"

"Absolutely — he's already prepared most of the material. There's a C-141 coming down to McGuire in the morning; everything you will need from here will be on board."

"Look, perhaps Tilton could come with you, as IO for the aircraft. I can send a replacement up on the rotator to cover the bases while he's on TDY."

"That's a good idea, Charlie. While you're at it, send up a C-130 crew, ski-qualified if possible, but that isn't essential. Ev Pritchard's office will handle it."

"Bill, since we're talking, can you bring with you any of the people who actually were in on that rebuilding job? That would be outstanding." The man in the Pentagon was rapidly making notes.

General Miller smiled. "You've just filled an inside straight," he said. "My copilot will be the man who actually found her on the ice cap. He won't take the credit; he insists it was his crew. However, I expect to bring them all with me."

"Absolutely superior. I'll call all of the top media people. Bless you!"

"One more thing," Miller said. "Do me a favor. Call Princeton and get hold of Professor Mafusky in the department of mathematics. Invite him to be present when we come in. Since he was part of my original crew, I think he'd like to be there."

Thule Operations showed Air Force three-six-zero due out at 0830 hours, bound for Andrews Air Force Base, Maryland. The crew met an hour earlier in Operations to take care of the necessary paperwork, pre-flight briefings, and the other formalities of departure. When the routine chores had been done, and the weather maps had been examined, General Miller reached into his pocket and extracted a coin. He flipped it into the air. "Call," he said.

"Heads," Ferguson responded.

The general looked. "Heads it is." He addressed the NCOIC. "The pilot will be Lieutenant Ferguson. I'll fly copilot. You have the rest."

"Yes, sir, the crew list is ready for signature."

Ferguson stepped up and put his name on the bottom of the form. As he finished, Sergeant Feinberg came in. "The bird is ready," he reported. Presently, he spoke to Ferguson privately. "Did you win the toss, sir?" he asked.

"Now look, Perry, there's no way you could have fixed that!"

The impressive sergeant gave a confident gesture. "Of course not, Lieutenant, no way at all. But I did take the liberty of mentioning to the general the sporting idea of letting the fates decide, as it were. That at least would give you a fifty percent chance. The general is well known as a sportsman and I suspected that he might go for it."

The operations clerk was lettering Ferguson's name on the board in the column marked PILOT. Lieutenant Jenkins handed in his flight plan; Andy Holcomb was right behind him with the weight-and-balance sheet, which already bore Sergeant Stover's signature.

"Since we've got some headwinds along the route," General Miller said, "let's go as soon as we're ready."

"We're ready now," Ferguson answered.

The *Penguin* stood on the ramp just outside. The ground-support personnel were ready with the fire extinguisher, battery cart, and other required equipment. It took ten minutes to get everyone settled in and the pre-engine-start checklist run through. All was well. With practiced efficiency Ferguson fired up and waited while the engines settled in. Then he called ground control and got clearance to the run-up area. He taxied slowly and carefully until he was in position, then he set the brake firmly and went through the routine of checking all four engines and propellers and all eight magnetos. With that behind him he called the tower and advised that he was ready for takeoff.

The tower came back with immediate clearance and supplied the latest altimeter setting. There had been no change since they had left the ramp.

Ferguson advanced the throttles and guided the four-engined Boeing bomber into position on the end of the runway. Before her was 10,000 feet of runway and the unlimited sky overhead. He pressed the intercom button. "Your takeoff, sir," he said.

Miller flashed him an appreciative smile. "I'll try to keep her off the ice cap this time," he said.

The engines picked up in tempo and then combined into a respectable roar. The plane began to roll forward, gaining speed. After only a short distance, the tail came off the ground and the weight rested on the main gear. The speed continued to build as the 2,000-foot marker went past. Then, gracefully as always, *The Passionate Penguin* lifted off the ground apparently of her own will. As she climbed up, her landing gear slowly disappeared and the wing flaps came up. Ferguson called departure control as the general turned the aircraft southward.

She climbed upward at a steady pace, her engines running smoothly, until those who were watching from the ground could no longer hear the sound, and the plane herself was little more than a diminishing speck in the sky.

GLOSSARY

A/C: Aircraft Commander, the pilot in charge.

ACM: Additional Crew Member, a term frequently applied to riders who have no actual function in the operation of an aircraft.

ADF: Automatic Direction Finder, a radio-navigation device that, in essence, has a needle that points directly toward the station to which it is tuned.

Advancing line search: One of several techniques for systematically searching a given area from the air.

A-frame: A simple, portable device, usually equipped with a block and tackle, which can be used for moderately heavy lifting jobs at field locations.

Aileron: A relatively small, movable control surface normally located at or near the wingtips of an aircraft. They are used to keep the wings level or to bank them while turning.

Airframe: The main structure of an aircraft, excluding the engine(s).

Airlifter: An aircraft specifically designed to carry freight. The term is sometimes applied to other aircraft that have been modified for cargo use.

Airscrew: Another, more technical, name for propeller.

Airway: A specific, frequently used flight path that is equipped with navigational aids. An air highway.

Alclad: A type of sheet metal used in aircraft construction. It consists of a strong aluminum alloy covered with a layer of pure aluminum to resist corrosion.

Altimeter: An instrument that shows the height of an aircraft above sea level. Most altimeters work by atmospheric pressure and need to be frequently reset. Radar altimeters read the distance above the ground or water directly underneath the aircraft.

Analyzer: A piece of electronic equipment which displays on a tube face a continuous report on the condition and functioning of an aircraft engine.

Angle of attack: The angle at which the wing of an aircraft meets the relative wind. Under normal flight conditions, increasing the angle of attack increases the amount of lift generated, up to a specific point.

AOK: A familiar military expression meaning "as good as possible."

APU: Auxiliary Power Unit. On large aircraft, the APU supplies power to operate various systems while the main engines are shut down.

Archie: The Thule designation for Arctic foxes.

ARRS: Aerospace Rescue and Recovery Service, a part of the Military Airlift Command.

Artificial horizon: An aircraft instrument that, by means of a gyroscope, can display on its face a miniature aircraft and a horizon line, which correspond to the relative positions of the actual aircraft and the true horizon.

ASAP: As Soon As Possible.

Atmospheric pressure: The almost constantly changing pressure of the atmosphere as it would be measured at sea level. The world standard for average conditions is 29.92 inches of mercury in a vacuum.

Autopilot (sometimes *Automatic pilot*): A piece of equipment normally capable of maintaining an aircraft's flight path at a preset direction, altitude, and attitude. Highly sophisticated units are coupled to radar altimeters and can thereby avoid terrain obstructions when flying at low altitude.

Avionics: Electronic equipment normally used for navigational purposes.

B-17: One of the bulwarks of the United States Army Air Corps during World War II, the B-17 (*B* for "bomber") was a four-engined heavy bomber, piston-powered and principally used for daylight bombing of the Axis strongholds. Thousands were built. The B-17 enjoyed a phenomenal reputation for durability; many of them flew home despite severe battle damage. The B-17 was designed and built by Boeing; when additional planes of the same type were needed, production lines were also set up at Douglas Aircraft Corporation at Vega.

Ballistic Missle Early Warning System (BMEWS): A very large, highly complicated, and extremely powerful radar installation kept in continuous operation to give warning in case of an attack launched against the United States or Canada by means of ballistic missiles.

Barrel roll: An aerobatic maneuver during which an aircraft is rolled completely around its longitudinal axis. (The longitudinal axis is an imaginary line drawn from the tip of the nose back to the end of the tail.)

Battery cart: A standard piece of ground-support equipment that carries a number of well-charged batteries (under most circumstances). It can be plugged into an aircraft and used to start engines, thereby sparing excess drain on the aircraft's own internal batteries.

Beeper: A small device that transmits a continuous electronic signal so that it can be easily located.

Belly in: To land an aircraft, usually deliberately, without putting the landing gear down. This is the accepted technique when making forced landings in rough terrain or on water.

Bendix Mixmaster: A very good, but quite complex, octant used during World War II for celestial navigation purposes.

Blind broadcast: A message put out with no assurance that it is being heard by the intended recipient.

Bluie West 8: The World War II code designation for the landing strip located at Söndre Strömfjord, Greenland. It is on the west coast of the island, slightly north of the Arctic Circle.

BMEWS: See *Ballistic Missile Early Warning System.*

Buddy system: A military regulation that, when in effect, prohibits anyone from venturing out without at least one companion, for mutual protection.

BX: Base Exchange, a military store operated for the benefit of the personnel stationed at a military facility; it normally sells civilian goods at reduced prices.

C-47: The Douglas DC-3 in all of its military variations. It is one of the most memorable aircraft ever built, and one of the best.

C-130: A Lockheed-built, four-engined, turboprop airlifter widely used by the Military Airlift Command, and by the Canadian Armed Forces. It is noted for its short takeoff and landing capability, and for its rugged reliability; its official name is "Hercules."

C-141: A Lockheed four-engine, jet, heavy airlifter with strategic (long-range) capability. This aircraft is the current backbone of the MAC fleet.

Carburetor heat: A system for deicing carburetor intakes in piston engines that do not have fuel injection. Carburetor ice is a frequent problem, even during good weather conditions, and almost all conventional piston-powered aircraft are equipped with this device.

Checklist: A schedule of items that must be checked and verified before each phase of aircraft operation. Usually there are several checklists, including *pre-engine-start, pre-taxi, before-takeoff, before-landing, after-landing,* and *shutdown.* Sometimes long and complicated, checklists are used to insure that no significant items are forgotten or overlooked. Checklists are religiously used during all properly conducted aircraft operations.

Chill factor: An equivalent temperature arrived at by taking into consideration both the actual temperature and the wind velocity. The wind has a major effect in determining the danger of exposure in the Arctic.

Chord: The width of an aircraft wing, measured from the leading (front) to the training (rear) edge. It is almost always greatest at the root, i.e., next to the fuselage or the main body of the aircraft.

Closed field: An airport where all operations are prohibited because of adverse weather conditions. (The term also applies, of course, to airports that have shut down permanently.)

Cocked: A term applied to a large or sophisticated aircraft that has been prepared for flight with all checklist items completed up to "start engines," or the equivalent. Generally, any aircraft prepared as far as possible for immediate use.

Command post: An especially equipped room, or site, that

serves as a headquarters for a specific type of operation. Normally command posts are equipped with communications, display boards, and other facilities.

Cuban 8: A fairly difficult aerobatic maneuver which consists, roughly, of vertical figure 8's. Cuban 8's are notoriously prone to induce airsickness in passengers who elect to ride through them.

CW: Continous Wave, or Morse code-type, radio communications.

DEW Line: A series of Distant Early Warning radar stations stretched across the Arctic; there are DEW Line stations on the Greenland Ice Cap, but they are different from, and should not be confused with, BMEWS.

Ditch: To put a land-based aircraft down on water, obviously an emergency procedure only.

DME: Distance Measuring Equipment, an airborne electronic device that can read out the distance in nautical miles from an aircraft to a suitably-equipped (usually TACAN) radio station. A pilot's dream come true.

Dope: A special compound used to coat aircraft fabric-covered surfaces.

Dorsal: A long, extended fin on the top of an aircraft which leads into the vertical stabilizer.

Double drift: A navigational technique used to determine the strength and direction of the wind. By measuring the observed drift accurately on two different headings, the navigator can make a very close determination of the wind at the altitude at which his aircraft is flying.

Driftmeter: A device by means of which a navigator can determine the drift of an aircraft by sighting the ground or water underneath. Drift, per se, is the amount of sidewise motion induced by the prevailing wind.

Driftpins: Very substantial and heavy steel pins used to fasten the wings onto the main body structure of certain aircraft.

They are slightly tapered and usually one to two inches in diameter.

Drink: Aviation slang for "refuel."

Elevator: A movable surface (or a pair of surfaces) that controls the pitch of an aircraft. It is part of the tail assembly.

Elmendorf: A United States Air Force base located near Anchorage, Alaska.

Empennage: The complete tail assembly of an aircraft.

Engine frame: The (usually welded) tube structure that serves as an engine mount on an aircraft.

ETA: Estimated Time of Arrival.

FAA: Federal Aviation Agency.

Fairings: Fillets, usually between the wings and fuselage of an aircraft, installed to insure a smooth, minimum-friction flow of air over otherwise awkward areas.

Feather: To turn the blades of an inactive propeller edgewise to the wind to reduce drag and prevent windmilling.

Feathering button: The cockpit control which when depressed will feather a specific propeller.

Field-grade officer: A major or higher.

Fillet: A concave piece of metal used to streamline the meeting of two aircraft surfaces, such as the wing and the side of the fuselage.

Firebee: A pilotless target drone manufactured by Ryan.

Firewall: A solid panel which separates the cockpit from the nose-mounted engine in single-engined aircraft. If there is no nose-mounted engine, the term is still used.

Fittings: The integral parts used to fasten one piece of an aircraft's structure to another.

Five-square: A code to indicate that communications are both loud and clear. The scale of values used is one to five, for both volume and clarity. Thus *three-by-three* would indicate marginal volume and also impaired clarity. *Five-square* is frequently used instead of *five-by-five*. The two values, of course, need not be the same; a signal could be very faint, but still clear.

Fix: A navigational term designating the exact location of an aircraft in flight at a specific time.

Flaps: Auxiliary wing panels which can be raised or lowered in flight. They are normally used to decrease speed and increase lift prior to landing. They are also used during takeoffs and whenever it may be necessary to slow an aircraft to minimum safe speed while in flight.

Flare: This word has two aeronautical meanings. Most commonly, when an aircraft is descending for a landing, just before or above the runway the pilot will raise the nose, slowing the descent to a minimum and putting the plane in a landing attitude. This is known as *flaring*. Expertly done, it produces a smooth and gentle landing. *Flare* also means a pyrotechnic signal light, as it does elsewhere.

Flight plan: A document filed by a pilot, or a responsible crew member, before departure. It supplies information concerning the pilot's identity, intentions, destination, alternate choice of destination in case of adverse weather, and other data. (Under some circumstances a flight plan is not legally required for cross-country trips, but prudent pilots file them anyway.)

463L (Four-Six-Three L): An efficient, palletized, cargo-handling system used by the Air Transport Command.

Fourteen-hundred hours: 2 P.M. See also *Time*.

Full bore: Wide open, i.e., a maximum effort.

Full feather: To turn an aircraft's propeller blades until they are directly edgewise to the relative wind.

Fuselage: The main body of an aircraft, excluding the wings or rotors.

G's: Multiples of the force of gravity induced by moderate-to-severe aircraft maneuvers. Two G's means twice the normal force of gravity; at five G's a normally 200-pound man would weigh 1,000 pounds. Astronauts and most test pilots regularly endure such stresses, and more.

GCA.: Ground Control Approach, a radar system by means of which a pilot on final approach to landing is given continuous information as to his exact position and distance from touchdown. This term has now been largely superseded by PAR (Precision Approach Radar).

Gear down: With landing gear extended. Also, the command by the aircraft commander to extend the wheels; normally it is done by either the copilot or the flight engineer.

Glide path: A precision approach path to an instrument runway. It is marked by two highly directional radio transmitters — the glide-slope indicator (GSI) and the localizer. The latter supplies right-left indications.

Glide slope: Specifically, the designated descent path onto an instrument runway. Also, the pitch, or angle, of that path.

Go-around: The procedure laid down for a pilot to follow if he approaches an airport but cannot complete his landing as planned. It is also known as a *missed approach* in instrument flying. The most common cause is inadequate visibility immediately prior to an intended landing.

Goose Bay: A widely known stop on North Atlantic and certain Arctic routes. It is located in western Labrador.

Ground control: The authority that handles the movement of aircraft on the ground, exclusive of takeoffs and landings, at major airports. Ground control normally has its own special radio frequency and personnel.

Ground effect: A phenomenon which gives extra lift to aircraft just before landing. Essentially it is an added cushion built up when the air deflected downward by the wings is slightly compressed against the ground.

Hardstand: A paved area at an airport where heavy aircraft can be safely parked.

Head: A military term, originated by the Navy, that means toilet.

Heading: The exact direction in which the nose of an aircraft is pointed. It can be, and frequently is, different from the path of the aircraft over the ground or water.

Head shed: The Pentagon, in Washington, D.C. (actually in Virginia). See also *Puzzle palace*.

Herc: Short for *Hercules*, the official name of the C-130 airlifter.

HH-3: The Air Force official designation for the twin-turbine Sikorsky rescue helicopter more popularly known as the *Jolly Green Giant*.

Hover-taxi: A frequently used helicopter technique; instead of rolling an aircraft along the ground on its wheels, the pilot will lift off a few feet and then fly just above the ground to where he is going. Some helicopters — those that have no wheels — do this of necessity.

Hundred-hour check: An inspection performed on aircraft after each 100 hours of use; normally it involves a minimum maintenance procedure.

IFR: Instrument Flight Rules.

ILS: Instrument Landing System.

Instrument approach: A precision approach to a properly equipped runway that can be executed by a qualified pilot solely by reference to instruments on the panel before him.

IO: Information Officer.

J Site: The common name for the BMEWS installation close to Thule.

Jigs: Tools used in the manufacturing of aircraft; essentially they hold components in proper alignment while the parts are welded or otherwise joined together.

Jolly: Short for *Jolly Green Giant*, the affectionate name for the

Sikorsky HH-3 rescue helicopter, which gained great fame in Vietnam.

Knot: One nautical mile per hour. In round figures, fifty-two knots equals sixty miles per hour.

Latrine: Toilet.

LEM: Lunar Excursion Module.

Letdown: An aircraft's descent from cruising altitude to a position where it can enter the landing pattern of its destination airport.

Loadmaster: A respected and highly skilled crew member who is responsible for the loading and unloading of an airlifter. He also makes certain that the load does not exceed allowable limits, is properly distributed, and is securely fastened down.

Long-legged: Having long-range capability.

Long-range cruise: An engine setting designed to get the maximum number of miles out of the available fuel at the sacrifice of some speed.

LORAN: An acronym for *LOng RAnge Navigation;* it is an electronic system, requiring specialized equipment capable of receiving two coupled transmitting stations simultaneously. LORAN is particularly effective over large bodies of water.

MAC: Military Airlift Command.

Mag drop: In almost all instances, aircraft piston engines have dual magnetos for greater ignition reliability. During normal operations both systems are continuously operated. Prior to takeoff, it is customary to run each engine for a brief test period on first one magneto and then the other to insure that both are functioning properly. The loss in rpm when running on either single magneto is known as the *mag drop.*

Mags: Magnetos, the alternators used to supply ignition to internal combustion engines; most aircraft piston engines have two for additional reliability.

Manifold pressure: The standard method for measuring the power output of an airborne piston engine.

Materiel: Military equipment and supplies.

Max gross: The theoretical maximum gross weight of an aircraft, including its fuel and payload, at which it can safely take off and fly.

Medevac: The transportation of medical patients by air; also, the special system set up to accomplish this.

Mixmaster: The popular name for the Bendix octant widely used by aerial navigators during World War II. See also *Bendix Mixmaster.*

Moonlight-requisition: A time-honored military technique for obtaining needed supplies or equipment which cannot conveniently be had through normal channels; it consists of helping yourself when no one is looking.

Mukluks: An Eskimo-invented foot covering worn inside boots in the Arctic for greater comfort and warmth.

Nacelle: The part of an aircraft's structure that contains an engine, usually wing-mounted.

Navaids: A convenient abbreviation for *aids to navigation*, usually electronic ones.

NCO: Non-Commissioned Officer. Included are Air Force sergeants, Navy chiefs, et cetera. NCO's frequently in positions of high trust and substantial responsibility.

NCOIC: Non-Commissioned Officer In Charge.

Non-directional beacon: A radio aid to air navigation that sends out a uniform signal in all directions.

NORAD: The North American Air Defense Command, a very complex and vital organization headquartered inside Cheyenne Mountain near Colorado Springs, Colorado.

BMEWS provides data input to NORAD, as do other sources.

Number one: "Number one to land" is a tower directive informing a pilot that there are no planes ahead of him and that he may proceed with his final approach.

Octant: A navigational instrument similar to a sextant that is used for determining the height above the horizon of stars and other celestial bodies. Octants are almost exclusively used in aircraft.

OMNI: A very widely used omnidirectional air navigation system; it is most effective over land areas.

P Mountain: An isolated site in the environs of the Greenland BMEWS.

PAR: Precision Approach Radar.

PA system: Public Address System.

Pax: Passengers.

Personnel door: A small door set inside a main hangar door so that people can conveniently go in and out without disturbing the main installation.

Phase: A condition of abnormally severe weather.

Phase Alert: A warning that phase weather is shortly expected.

Phase One; Phase Two; Phase Three: Progressively more severe Arctic weather conditions (which are described in detail in the text). Phase Three can bring winds in excess of 200 miles per hour and chill factors which make survival out of doors very marginal, even with the protection of full arctic clothing. Phase storms have an intensity all but unknown in the continental United States.

Phase markers: Steel posts with bright reflectors on top that are set on each side of the roadways at Thule and along the route to BMEWS. They are only a few feet apart and are intended to mark the edge of the roadway for any driver unfortunate enough to be caught out during phase conditions.

Phase rations: Emergency food supplies stored in almost every building at Thule for use during extended phase weather conditions.

Phase Warning Card: A small blue card issued at Thule which states the rules that apply under each set of phase conditions.

Pitch: The angle at which the blades of a propeller meet the relative wind.

Pitch control: The means by which a pilot can change the pitch of his propeller blades. Pitch control is particularly important in turboprop aircraft.

PJ's: The parachute rescue men of the ARRS. They are, among other things, scuba divers and trained medical technicians.

Proficiency flight: A flight made principally for the purpose of crew training and to maintain proficiency.

Prop: Propeller.

Puzzle palace: The Pentagon.

R and R: Rest and Recreation.

Radome: Short for *radar dome*, a piece of nonmetallic aircraft structure behind which a radar antenna is mounted and operated.

RAL: Radar Assisted Landing.

Range-leg: A now all-but-obsolete method of air navigation. A radio range station would transmit four different legs a pilot could fly inbound or outbound. This system has been effectively replaced by the much superior OMNI and TACAN.

Red-line speed: The "never-exceed" speed of an aircraft, usually marked with a red line on the airspeed indicator.

Reefer strap: A canvas strap that is frequently used to fasten loads onto hand trucks or dollies.

Relief tube: A simple, flexible urinal found in most military aircraft, including fighters.

Roger: A standard radio communications term. It means "received and understood."

Rotate: A technical term which applies principally to turboprop and turbojet aircraft. During takeoff the aircraft gains speed on the runway with the nosewheel on the ground. When flying speed has been attained, the pilot will rotate the plane around the transverse axis a specified number of degrees. Put another way, he lifts the nosewheel off and increases the angle of attack. This generates the necessary added lift and the plane comes off the ground.

Rotator: An aircraft which arrives on a regular schedule at a military base, bringing replacement personnel and taking back those who have completed their tours at the installation. The Thule rotator arrives weekly, weather permitting.

Rpm: Revolutions per minute.

SAC: Strategic Air Command.

Secured: Completely shut down. Also, closed and locked, in some contexts.

Sikorsky: A major American manufacturer of highly esteemed helicopters and, formerly, flying boats.

Single sideband: A form of long-range voice communication between a suitably equipped aircraft and the ground.

Six-pack: A fairly heavy pickup truck with a rear seat in the cab. It will carry six persons inside, including the driver.

Slipstream: The flow of air past an aircraft while it is in flight.

Snow cat: A tracked vehicle capable of operating on snow-covered surfaces. It is frequently used for towing sleds.

Socked in: A term applied to an airport or airstrip that has been closed because of adverse weather conditions.

Spin: An aerobatic maneuver during which an airplane is fully stalled and then allowed to autorotate like a falling maple seed. It is dangerous when performed — voluntarily or otherwise — too close to the ground.

Squawk: To signal by means of a transponder. See also *Transponder.*

Stabilizer: The (usually fixed) horizontal surface that is part of a conventional aircraft's tail assembly.

Stall: A condition of flight in which the even flow of air over the wings is broken, either by having too high an angle of attack or by slowing below a safe speed (or both). Stalled aircraft will drop down until they regain flying speed — some more drastically than others.

TACAN: TACtical Air Navigation, an excellent electronic navigation method at present used largely by the military for over-land operations. TACAN is somewhat similar to OMNI in practical use, but is an entirely different system.

Tail-dragger: An airplane equipped with what used to be called a conventional landing gear, i.e., with a main gear in front and a relatively small tail wheel at the back.

Tail number: An identifying number normally painted on the vertical stabilizer of all military aircraft.

TDY: Temporary Duty.

Thule: An actual air base located high up on the west coast of Greenland. It takes its name from *Ultima Thule:* "the utmost limit."

Time: The United States Air Force uses the 24-hour clock and expresses time accordingly. The hour and minute are written together as a single four-digit number; thus *0630* means six-thirty in the morning. Six-thirty in the evening would be *1830.* Two P.M. would be *1400.* This system removes all ambiguities and is highly efficient in use.

Trackmaster: A special rescue vehicle designed and equipped to operate over unprepared terrain, ice, and snow under the most severe weather conditions; riding in one is somewhat similar to being inside a concrete mixer.

Transceiver: A piece of radio gear that will both transmit and receive.

Transponder: A piece of airborne radar equipment by means of which an aircraft can identify itself or alert ground controllers to any unusual situation. The transponder produces a bright visual display on the controllers' radarscopes. Transponder use is known as *squawking*; thus, an aircraft may be asked "to squawk" a certain code number so that it can be positively identified. An aircraft in distress will squawk 7700, a signal that gets immediate attention. The code 7600 indicates radio failure. There is also a code to be used if hijacked.

Tricycle gear: The now very popular arrangement of a main landing gear, usually somewhere under the wing area, and a nosewheel. It is used on aircraft of all sizes.

Trim tab: A relatively small movable surface that is part of a larger aircraft control surface. It is used to make minor, semi-permanent adjustments.

Truculent Turtle: The name of a famous U.S. Navy aircraft that set an impressive long-range record. The *Turtle* is a Lockheed P2V Neptune; Commander Thomas D. Davies and crew flew her nonstop 11,236 miles.

Turboprop: An aircraft powered by turbine engine(s) that turn propeller(s). Turboprops are roughly halfway between piston-engined aircraft (all of which are propeller driven) and pure jets.

Twin Otter: A DeHavilland (of Canada) aircraft particularly suitable for operation in undeveloped areas. It is a twin turboprop STOL (Short Take Off and Landing) transport able to carry up to twenty passengers and suitable for ski operations.

Urp bucket: A wax-lined bag, or other container, provided to receive vomit in case of airsickness. (The next time you fly, you will find one in the seat pocket in front of you.)

Very pistol: A flare signaling device carried on most aircraft likely to be operated over desolate regions.

VFR: Visual Flight Rules, i.e., flying in clear, unobstructed weather.

VHF: Very High Frequency.

VIP: Very Important Person, now more commonly DV (Distinguished Visitor).

VORTAC: A radio aid to air navigation which combines VOR (VHF Omnidirectional Range) and TACAN transmissions—two entirely different systems—at one location.

Walter Reed: A large military hospital in Washington, D.C.

Weather radar: An airborne radar system that will show a pilot weather conditions ahead of him, particularly such things as thunderstorms. It is especially useful at night.

Weight and balance: A computation made before flight to establish that an aircraft's load is within established limits, both as to gross weight and placement within the cargo hold.

Whipstall: A violent aircraft maneuver in which a stall is induced at an extreme attitude, such as with the nose almost straight up. Under such circumstances, the aircraft will literally whip around as it recovers. Unless stressed for such maneuvers, it could experience structural failure.

Whiteout: A condition in heavy fog or snow when the pilot of an aircraft cannot see anything but white out of his windshield, and cannot distinguish snow-covered ground from the equally white atmosphere.

Wilco: Will comply. Used in radio communications, it also implies that the preceding transmission has been fully understood.

Wing-root section: That section of an aircraft wing closest to the side of the fuselage.

Yoke: The aircraft control column, usually in duplicate in aircraft that have provisions for a copilot. The yoke moves backward and forward to control the elevators; the control wheel is mounted on top.Normally, *yoke* implies the entire control assembly.

Zero time: By law, or military regulation, a very careful record is kept of the amount of time that each aircraft is in actual use. This time accumulates until the aircraft (and/or its power plants) undergoes complete overhaul. When all worn parts have been replaced, and the aircraft has been restored to new condition, it is then considered to have zero time, since it is the equivalent of a brand-new plane. *Zero time,* therefore, does not imply total newness, but rather implies no time since exhaustive overhaul and restoration to new condition. The total time on each aircraft and engine is also progressively accounted for. An aircraft may therefore be described as having "total time 2,345 hours, zero time since overhaul." (Such periodic overhauls are mandatory.)

Made in the USA
San Bernardino, CA
17 March 2019